Love Lessons

He taught her the meaning of passion.

Cheryl Holt

ST. MARTIN'S
PAPERBACKS

U.S. $6.50
CAN. $8.50

ISBN 0-312-97840-5

9 780312 978402

50650

S EAN

SHE WANTED ONLY TO LEARN . . .

"I will go to great lengths to ensure that no one discovers we have met. However"—James sipped his drink pensively—"should our liaison be exposed, it will cause quite a scandal."

"I'm aware of that fact."

"If the worst should happen, I will make no move to save your reputation. I will fight no duels in your honor. I will not marry you. I will do nothing."

"I understand." Abigail nodded firmly. "I am a woman full grown. As this has been at my instigation, I would expect no reparations from you."

"Then, we are agreed?"

"We are agreed," she repeated, standing, and he towered over her so closely that she could have reached out and laid her palms on his broad chest. She liked having him here, liked being shamefully alone with him, liked smelling him and seeing the way he caressed her with his eyes. They roved brazenly, across her face, her breasts, her stomach. She should have been uneasy with his bold regard, but she wasn't. There was approval in his assessment that made her feel feminine and beautiful.

"Well, then . . . are you ready to begin?"

Her heart pounding, her skin heating, she squirmed with anticipation. "Yes, I'm ready."

In all actuality, she felt as if she'd been *ready* her entire life.

"Arranged marriages have a way of working out as Ms. Holt proves in this emotional debut romance. Jane couldn't have a better teacher in the art of love than Phillip and each learns to meet the emotional as well as physical needs of one another." —*Romantic Times* on *The Way of the Heart*

Love
Lessons

Cheryl Holt

St. Martin's Paperbacks

LOVE LESSONS

Copyright © 2001 by Cheryl Holt.

All rights reserved. No part of this book may be used or reproduced in any manner whatsoever without written permission except in the case of brief quotations embodied in critical articles or reviews. For information address St. Martin's Press, 175 Fifth Avenue, New York, NY 10010.

ISBN: 0-312-97840-5

Printed in the United States of America

St. Martin's Paperbacks edition / October 2001

St. Martin's Paperbacks are published by St. Martin's Press, 175 Fifth Avenue, New York, NY 10010.

10 9 8 7 6 5 4 3 2 1

CHAPTER
ONE

James Stevens entered his office and closed the door with a soft click. He didn't bother to lock it. His staff was well trained, and none would dare enter while he conducted the coming interview. Not because they feared his wrath if they interrupted, but because not a single one of them could bear to witness what they uneasily called the *pleading* session that he was about to endure. The meetings were always distasteful, but he'd learned early on that the encounters were just one of the more unpleasant facets to owning a gambling establishment.

The woman waiting for him in the small room hadn't bothered to sit or help herself to the tea tray his servant had left for her. As with nearly all the others who had come before her, she was too distracted to enjoy the comfort offered by food or drink. She had remained by the window, staring out at the busy, cobbled street, her eyes looking at, but not really seeing, the multitudes of people and carriages passing by. The stiff set of her shoulders gave evidence of her resolve.

The dreary March rain drummed softly against the window, the gray sky shadowing her figure in interesting ways. Upon arriving, she'd relinquished her cloak, so he was able to study her openly, his eyes taking in every curve and valley accented by the cut of her expensive dark blue gown. It was a simple dress—one that she had probably spent hours selecting before deciding it was befitting of the occasion—but the excellent tailoring told him she led a life of incomprehensible affluence and privilege.

She was short, the top of her head just reaching his shoulders, and she was more thin than he typically liked his women to be. But, very likely, stress over her current life circumstance had caused a recent loss of weight. Her waist was tiny; he probably could have fit his hands around it, so tightly laced was her corset. The rest of her shapely torso was hidden by the curve of her skirt, but he'd always had a vivid imagination. With ease, he could visualize the flare of her hips, her long, long legs, her dainty feet.

Narrowing his eyes, he studied the back of her head, wondering as to the color of her hair. Most of it was hidden by her hat, but one perfect ringlet dangled free. It was blond, which made him think her eyes would be blue. A hint of bare skin about her neck showed it to be pale and creamy, the kind possessed by only the richest ladies who could afford the expensive creams and powders necessary to keep it smooth and young-looking. A delicate rose-scented perfume, French from the smell of it, wafted across the room and tickled his male senses.

From the feather in her hat, to the fabric of her gown, to the soft leather slippers on her feet, she was the absolute picture of English wealth and nobility.

Her gloved fingers distractedly worked her reticule, hideous scenes, no doubt, playing through her mind. Scenes of ruin, of poverty, of disgrace. Of no roof over her head, and no food for her children. Of the loss of her entire way of life.

She had to be terribly frightened, but as with all the other English ladies whom he'd met over the years, she was simply too well bred to display any sign of the strong emotion that had to be lingering just below the surface. Besides, if he'd learned anything from these heart-wrenching dialogues, it was that the women with whom he spoke had barely an inkling of what was truly coming. Her lack of agitation was presumably caused by her inability to rationally grasp the seriousness of her situation.

Invariably, she could foresee all sorts of horrors lurking just around the next bend, but the fates over which she postulated were still just possibilities. Her fear wasn't evident, because she still refused to believe that the worst could truly happen. In her world, bad things never did.

He could hardly blame her; he could hardly blame any of them. They were all positively certain that, whatever ghastly sin their wayward husbands had committed, it could be absolved by rational discussion, and if not by talking, then by other means. Nauseating as it sounded, he almost enjoyed seeing to what lengths his visitors would go to safeguard their domains.

All manner of bribes had been flashed before his eyes: cash, jewelry, the family silver, priceless works of art. Whatever the women possessed, they were prepared to offer in exchange for keeping their existences secure. Those who were most frantic always ended up offering themselves. When the meetings fell to that level, he wished he'd taken his father's advice and bought himself a commission in the army.

How desperate was the woman standing across the room? Who was her husband and what had he gambled away? Their estate? All their funds? Their children's inheritances? What would it be worth to her to stave off the future that was winging toward her like a runaway carriage? What humiliating act would she be willing to perform in her misguided attempts to save herself and her family?

How he hated this!

When the encounters ended, he was always so upset that his brother, Michael, insisted he should stop seeing the women who came begging for help. But James couldn't turn them away without letting them say their piece. Although he'd never been an admirer of the type of gently reared females who called, he couldn't help appreciating the bit of pluck they exhibited by daring all in a futile attempt to fix their predicaments.

It took such courage for them to come, in their anonymous rented hansom cabs. They knocked softly at the servants' entrance, dressed in their discreet clothing, their veiled hats, as they made their polite requests for an audience. Just showing up unescorted in his neighborhood, where a lady of Quality had no business being, was evi-

dence of their determination. He felt an obligation to talk
with them, and he'd managed to convince himself that he
was doing them a service.

Few of them had an accurate understanding of the re-
alities of their situations. Typically, they had no control
over their lives. They'd been so sheltered by fathers, brothers, and spouses that they had no idea about the value of
money, where it came from, where it went. They truly believed that they could repair the damage done by their male
relatives.

If nothing else of substance occurred during the heart-
wrenching discussions, he was usually able to open their
eyes to the true state of their dilemmas. While not an intentionally cruel person, he nevertheless exhibited a ruthless
bearing in dealing with his guests. He was not kind, he was
not patient, but he couldn't afford to be. There was nothing
he could do for any of them, and they needed to realize
that fact. Because of his behavior at times such as these,
he'd earned a reputation as a brutal, hard man.

He wasn't, but he couldn't show any weakness, lest the
despairing women go away mistakenly believing that res-
cue was feasible. They all had to begin preparing for the
approaching calamity. If he scared them into confronting
their dire plights, then he'd succeeded in his efforts.

"Good afternoon, madam," he said. He didn't intend to
ask her name. At this stage, they rarely gave it truthfully.
Obviously, she wasn't aware that he'd entered, and she
swung around at hearing his greeting. "I am James Stevens.
I was told you would like to speak with me."

"Hello, Mr. Stevens. Thank you for agreeing."

Her voice sounded low and husky, intimate, as though
she'd just whispered something deliciously erotic. Its tim-
bre conjured intense images of a hot room, sweat-soaked
torsos, stained sheets, the smell of sex heavy in the air.

His attention was immediately captured by her breasts;
he couldn't help noticing. Even though her dress was mod-
estly designed, the neckline was cut low in the current fashion, her corset raising and pushing, until he was presented

with an arresting view of tempting flesh. The flawless mounds were full and rounded, and strained against her bodice as though wanting to spill themselves out for his perusal. He could imagine them filling his hands, her skin warm against his own, her rose-colored nipples hard and elongated and pressing against his palms.

The unlikely prospect caused him to chuckle inwardly.

What would this troubled creature think if she could read his mind at the moment? She was here on a wretched mission, hoping to protect her family; while he could merely envision her naked, stretched out beneath him, and servicing his carnal needs.

But such was life. He'd sat through too many of these appointments, knew how it would end—badly—and he would much rather concentrate on more interesting topics. Such as the fabulous swell of her bosom. The cleavage she exhibited was dreadfully enticing.

Her face was shielded from view by the netting woven into her hat. All that remained visible was her mouth, the lips lush, moist, and crimson as a ripe cherry. It was the kind of mouth that made a man lose his concentration. Just by staring at it, he began to conjure the varied uses to which it could be put. Quite distinctly, he could conceive of her kneeling down, taking him far inside, giving him frightful pleasure.

Nervously, she ran her tongue across her bottom lip, the pink tip just visible as she wet it delicately. As he watched, he felt a keen stab of desire that took him far beyond fantasizing and into the realm of potentialities. To his great consternation, he could picture himself partaking of what she would eventually suggest once she realized that words would do her no good. The discovery was an extraordinary one.

In the decade that he'd owned the gaming house, he'd never taken advantage of any of the overtures the distressed women made. Not to say he hadn't been tempted, because he had been. Many of them were incredible beauties, and denying their proposals—to become his mistress, to provide regular sexual favors in exchange for promissory notes, to engage in a brief coupling in the manner of his choosing—was often difficult. He was only human, after all. Plus, taking into account his life experiences, one could hardly blame him for wanting to bring some of them down a peg or two.

Still . . . to consider breaking his self-imposed rule was immensely out of character, which intrigued him. What was it about this woman? Evidently, she gave off invisible signals to which his body was reacting. He was attuned to her as only a man could be. Attuned to her smell, to the smallest shift of her muscles, to the heat of her skin. Like an untamed animal, he was cognizant of everything about her, as though he knew in some primal way that he had selected the choicest female in his herd.

For some reason, he was tremendously curious as to the color of her eyes. He thought they would be blue, but he needed to know for certain, which irritated him in the extreme. His mental wanderings had led him too far afield, so he forced himself to the tedious task at hand.

"Lift your veil," he ordered. He never allowed any of his female guests to hide their identities. By the time they arrived in his office, they had few secrets worth keeping.

"Pardon?"

"Lift your veil," he repeated, stepping behind his desk and reaching for his favorite bottle of brandy. He poured a glass half full, drank it down, then turned back to her. "I assume you wish to have a discussion about a serious topic, and I refuse to engage in such unless I can see your eyes."

"I fail to understand how viewing my . . . my eyes is necessary."

"It will help me to judge if you are being candid." She prevaricated for the longest time, until he decided she was going to refuse, so he cautioned, "If you don't do as I ask, I will have my servant show you to the door. What a waste it would be to have come so far . . ." He let the thought trail off, let the implication linger.

Another silence ensued, and he could almost see the internal battle raging within: She had been brave enough to face him, but she had hoped to retain the bit of anonymity afforded by her hat. Just as he resolved to put an end to the charade by having her escorted out, she spoke again.

"I have something quite delicate to discuss with you," she said, "but if you should deny my request, I would rather that you not be able to recognize me at a later date."

"I realize that."

"Then perhaps I could—"

"No." Taking pity, he added, "I have discussed any number of *delicate* topics in this room. Whatever you have to say will neither surprise me nor shock me. Nor will it ever be repeated to another living soul. You have my word."

She assessed him, trying to decide the verity of his last statement. Would he keep her secrets? What value did his assurance hold? After all, his lineage was deplorable: a nobleman's by-blow, his mother a famous actress. He'd made his living the best he could, becoming quite well off in the process, but along the way, he'd rolled in the gutter with the worst sort of vermin, and none of them were of the lower classes.

On a daily basis, he gambled, drank, and consorted with women of dubious character—the only type he enjoyed—and his mode of employment required that he regularly intermingle with the most despicable sorts of human beings. He had seen and done things that would have slain lesser mortals, yet he persevered. How must one such as himself appear to the woman who was regarding him so meticulously? Could he be trusted?

A second lengthy inner struggle ensued, and she ultimately arrived at a decision.

"Very well," she said, resigned. Grasping the pin that secured it to the back of her head, she removed the offending hat and tossed it on a nearby sofa.

Her eyes were not blue. They were green, a deep emerald, as deep and vibrant as mowed grass on a summer day, and they were ringed by long, light-colored lashes, winged brows. Her skin was smooth as silk, her cheeks still rosy from the cold, her nose pert with an upturn at the end, a smattering of freckles across it. The hair he had originally theorized to be blond was much more than that: blond with streaks of auburn and gold as highlights. It was pulled up on her head, but he could imagine how it would look hanging free and spilling across her shoulders and down her back.

The man in her life who had sent her to do his begging had chosen well. She was an irresistible enchantress. Whatever her request, it would be difficult to refuse, but refuse he would.

"How may I help you?" he asked.

"I have a proposition for you."

"Really?" She intended no small talk! Most of them wanted to chat endlessly about their boring schedules or children, completely skirting the issue that had brought them sneaking into his establishment. He couldn't prevent himself from inquiring, "What kind of proposition?"

"It may sound quite odd," she said, not answering his question and only serving to pique his curiosity further. "In fact, considering that you don't know me, you might find it rather astonishing."

"I doubt that. As I said, I've had any number of amazing topics reviewed in this office."

"Yes, well . . . I don't expect you've ever heard anything like this."

"What is it?"

"Before we begin"—she glanced out the window, suddenly embarrassed to meet his gaze—"I must admit that I've listened to gossip. Others insist that you are remarkably circumspect."

"I am."

"Previously, you vowed that you would never disclose what we discuss, but I must ask anew for your guarantee that what I'm about to say will be held in the strictest confidence."

"What you have gleaned from others is true. I will never

divulge your secrets to anyone. As we are not acquainted, I don't know how to convince you other than to repeat myself: I am discreet."

She found the nerve required to look at him once again, and she stared, taking his measure. "Yes," she eventually mused, "I can see how you might be."

"Why don't we make this easier by your telling me who your husband is. I shall then have a frame of reference about of what and of whom we are conversing."

"My husband?" she queried, her brow wrinkling attractively. "I'm not married."

"Oh, I see." Perhaps a brother or her father had asked her to come. "Then who is it who has sent you to plead so prettily on his behalf?"

"I'm alone. No one knows I'm here."

"So . . . this is your own mission of mercy. Well, what is it you would have me do? Refund the money? Tear up the promissory notes?" When it appeared as though she might comment, he held up a hand, stopping her. "Before you respond, let me point out that I can very probably do none of those things. I hold few men's markers, and they are all for small amounts. Whatever your family has lost is most likely not mine to return."

"I think perhaps you have . . ."

"Aren't you listening?" He rudely cut her off, angry because she was disposed to sacrifice all, prepared to completely demean herself for an undeserving man. "I doubt I can be of service, but if I can, what will be my reward should I grant you a favor?"

"I'm not here to ask for a favor," she declared, clearly offended. "I fully intend to pay you for your services. I realize you are a busy man, and I would never dream of occupying your time without remuneration. I had thought fifty pounds might be about right." Apparently ready to retrieve the cash and hand it over, she glanced down at her bag.

"Fifty pounds?" He wasn't certain he'd understood correctly.

"Well, I'll go as high as seventy-five, but no higher."

Just when he'd deemed that nothing could surprise him, he was halted in his tracks. She wanted to pay *him*? "I guess I am confused. About what are we speaking?"

"I need to hire you with regard to a very personal undertaking."

"Hire me?" Coming around the desk, he rested against the edge directly in front of her. She was only a few feet away, and if he'd desired, he might have easily reached out and touched her waist or gripped her hand. At his unanticipated nearness, he could sense a prickle of sensation moving across her skin, see the manner in which her eyes widened, how she struggled to steady her breathing. Clearly, the lady felt the same strange attraction he was experiencing, and she had no immunity from these bizarre physical responses, either.

"What would you engage me to do?" he inquired.

"I need you . . ." she began, then paused, swallowed, started over. "Rather . . . I need your knowledge and skills."

"I'm good at so many things," he said facetiously. "In what arena do you require my marvelous attendance? My pugilistic abilities? Marksmanship? Swordplay? Gambling? Drinking? What?"

"Don't tease me. Please." She requested it quietly, fervently. "Simply being here is difficult enough."

"You're right, of course." He nodded his head in agreement. "My apologies."

"No. 'Tis I who apologize. I'm handling this poorly." Sighing in frustration, she added, "Perhaps, I should explain."

"Perhaps you should."

"I have it on good authority that you have quite a way with the ladies."

A muscle twitched in his cheek, but he did not immediately respond.

His reputation with the women of her social circle was shocking, contemptible, and mostly accurate. After his wife's death, he had blazed a carnal swath through the

Quality, making certain that he enjoyed the sexual company of those females who had shunned her in her short life. He'd intentionally broken hearts, strained marriages, and corrupted any number of women, but he had no regrets.

For her untimely demise, he had made them pay, and pay dearly.

"And your point is?" he asked.

"I would like . . . that is . . . well . . ." She wrung her hands in dismay. "Oh, this is so dreadfully difficult."

"I find it's easiest to just say what's on your mind. Whatever the subject matter, it can't be as hideous as it seems."

"All right." She took a deep breath, let it out, then turned toward the window, toying with the drape while she gazed outside, much as she'd been doing when he had first entered. "I am twenty-five years old. I have never been married, and therefore I am not overly familiar with the interactions of men and women, but . . . but I have need of instruction on what occurs between them during their private moments."

"To what *private* moments do you refer?"

"When they are . . . are . . ." She stammered, blushed fiercely, then whispered, "Intimate." Facing him once again, yet staring at the floor, she massaged a finger and thumb across the bridge of her nose as though she suddenly had a brutal headache. "You see, I find myself in a somewhat awkward position, and I am at a loss as to how to resolve it without someone to tutor me. The knowledge I pursue is not the type I can garner from any of my personal acquaintances."

No doubt about it, their meeting was becoming more peculiar by the second! He crossed his arms over his chest and studied her. "What is it you hope to learn?"

"Everything!" Suddenly agitated, her head came swinging up, and he was impaled by her earnest gaze. Her eyes were open wide, two rich pools of emerald green. She waved her arm, gesturing as though to encompass the entire world. "I want all the details. What happens. How it starts. How it ends. What goes on in between."

Over the years, women had invited him to do many things, but he'd never received a request that was remotely comparable to this one. He scowled, thinking he was hardly the man to instruct an untried woman on the intricacies of physical love. She'd said that she was aware of his reputation, but plainly she'd not caught the true facts. If she had, she'd never make such an outrageous solicitation. The type of *lessons* he could provide were a far cry from what such a sophisticated lady should ever be taught.

"I am of the opinion," he contended, "that you do not entirely realize what kind of man I am."

"I have no illusions." Her verdant eyes seemed to penetrate inside his being, her astute gaze piercing all the way to his black heart. He did not care for the impression at all, and he had the sharpest desire to hide from her comprehensive assessment, when she added softly, "I appreciate the sort of scoundrel you are. That is why I am here."

Not certain if he'd just been complimented or insulted, he growled low in his throat. "Have you no females who could assist or advise you?"

"Nary a one. Even if I dared ask, I'm not sure they would give me the guidance I'm seeking."

"Are you to be married?" Pending nuptials must be the reason for her odd proposal. "If so, your husband"—she made a derisive sound and rolled her eyes at the mention of a *husband*—"will instruct you on what you crave to understand. You need have no fear about that . . ."

"No," she cut in. "I shall never wed. I simply inquire for my own reasons."

"What are they?"

"I don't wish to say."

"So . . . you would like us to be lovers." He'd hoped that using the word *lovers* would shock her, but he was wrong.

"Well, not lovers specifically." Her response couldn't have been more casual if they'd been discussing the weather. "As I hardly know you, such familiarity wouldn't be appropriate, now, would it?"

"Then just what is it, precisely, that you're asking?"

"I thought we could . . . chat . . . and you could explain the . . . the mechanics, and the order in which things occur."

"The *mechanics* . . ."

"Yes. And the sequence of events."

He ran a wary hand through his hair, pondering, calculating, evaluating each and every word she spoke, but making no sense of her scheme. As he kicked it around in his head, several possibilities occurred.

Could this entire episode be a joke? Perhaps his brother was behind it. Even now, were Michael and others breathlessly waiting in one of the gaming rooms, ready to hear how he'd handled the woman's exceptional overture?

Perchance her appearance was an attempt at revenge for the havoc he had wreaked in his destructive vendetta against numerous members of the *ton*. Although it had been quite some time since he'd trifled with any of them, their memories were protracted and vicious.

Or it could be just as she said it was: a plea for help from a beautiful woman who needed a kind of sexual assistance that only he could supply. The very idea caused a tightening in his loins.

If her petition was genuine, the possibilities were endless. He'd start by talking to her, about carnality, about desire, about mouths and hands and tongues. His captive pupil, she would be an eager, zealous student who would want to learn all he could teach. No doubt she would quickly progress from a passive listener to an active participant who would need more detailed instruction.

What man could fail to be titillated by such a prospect?

Rising to his feet, he leaned close until they were face-to-face, eye to eye. Her skirts swirled and tangled about his legs. To her credit, she stood her ground, refusing to be intimidated by his size, by his nearness, by his masculinity.

Quietly, he insisted, "Tell me the true purpose behind your request."

"I don't wish to disclose my motivation to you."

"That's not an acceptable answer, for if I agree to help you . . ." Dear Lord, where had that come from? He absolutely was not going to consider this risky, foolish endeavor. Or was he? As he gazed down upon her comely face, her trim physique, he felt a stirring between his legs, a heating in his blood, a tingling in his fingers.

They hovered, touching but for the shape of her dress, and her unique musk overwhelmed him. She smelled like fresh-cut flowers, yet, at the same time, tangy like lemons or tart apples. If they had found themselves in a room of a hundred people, he could have been blindfolded and picked her out by that distinctive scent alone.

The aroma called to him on an ancient level of which he was hardly conscious, but he had intellect enough to realize that it resided at the very core of his manhood. His heightened state of perception was animalistic, a sort of chemical reaction that was impossible to resist, so why try to fight it?

Too long, he stared into her penetrating, shrewd green eyes, and he finally forced his gaze away, lower, coming to rest on the snow-white swell of her bosom, the press of her cleavage. The rigor of her breathing had increased with his proximity, and her chest rose and fell in a quick motion. With each intake of air, her breasts pushed against the rim of her bodice, continuing their struggle to burst free. Her nipples were aroused by the excess friction, and even through all the layers of fabric in which she was attired, he could make out the hard nubs.

Explicitly, he could imagine himself baring that superb chest, seeing those two delightful mounds for the first time. Gently and roughly, he would fondle them before sucking them far into his mouth. The ecstasy would be exquisite, and she would groan and sigh with pleasure.

Yes, he could definitely picture himself doing all that and more.

"If I agree," he reiterated, "there can be no secrets between us. Why do you demand this of me? What is the actual objective that makes you willing to engage in this impetuous exploit?"

" 'Tis hardly *impetuous*," she answered, affronted that

he would have such a low opinion of her capabilities. "I have been thinking about how to solve this dilemma for months. Only recently have I formulated this plan, although I must say, it has taken me some time to locate the courage to approach you. I've endured many a trying moment as I debated whether or not to go through with it."

"I'm sure it's been difficult. It isn't the type of discourse one would expect from a lady such as yourself."

"Then perhaps, in this instance, it is time for me to quit behaving as I usually do. I am willing to take whatever steps are necessary to obtain the information I require."

The admission seemed full of sexual promise and innuendo but also vaguely threatening, and he repressed a shiver that worked its way down his spine.

If he did not support her, would she seek assistance elsewhere? He couldn't bear the notion of her contacting some of the other men with whom he was acquainted. The very idea of how others might use and abuse her, how they might talk and spread stories after, terrified him. She could promptly land herself in a desperate circumstance without realizing what she'd done to cause it.

Better than anyone, he understood the ruthless environment in which she passed her days. Even the hint of scandal would end her life as she knew it to be. Amazingly, he didn't want any intolerable eventuality to happen to her. Just as she inspired an unusual physical attraction to swell through his veins, she also lit fire to his protective instincts, the ones he thought he'd properly buried years earlier. Being around her made him want to act the gentleman, to let chivalry rear its ugly head. He needed to guard her from harm and dishonor, but astoundingly the only method he could think of was to aid her in her search for knowledge.

If he didn't help her, to whom might she turn?

Still, one question nagged at the back of his mind. "As we have never met, why did you decide to come to me rather than another?"

She smiled, the intensity of it lighting up the room. "I hate to tell you."

"Why?"

"Because I don't think your masculine pride needs further inflation." She looked smug as she chuckled softly and admitted, "I inadvertently eavesdropped on some women who were talking about you. In explicit detail, I might add. They said some things that intrigued me very much."

When she did not elaborate, he prodded, "What things?"

She raised a brow. "That you are a man of much passionate experience, a dramatic and thorough lover, and that women flock to your side because of your amorous abilities."

His curiosity flared with his desire to discover who she had heard conversing and what, exactly, they might have disclosed that would have led her to brave this moment in time. "I guess I'm flattered."

"I don't know that you should be." She pursed her lips in slight disapproval. "To my untrained ear, your escapades sounded quite naughty. However, their stories also made you appear perfect for my purposes." She smiled again. "Now, then, since I have apparently been successful at stroking your male vanity regarding your female conquests, may I also hope that I have convinced you to do this vital service for me?"

He grinned in response, at her humor, at her mettle, at her ability to read him so well. They stood, not talking, the bit of mirth they shared gradually fading, the silence lingering. Long and hard, he stared into her eyes, looking for either lies or candor.

Perhaps he didn't recognize what he saw, perhaps he was being played for a fool, but he perceived only truth. There was something about the woman—a strength of character and resolve—that made it seem as if he had always known her, as if he could ascertain what she was thinking, what she was feeling, simply by being near and sharing a period of quiet contemplation. She was a woman to be admired. To be trusted. However . . .

His instinct for self-preservation was strong, and he needed to ensure that he wasn't walking into some sort of carnal trap from which he could not readily extricate himself. While he was now a grown man who would never succumb to the kinds of societal pressures from his father and others that had led to his marriage, he didn't intend to become embroiled in any type of public calumny over another virginal member of the Quality. The pressures from such an occurrence would be too oppressive. Also, there was his mother's peace of mind to consider, so he required time in which to ponder all the angles and consequences.

"I will need a few days to contemplate your request. When I have reached my decision, how may I contact you?" She retrieved a card from her reticule and handed it to him. He examined the direction she had jotted down.

"Are you familiar with this section of London?" she asked.

"Yes." It was in the theater district, a busy, bustling area filled with actors, musicians, and artists coming and going at all hours. Near, in fact, to his own domicile. It seemed the oddest location for the residence of the woman he believed her to be.

"Are you free this Thursday afternoon?"

"Yes," he responded again, not bothering to check his calendar but knowing that, if his resolution was positive, he would arrange his affairs accordingly.

"Should you decide to assist me, I've taken a small apartment in the neighborhood. Show yourself at the appropriate door at two o'clock, and I shall welcome you. 'Tis as simple as that." She reached for her hat and, with an efficient movement, secured it to her head. "After some reflection, should you find that you cannot help me, ignore the engagement. I will be disappointed, but I will understand. I realize I ask a great deal."

She was set to depart, but, curiously, he didn't want her to go just yet. There were many questions he wanted answered about why she was doing this. Regretfully, she wouldn't confess her rationale, but it was no matter. There were other methods of discovering what he needed to know.

"What shall I call you?" he queried, discomfited by a strange desire to learn her name, even if the one she provided was false.

She tipped her head one way, then the other, considering her reply. "If I see you on Thursday, I shall give you a name. If I don't see you, my name is of little import."

"I suppose not."

Unexpectedly, he was overcome with a desperate desire to touch her before she left. He reached out and took her hand, wishing it bare, the glove gone, so he could feel her smooth, warm skin against his own. He raised it to his mouth, his lips tarrying on the back, but as he did so, he kept his eyes fixed on hers. To his surprise and delight, she did not flinch or pull away, but viewed the incident inquisitively, as though trying to decide what to make of the intimate connection.

"*Au revoir,* madam," he said.

"Good-bye, Mr. Stevens. Thank you for meeting with me."

"Believe me, my dear, it has been an interesting and enlightening pleasure." He patted the back of her hand, then relinquished it, and she dropped it to her side.

An efficient servant appeared with her cloak and showed her out. He watched down the hall until she proceeded outside into the cold March drizzle, then he returned to the window and gazed at the street, tracking her progress as she crossed to the other side and walked down the block toward a rented hansom cab.

Just then, his younger brother, Michael, entered the room, lured by his desire for information about their latest secretive visitor. They were two years apart in age, James at thirty and Michael at twenty-eight, alike in many ways, but different in many others. They both possessed their father's tall, broad-shouldered stature and dark good looks, but they were made more striking by the receipt of their mother's startling blue eyes.

"How did it go?" Michael asked. "Not too disturbing, I trust?"

"No. Not disturbing in the least," James answered, turning to look at his sibling. "Actually, it was quite fascinating."

"Really?" Michael smiled in relief. "And to think I've been lurking down the hall, pacing, and waiting to rush in with comfort and brandy as soon as she quitted the premises."

"Unnecessary," James murmured distractedly. "Come closer," he commanded, and Michael stepped next to the sill. "Do you see that woman heading toward the cab stand?" He pointed at the street.

"That one there?"

James nodded, keeping an eye on her and the vehicle. "Do you have any idea who she is?"

"Actually . . . yes." James whirled, brow raised in question and, unabashed, Michael returned his probing stare. "You can't blame me for peeking when she walked by my office."

"No, I guess not. . . ." James glanced back to the street just as the woman climbed into the cab. The driver prepared to advance into traffic. "Her name?"

"Lady Abigail Weston."

"Marbleton's sister?"

"The older one. She's been secluded in the country for several years now. She's just arrived in Town."

It was hardly a surprise that Michael would know about Abigail Weston's appearance in London. Her older half-brother, the Earl of Marbleton, was a regular at their gambling tables, and Michael made it a point to uncover the paltry details of the lives of every customer. The information always came in handy sooner or later.

James carefully mulled the woman's exalted identity, trying to sort through the possibilities of why she'd come and what she truly hoped to accomplish. Marbleton was a man of despicable character, a self-righteous prig whom the two brothers couldn't abide. For his sister to have made her stunning approach, for her to have initiated such a shocking request, was absolutely the ultimate puzzle.

"Tell me all you recall about her," he urged. "Don't leave anything out."

TWO

Abigail Weston paced across the floor of the parlor in the cozy house she had rented in order to meet clandestinely with James Stevens. It was Thursday afternoon, five minutes before the hour of two. Carriage wheels sounded on the street below, and she couldn't prevent herself from rushing to the window to see if he had arrived.

He hadn't.

The carriage lumbered past without stopping, and she couldn't decide if she was relieved or disheartened.

"Five more minutes," she murmured, glancing at the clock over the mantel, although she had already decided she would wait an extra hour before giving up on him completely.

Would he show?

Nervously, she examined the furnishings of the unpretentious residence. The room was neat and tidy, a refreshment tray set on the table in front of the sofa. A cheery fire crackled in the grate. He had been drinking spirits during their brief meeting at his office, so even though it was the middle of the afternoon, she'd added a bottle of brandy to the sideboard in case he wanted something stronger than tea.

Everything appeared to be ready for his arrival, but still, she wished she was in familiar surroundings rather than this unknown, slightly worn dwelling. The strange environment added to her discomfort, though it was too late to worry. The site she'd selected couldn't be helped.

She'd had no choice but to pay for the temporary, covert location for their planned appointment. Before going to speak with him, she'd nearly driven herself mad trying to come up with a suitable solution in case he agreed to her demented scheme. Yet she could not think of a single site where the two of them could talk candidly.

In her sheltered, stilted world, a woman simply did not cross paths with men like Mr. Stevens. He was too unrestrained, too infamous, too scandalous a personage for a refined female to know. Therefore, she could hardly have asked someone to introduce them. They couldn't have had a *chance* encounter on the street, in the park, or in one of the city's more prominent establishments where the Quality liked to see and be seen. Word would have swiftly gotten back to her half-brother, Jerald, or—perish the thought!— his wife Margaret, and there would have been no end to the pandemonium any type of association with Mr. Stevens would create.

As Earl of Marbleton, Jerald was a stuffy, boorish man; his wife, righteous, vain, and self-centered. Their lives were ruled by propriety and social status, and neither of them would ever understand Abigail's need to mingle with someone from the lower classes. If she was caught with Mr. Stevens, even in the most innocent of circumstances, there would be no excuse she could give for her behavior.

As the notorious bastard son of the Earl of Spencer, James Stevens was the most insulting, disreputable, and inappropriate type of person Jerald and Margaret could imagine. No matter what type of man he was on the inside, for them, his birth status said all.

But she was determined to succeed, so she'd eventually settled on renting in the out-of-the-way neighborhood where they could both come and go with relative anonymity. Indeed, she'd found herself relishing the bit of daring and deception it had taken to secure their secret hiding place, and she eagerly anticipated what would occur during their conferences, however few or many they might turn out to be.

She had no idea how many visits would be required, but she assumed it would take at least two or three discussions to learn all. If they needed more time, they would have it. A six-month lease had been signed to retain the property, but she didn't mind. Money was not a problem, and the insignificant expense was worth it if it helped to bring her the information she sought.

The rendezvous at his office had been the most exciting event of her rather eventless life. It had also been the most difficult, but she thought she had pulled it off well. In spite of the fact that she had been frightened and apprehensive, she'd hidden her trepidation, appearing assured and confident.

She'd hoped he would believe she was a mature, worldly woman who could converse about adult topics without stammering or swooning, and not what she actually was: a shielded spinster who had few clues about how men and women interacted. She was certain she'd come across as a bold person, despite her thinking that nothing could have been worse than looking him in the eye and making her strange request.

However, as she'd learned in the past few days and hours, asking for his help had been the easy part. Keeping their planned assignation was another matter altogether. Showing up for their second rendezvous took much more temerity than the original appointment.

Oh, what madness had ever possessed her to decide this was a good idea?

For twenty-five years, she'd stumbled along without knowing the details of marital relations. Very likely, she could stumble along for twenty-five more.

Just pondering what was coming caused her heart to begin pounding all over again, and she rubbed her hand across the center of her chest, attempting to ease its furious beating. The motion brought her wrist in contact with her right breast, so she quickly stopped herself. Since her meeting with Mr. Stevens the previous Monday, her breasts had become overly sensitive. They were fuller, heavier, her nipples constantly working against the lace of her chemises, pressing in an irritating way against the bodices of her dresses.

At the strangest times, she'd find herself feeling too hot

when there was no reason to be, and she'd be fanning her face while others were complaining about being too cool. Eventually it had dawned on her that these moments of overheating coincided with the straying of her thoughts in Mr. Stevens's direction.

Restless and aching, she was suffering in bodily spots she had never noticed before. Her skin felt too tight, as though she needed to molt it off. At night, she couldn't sleep, but tossed and turned, trying to get comfortable, all the while imagining what sorts of wicked subjects they would inevitably review.

She kept picturing Mr. Stevens and how he had looked that day in his office. Heat had seared up her arm when he had kissed her hand in good-bye. The brief sensation had been unlike anything she'd previously encountered. How she wished she had not been wearing a glove so that he might have touched his lips directly against her skin!

After arriving in London from the family estate in early January, her only visit since her debut at age seventeen, she had barely been in Jerald's Town house an hour when she'd heard Mr. Stevens's name for the first time. Two of the servants had been gossiping about him when they thought no one was listening. Apparently he had been keeping company with a widow for whom one of them had been previously employed. Mr. Stevens had broken off the relationship, and the spurned widow was beside herself, furiously striving to regain his attention.

Both servants insisted the widow wouldn't prevail. When Mr. Stevens finished with a woman, he never went back, and rumor had it that he was already seeing another.

Abigail might not have remembered his name at all had it not been whispered and bandied about on five different occasions during her initial week of social calls. Numerous women appeared to know him quite intimately, and those who did not had no qualms about discussing him at great length. She had been in a retiring room, unseen and unnoticed, when she'd finally gleaned shocking specifics.

Two giggling women—both were slightly inebriated—

had been recalling their previous evening's entertainments, how the two of them had gone to his bed together. Most of what the pair had uttered was beyond her comprehension, but she couldn't prevent herself from listening. Long after the women had departed, she remained where she had been standing, aghast and, for some reason, stimulated by what she had learned, though she couldn't have said why.

Generally, she was left with questions: Why would two women go to one man's bed? Why was the experience so thrilling for them? What exactly was it that they had done to him with their mouths? Where did this indisputable joy come from that had them waxing on in such an indiscreet fashion?

Although she had eavesdropped in the worst way, she was frightfully glad for the sexual tidbits she'd uncovered while hiding behind the ferns. Up until that moment, she had earnestly believed that men and women shared the marital bed in order to breed children—the hows and whats of it still a mystery—and for no other reason. Clearly, she'd been wrong, which made her understand that much had been skimmed over and downright omitted in her limited education regarding procreative matters.

Obviously, there were people in the world who truly enjoyed the marital act and who engaged in it on a regular basis for the sole purpose of finding pleasure. The women whom she'd stumbled upon were from lofty families, so she couldn't attribute their delight to their having common natures. They were both highborn ladies who had sought out a man who was not their husband, who had committed unspeakable acts with him, and who couldn't wait to do it all again at the earliest possible opportunity.

During their hushed conversation, they had made much of James Stevens's good looks and broad physique. So, when she had turned to face him in his office, she had been expecting to encounter a comely gentleman. Instantly, however, it was clear that the words used to describe him had fallen far short of their mark. By far and away, he was the most handsome man she'd ever seen.

He was tall, six feet at least, with dark hair, so dark it had looked black in the dim light of the rainy afternoon. It was neatly trimmed in the front, the back strands curling deliciously over his collar, the style only serving to emphasize his beautiful face, his high cheekbones, his aristocratic nose. And his eyes!

They were a fathomless blue, a deep striking sapphire that drew her in and held her spellbound. When he had looked at her with those magnificent eyes, his gaze boring into hers, she felt as though he could peer to her very core where all her insignificant heartaches and loneliness quietly rested. He seemed to know things about her that no one else had ever guessed. The sensation was disconcerting, but new and interesting, and therefore welcomed at this period in her life.

Did he look at all his women that way? Was it a special gift he had? Was that why he was so popular with the ladies?

Perhaps he made them all feel that he saw something unique and special that no one else had ever noticed. She herself had come away from their appointment with the particular impression that they shared a distinct affinity, that she could tell him secrets she would never have dared speak to another, and because he understood her so well, he would neither judge nor condemn . . .

More carriage wheels sounded below, and she jumped toward the window, furtively glancing into the street just as the knocker banged on the front door. Though she had retained a woman to do minimal cooking and cleaning, Abigail had arranged it so that the servant would never be present if Mr. Stevens came to call, so there was no one to answer. Her hand fluttered to her throat, and she physically stopped herself from making such a silly motion. She'd never been a *flutterer,* and she wasn't about to start now.

Taking a deep breath, she headed for the stairs and started down, relieved that he had arrived promptly, thus saving her from endless minutes of further torment. At the bottom, she paused briefly by the mirror, making a last check of her appearance.

The dark green dress she'd chosen for their afternoon engagement was simple but elegant, with a high neck and long sleeves. She had spent hours agonizing over what to wear, finally deciding that the rich color and plain style would help her to appear serene and self-possessed. Since she was neither, she appreciated aid from any corner, hence the unassuming gown.

Her hair was neatly braided and pinned up on her head, her cheeks rosy from the past hour of fervent pacing. All in all, she looked quite fetching, which made her more certain of her intentions.

With a trembling feeling coursing through her body, she forced a smile, then reached for the door and opened it.

"Hello, Mr. Stevens," she said, encouraged to discover that she sounded calm and collected. "I'm so glad you decided to join me. Do come in." She stepped aside to allow him space to enter.

In his perfectly tailored light blue coat and snug-fitting tan breeches, he was more handsome than she recollected. His snowy white cravat was perfectly tied, his tall black boots buffed to the brightest shine, and he appeared to be a gentleman out taking an afternoon stroll. There wasn't the slightest hint that he was an earl's bastard, that his mother was a woman of supposedly low moral character, that he made his living by owning a gaming establishment. Gallant and refined, he seemed perfectly comfortable with the idea of meeting an unknown woman for a few hours of sexual discourse.

As he moved inside, wonderful masculine aromas, of fresh air, horses, and tobacco, filled the foyer, and she couldn't prevent a sudden flight of feminine fancy from creeping over her, which made her feel she was welcoming him home.

What would it be like to have a man as part of her life, to wait impatiently, ready to greet him after his long, hard day? Up until this instant, she hadn't realized she'd missed having her own husband and family. Perhaps the peaceful years she'd passed in the country had lulled her into a false sense of personal serenity.

He carried a brown satchel, a sort of portfolio, made of soft leather. The flap was tied at the front with a black ribbon, and she tried to avoid showing any overt curiosity. As he began to remove his outerwear, he held on to it with one hand. His eyes never left hers as he did so, and she hung his damp cloak on a peg next to the door, rested his hat on a nearby chair. There was a closeness generated from handling his belongings that she enjoyed very much.

"If we meet a second time," he mentioned, the soft baritone of his voice brushing across her skin and reverberating through her nerve endings, "you should leave the door unlocked, and I shall admit myself. 'Tis not advisable for me to linger on the stoop, even if it is only for a few moments."

"You're right." She gestured toward the stairs, finding it amazing that they could converse casually as though nothing unusual were occurring. "Shall we go up?"

"After you," he responded politely.

She ascended to the drawing room and, even though he was behind her, she was aware of every single thing about him. The way he smelled. The way he moved. Where he was concerned, she had developed an extra sense that made her cognizant of him in a manner she'd never been with another person.

Once inside the parlor, he shut and locked the door behind them, and she wasn't certain if she was frightened or reassured. Due to the traits she'd ascertained about his character, it had never occurred to her to be afraid of him, and now they were totally alone. At the sound of his laying his mysterious pouch on the table, she located the fortitude necessary to confront him. She turned.

"Your name," he said, without preamble, "is Abigail Weston."

She gasped. Her knees suddenly weak, she collapsed against the sofa. "How did you know?"

"Your half-brother"—he continued without answering her question—"is Jerald Weston, Earl of Marbleton. You had the same father; different mothers. You are twenty-five years old. You have never been married, although you were once engaged for a short time when you were seventeen. Your fiancé died of the influenza shortly after your betrothal was announced. As far as anyone can determine, you've never had another beau. Your mother died when you were eighteen, and since that time, you have remained in the country, efficiently finishing the raising of your younger sibling, Caroline."

"Oh, my. . . ." She pressed the tips of her fingers against her mouth, feeling as though she might be ill all over the rented carpeting.

"Caroline is now seventeen. The two of you have come to London and are staying with the earl at his Town house, where you will chaperone and supervise her during her presentation at court and her debut. It is expected that she will be one of the belles of the coming Season, and that she will become engaged in the months ahead. Under your guidance, she is expected to make a grand match due to her familial connections, attractiveness, friendly manner, and large dowry." Casually, he walked to the sideboard and poured himself a brandy. Taking a prolonged sip of the amber liquid, he watched her over the rim of the glass and asked, "Have I left anything out?"

"Oh, dear Lord . . ." she murmured, at a loss as to how to proceed. She had no background for enduring this type of confrontation or for dealing with this kind of man, and she should have known better than to think she could enter his domain, yet exit unscathed. Complete mortification flowed through her entire being.

She had to get out of there! Immediately! She needed to scurry back to her safe, secure world, where she knew the day-to-day routines, the rules and strictures by which she was to live. Not daring a glance in his direction, she rose to leave.

"Sit!" he ordered calmly but forcefully, and because she

had spent a lifetime obeying male dictates, she did as he commanded, perching against the edge of the sofa like a trapped animal awaiting the opportunity to flee.

He let the silence linger until it became so unpleasant that she was afraid she might embarrass herself by screaming in frustration. Her eyes remained fixed on the floor, but she could sense his gaze like a tangible object, sweeping across her, assessing her defeated form, her sagging spirit. How she wished she could simply vanish into thin air! That the floor would open and swallow her whole!

When she could no longer tolerate the quiet, she queried, "How did you detect my identity?"

"You're an eminent personage. My brother recognized you as soon as you entered our establishment."

His words stung like a betrayal and hit like a blow. She flinched. How stupid she had been, believing herself clever, unknown, covert! How he must have laughed when she'd departed his office!

A disturbing possibility arose. "What will you do with the information you have gathered?"

"Nothing," he responded firmly, the simple word making her yearn for the necessary bravado to look him in the eye, but she honestly could not bear it. "I gave you my vow that our meeting would remain private, and so it shall."

"Then why . . ." Her question trailed off.

"Because I am a cautious man who likes to establish all the facts before making a decision, and after uncovering your prominent rank I have spent many agonizing hours trying to figure out the actual purpose behind your request. I must confess that your intention eludes me." He took another sip of the brandy. "So tell me, Lady Abigail, what is the true reason you have asked me here?"

"It doesn't matter now." She rose on unsteady legs. "I shall take my leave, and I hope—actually, I beg of you—that if you ever encounter me again, you will have the decency to pretend we have never met."

In a quick, graceful move, rather like an advancing predator, he stepped in front of her, blocking her way to the door. "Has your thirst for carnal advice suddenly disappeared?"

"I find that it has," she admitted. "Now, if you will excuse me . . ." She tried to slide around him, but he shifted with her, and she couldn't pass.

"I do *not* excuse you," he asserted. "I am perfectly willing to instruct you. All you need do is answer my question: What is the reasoning behind your inquiry?"

He inappropriately rested a hand on her waist, and she recoiled from the heat of his unexpected touch. Her skittishness caused him to chuckle, which made her furious. More forcefully, she repeated, "It doesn't matter now."

"It does to me."

The solemnity of his statement provided her with the strength she needed to meet his gaze. "Why would it?"

"Discovering your elevated status has only served to increase my sense of how important this quest is to you. That a woman in your position would seek out a man like me . . . that you would ask me for sexual counsel . . . Your behavior shows me that you are serious and resolute and in need of my help. I am, therefore, glad to give it to you. But you *must* answer my question."

She hesitated, not certain what to do. He seemed sincere. What could it hurt to confide in him? As he had previously pointed out, if they commenced down this road, there would be no secrets between them. Surely she could divulge a bit of the truth.

Utterly perplexed, she sighed. "Oh, I don't know what's best."

Appreciating the depth of her confusion, he leaned down to the folder he'd laid on the table when he first entered. He ran his hand over the soft cover, stroking it as one might lovingly pet a favorite animal. "I am ready to begin your first lesson," he said. "Surely that's what you still want, what brought you here." His fingers were hypnotic, massaging the leather. "Share your rationale with me, and the knowledge shall be yours."

Because he would not let her reach the door, she turned

the other way, walking to the window and looking out at the gray day, the busy street. The glass felt cool against her palm as she mulled her situation.

What could it hurt? The question played over and over in her mind. She'd come this far. What could it hurt?

"Tell me," he coaxed from across the room. "I will not betray your trust. I swear it on my mother's life."

The very idea, that he would invoke his mother during this debacle, sent her defenses crumbling. Apparently he had a different view of his mother's character than that shared by the rest of the world, making his pledge sound dramatic and unquestionable. She couldn't discredit it. Besides, she rationalized, the damage was done. If he wished to blackmail her in some fashion, he already had the details with which to ruin her life. She had to rely on him. What other choice was there?

"You are correct," she said, still staring outside, "that my sister, Caroline, is in the City for her come-out. And yes, I fully expect that she will have a grand debut and that we will find her a wonderful husband. That is why I have come to you."

"Because she is marrying?"

"Because I am her sister, but also her friend." Gathering all her courage, she faced him. "She looks to me for guidance in this matter of selecting a husband, and already she has been asking me questions."

"About what?" he prodded gently.

"About men and their wives. What they do when they are alone together. How it will be." He accepted her explanation so calmly and readily that she was greatly encouraged. "I find myself completely in the dark about how to advise her."

"No one has taken the time to enlighten you?"

"I suppose I could tell her what my mother told me." She blushed bright red, which she was quite certain was going to be her perpetual state while she was in his company.

"And what is that?"

She couldn't believe that she was about to address such an indiscreet topic, but on observing nothing but curiosity and understanding in his eyes, she pressed ahead. "Mother said that my husband would inflict himself upon me in a foul and disgusting manner."

"Oh, for pity's sake—" He bit off a curse.

"She explained that my *wifely* experience would be painful and humiliating, but that it was my duty to suffer through any indignity to which my spouse would like to subject me. Let's see . . . what else?" She tapped a finger against her lip, remembering every detail of that horrid conversation. "Oh, yes . . . that his revolting attentions would occur with regular frequency, and I would need to mentally compose myself during the months preceding my marriage so that I did not overly embarrass myself—or him—on my wedding night."

He refilled his glass, silently pondering her astonishing statement, eventually shaking his head in derision. "I never cease to be amazed by the women of your station, Lady Abigail."

"Neither do I, Mr. Stevens."

They shared a keen look that broke the tension. Tentatively, she stepped toward the couch and balanced herself on the seat, taking overly long in adjusting her skirts. "Recently, a friend of Caroline's was married," she stated. "She's a year older than my sister and made her debut last Season, but apparently she was totally unprepared for what her marital duties would entail. Being unwed ourselves, we were not allowed to visit with her, but rumor has it that she was so stunned by what happened on her wedding night that she has been under a physician's care ever since. She has retired to the country."

"Yes, I had heard the same rumor."

"Is there no sordid transpiration about which you don't know?" she asked, smiling.

"I make it my business to be aware of the affairs of my customers," he replied, shrugging.

"I can see where that might be helpful to a man in your

position." She fiddled with her skirts, once again letting the silence linger on, until she mastered the daring to confess her greatest wish. "I want Caroline to find joy, Mr. Stevens." She let her gaze settle on his astute, sapphire eyes, needing him to understand how vital was her objective. "My sister is a wonderful girl, and she should marry for love, and be happy and fulfilled through her choice of a spouse. When she comes to me with questions, I pray that I will be able to give her the proper answers, and the tools with which to flourish at the more private side of her wedded condition."

"I think you are being very wise."

"You do?" She was pleased and startled.

"Yes."

She was so elated to have his approval that she felt as if all her bones had suddenly turned liquid. "Do you think it is possible for a woman like Caroline to enjoy what will unfold in her marriage bed?"

"I'm certain of it."

"I had always suspected as much"—she nearly slid to the floor, her relief was so tremendous—"despite what I have heard over the years. Will you teach me the details so I may share the information with her when the time is right?"

"Of course, I will," he responded without equivocation, "but upon one condition."

Her heart sank. Would he now speak of blackmail? Of terms? "What is it?"

"I will go to great lengths to ensure no one discovers that we have met. However"—he sipped his drink pensively—"should our liaison be exposed, it will cause quite a scandal."

"I'm aware of that fact."

"If the worst should happen, I will make no move to save your reputation. I will fight no duels in your honor. I will not marry you. I will do nothing."

"I understand." She nodded firmly. "I am a woman full

grown. As this has all been at my instigation, I would expect no reparations from you."

"Then we are agreed?"

"We are agreed," she repeated, standing, and he towered over her so closely that she could have reached out and laid her palms on his broad chest. She liked having him here, liked being shamefully alone with him, liked smelling him and seeing the way he caressed her with his eyes. They roved brazenly, across her face, her breasts, her stomach. She should have been uneasy with his bold regard, but she wasn't. There was approval in his assessment that made her feel feminine and beautiful.

"Do you own this house?" he asked.

"No. I have only let it so we would have a location to carry out our discussions."

"How long is your lease?"

"Six months."

His brow rose, and he laughed, a full, rich sound that made her pulse accelerate. "Were you anticipating need of protracted tutoring, or were you thinking you might prove a slow pupil?"

"It was the shortest lease I could negotiate." She smiled in return, being forward and flirtatious. In his company, new behaviors were popping up every second!

A dimple creased his cheek, making him look like the devil himself come to call. "All right, then. I propose that we meet twice a week. Monday and Thursday afternoons. For the next month."

"Eight times." She sighed, thinking that *eight* times was not very many! There was definitely a part of her character she had never recognized before, because she craved this bit of stealthy adventure, this notorious secret to keep between the two of them. Mostly she relished being so improperly sequestered with him, but despite what she had done so far, it went against her nature to act immodestly, so she couldn't propose a longer tryst.

"Eight times will be fine," she concluded.

"If we decide that's too few, you'll still have this place. We can extend our appointments."

She couldn't believe her surge of excitement: a drowning woman thrown a rope! "I would like that," she admitted, pretending a calm she hardly felt.

"Along the way, should you need to cancel, just send a note 'round to my office."

"And if *you* should need to cancel," she echoed, "I would prefer that you not contact me. I will simply come here to learn that you have not arrived."

"As you wish."

" 'Tis safer. For both of us."

"Yes, it is," he couldn't help but acknowledge. "Well, then . . . are you ready to begin?"

Her heart pounding, her skin heating, she squirmed with anticipation. "Yes, I'm ready."

In all actuality, she felt as if she'd been *ready* her entire life.

THREE

"Do you have any idea of what occurs between a man and a woman when they are alone together?" James stood next to the sideboard, eyeing her where she sat on the short sofa.

"Not really," Lady Abigail answered honestly. "I know they lie down in the same bed, and somehow babies are magically created." She shifted uncomfortably. "However, I've always suspected that there was a little more to it than that."

He chuckled, asking, "Have you ever seen a naked man?"

"Of course not!" she maintained vehemently. "When would I have?"

"How about a painting? Perhaps a statue." She shook her head. "Maybe one of your brothers when they were bathed as children?"

"I was never allowed to watch or help. It simply wasn't done."

James crossed the room and settled himself next to her, not touching but nonetheless feeling the caress of her all the way down his body. Her unique smell filled the space around him, and it flowed over him like a carnal cloud, stimulating his senses.

In profile, her face was perfectly assembled. The high, smooth brow, the long lashes, the adorable nose, the full lips. Combined with the swell of her breast, the tuck of her waist, the flair of her hip, she was an outrageously beautiful female who had tickled his fancy on more than one occasion during the past few days and nights.

Remarkably, he'd suffered numerous moments of physical and emotional turmoil as he'd pondered her request, where their assignations could lead, what her acquiescence would mean. Especially after Michael had provided the information regarding her lofty station, he had been unable to keep her far from his thoughts. Even his dreams had been disordered by her, and upon rising, his tangled sheets were proof of how he'd tossed and turned, fantasizing about her both consciously and unconsciously.

As he'd grasped when they first met, aiding the woman presented numerous erotic possibilities—none of which he had the least interest in resisting. He'd always been called a bastard, for reasons having nothing to do with his birth, and in light of his plans where she was concerned, many would likely consider his base character to be showing its true form. But he didn't care.

He wanted her. It was as simple as that. And he intended to have her—eventually.

From the start, he'd been devastatingly attracted to her. She stroked his male temperament in a fashion that had only happened previously on the rarest occasions. He was a man of vast experience with women, possessed of a strong sexual drive, and he seldom declined what was offered, so he understood well what was occurring whenever he drew near to Abigail Weston.

They were intimately compatible in a manner he could not deny. Whether she gave off a specific scent, a vibration, a chemistry, he didn't know, but he was aware of her on a plane that was different from the other females who orbited his universe, and he was glad. For so long, he'd been searching for a diversion from the lackluster carnal encounters in which he regularly engaged. The lovers with whom he consorted were always possessed of great skill. They could and would do the most flagrant, wanton, even perverse things in their attempts to please him, but, quite simply put, he was bored with all of them.

Discontented, unhappy in his personal affairs, he was perpetually seeking the type of hot desire that had come so easily when he was young and sexual congress was still so new. Without exception, each moment of each encounter had been breathtaking. He wanted to discover the path back to those heady times, and he couldn't prevent himself from hoping that perhaps he'd found it in the slender blond sitting next to him. Everything about her aroused him.

Even now, just from being near her, his trousers were tight, his loins uncomfortable, and the two of them had yet to commence. He simply couldn't quit thinking about her and what he would like to do with her, and he didn't intend to stop himself from enjoying any pleasures he might ultimately encounter. Of course, she didn't realize his plan; she thought she was here to learn the variations of marital intercourse so she could interpret them for her younger sister.

But James understood more about women than any other subject, and he appreciated where their innocent talking would lead. She was an untried, twenty-five-year-old virgin, her body primed and ready for a sexual upheaval. He, with great delight, was prepared to make sure she experienced one.

From the straightening of her spine, and the nervous opening and closing of her fists, he could tell he disturbed her. These were very good signs of the sensual future they would inevitably share.

"You've never seen a naked man?" he asked again. "Not even when you were engaged?"

"Mercy, no!" she asserted, blushing delightfully. "How could you imagine such an occurrence would have happened?"

"Many betrothed couples decide they cannot wait for their wedding night."

"Not me. And certainly not my fiancé!" She dared a sideways glance, looking at him through veiled lashes. "What kind of woman must you believe me to be?"

"I think you are the finest lady," he responded truthfully, while contemplating how dreadfully pretty she was up close. All smooth skin, moist lips, and pink cheeks. "I make no judgments through my questions. I only wish to determine where we should begin, and I had wondered if perhaps you and your fiancé . . ."

"No." She laughed softly. "I hardly knew him, and I was never alone with him."

"Very well," he said, intrigued by the sheltered life she'd led. She was five years younger than himself, yet in many ways innocent as a child. Her upbringing had been so contrary to his own. Just by the fact that his mother was an actress, he'd been raised around theater people and other artists, so he'd nearly always associated with women who were cognizant of the facts of life from an early age. With the exception of his wife, his lovers had always been adept, uninhibited women.

Her naïveté captivated him; it thrilled him, as well. He relished the chance to act as her tutor. What sort of willing pupil might she eventually turn out to be?

"Let us start," he said, "by my explaining the basics. We will expand from there."

"That sounds like a good idea."

One corner of her lovely mouth lifted in a tentative smile, making her appear as if she couldn't quite decide if she wanted to hear what he had to say or not. Despite her insistence that she was ready to learn all, she was about to be tremendously shocked—perhaps even alarmed—by what he would impart.

"This will be difficult for you. We are going to discuss things you've never imagined, and we will speak of body parts and bodily functions. I don't want you to feel overly embarrassed or shamed about the topics we will mention. Please ask me any questions that come to mind. Can you do that? Can you ask me questions?"

"I think so," she murmured quietly. " 'Tis very easy to talk with you."

"Good. I promise that I will do my best to respond openly and honestly." She nodded hesitantly, accepting his gesture, and he continued. "A man and a woman are created differently," he said. "In their private parts between their legs."

"Why?"

"Because their private parts are used for sexual mating.

Unclothed, a man and a woman look completely dissimilar."

"Really?" She held her eyes bravely affixed to his, but he could sense that she wanted to peek lower, as though she could peer through his trousers to see if his statement was true. The thought of her viewing his naked form and assessing his aroused state sent a jolt of heat straight to his groin, and he had to fight back a lusty groan. Amazingly, she could instill such stinging desire, not by doing anything, but solely through her proximity.

"Really," he eventually replied, then he paused for a lengthy period, pondering his unruly cravings—so long, in fact, that she finally broke the silence with a chuckle.

"Might I hope," she inquired, "that your hesitation means you're having as much difficulty with this as I am?"

"No, it's not that," he said, smiling while he lied. "I'm just trying to think of the appropriate way to describe the process."

Leaning forward, he braced his elbows on his knees, deciding that the details would be easier to supply if he avoided her gaze. "A man is constructed differently from a woman. Mainly in the spot where his legs are joined. He has a sort of . . ." Deep in thought, he stared at the opposite wall, choosing words. How could he accurately describe the bloody thing to someone who'd never seen one? "A sort of protrusion."

"What is it called—this protrusion?"

"Many things. A phallus, a penis, a cock." There were many other names, but for the life of him, he couldn't recall any of them.

"How do you refer to it?"

He cleared his throat. "I suppose I use *cock* most often."

"Then I believe that's the term I shall use."

He hardened instantly. Just the notion of the word coming from her pristine lips was unbearable, and he caught himself shifting from side to side, trying to ease the fullness of his trousers.

He forced himself onward. "A cock is usually flaccid as

a man goes about his day-to-day affairs, but during a time of sexual stimulation, it becomes very hard and erect. It is from this *hard* member that a white cream erupts during mating. The white cream carries his seed with which he impregnates a woman. The release of this . . . this cream is a highly pleasurable development, one that men seek to enjoy before all others."

"What causes this *eruption* of a man's bodily cream?"

"A man places his cock betwixt a woman's legs." Realizing that the next might be the most embarrassing topic she'd hear all day and wanting to observe how she withstood it, he compelled his gaze to meet hers. In her world, for a gentleman to even know about female menses, let alone to comment on it, would be the height of indecorum. "He pushes the tip into the spot from which her monthly blood flows"—no visible reaction—"where there is a bodily opening to her womb, then he shoves the entire cock inside—"

"Inside?" She sounded incredulous, aghast.

"Yes . . . inside, and by stroking himself back and forth, a captivating friction is created which causes him to spill his seed."

A long silence ensued, and she finally murmured, "I see," although from the bewilderment on her face, he was fairly certain she didn't see at all. She nervously wet her bottom lip, then asked, "Are the parties undressed?"

"Sometimes," he responded. "Sometimes not."

"Why is that?"

"They might be so overcome with passion that they hope to accomplish the act as quickly as possible, so they wouldn't want to waste time disrobing."

"And how about during more normal circumstances?"

"If a husband wished to preserve his wife's modesty, he could simply lift the hem of her nightgown. However, I do not know of a single man who takes his marital pleasure that way."

"Why?" she asked again. So many whys.

"Well . . . most men enjoy the extra luxury created by

touching their wives' skin. They become more excited when their wives are naked."

"A woman would most likely be completely unclothed from the very first?"

"Yes."

She inhaled, then let the breath out slowly, almost painfully. "I suppose this sounds dreadfully improper, but I must admit that I am utterly fascinated. And astounded. I had no idea. . . ."

" 'Tis amazing, really," he agreed. "Imagine how shocked a gently raised girl could be on her wedding night."

"As Caroline's distressed friend is said to have been."

"Yes. Just like her, and your sister could easily end up in the same predicament. A bride's initial marital experience can be very frightening if the husband is not a considerate lover. As I said earlier, I think you're being very wise by planning ahead."

She searched his eyes for the truth of his statement and found it. "Thank you."

"You're welcome."

"I have a question," she said, suddenly eager to go on. Apparently, receipt of this thimbleful of knowledge had only served to pique her curiosity. Already she desired more. "I don't exactly understand how the man and woman fit together. . . ."

"I thought you might wonder, so I have something to show you." He grabbed his satchel from the table and rested it on his lap, her eyes following his every move. "I've brought some pictures that will illustrate what I'm telling you."

"What kind of pictures?" she asked.

"Sexual pictures. They were painted by a friend of mine in Paris many years ago. They're quite enlightening."

"What do they depict?"

"They portray a man and woman progressing through the steps of a sexual joining." He relocated himself on the sofa so that their arms and thighs were pressed together, the fabric of her skirt flowing across his leg and boot. "Obviously, they are motionless renderings, so they can't give you the entire flavor of how it goes, but the drawings are very detailed."

"Why would an artist make such pictures?" She squinted at the flap of the envelope as though she could compel her vision to pierce through the leather so that she could view the first sketch.

He stated the obvious. "For money."

"No!"

"There is quite a market for this sort of thing." He grinned as he recalled Pierre, Paris, and the wonderful days he'd spent there as a young man. "The demand is much greater for these than it is for my friend's innocuous watercolors of Paris street corners."

"How come?"

"Most men regard erotic pictures as highly arousing. The visual images increase a man's sexual urges."

"Does it work that way for you when you look at them?"

She was extremely proud of her ability to ask such a bold question, so he answered candidly and without vacillation. "Yes. I suppose it is due to my animalistic nature. I am a man, and men are simply beasts at heart, ready to copulate at the drop of a hat."

"So I've been told all my life." She laughed heartily. "Do you truly believe it?"

"Absolutely," he responded, smiling. "No matter what we males pretend, mating is all we think about. Nature has endowed females with numerous charms that lure us to our doom. Bare skin, a woman's lips, her breasts, the springy hair that cushions her alluring cleft"—he let his attention drift and linger on each site he mentioned, and she shifted uncomfortably under his bald assessment—"all of these are enormously stimulating to a man. Just seeing the curve of a woman's bosom makes him think about nothing but the sexual event."

"Perhaps that it why we dress so thoroughly, so that

there is not a hint of femininity remaining to be appreciated by male eyes."

"I'm sure you're right," he said, encouraged by how easily she adopted the casual banter. "If we were constrained to gaze upon women's flesh all day, we would very likely pass all our time rutting like creatures in the field."

She laughed again and shook her head. "I can't believe that I'm sitting here, discussing all this with you. If you knew me . . . knew what my life is like . . ."

"I have a fair idea." He took in her coifed hair, her pale skin, her manicured nails, the hands that had never seen a day's work. In every fashion, she was the grandest of ladies.

"May I look?"

She held out her palm, and he removed the contents of the portfolio. It contained only twenty portraits, each one executed on stiff, specially treated pieces of parchment. The figures had been originally sketched in stark lines with black ink, then bits of color and shading had been added for dramatic effect. He gave her the first drawing, and she studied it intently. To his jaded eye, the picture was simple enough, but for a woman with Lady Abigail's background, it was probably fairly astonishing.

A nude female reclined on a daybed, her back propped against a pile of pillows. She was rounded and pleasingly plump, with full, heavy breasts, and large, elongated nipples. One hand was slipped behind her head, the other rested low on her stomach as though she may have just been touching herself or was about to. The hair under her arms and on her mound had been removed. From the gleam in her eye and the provocative pose, there was no doubt that she was awaiting her lover.

Lady Abigail peered at the rendering forever, and he waited impatiently, wondering what she was thinking. The silence became oppressive, and he decided she was never going to comment, so he reached to the illustration and stroked his thumb across the woman's nipple, much as he might in real life, circling slowly around the peach-colored tip.

"Have you ever seen a woman's breasts?" he asked.

"No." She was mesmerized by the motion of his hand.

"Have you ever seen your own?"

"No!" she answered more vehemently, and she reddened, the blush beginning somewhere deep inside, then working across her shoulders, her neck, her cheeks, into her hair. She was completely flushed, and he had the strongest urge to take pity on her, to leave off the discussion and fan her heated face, but he didn't. He wanted her hot—but not really understanding why.

"A woman's breasts," he maintained, "are the most sensitive location on her body. A man fondles them, bites them, and pinches them. Her nipples, especially, are responsive, and a man sucks them far into his mouth, much as a babe would, only he does it roughly, using his tongue and teeth abrasively."

"And this abrasion . . . this sucking . . .'tis pleasurable?"

"Extremely pleasurable. To both the man and the woman." He glanced down at her chest, which was rising and falling quickly, her breathing unexpectedly labored. Even through all the layers of lace and fabric, he could see the shape of her nipples. They were irritated and pushing against the bodice of her dress.

" 'Tis so difficult to imagine . . ." she whispered.

"Is it?" he queried, willing her to conceive of it in great detail.

He could almost hear her brain working as she continued to stare at the nude. Finally, she said quietly, "She has no hair . . . on her lower parts. . . ."

"No. 'Tis a French fashion."

"How is it removed?"

"Some women keep a special maid to shave them, others visit parlors that specialize in waxes and other concoctions. There are several methods of having it accomplished."

"Why would she?"

"Many men find it excessively stimulating to feel and

see a woman's smooth, unimpeded skin." He touched the woman's shaven genitals. "They like to kiss a woman here, between her legs—"

"Truly?" she interrupted, her troubled eyes swinging to meet his.

"Yes."

"Why? Why would a man want to do such an outrageous thing?"

"Pleasure, milady. 'Tis all about pleasure."

"Have you ever . . ."

She swallowed. Paused. He knew exactly the question she wanted to raise, and he couldn't help thinking that she was incredibly brave to be wading into these deep waters without a clue as to where it might all lead.

Calmly, he prompted, "You're wondering if I have ever kissed a woman like that."

"Yes," she breathed as her cheeks turned another delightful hue of red. He hadn't realized a woman's skin encompassed so many different shades for marking the stages of her embarrassment.

"Ask me." When she continued to hesitate, he said, "Go ahead. 'Tis all right."

"Have you . . . have you . . ." She looked prepared to jump from a high cliff into a raging torrent. "Have you ever kissed a woman between her legs?"

"Yes. I do it all the time with my lovers."

"You find such a thing enjoyable?"

"Immensely."

"And your . . . your . . . lovers, they derive satisfaction from it as well?"

"Well, I like to believe they do." He laughed; he couldn't help himself. "I do not brag when I say that I am quite renowned for my sexual prowess."

Skeptically, she shook her head. " 'Tis difficult for me to fathom that a woman would intentionally agree to undergo such attention, even if the man doing it to her is exceedingly experienced. It seems too personal."

"That's one of the reasons it's so exhilarating." He

flashed her a wicked grin. " 'Tis also a bit naughty. I typically note that the *naughtier* something is supposed to be, the greater the gratification I derive from doing it."

"You're horrid." She chuckled in response, then her brow wrinkled in consternation. "There's one point I want to be clear on, though."

"What's that?"

"All this fondling and sucking and kissing . . . I assume it's a necessary prelude to the marital act?"

"Well . . ." he mused, "I wouldn't say *necessary,* but it certainly makes the proceedings more interesting."

"But why must all this . . . initial touching . . . occur?"

"Simply because it is tantalizing; however, a woman is not as easily excited as a man, so it can be painful for her if he rushes to implant his hardened cock too quickly."

"Aah . . ." she said pensively. "That's the *pain* I've heard whispered about."

"What you've heard talk of is a virgin's pain on her wedding night. A woman is born with a thin piece of skin covering the opening to her womb. It is called her maidenhead. This a man tears when he enters her for the first time. The moment can be quite terrible if the woman is not properly relaxed. Even with adequate stimulation, it can still be . . . unpleasant."

"So this *stimulation* results from all the caressing?"

"Yes." He nodded. "A woman has many sensitive places on her body. When they are appropriately aroused, she is ready for mating."

"And while the man is so busy, what is the woman doing?"

"She is kissing him and touching him in return. Usually a woman will take a man's cock in her hands or in her mouth"—her eyes widened at this—"in order to stroke him in a sexual rhythm. It is extremely invigorating and increases the man's anticipation for the coming event."

"A man would expect the woman to touch his private parts?"

"Perhaps not during their early encounters, but . . . yes,

he would come to desire it on a regular basis as the woman learns more of her wifely duties."

Her eyes worked their way back to the parchment again, but not before engaging in a quick inventory down his front, her furtive, curious gaze lingering briefly on his crotch. Luckily, he continued to lean forward, so she couldn't detect the bulge she'd created. He was still hard as a poker, none of his sexual agitation having waned in the least.

While he loved the fantasy that she might one day slip a hand inside his trousers in order to manipulate him with those long, slender fingers, that she might eventually suck at him with those lush, ruby lips, now wasn't the time for her to discover what size a man's phallus could actually grow to be. Any illusions she had were best humored until she was equipped for a more intimate lesson.

He laid the first painting on the table in front of the sofa, then he handed her the second in the stack. "Look at the next."

The voluptuous woman had rolled to her side, and a nude man had joined her. He was mostly hidden from view, stretched out behind her with a leg casually tossed over her thigh, a hand twirling her nipple. Lady Abigail stared for long moments before the obvious appeared to her.

" 'Tis you!" she hissed, turning to him with accusing eyes. "The man in this picture is you!"

"Yes."

"You're naked!"

"Yes," he said again.

"Is there more of you?"

"In nearly every portrait." She reached out as though she wished to flip through the pile quickly, but something undefined prevented her from peeking ahead.

"So, I am going to see you in your . . . your altogether?"

"I'm afraid so."

For that very reason, he'd debated endlessly on whether to show her the drawings or not. He couldn't care less if she saw him naked. In fact, he was hoping that she'd see the genuine article before too much time had passed, but he'd known the images would make her ill at ease. After much deliberation, however, he'd brought them simply because he didn't have anything else. He possessed two other collections that were similar, in which he was also in the starring role, but they were much more risqué.

"Won't you be embarrassed to have me gaze upon you like this?" She ran her hand in the air over the picture, indicating his bare state.

"Not really." He shrugged off her concern. "Many women have seen me naked in my life. I have no great qualms about it."

She studied his likeness. "You were much younger."

"Nineteen years."

"What caused you to do such a thing?"

"I was brash. Foolish. I had no better sense. As I said, the artist was a friend, and he asked it of me. It seemed a great lark at the time." Once again, he chuckled at the memories of Paris. Ah . . . what a life he'd led growing up on the Continent! "I should mention that my mother brought me back to England shortly after she discovered what I was about. She decided that I had adapted to the French ways much too readily, and that my behavior had become entirely too indecent. She felt I could benefit from the more socially restrictive world I would encounter here."

"Have you?"

"It's been over ten years now, and I would say"—he grinned impishly—"that the jury is still out."

"I think your mother was very wise in forcing you to return." She sounded too fussy, too stuffy, and much older than her years.

"I don't know that I would agree with you," he said, and, unable to believe he'd admit such a thing, he added, "I seem to draw female trouble no matter the country in which I reside."

"And the woman?" she eventually asked, after staring

much too long at how his hand manipulated that breast. "What was her name?"

"Lily. She was the artist's wife." Her eyes widened with shock, or perhaps dismay.

"And your friend did not mind?"

"We were young. In Paris. The times were more open. He considered the entire episode to be totally erotic."

Without responding, she slid the second drawing onto the table, then she reached for the third. The couple had moved so that Lily was now on her back with James stretched out on top of her. They were embroiled in an animated kiss, their lips melded, their tongues entwined. James's hand squeezed her breast as his fingers pressured her nipple.

"Your tongue is in her mouth," she commented after a long perusal.

" 'Tis the most passionate way to kiss a woman," he answered, fixed on her profile, but her attention was glued to the enthusiastic embrace. "A man moves his tongue in and out of the woman's mouth in a tempo meant to simulate mating."

"More of the *preparation*?"

"Yes." She was so wrapped up in the lovers that he dared move closer. "Have you ever been kissed?" he asked.

"Once," she replied, smiling with the memory. "My fiancé was allowed to kiss me, on the cheek, immediately after he proposed."

"That was the one and only occasion?" He inhaled deeply of the scent of her hair, the smell of her skin.

"The one and only. . . ."

She finally managed to wrench her focus from the painting, and as she did, her breast brushed against his arm, her thigh crushed into his. He could see the gold flecks in her emerald eyes, see his face reflected back. Her pupils dilated, her nostrils flared at finding him hovering so near.

"So . . . you've never been properly kissed?"

"No," she admitted.

They sat unmoving, paralyzed by the promise of what might happen.

"Would you like to be?" His heated gaze dropped to her mouth and lingered.

She seemed to surprise herself with her response. "I believe I would."

"Would you like to be kissed by me?"

He might have jabbed her with a pointed stick, so rapidly did she jump to her feet and head to the window, the sofa becoming a barrier between them. She braced her back against the panes of glass, glaring at him accusingly, as though he'd actually kissed her instead of simply considering it.

"This is not about me!" she insisted. "This is about Caroline, and my need to assist her with accurate information."

"But how will you give her *accurate* information if you have no firsthand knowledge?"

"You said you could teach me!"

"I can. I merely indicate that your understanding will be greater if you experience something of physical desire yourself."

"No," she declared, shaking her head. "That is not what I want. Or what I came for."

"Are you certain?"

"Absolutely positive," she ultimately answered, but not until after a protracted delay, which provided him with ample evidence of her confusion over what was just beginning.

He stared calmly in return, as if he couldn't care less about which choice she made even though he was dying to feel the press of her lips against his, but he was a patient man. There was plenty of time to wear her down.

"Come," he coaxed. Missing her adjacency much more than he ought, he patted the empty spot next to him on the sofa. "I have some more pictures to show you." But like a skittish animal, she did not move closer, so he added assuringly, "I give you my word that I will do nothing unless you ask it of me."

"Swear it," she fervently required.

"I swear."

Unfortunately, his pledge failed to mollify her, and she remained where she was. Her chest heaved, her cheeks burned, her teeth worried her bottom lip, and she kept a hand pressed against her stomach as though she might be ill.

"I think," she finally said, finding her voice, "that will be enough for today."

He intended to argue against quitting so soon, needing the extra time to figure out how he could change her mind. Then he looked at her again, and decided she'd heard all she could bear for one encounter.

"As you wish." He nodded in agreement, then stood to go, but not before scooping his lewd pictures into a pile and stuffing them into their protective portfolio. The collection was too precious a memento to leave behind, and he couldn't stand the thought of possibly losing it. Besides, rogue that he was, he wanted to be with her as she viewed every rendering. "Will we meet on Monday as we planned?" He tried to ease her distress with a smile. "Or have you had enough?"

He held his breath, waiting for her answer. If she said *no,* he'd have to find a method of inflicting himself into her world, because he *was* going to see her again.

"Yes," she ultimately concurred, "I would like to meet again on Monday."

His knees weak with relief, he just managed to suppress a satisfied grin. As he'd suspected, the woman was being gradually lured toward the dark pleasure that so easily tempted. While she still believed she was enduring this for her younger sister, she was a grown woman—a woman who yearned to know all. Which meant he could push her limits a bit further.

"I find you very beautiful, Lady Abigail."

"Mr. Stevens . . ." She groaned his name.

"No secrets, milady, and no shame. Not when you're here with me like this."

"Your comment is overly personal . . . and it doesn't have anything to do with Caroline."

"No, it doesn't." He made a step as though to depart, then stopped himself. She was still huddled by the window. "Tonight, after you've sent your maid to bed, go stand in front of your mirror. Completely unclothed. I want you to touch your breasts. . . ."

At hearing his astonishing suggestion, she inhaled sharply. "I never could!"

"Yes, you can," he contended. "Squeeze your nipples. Discover for yourself how quickly and painfully they become aroused."

Before she could retort or protest, he rushed out, taking the stairs two at a time, grabbing his belongings and heading into the wet day. Already he was anticipating, counting the hours until he would see her once more.

FOUR

Abigail regarded the elaborate supper assemblage, trying to follow the conversations going on around her, but concentration was impossible. All she could think about was James Stevens, so she gave up listening to the ebb and flow of the discourse from those sitting on either side, and she quit offering interesting responses to remarks directed her way, wallowing instead in her memories of the afternoon she had spent at her rented house.

Several hours had passed since she and Mr. Stevens had parted, but in that small expanse of time, the world had tipped off its axis. Even the floor seemed to tilt slightly as if everything had shifted, and she had to fight the urge to hold on to the furniture to keep from losing her balance.

Nothing was the same.

With his descriptions of sexual coupling fresh in her mind, she'd found herself in the parlor before the meal was announced, furtively glancing at all the gentlemen's crotches, looking for the telltale bulges hidden by their clothing. She couldn't believe she'd never noticed such a physical difference before.

Once in the dining room, her condition hardly improved as she took surreptitious peeks at the various couples, unable to prevent herself from imagining how they would appear when joined together in the throes of passion. The notion that any of the balding, gouty men, and the obese, churlish women could find pleasure in each other's naked company was so far-fetched that she had to focus on her plate lest she be caught staring in discourteous, wide-eyed wonderment.

Her gaze came to rest on her half-brother, Jerald, who reigned supreme at the head of the table. Twenty-three years her senior, he was short and portly, with thinning hair and huge sideburns that fanned across his cheeks and covered the ruddy complexion he'd developed through excessive drink. His belly protruded over the waistband of his trousers so that his chair had to be placed quite a distance away from the table in order for him to fit in his seat. While not a handsome man in his younger days, he'd nevertheless been good-looking enough, but he'd let himself go, and she couldn't help speculating as to what her sister-in-law, Margaret, thought of his current condition. They had been married for almost thirty years. Did she even notice any longer?

At the other end of the table, Margaret sat, regal as a queen. Her graying curls were piled high and adorned with feathers, and the style accentuated her plump face, jowls, and the sag under her chin. The bodice of her dark purple gown dipped low, emphasizing her enormous bosom.

Did Jerald still visit Margaret's bed? Did the two of them undress and roll around in torrid ecstasy?

The concept was so ludicrous that she reached for her wine glass and sipped in order to stop herself from laughing aloud. In her haste, she swallowed more than intended, setting off a fit of coughing that had people staring. To cover the torrent of mirth wanting to burst out, she pressed a napkin to her lips and inhaled deeply.

How would all these noble ladies and gentlemen react if they realized where her curiosity strayed? Despite the inappropriateness of her musings, she couldn't help but strip them with her eyes while pondering the level of their sexual passions. James Stevens had opened a secret door to an entirely different world, and like the worst sort of voyeur, she couldn't resist gawking.

Across and down a few chairs, her sister, Caroline, conversed jovially with two possible beaux. Caroline was a beautiful girl, blond and blue-eyed, with creamy skin, perfect features, a pleasant voice, and a refreshing demeanor. Contrary to Abigail's opinion of the other guests, she could easily picture her sister in the arms of one of her two suitors, just as she could picture herself. Previously, she'd have denied it, but not after her meeting with Mr. Stevens.

From that one fleeting lesson, she'd made a shocking discovery: There was an earthy, lusty side to her personality that she'd never suspected. She hadn't grasped that she'd been missing the type of physical interaction that marriage would effect. Now she couldn't understand how she'd managed to survive without it.

Surprisingly, she possessed an uncanny ability to fantasize. Every time she closed her eyes, she saw the nude drawings Mr. Stevens had shown her, the ones of himself lying on the sofa with the woman named Lily. However, the woman she conjured wasn't Lily at all, but herself! *She* was the female who was so tightly entwined with James Stevens. *Their* legs and tongues tangled, his weight pushed *her* down into the pillows, his hand was at *her* breast, squeezing and manipulating *her* extended nipple.

To her dismay, her mental renderings were so vivid that she could perceive the warmth of his skin, the brandy on his tongue, the thickness of his hair as she sifted her fingers through it. Uncomfortable, she shifted in her chair, the friction against her thighs and bottom setting off a strange maelstrom of agitation.

Oh, how could Mr. Stevens have brought about such agony? Had the scoundrel realized that his brief tutoring would leave her in such a state? She couldn't contemplate anything but him! The rat! Every second of their appointment maddeningly replayed inside her head: everything he'd said, everything he'd done, everything she'd said and done, as well.

Mostly, she continued returning to the moment when they had discussed kissing, when he had asked her if she would like to be kissed. With all her heart, she'd craved the opportunity to have his lips pressed against her own. She'd wanted it with a longing that was as desperate as it was frightening. The prospect made her limbs weak. She was aching and restless. And her lips . . .

They tingled and burned, and she repeatedly ran her tongue over them, aware of their presence in a fashion she'd never been before. Mad as it sounded, they felt dry and unused, as if they'd been in storage for a lengthy respite and were just now reattached and ready to be utilized for their main purpose. That being for kissing James Stevens.

The notion set her senses to reeling. What would it be like to be kissed by him? He had said that she would have to ask if she wished it to occur. What if she braved that necessary giant step?

She could reflect upon nothing else.

While contemplating their next rendezvous, she was compelled to admit an insane urge to wear her hair down, but, as no man had seen her locks unbound, the concept was almost too scandalous to consider. Yet, she could imagine Mr. Stevens looking his fill, touching, toying, letting the long strands drift across his palm. He would press it to his face, inhale the tangy scent of her soap, then wrap the blond wave around his fist, pulling her close, closer. . . .

Stifling a groan, she glanced about, baffled to find that the meal had ended without her realizing. The ladies were headed for the drawing room and, thankfully, Abigail slipped past without having to talk to anyone. Since she'd arrived back at the Town house, she hadn't had a single quiet moment for solitary retrospection. Servants had been hurrying to and fro. Margaret had been in a dither over the seating arrangements. Caroline had insisted on incessantly reviewing the excitement over her first London party.

While Abigail typically exhibited the utmost patience and forbearance, it had been all she could do to keep from snapping at everyone. She yearned to sneak off to her rooms where she could fret and stew over the carnal information she'd just received, but departure would have been the height of rudeness.

She snagged the small sofa in the corner, hoping no one would join her, but to her dismay, her sister-in-law made a beeline in her direction. In Abigail's distraught state, she couldn't tolerate Margaret's blathering.

"I think supper was a success," Margaret declared as she worked at adjusting her full skirts until she was able to perch serenely.

" 'Twas delicious," Abigail lied. She was so befuddled that she couldn't have said what was served. Vaguely, she recalled drinking some wine, and it was gurgling and fermenting in her empty stomach.

"I just heard the most exciting news." Margaret leaned in. "I had to share it with you right away."

"What is it?" Abigail was almost alarmed by the zealous gleam in Margaret's eye.

"The Earl of Spencer is going to marry again."

Abigail's entire body went rigid. The earl was James Stevens's father. The mention of the man, coming so soon after her assignation with his illegitimate son, panicked her. For a frantic instant, all sorts of alien impressions swirled through her, causing her to worry crazily that the earl's appearance at Margaret's soiree would unmask her bizarre scheme. With determined effort, she pushed the errant concern aside. There was no way anyone could discern how she'd passed the afternoon, and she simply had to get a grip on her careening sensibilities.

Searching for calm and steadying her breathing, she gradually realized that she didn't understand the significance of Margaret's pronouncement that the earl might wed. She asked, "So?"

"He would be perfect for Caroline."

Abigail had never met Edward Stevens, but she knew quite a lot about him. He was a widower who had just completed a year of mourning for his late wife. Three decades earlier, he had sired two bastard sons with the actress Angela Ford, plus he had four grown, legitimate children. While she wasn't certain of his age, she assumed it to be somewhere in his mid-fifties. "Honestly, Margaret," she chided, "what would make you even conceive of such a match?"

Margaret glared at her as though she were an idiot. "Rank and fortune, of course."

"Of course," Abigail murmured, biting her tongue against numerous rude retorts. "But Caroline is only seventeen."

"An older man might be just what she requires." Margaret's gaze roamed across the room to where Caroline chatted merrily with several friends, and Abigail fought the urge to gnash her teeth. Margaret had always predicted that Caroline was too pretty, too lively, too uninhibited.

"She'll do fine with someone her own age," Abigail insisted. "Besides, I can't fathom that a widower would be interested in a girl who's young enough to be his granddaughter."

"Older gentlemen like youthful wives. They find them more biddable. More easily trained."

"For pity's sake, Margaret!" Abigail snarled. "You talk about Caroline as if she's a pet dog." A waiter strolled by offering wine, and anxious for something to do with her fingers lest she wrap them around Margaret's throat, Abigail grabbed a glass.

Undeterred by Abigail's sharp tone, Margaret said, "Girls have many wifely duties to learn, and someone as . . ."—she paused, seeking the appropriate word, and Abigail tensed, waiting—"as *vivacious* as Caroline could definitely benefit from the firmer hand a more mature husband would provide."

"Caroline will secure an excellent husband. Don't fret over her." But she made a mental note to speak with Jerald as soon as she had the chance. Although it was out of his character and terribly modern, she had gotten him to acquiesce that Caroline would be consulted over any proposal, and that she could turn down those suitors who didn't interest her. With the kind of determination only a seventeen-year-old girl can exhibit, Caroline had taken his assurance to heart and was determined to wed only for love.

Jerald's decision had never set well with Margaret. Her opinion was that Caroline should marry whomever she was told to marry, with no complaints, and Abigail's greatest fear was that Margaret would convince Jerald to renege on the promise he'd given. If Jerald changed his mind at this late date, it would be an unqualified disaster.

Hoping to placate her overbearing sister-in-law, she

smiled. "Let's not fuss about it now. We've only just begun our search. We have plenty of evenings to decide who might be best for her."

"Yes, indeed," Margaret concluded. "You know, if the earl doesn't fancy Caroline, you might throw your cap for him yourself."

"What?" she gasped. As if she could marry James Stevens's father! The concept was preposterous! Her ragged mood was motivating her to fervently deny the possibility, so she forced herself to appear nonchalant. "You're joking."

"Why do you say so? What are your intentions? You're twenty-five years old. Caroline is raised. Your obligation to the family is finished. Do you mean to simply return to the country and live out your days as a spinster? Surely you want more for yourself than that."

Abigail glanced around the salon. The gentlemen had finished their cigars and port and were trickling in, and she tried to picture herself wedded to one of them, but it was not a view she could bring into clear focus.

After discovering the truth about a wife's intimate commitments, she doubted she could ever walk down the aisle. Not with any of the men of her acquaintance. For love, she might risk it. But only for love. Her husband would have to be someone dashing and spirited. Someone who stirred and captivated her.

He would have to be someone like . . . someone like Mr. Stevens, she thought, her already-hot cheeks blushing a darker pink.

"I don't know what my plans are," she contended. "At present, I'm concentrating on this Season and Caroline's future. After we're finished with hers, I'll start plotting my own."

"Well, good. I'm glad you've resolved to be sensible." Margaret patted her arm. "Jerald did you a gigantic disservice by not obliging you to wed after . . ." Her voice trailed off as a new group of guests entered, and she rose to greet them, but not before whispering, "I noticed that your lips are terribly chapped. I have a nice balm that might help. Ask me later."

Margaret departed, and Abigail slipped her hands under her skirts, sitting on them so she wouldn't distractedly massage her mouth. She hadn't realized how incessantly she'd been licking and rubbing with her fingertips as she'd ruminated on kissing Mr. Stevens.

Irrationally, she suffered a wave of anger at Margaret for raising the subject of marriage when Mr. Stevens was still overwhelming her senses. She didn't want to think about men, marriage, or marital behaviors. She just wanted to think about Mr. Stevens and what his appearance portended, and she didn't care to have Margaret upsetting her peaceful reveries.

Over the years, she'd had copious discussions with Jerald and Margaret as to whether or not she should become engaged again. Margaret claimed that it was unnatural for Abigail to be single, and the arguments went around and around, but Abigail had always won. Rearing Caroline had kept her plenty busy, so the potential for her own husband and family had never blossomed.

Now Caroline was grown, and Abigail conceded that Margaret was correct. What was she to do? She could hardly putter about Jerald's country estate, Marbleton, with no duties and no responsibilities to oversee.

Marriage was the only option for a woman in her position. But in light of her recently acquired knowledge, she didn't see how she could ever choose a husband. Any decision would be impossible. Compared to Mr. Stevens, every other gentleman she'd ever encountered seemed positively tame—and therefore completely unacceptable as spousal material.

In a mere matter of hours, her tastes had changed. Apparently, she now liked her men ribald and totally unrestrained. None of her staid, stodgy acquaintances would suffice. She desired spice and heat and the type of intense longing she suffered whenever she recalled Mr. Stevens. How she was supposed to stumble upon such a marvelous fellow among this limp crowd was a mystery she'd mull another day.

Caroline flitted to her side, a lovely vision in white satin and pink lace. Full of good cheer, she queried, "What do you think?"

"Supper was excellent," Abigail fibbed again, "and the party is fabulous."

"Not the party, silly," Caroline said. "What about the boys who've come to call?"

"Oh, pardon me." Abigail smiled. "You must intend to analyze the *really* important aspects of the evening."

"Exactly," Caroline responded, smiling as well.

"Let's see . . ." Abigail surreptitiously glanced to where a quartet of elegant, strapping lads was huddled. Theirs was a small world, and the suitors always knew each other. Usually they were friends who had attended school together. All came from aristocratic families of impeccable wealth and breeding; all would eventually hold titles, so any of them would be an appropriate husband for Caroline.

After a thorough perusal, Abigail declared, "I suppose I'm rather partial to the dark-haired boy."

"He is darling, isn't he?" she acknowledged. "His name is Charles."

Caroline sighed with such sweet affection that Abigail could barely hide her envious delight. How wonderful to have such romantic adventures lying ahead. "He's charming," she agreed.

"He's asked me to go riding tomorrow afternoon. Actually, they've all asked me to go one place and another. May I?"

"Certainly," Abigail consented. "With the way the requests will be rolling in, I suspect we'll need to begin a calendar to chart your myriad invitations."

"That's a grand idea. I'll start on it first thing in the morning."

"And I think you should accept as many as possible."

"I'll try hard to garner all I can." Caroline laughed amiably, her blue eyes twinkling.

They'd discussed the courtship rituals on hundreds—perhaps thousands—of occasions, and Abigail was resolute that Caroline not set her sights on any one admirer too early. After meeting Caroline, none of her admirers would be able to resist her, and she would receive many offers, so Abigail insisted Caroline get to know all the candidates as thoroughly as was viable, thus providing herself with the opportunity to make the very best decision.

"What a dreary chore it must be," Abigail mentioned facetiously, "having to decide how to fill your days with one handsome boy after the next."

" 'Tis a desperate burden," her sister replied, "but I'm up to the challenge."

More guests arrived, two young men among them, and Abigail nodded toward the group. "Your cadre of swains has just increased."

"Ooh, the blond one is quite adorable."

"Off you go." Abigail chuckled as she helped Caroline to her feet. "Be dazzling!"

"I shall!"

She swirled away, majestic as any princess, and as Abigail watched her, she experienced a rush of sadness. Had she ever been that innocent? That gay and carefree?

Her own come-out was a nebulous recollection of dances, gowns, and parties, but she saw it all through a hazy filter, watered down by the passing of the years. She'd endured the same anticipation and high hopes for the future, but none of it had become reality, and she was just recognizing that she'd ended up settling for so little. With no family or home of her own, she was existing rather than living, forced to vicariously enjoy Caroline's successful journey to matrimony, rather than making the trip herself.

How had it happened that she found herself in this predicament?

She seemed ancient and worn out, a tedious, uninteresting woman for whom discontentment prevailed. Though she was only twenty-five, she felt herself to be a *hundred* and twenty-five, and as she stared down the road, the view was terribly depressing. What destiny awaited?

What was to become of her once Caroline was wed?

Her outlook was so disheartening that she couldn't bear further personal evaluation, so she abandoned her safe haven in the corner and floated through the throng of callers, hoping activity would keep her disturbing reflections at bay, but try as she might to ease her disquiet, nothing worked. Gradually, she migrated down the hall, to the more private family rooms at the back of the house, and she slipped into Jerald's library, welcoming the solitude. But as the heavy door clicked shut, she realized she wasn't alone. An unknown male was standing in the shadows behind the desk, and he whirled to face her.

James! she nearly called, but she just managed to swallow the name, and she was so glad she had, for the gentleman *was* James Stevens—as he would appear in another twenty or thirty years.

From the remarkable resemblance, he could only be James's father, the notorious Earl of Spencer, Edward Stevens. He had the same tall, lithe grace, ravishing face, and piercing eyes, though his were brown instead of blue. The dark hair matched, too, except his was peppered with gray. A striking older man, he was the type who grew more attractive with the passage of time.

"If you would be so kind," he said in a voice that was the exact duplicate of his illegitimate son's, "would you open the door? And please be quick about it."

The request was politely made but definitely an order, and she hastily complied. "My apologies." She pulled the door back as far as the hinges would permit. "I hadn't noticed this room was occupied."

"Really?"

"Yes, *really.*" She was piqued by his blatant disbelief. "Why would I intentionally want to close myself off with . . ." Then, she remembered her brief conversation with Margaret, and awareness dawned. Any number of unmarried females were now scheming to meet him privately, and he couldn't allow himself to be caught with any of them or untold scandal would result.

"Truly, Lord Spencer," she said earnestly. "I hadn't expected anyone to be about."

"You know me?"

"I know *of* you."

After a cautious assessment, he asserted, "I see that you grasp my predicament."

"I was merely trying to escape the swarm of visitors."

"As was I. With each Season, I have less tolerance for such folderol."

"I feel the same."

"Ah . . . a kindred spirit."

She smiled and, when he smiled in return, her heart melted. With those dimples in his cheeks, and that air of mischief in his eyes—so much like his son's—what woman could have remained unmoved? It seemed they shared a precious secret, making them intimates and confidantes, instead of two strangers.

"If you detest these affairs so much," she asked, "why are you here?"

"I hadn't intended to come, but my son insisted."

"Your son?" She panicked, and she was powerless to prevent herself from glancing around as though James Stevens might step out from behind the drapes.

"Yes, my only boy, Charles, wanted an introduction to Lady Caroline."

Oh, that son! Her pulse slowed to its normal rate.

His legitimate son, Charles, was an invited guest, and Abigail understood why the earl would claim him as his *only* son, but she couldn't forestall the instant swell of sorrow that had her cursing their Polite Society.

What must it be like for the earl to be the father of a magnificent man such as James, yet forced to deny his existence at every turn? What must it be like for James to be the offspring of this vibrant, astute aristocrat, but to continually have their blood connection discounted? What could their relationship possibly be like?

Habit kept her smile firmly in place as she inquired, "How did your Charles convince you?"

"He dragged me out of the house."

"Kicking and screaming?"

"Well, mumbling and grumbling anyway," he admitted. "I refused to show up for supper, but he was adamant that we attend the gala afterward." He moved to the sideboard, poured a brandy and a glass of sherry, then he walked closer and handed her the wine. "Have we met?"

"Not officially. I am Lady Caroline's older sister, Abigail."

"So you are." He studied her curiously. "You wouldn't remember, I don't suppose, but I spent a week at Marbleton when you were just a girl of eight or ten. My . . . how time flies."

"Yes, it certainly does." She'd just reached the same dreadful conclusion, which was precisely the reason she'd sought refuge in the library. She needed to regroup before facing the guests again. The earl's son—his *illegitimate* son—had stirred too many disturbing insights.

"I have not seen you about. . . ."

"No, I stayed in the country after Mother died. What with overseeing Jerald's staff and acting as a companion to Caroline, I haven't made it to Town."

"And you haven't missed it a whit, I'll wager."

"Not a whit."

He sighed miserably. "I simply can't abide going back to the party just now." Astonishing her, he asked, "Would you sit while we enjoy our beverages?"

"I should like that very much."

She eagerly seized the opportunity. The solitude was appreciated, but more importantly, she simply couldn't pass up this pretext to learn more about James Stevens's father. Who was Edward Stevens, this man who had seduced James's actress-mother, then left her unwed to carry on alone with two small children in tow?

She started toward the fireplace, to where two chairs awaited, but the earl walked around the desk and positioned himself behind the massive slab of mahogany.

"I doubt if Jerald will mind," he declared, "and I regret to say that if anyone happens by, I simply must have as many pieces of furniture between you and myself as I can possibly manage."

She grinned. "If you're not careful, I'll think you're questioning my intentions."

"Yours and everyone else's," he muttered in disgust. As soon as the words left his mouth, his cheeks flushed bright red. "Forgive me, Lady Abigail. I hadn't meant that to come out so harshly."

"No harm done. And please . . . call me Abigail."

"If you'll call me Edward."

"I will." She liked his informal way, his direct manner. "I had heard you were out in Society again. Are the ladies being troublesome?"

" 'Tis the absolute worst! You can't imagine. . . ." He repressed a shudder of distaste. "I was married for twenty-eight years, and now that I'm a widower, everyone assumes that I will tie the knot a second time. Immediately."

"Which obviously you don't wish to do. . . ."

"As if I'd jump off that wretched cliff again!" Abruptly, he stopped himself, flushing anew. "Pardon me. I don't know what's come over me. Pay me no mind."

At his amazing disclosure with respect to his lengthy marriage, she was dazed by the information. What a time she was having with the men of the Stevens family! "That's quite all right if you're a tad bit disordered," she comforted. "I'm not exactly having the best day, either. After all, I'm hiding back here with you." He chuckled at the observation. "Perhaps 'tis the weather afflicting us."

"Yes, let's blame it on the weather," he agreed pleasantly, "although in my case, it might have something to do with the fact that I hadn't been in the door five minutes, and your sister-in-law was introducing me to Caroline and telling me all her gory details."

"She didn't!"

"She did! I now know the amount of her dowry down to the last farthing."

"How embarrassing! I told Margaret to leave you be."

"At least someone in your family has a lick of sense." He leaned back, weary and exasperated. "No offense, Abigail, because Caroline is a very sweet girl. But she's a *girl*, for God's sake. And I could say the same about you, too, no matter what sorts of vivid fantasies you might be indulging."

He said it with such vehemence that she couldn't help laughing. "That's fine, because I'm not looking for a husband."

"You must be the only woman in London who's not! I'm fifty-six years old. What are people thinking?"

"They're not, Edward," she responded gently, relishing the chance to use his given name.

"You're right about that!" He stared at the fire. "I've missed attending certain functions, such as the theater, but I can't stand being hounded wherever I go. Have you any wise recommendations?"

"I haven't. I've been wondering myself how Caroline and I will proceed. Caroline is planning all manner of entertainment and diversions, but Jerald is a busy man, so we can hardly expect him to drop everything if we want to go somewhere."

They were silent, enjoying their refreshment, as well as the isolated company. Through it all, Lord Spencer watched her, and when the creases on his worried brow relaxed, she knew she'd passed some type of internal test to which he'd subjected her.

"I have an idea," he said.

"What's that?"

"Charles is interested in escorting Caroline to various events. Perhaps the two of us could accompany them as their chaperones. That way, I could frequent some of the more pleasant distractions this Season."

"You'd have a woman on your arm"—she nodded pensively—"but you'd be able to carry on with greater flexibility."

Evidently, with very little cogitation, she was endorsing his deranged suggestion. In light of what she was secretly doing on Mondays and Thursdays, she should have been running fast and furiously beyond his sphere of influence, but she couldn't seem to adopt the wiser course of staying far away from Edward Stevens.

Almost against her will, she was being drawn into the circle that enclosed James and Edward. Before long, she'd be trapped, unable to budge in one direction or the other without bumping up against either father or son.

This is wrong, wrong, wrong! an inner voice shouted, but she rashly ignored its warning. Her coming association with Edward couldn't be avoided or changed.

Unable to prevent herself from forging ahead, she said, "I would welcome the opportunity to have you as my companion."

His smile, and her own, sealed their bond. They were now friends, associates, conspirators against all the eager parents and daughters of High Society. With much more delectation than she ought to feel, she couldn't wait to become better acquainted, and she was already refining the devious methods she could use to glean information about James.

They'd tarried too long, so they returned to the party. Separately. They hadn't another occasion to converse, but Abigail glanced up sporadically to find Edward watching her as though they shared some private jest.

It was almost three in the morning before she slipped off to her room. After quickly disrobing, she sent her tired maid to bed, then snuggled beneath the cool sheets. As she was extremely fatigued herself, she'd thought she would fall asleep instantly, yet she tossed and turned as she had each night since meeting James Stevens. She couldn't quit remembering how he'd wanted to kiss her, how close she'd come to saying *yes.*   •

Stand in front of your mirror. Completely unclothed,

he'd said, in that low sensual way that made her wish to carelessly do anything he asked. *I want you to touch your breasts . . . squeeze your nipples . . .*

Disturbed by her dark imaginings, she threw back the blankets and tiptoed to the mirror. There was a candle next to it, and she considered lighting it, but she simply could not. A hint of moonlight glinted through the window and provided more than enough illumination for her shocking behavior.

For the longest time, she stared at her reflection, trying to see herself as James Stevens did. As a woman. As an alluring female. Slowly, she untied the ribbon at the front of her nightgown; then, before she could muster the courage to stop herself, she tugged it off one shoulder.

In the silvery shadows, she viewed her breast. It was pretty, round, shapely. The cold air had aroused the nipple, and she surveyed the nub, fascinated, as it peaked and hardened. Carefully, as though observing someone else, she raised a hand, cupping the weight, judging the abundance. Then, gingerly, she covered the center with her palm.

Her nipple contracted further in an irritating, intriguing manner. Meticulously, she gauged the novel sensation, letting it register adequately before she laid her finger and thumb to the raised tip. Scrupulously, tenderly, she gave it the barest squeeze, and the action brought such a surge of agitation screaming through her entire body that she dropped her hand as if she'd been burned.

Scrambling, she hustled back to her bed and scurried under the covers. Her pulse raced, and her nipples throbbed with each beat of her heart. Her breasts felt heavy and too tight for the skin in which they were encased. All from the merest caress!

Stars, but she yearned to touch herself again! To continue on until . . . she knew not what!

Lest temptation strike, she tucked both her hands under her pillows and kept them there—out of mischief—through the endless, sleepless night.

CHAPTER

FIVE

James reached for the front door of Lady Abigail's rented house. As they'd previously arranged, it was unlocked. He stepped through, then quickly closed it, leaving the rest of the world on the other side. Alone in the foyer, he hastily shed his outer garments and climbed the stairs, much more eager than he should have been.

Four days!

Four days had passed since he'd last seen her, and like an infatuated swain, he'd spent nearly every second pining over the fact that they were apart. His longing for her was entirely out of balance with the actual facts of their situation, but nevertheless, he couldn't bring himself under control.

At the oddest times, he'd think about her, wondering where she might be, what she might be doing. During the night, he'd try to concentrate on the flow of money, food, and liquor, on the games and customers' entertainment, but more often than not, he'd stare off into space, imagining her in her bed. He'd fantasize at length about what her bedchamber looked like, what she wore for nightclothes, how she appeared without them on.

Because of his distraction, he'd wasted a thousand pounds on a turn of the cards—an amount he rarely wagered anymore—simply because he couldn't focus his attention. The loss was so out of character that his brother, Michael, had asked if he was feeling all right, if he'd been working too hard and required a holiday.

While escorting his mother to the theater, he hadn't spared the stage a glance. Instead, he'd perused the other boxes like a love-struck lad, hoping Abigail Weston might be in attendance and that he'd be lucky enough to catch a glimpse of her.

This was madness! Yet on light feet, he fairly flew up the stairs, overly thrilled. The uncountable hours were finally at an end!

For some reason, he kept repeating, he had inflated his craving for her all out of proportion to reality, and he'd told himself over and over that a second rendezvous would quench the thirst she'd generated. His recollection of the events on the previous Thursday *had* to be incorrect, and once he saw her again, this gnawing, empty well of yearning would slowly be filled by the realization that she had no special hold over him.

However, as he walked into her private parlor, he was abruptly forced to concede that his careful assessment was utter nonsense. His heart leapt at the sight of her. There was just something about the woman that tickled his fancy as no other ever had. He fiercely desired her, and he wanted to jump ahead to their future carnal relationship. On a primitive level, he sensed that this bizarre need could only be pacified by possessing her completely.

Across the room, she stood next to the window. Sunlight had poked through the clouds and flooded the area where she lingered, bathing her in a halo of amber light. She'd donned another dark green dress, but the fabric of this one was lighter and woven with an exotic thread that shimmered with silver highlights when she moved. The color intensified the emerald shade of her eyes, making her seem ethereal, mysterious, as though she could see more than she rightly should. Her skin was translucent, her cheeks and lips rosy red. And her hair . . .

She'd worn it down! With unrestrained admiration, he gazed upon it. The golden mass flowed free and long, the curled ends just brushing her hips. In a compromise, she'd tied it loosely with a green ribbon.

Furiously, he evaluated what the gesture meant. It was a capitulation of sorts, a signal, an indication of trust. As he contemplated how far he might be able to push her during their lesson, his loins tightened, his trousers promptly becoming uncomfortable. With a single snap of his wrist, the ribbon could be gone, the silky strands available for his unimpeded exploration. His nerves tingled at the idea of massaging through it.

With a kind of crazy recklessness, he could picture her on the big bed in his own bedchamber—a private location he never let his paramours inhabit!—stretched out beneath him, her flaxen locks fanning across his pillows. What a spectacle she would be!

As he entered the cozy salon, she was so well schooled in masking her emotions that, for a fleeting moment, she assessed him casually, ostensibly expecting him or someone else. However, her indifference lasted only a brief instant; then her eyes shadowed, her pretty brow creased with concern, her hands toiled over a kerchief she grasped between unsteady fingers.

"Hello, Mr. Stevens," she said in that husky voice that never failed to arouse him. "I'm so glad you've come."

"So am I." Hesitantly, he took a few steps into the room. As he'd done formerly, he shut the door and secured it, sealing them in, not really worried about intruders or discovery, but liking the added bit of intimacy the barred door implied.

Wanting to extend their initial greeting, he tarried, languidly placing his satchel on the table, yet even as he bent over to relinquish it, he kept his steady gaze fastened to hers. As had happened during the two preceding encounters they'd shared, it seemed as if he had known her for a thousand years, that he could cut through the walls of propriety that separated them and shoot directly to the heart of whatever was troubling her.

"You're distraught."

"I guess I am. I just . . ." She smiled tentatively. "Would it be terribly inappropriate of me to say that I am relieved you're finally here?"

So . . . she felt it, too, this powerful sense of connection and expectation. Perhaps he was not the only one who had passed the time daydreaming, tossing and turning on a lonely mattress. He divulged, "I've been thinking about you. I couldn't stop myself."

"Nor I, from thinking about you."

"Your hair . . ."

Blushing, she patted her temple in a self-conscious attempt to straighten what didn't need straightening. As though confessing a horrid sin, she disclosed, "I have never taken it down before . . . not for anyone. . . ."

"But you did for me." A great wave of hope swelled to the surface, and he steeled himself against the tempest of excitement rising through every part of his being. "Your hair is very beautiful. *You* are very beautiful." She was obviously flattered but also surprised, and he surmised that no man had bestowed such a compliment before.

"Thank you," she murmured, outwardly nervous, then she meandered to the sideboard. "I had tea prepared, but it's occurred to me that you're not a *tea* type of person, are you? Perhaps you'd like a brandy. I'd be happy to . . ."

Off she went, talking a mile a minute. Fidgety and apprehensive, she'd lost her unruffled aplomb, and he watched curiously as she rifled through bottles and yanked at corks. Quietly, he came up behind her, striding close, the fragrance of her perfume and the lavender of her soap pervading his nostrils. He narrowed his eyes and inhaled deliberately, allowing himself to be overwhelmed by all the aromas that made her so unique.

He moved nearer still, her skirts swirling around his calves, his toes buried under the hems, his legs cognizant of hers through her petticoats. He reached out, covering her busy hand, arresting it with gentle pressure.

"Calm yourself," he whispered over her shoulder, his mouth next to her ear, his warm breath brushing across her lobe and tickling the hairs on her neck. "What has put you in such a state?"

Involuntarily, she shuddered, then turned to face him. "Everything has changed. These meetings will be so difficult."

"Why?"

" 'Tis nothing like I anticipated."

She shifted, and one of her thighs wedged between his own. Although the multiple layers of her clothing offered plenty of padding, he could discern form and substance. His cock hardened; he ached to pull her tightly against him in order to allay some of the sudden pressure, yet he managed to restrain himself, traveling the more innocent route by resting a hand on her tiny waist.

"In what way?"

" 'Tis so much more personal than I imagined. And physical. I thought we could just . . . just . . ."

Her gaze fell to his lips, lingered. A frown creased her forehead, and he had the answer to her upset. As he'd suspected from the beginning, her body's fervor was quickly outpacing her mind's clamoring for boring verbal discourse. Remarkably, the perception provided none of the elation he'd expected. She appeared utterly wretched, overwrought, distressed, and he felt acutely sorry for her predicament.

With any other female of his acquaintance, he'd have immediately pressed ahead, but because he enjoyed such a peculiar kinship with her, he couldn't seize the advantage. His affection for her overruled his masculine drives, urging him to protect and cherish rather than exploit. He couldn't have behaved badly toward her any more than he could have cut off his right arm.

"I knew this would be hard on you," he admitted.

"You did?"

"Yes." He smiled at her, and her attention remained fixated on his mouth. "Perhaps we proceeded a tad too rapidly the other day."

"No. 'Tisn't that at all." With the greatest of effort, she returned to staring at the bottles of liquor, showing him her back. "I suppose I will sound exceedingly forward, but I'm impetuously anxious for more than mere words. I need to experience what you're telling me. I crave an understanding of how a woman feels when a man . . . when he . . ." A blush started across her shoulders and rose into her cheeks.

"Oh, I'm a mess!" she wailed, and he couldn't help chuckling at her plight.

" 'Tis only natural."

"What is? Thinking and acting like a brazen hussy?"

"No." He chuckled again. " 'Tis only natural for you to be curious." With both hands at her waist, he maneuvered her until she reluctantly faced him once again, though she seemed to be extremely fascinated by his shirtfront. "A woman needs sexual stimulation just as a man does," he explained. "Your body has been disposed and waiting for many years. You're simply aware of it for the first time. The realization is disquieting for you, but we'll deal with it together."

"I want you to kiss me," she whispered, her lashes sweeping down. "With your tongue in my mouth. Like you kissed Lily in your erotic drawings."

A groan of frustration charged to the surface. She was offering the initial step toward everything he eventually hoped to receive from her, so he couldn't help wondering if he'd gone completely insane when he responded, "We'll talk about it."

Instantly he deduced that it had been the absolute wrong comment. She stiffened, reddened further, then whirled toward the sideboard. "Oh, you don't wish to! You don't find me . . ." Patting her scalded cheeks, she muttered, "The thought had never occurred to me! I'm so embarrassed!"

"No, milady, no." He raised his hands to her shoulders. She was wedged quite nicely, her back against his chest, the hint of her bottom against his groin. "I would love nothing more than to kiss you, but you are a maid, and these are dangerous waters. We must both be certain of the depths before we dive in. . . ."

He let the statement trail away as he brushed the sweep of her hair off to the side. The creamy slope of her nape beckoned. Leaning forward, he rested his lips on her heated, smooth skin, and he dallied there, tasting, nuzzling, and nipping until gooseflesh prickled.

Barely breathing, she asked hesitantly, "You desire me, then?"

"Very much." At his admission, she sagged with relief, and he added, "But I am more enlightened in these matters. I grasp where kissing may lead. It can quickly spin out of our control, so you need to learn more of what you're truly contemplating." He dropped his hands to hug them around her middle, cradling her but not tightly, loving the way she fit so neatly into the circle of his arms.

"Of course, you're right," she said, on a shaky laugh. "I hadn't thought ahead. I've just been so distressed. It seems as though it's been forever since Thursday, and I had so many questions for you. . . ." She stopped. "Oh, but my imagination has been driving me mad!"

"I can tell." He kissed her hair, her cheek, encouraged by the manner in which she accepted his embrace as though it were the most natural thing in the world. "Come sit with me. We must talk. And look at more renderings."

"Yes."

He moved away so that she could proceed to the sofa while he poured a stout brandy, then he walked over and held out the glass. "Try this. It will soothe you."

"I don't think anything will help." Yet she reached for it with a trembling hand. Her fingers wrapped over his own as he guided it to her mouth. She accepted a prolonged sip, then flinched as the delayed sensation burned her throat. Her eyes watered.

"That is ghastly." She shivered.

He took a drink, fitting his lips over the spot where hers had touched the rim, then he proffered it again. "Another."

As he had just done, she twisted the glass in order to partake from the same site. An apt pupil. The liquor went down more easily the second time. Already she was relaxing; the tense set of her shoulders, the crease on her brow, were disappearing.

"One more," he insisted, and she did as he asked, draining the contents.

She sighed, then chuckled. "So now I've become not

only a wanton, but a daytime drunkard, as well. You're having a fascinating effect on my character, Mr. Stevens."

He shrugged, saying philosophically, "A few bad habits never hurt anyone. They make a person more interesting."

"You would say something like that."

The strong spirits had brought a becoming blush to her cheeks and further reddened her ruby lips. They were lush and moist, and she was staring at him with such wide-eyed, innocent appeal that it was all he could do to keep from kneeling in front of her and propelling her back against the sofa. But for once in his despicable life, he behaved himself, despite his desperate crescendo of lust, fearing that if he started kissing her, he might never desist.

He settled next to her, sitting much nearer than he had during their earlier assignation and touching her down his entire length; arms, hips, thighs—all were connected. Events were spinning out of control much faster than he could contain them. The fantasy was turning out to be nothing like the reality. She was animated and enthusiastic, downright eager to advance their acquaintance to a higher level, and the only obstacle to her longed-for ruination was his little-used, much-abused, barely recognizable sense of honor.

Who would have thought?

On tenuous new ground, and feeling as if it were constantly shifting beneath his feet, he grabbed for his portfolio, needing to hold on to something tangible. "Let's begin again, shall we?"

"Let's do. I've been beside myself, wondering what's coming." Seizing the lead, she retrieved the stack of parchments and centered it on her lap. She skipped the first two renderings, glancing only briefly at the initial nude sketch of Lily, at the second where he'd joined Lily on the daybed, but hurrying to the third—the drawing where they were luxuriating in an intimate kiss. Relishing a drawn-out examination, she studied the stretch of their bodies, the angle of their hips, the squeeze of his fingers around Lily's nipple. Then, apparently satisfied, she tossed it on the table and turned to the fourth picture before he had a chance to warn her as to what she would find.

He was there for her avid inspection, reclining against the pillows, an arm tucked behind his head. His body hair looked coarse and dark, contrasting starkly with his pale skin. It was matted across his chest in a thick pile, circling his brown nipples and descending in an arrowed line past his navel.

Only Lily's hands were in the picture with him. With one, she cradled his rock-hard balls. With the other, she gripped his solid length, her thumb at the sensitive tip. The erotic image easily brought back to him the memories of how learned and agile those knowing hands had been, of how much pleasure they had been able to incite.

Bothered by his recollections, he closed his eyes against them, when he grasped that the woman he was visualizing between his legs wasn't Lily at all, but Abigail Weston. It was *her* slender fingers tightened around his rigid shaft, *her* hair flowing across his abdomen, *her* tongue geared to moisten his enthusiastic phallus. In his vivid fantasy, she was practiced and adept, and the depictions were so lifelike that he could only assume that they would, one day, become reality.

"Oh, my. . . ." She reached out a tentative finger and traced over the length of his erection. The sexual jolt he received was so strong that he felt she was actually touching his flesh. "It's so . . . so big. . . ."

She said it with such awe that he couldn't help laughing full and long at her guileless statement. Tears of mirth stung the corners of his eyes.

Amused and perplexed, she asked, "What did I say that's so funny?"

"Oh, milady, you are sweet." He struggled to contain his raging humor. "A man always loves to hear how big his cock is."

"You mean they come in more than one size?"

Her question was so genuine that he hated to pleasure himself at her expense, but he couldn't remember the last occasion when he'd so completely enjoyed conversing with a woman. He swallowed a second eruption of laughter that begged to burst out. "They are mostly the same shape, just like a man's nose or his hands or feet, but no two are exactly alike."

"How would you describe yours as compared to others?" When he stifled another snort of hilarity, she elbowed him good-naturedly in the ribs. "Quit laughing at me."

"I'm sorry. I'm just not used to spending time around a woman who is so unfamiliar with all of this." If he could just demonstrate, it would be so much simpler! "Suddenly our situation seems particularly absurd."

Her brow creased with concern. "But you said I should ask questions."

"So I did," he agreed, patting her thigh. "Forgive me my outburst. Now, what did you wish to know?"

Displaying the utmost fortitude, she pressed, "What size would you consider yours to be?"

"Bigger than most." He sighed, reining himself in. "Not as large as some."

She nodded thoughtfully, her attention returning to the drawing. "Why would a man like hearing that a woman found his male member to be an enormous specimen?"

"Masculine vanity, my dear," he said. "We're beasts at heart, and we all want to believe that we're the biggest bull in the herd, so you've given me a vast compliment without even realizing it."

Against his will, he was overcome with a wave of protective feeling for her. He cherished her brash naïveté, her originality and temerity, and he was tickled with the idea of what it would be like to make her his own. The notion was ludicrous, of course. There was no future for them beyond the next few meetings. However, he couldn't prevent the whim from toying at the outer fringes of his good sense.

What would it be like to claim her and keep her?

Luckily, her inquisitive mind lured her back to the lesson much before he was prepared to resume, and he was forced to abandon his opportunity to speculate about any possible destiny between them.

"What's that she's holding in her hand?"

"My balls." Tired and confounded, he answered without thinking.

The session was growing more difficult by the moment. He hated having to instruct her in this analytical fashion. He despised having to provide her with explicit carnal information that she might one day use with a man other than himself. With a flash of amazement, he was dumbfounded by his desire that she ever only view his naked male form, and that she never see another with which to compare it.

For the first time, he pondered what it would be like to practice fidelity with a woman, and he didn't care at all for the gloomy impressions that flitted through his mind— those of her in the arms of another lover. Bad enough to have to instruct her, worse still to ponder where she might head with her newly learned skills!

"What are they?"

"Two sacs at the base of a man's cock. Usually they're soft, but during sexual intercourse, they grow very hard. They're remarkably sensitive, as well, and it's marvelous to have them caressed." Nothing could shock her now, so he said, "Frequently, a woman will lick them or suck them into her mouth. It's highly arousing."

"Do you enjoy it when one of your partners does it to you?"

"There is very little about bedplay that I don't enjoy."

A long silence played out, and she squirmed in her seat. "What is she doing with her other hand?"

"Stroking me. In a sexual rhythm."

He lifted her wrist and squeezed his fingers around it while massaging back and forth. "Like this," he described, directing her in the appropriate tempo.

He hadn't intended to handle her so explicitly, but now that he had, he couldn't seem to withdraw. She remained perfectly still, staring at the parchment, while he played with her arm. Each manipulation distinctly reminded him of being fondled lower down, and the sensation was painful.

Eventually, he dropped her hand to her lap, although he maintained contact by linking his fingers through hers. Lady Abigail gazed at their united hands, inspecting them intently, contrasting her pallid skin with his dark, her smooth with his rough. She outlined the ridges, exploring bone and knuckle. Opening her palm, she flattened the heels together, as she noted the difference in proportions, how much larger his was, how wide, how long.

Finally, she slipped her fingers into his once again, and they sat in the quiet, the only sounds the ticking of the clock on the mantel, and their slow, steady breathing. Refusing to pause so he could decide if what he was about to do was a good idea or not, he kissed her.

By anyone's standards, it was not much of an embrace, but from the minimal impact, his senses careened wildly. He brushed her lips lightly, barely connecting. She was soft and warm, supple, made for kissing, and he had to do it again immediately. He hesitated, offering her one last chance to save herself, but she didn't grasp it, so he closed the short distance between them a second time, and he was lost.

Effortlessly, he maneuvered her into the corner of the sofa, using only the urgency of his mouth to tip her back. He dared not touch her with his hands. If they so much as hovered over her torso, he'd start removing clothing, which would be a quick disaster, so he learned his way almost chastely—by tasting. She was a heady mixture of peppermint and the brandy he'd given her, and he savored and sampled her honeyed variety of delights.

Unsatisfied, he delved deeper, flicking with his tongue. Asking. Asking. She opened and welcomed him inside, and the strangest perceptions washed over him: that he'd arrived at a special place, that he'd finally come home.

He could not have said how long he kissed her. Their tongues toyed and trifled, as he tarried and let the absolute joy of her flood over him time and again. When he eventually pulled away, he was permeated by the foreign emotions of loss and regret.

How he wanted from her! Anything and everything, and with scarcely concealed dismay, he blazed a path across her cheek, down her neck, to where he nestled his forehead against her nape.

"Don't stop," she whispered, her palm gliding to his neck, urging him nearer.

"Oh, Abby," he whispered in return, desperate to call her by her name. "We have to." Closing his eyes, he inhaled sharply, and her scent enveloped him. On some ancient plane, he could detect the aroma she was emitting. She was ready to mate, her body primed for the next step. All he need do was take it, but he couldn't.

Beginning at her hip, he allowed one hand to drift over her abdomen, her stomach, her chest. At the slope of her breast, he meant to move off quickly, but she captured his wrist and held him just there, and he couldn't resist spreading his palm wide and caressing against the soft mound. Through all the layers of fabric covering her, he could feel the tight bud of her firm nipple.

Quietly, she acknowledged, "I touched my breasts as you asked me to."

He could picture her standing in front of her mirror, assessing their mass and shape, observing the nipples as they stiffened under her visual scrutiny. "I wish I'd been with you."

" 'Twas very disturbing for me."

"Good! I want you *disturbed*."

He stared at her breasts, imagining how beautiful they would be fully bared, how round, how creamy white, how rose-tipped. They would fill his hands to overflowing. Tormented with his need for more of her, he pinched her nipple as much as he was able through her dress, and she squirmed.

"James . . ." she hissed.

"Say my name again."

"James . . . please . . ." But he couldn't tell if she pleaded for him to cease or persevere. Her corset had created an extraordinary cleavage, and he buried his face in it, for a fantastic moment letting the smell of her skin and sweat inundate him while he regained some of his equilibrium.

He lingered above her, one knee resting on the sofa cushion. She was trapped between his arms, and she looked thoroughly ravished as she reached out to tenderly lay her palm on the center of his chest. He clasped it and guided it lower, so she could feel the hard jut of his erection straining against the front of his trousers. Showing her how to please him, he used her to fondle himself, dipping her down, having her coddle his balls before coming back up. Deftly, she explored his severe magnitude on her own. Gritting his teeth, he held himself motionless as she investigated.

With a flick of his thumb against one of the buttons, his trousers could be open, and he could be fully exposed for her ardent perusal—a dangerous idea for both of them—so he relented and removed her hand from his person much sooner than he would have demanded it gone.

Determinedly, he advised, "I don't know if I can carry through with these lessons."

"Whyever not?"

"I desire you too much. I hurt with lusting after you."

Concern marred her features. "I don't mean to—"

" 'Tis simply the way of these things," he curtly cut in. "I've pilfered a small taste, and I will only steal more and more from you until I've had all."

"I don't mind. I fancy the same outcome."

"But you don't understand about what we're truly talking."

During their fervent embrace, the stack of pictures had fallen to the floor, and he grabbed for it, leafing through to the next portrait. Lily had returned to the etching, and she was serving him with her mouth, and he was buried deep. As he remembered the tension of that long-ago episode, he hardened further. Pierre had asked them to remain stationary as he'd struggled to get the facial and bodily expressions just right, but once he'd told them they could move, James had come so forcefully. Almost violently. And Lily had happily accepted all he'd had to impart. He craved that style of raucous passion now.

"I want you kneeling before me. As Lily did," he declared coarsely, angry that she aroused him so acutely when she could do nothing to assuage it. "I want to make you suck me so far inside that you are choking with the size of me and begging me to quit. I would demand that you swallow my seed, then I'd have you licking the tip until I decided that I'd had enough."

Unaffected by his display of temper, she stared at the sketch, then at him. To his horror, she was brimming with anticipation. "I would like to do that to you. If you would just show me how to—"

Moaning with frustration, he leapt from the couch lest he take her up on her insane offer. Huffing and puffing as though he'd run a long race, he stalked to the window and stood with his back to her. Ominously trying to calm himself, he pushed against his vertical phallus, unsuccessfully attempting to alleviate his pained situation. Only when he'd regained minimal restraint did he turn to face her again.

"I have to go."

"Will I see you again on Thursday?"

"I don't know," he answered truthfully. "I don't know if I can proceed."

"I didn't mean to disconcert you. I didn't realize I was."

" 'Tis not anything you did," he assured her. "Of a sudden, I want you without regard to any consequences, and I understand what will happen if we forge ahead."

"But I want it to happen, too."

"You say that now, but one of us needs to keep a level head."

Flashing him a weak smile, she said, "I guess we can both see that it won't be me."

"No, I don't think it can be you."

So it must be me, he warned himself, wondering why he was so upset. After all, when he'd commenced this affair, he'd suspected that her body would betray her, that he'd be able to lead her down a carnal path.

Yet now, as they contemplated this fork in their road, he couldn't fathom continuing. Though he hardly knew her, and had scarcely passed any time in her company, he cared for her and about her, and he couldn't commit a dastardly act against her.

While she might wish they could become lovers, it was no more than the nebulous, romantic fantasy of an untried woman. She had no clue what she was actually proposing, and from his past experience, he appreciated only too well that a physical relationship would lead directly to heartbreak. He was totally incapable of offering a woman more than limited sexual interplay, so if he deliberately compromised her, she would eventually grow to hate him, just as he would ultimately grow to hate himself. He simply couldn't behave so badly toward her.

So . . . he had to call a halt while the opportunity was ripe. But try as he might, he couldn't imagine missing their next assignation. Already she'd wheedled under his skin to the point where he didn't know how he could ever be shed of her.

"I have to go," he repeated. "Now. While I still can."

After a lengthy equivocation, she nodded, accepting his determination as the only possible course. "When will you decide if you'll come again?"

He struggled with the question, mulling it over, but there was no viable answer he could give her on such short notice. "I suppose I'll either be here on Thursday—or I won't be."

She nodded again.

Before she could respond, before *he* could do anything more rash, he hastily crossed the room, snatched up his pile of erotic pictures, and raced from the chamber and down the stairs as though the very hounds of hell were chasing him.

CHAPTER

SIX

James sat behind his desk, staring at the papers Michael had placed there, but he couldn't make sense of what they said. They might as well have been written in some strange hieroglyphic, for he simply could not concentrate long enough to decipher the details, despite how pressing the subject appeared to be.

His thoughts were too distracted by other weighty matters. By things like the smell of Abby's perfume, the creamy color of her skin, and the thickness of her glorious blond hair.

What was happening? Had he gone mad?

They had only passed but a scant number of hours together, had conversed about hardly any topic other than sex, but he was thoroughly infatuated. In his mind, she'd jumped far past the cool, sophisticated Lady Abigail with whom he was barely acquainted, and she'd quickly and easily become *his* hot-blooded, sexy Abby in a manner that was as unusual as it was frighteningly possessive. He couldn't quit thinking about her for a mere second. What would become of his mental faculties if he continued to meet with her?

That was not to say that his physical condition was faring much better. Behaving like a randy lad of thirteen again, he was ready to spill his seed at a moment's notice. Just from kissing her, he'd grown so hard that, all these hours later, his body was still reeling from the aftereffects. He was surly and short-tempered, his balls were aching, and all he could contemplate was how he wished he'd taken her up on her offer to relieve his carnal distress.

He should have unbuttoned his trousers! He should have made her reach inside! Instead of hesitating, he should have taught her how to stroke him, lick him, satisfy him. With the desperation of a starving man, he'd hungered to have

her touching him and fondling him, perhaps sucking him
between those ruby lips. If a tiny bit of her feminine attention had been directed his way, he wouldn't now be suffering so terribly.

She was eager to leap beyond the steady pace he'd initiated, but he crazily resisted. Why? The only answer that
occurred to him was: He liked her. For some reason, he
simply did, and he didn't want to hurt her.

If they became lovers, he realized exactly how it would
go. They would enjoy a glimmer of romance, a brief sizzle
of erotic assignations, but then the newness would wear off.
As always transpired, his fascination would gradually wane,
his desire for her cool, and he would be inclined to move
on to another. That had been the sorry state of his sexual
life; a woman never retained his interest for long.

But where would that leave her?

In her world, true ladies believed that love and sex were
inextricably bound, that one created an unbreakable responsibility regarding the other. Unfortunately, she wasn't
like the other women with whom he dallied, so she didn't
grasp that, sometimes, sex was just physical release and
nothing more. She'd never been instructed as to how deeply
lust could penetrate, how fiercely it could burn, or how
readily it could diminish. Nor could she possibly understand how horribly a sexual relationship could end, with
hurt feelings, recriminations, and harsh words.

He didn't want her to suffer through any heartbreak. So
. . . what to do?

Obviously, he couldn't keep meeting with her; he was
on a fool's errand. Yet, as he pondered how wonderful it
had been to finally hold her and kiss her, when he remembered the sparkle and longing in her eye as she'd asked if
he would return on Thursday, he couldn't imagine not going. To never see her again was an impossibility. To continue, the greatest folly.

He was a smart man, who prided himself on always
being in control, who never allowed himself to wander into
hopeless situations, so how had it eventuated that he now

found himself in this predicament? And how, pray tell, was he to extricate himself?

His options were few. He could simply never show up again, forcing her to forlornly wait on him until she deduced that he wasn't coming. She'd likely conclude that his decision had been her fault, that she'd offended him in some manner, which he hated to consider.

Or, he could make his meaning more rudely clear by sending her a parting gift. It would be some meaningless token of his affection, a worthless trinket that she could stare at occasionally so that she would always be reminded of what a cad he truly was. She'd forever recollect how he had entered into an important agreement with her but hadn't had the fortitude to follow through.

The only other alternative he could discern was to progress until she felt she'd seen and heard enough. And those unbearable meetings could go one of two ways: Either he could use every fragment of his resolve to keep the discussions on an intellectual level whereby he would end up sexually frustrated, sore, and wretched, or he could advance down the path his body was begging him to walk. He could begin her final seduction.

While he was suffering the discomfort of his musings and his choices, the door opened and his brother, Michael, stepped through. He gestured to the papers he'd earlier laid on James's desk and asked, "What do you think? Should we cut him off?"

"What is the total of Lord Rosewood's debt to us?" James was well aware that he should have gotten to the bottom of the stack by now and that, but for his scattered introspection, he would have long ago arrived at the answer himself.

On an exasperated sigh, Michael crossed the room. "What is it with you these days? You're absolutely distracted." He flipped to the last page and pointed his finger at the debit column.

James covered a wince that the substantial number had been so easily located. "I just have several important business matters on my mind," he fabricated. "I'm preoccupied."

"Right!" His brother snorted in disbelief. "If I didn't know better, I'd say some new woman has turned your head. . . ."

James stiffened but fumed silently. Given the slightest indication, his younger sibling would guess all. He and Michael had shared much over the years, and Michael safeguarded many of James's most vital secrets. He was an inestimable friend, a valuable confidant, and the only person in the world James trusted implicitly. But he could not learn about Lady Abigail Weston.

Yet, despite James's best intentions to hide his involvement with her, Michael stopped in his tracks. "Oh, give me strength. . . ." His voice trailed off, and he shifted so he could look James straight in the eye. "You're completely smitten!"

"That's ludicrous."

"Is it?" He focused in, as though by staring tenaciously he might be able to penetrate to the truth lurking inside. "Is she anyone I know?"

"I tell you: There's no one."

"You were always the worst liar." He stomped to the sideboard and poured a brandy. Facetiously, he inquired, "So, who's the lucky girl? Will you be bringing her home to introduce her to the family? Seeking Mother's blessing? Are there wedding bells in your future?" He paused, sipping the amber liquor, as James remained sullenly noncommittal. "I didn't suppose so," he muttered. " 'Tis that woman who came here, isn't it? Marbleton's sister. What was her name? Abigail?"

"You're talking nonsense," James insisted, but with much less intensity than he'd have liked to exhibit.

Their gazes met and held, and Michael bluntly questioned, "Are you mad? Have you so quickly forgotten how it was the last time you did something this reckless?"

James detested Michael's ability to so aptly pierce to the heart of the matter, mostly because he knew his brother to be correct: He was playing with a deadly fire, as he had once before, and they'd all gotten charred by the treacherous flames of the debacle his licentious behavior had created. Apparently, he'd learned nothing of import from his past actions. He was ready—no, eager!—to once again toy with prurient disaster.

As a lad of nineteen, he had disregarded his father's admonitions and his mother's warnings regarding the girls of the aristocracy, chasing after any young woman who appeared interested. And they all had been. His father's oldest, but illegitimate, son, he had hovered on the fringes of their exclusive world, had been seen, known, but not welcomed into it. His good looks and tall physique drew them to his side, but it was his status as an earl's bastard that held them captivated.

A dangerous boy, he was wealthy and wild, with no detectable scruples. He was the one to whom their mothers insisted they never speak, which only served to make him more desirable in their innocent, sheltered eyes.

Overly proud, rebellious, and heedless of the consequences, he had dallied once too often, been caught, and abruptly found himself wed to the daughter of a duke. Patricia had just turned seventeen. She was a stunningly beautiful girl, full of herself, and assured of her rightful place at the top of the world after a lifetime of pampering.

The golden prize of her Season, she'd been the most unattainable of females, the most forbidden to a man of his low station, so of course she was the one he'd sought out. They'd managed a handful of clandestine meetings, each one causing her to grow more certain that he was the husband she wanted above all others—even though they were virtually strangers.

Immature and foolish, brimming with nonsensical romantic notions, she'd naively assumed that theirs would be a grand passion to set Society on its ear. How blissfully unaware she'd been of what the future held!

Her first inkling had come at their wedding. Up until the last moment, she'd been convinced that her parents would relent, her transgressions would be forgiven, and he'd be welcomed into the family. She'd been so sure that she would ultimately be allowed the magnificent ceremony of which she'd always dreamed.

Instead, their vows had been hastily and secretly ex-changed in a minister's sitting room, without so much as a vase of flowers to enliven the surroundings and only her father in attendance. The exalted bastard had hovered sto-ically in the back, then departed directly after, not even pausing to say good-bye or wish them luck.

The closed doors had followed.

While James couldn't have cared less what others thought of their marriage, she'd suffered profusely. Dis-couraged and despondent, she'd waited at home for the in-vitations that never arrived, but no one would see her or speak to her. No one would answer her letters or reply to her inquiries. She was ignored on the street, regularly cut by people with whom she'd been acquainted all her life. The final straw was on a night he'd forced her to attend the theater. They'd encountered her parents and been pub-licly snubbed.

She'd never ventured out again.

Through it all, Patricia had loudly and continually pro-tested and accused that he was the source of all her woe, that he had brought about every wicked development. He had never denied her charges, feeling that he really was to blame, while silently suffering incredible guilt over the fact that he was a terrible excuse for a husband.

Early on, he'd abandoned any attempts at appeasing her. Her state of wretchedness and her level of melancholy were impossible to tolerate. Struggling to find a resolution that would restore his family's equanimity, he'd bought a sec-ond home and moved her into it, then he'd left her there to wallow in her own peculiar misery.

When he'd received word that she was gravely ill and had been for many days, the news had hardly affected him. She was an unpleasant, dismal woman whom he'd never understood. On her deathbed, while wracked with fever and cough, she'd offered no kind sentiments, no statements of remorse or regret for the way their short union had flashed, then floundered.

After her passing, a physician who had treated her mentioned that her lung fever hadn't been that severe and shouldn't have been life-threatening. That she'd simply faded away, despite his best efforts, as though she hadn't intended to go on living, and James still believed that she'd died of a broken heart, grieving over all that she had forfeited due to his reckless impulses.

Daily, he thanked his lucky stars that they'd bred no children!

Needing to produce some type of rejoinder, he maintained, "It won't be like the time I ended up wed to Patricia."

"How can you make such a guarantee?"

Michael had good reason to worry. Perhaps more than any of them, he had suffered in trying to deal with James's spoiled, miserable bride. She had directed much of her gloom at him, and the more accommodating he'd become, the more hellish had been Patricia's demeanor.

"The lady and I have decided . . ." James started to elucidate that part of their arrangement where Abby promised to issue no demands of him should they be discovered, but, recognizing how ridiculous the pact sounded, he checked himself.

"Oh, really?" Michael scornfully jumped into the void left by James's conundrum. "What have you agreed? Not to compromise her? Not to offer for her once you've utterly shredded her reputation? Not to wed her once she's increasing with your child?"

The cut was deep, incisive, firmly thrust. The idea that James might leave a woman with a bastard child was inconceivable. They both realized it. Having witnessed how their mother struggled to raise two boys on her own, they had both vowed that they would sire no illegitimate offspring.

"We haven't done anything," James ultimately said.

"And you won't?" Michael mocked. More gently, he cautioned, "Have a care, James. If you won't think of yourself, then think of Mother and what it would be like for her to endure another vicious scandal."

"I have, and I give you my word—"

"Oh, spare me," Michael interrupted. "When you're reasoning with your cock, your word means nothing. Less than nothing."

Angrily, they regarded each other, the tense quiet playing out. James felt like a chastened boy, and he despised his brother for displaying such disdain, despised himself for his uncontrollable desires. The lust he harbored for Abby was precarious. It threatened and overshadowed everything—their family's harmony, their peace of mind, even their livelihood.

Aspiring to ease the strained confrontation, he promised, "I'll be circumspect."

"That's something, I guess," his brother concluded, accepting James's attempt at conciliation, and the acrimonious moment dissipated. They were too close, and had endured too much, to be at odds. "And what of Lord Rosewood?" Michael asked, indicating the papers once again.

"He's finished at our tables," James concurred. "Have him sent to me."

Michael went to fetch the earl, and James stayed at his desk, calming himself as he waited for the aristocrat to arrive. Many minutes passed before Rosewood rapped on the door, and James almost felt sorry for him. The man would have no idea what was coming. Considering their protracted history, Rosewood, no doubt, would assume he'd been summoned to the back of the establishment for some type of dubious entertainment, the likes of which the two of them had partaken of on numerous occasions.

But, as the poverty-stricken earl was about to learn, James was a ruthless man of commerce. Friend or no, acquaintance or no, the business was always his first priority. His family relied on its steady income, and with James, his family's needs were paramount. By devoting himself to their welfare, he'd resolved to never be like his father who had tossed them aside with nary a backward glance when he and Michael were just lads. James was determined that his behavior toward those who depended on him would always set him apart.

"Rosewood." James nodded his acknowledgment of the earl's presence, as he waved away the servant who had brought him to the office.

Wanting only to be finished with the dreadful chore as rapidly as possible, he commenced with no preamble, explaining the man's exorbitant debt and watching as the nobleman became perturbed by the audacious airing of his finances. This wasn't the first such appointment James had had, and it wouldn't be the last, and he exercised a well-controlled, practiced patience. When James reached his final point, informing the disreputable earl that he wouldn't be welcomed inside again, Rosewood seethed with fury.

After much blustering, the discussion fell to the level to which they all descended. With no method of paying his bills, and no leverage to pressure James into changing his mind, the earl sank to using threats—just as James had known he would.

"I'll see you ruined for this!" the angry earl declared, but James didn't flinch. Even as the man voiced the warning, they both knew it to be idle posturing. Poverty had a wonderful way of making them equals, of stripping a fellow of much of his power. As the earl stormed off in a huff, James let out a long, slow breath, massaging at the headache forming behind his eyes.

Unmoving, he stared at the clock, calculating the time it would take for Rosewood to depart the premises. Michael would be discreetly observing to ensure that he left without causing any trouble. Exactly fourteen minutes later, the office door opened and Michael entered once again.

"Any problems out front?" James asked.

"None," Michael answered. "How about in here?"

"More of the same." James shook a finger and mimicked the earl's stern tone. "He'll 'see us ruined for this'!"

"Cheeky bastard, isn't he?" Michael rolled his eyes in disgust, then glared down at the papers that detailed Rosewood's outstanding debt, one they would be forced to carry for years, one that they most likely would never even partially recover.

"No worse than any of his kind," James responded.

"High praise, indeed," Michael declared, and they both chuckled. He walked to the sideboard and poured two brandies, then handed a glass to James and toasted. "To the earl's financial improvement. May it be substantial, and soon."

James angled his glass in return, adding, "And may we be the first creditors in line for repayment."

"Here, here," Michael said.

A silence began, lingered, grew jarring. James squirmed in his chair. "I must get out of here for a few hours."

"So . . . go." Michael shrugged.

"You'll be all right?"

"Of course."

He always was, but James invariably felt it necessary to inquire. "I'm not sure when I'll be back."

"Don't hurry," Michael advised. He downed his beverage, then headed for the door and the gaming rooms. "Dawdle until your mood has improved, or at least until your cock is limp. I'd like to hope you'll be more sensible by the time I encounter you again. Stay gone a few weeks—if that's what it takes." His farewell remark deftly delivered, he hustled away rapidly, so he missed the several snide comments James muttered in his wake.

The lamp sputtered out, and James hunkered in the near-dark while he considered his next move, and without any laborious cogitation, he concluded that there was no reason to obsess over Abby—no, Lady Abigail. Their relationship, as it presently existed, was the sole extent of what would ever occur between them. They could never become friends or paramours. They were two people who had come together under odd circumstances, for an invalid purpose, and who would part forever when that purpose concluded.

What the lady deserved, and would expect from life, was a romantic courtship, followed by an extended engagement and a happy marriage that led to a house full of boisterous children, but James couldn't bestow any of those things upon her. In the first place, even if he wished to wed her—

which he didn't—her family would never allow it. In the second, he was hardly the sort of husband a gently raised woman should have to endure for the remainder of her days.

A creature of the night, he'd been raised around prostitutes and actresses. His adult years had been spent cultivating the underworld of Polite Society, enjoying the amusements and sordid dissipations it had to offer. Even his employment matched his lifestyle. He slept in the day and worked in the evenings, arriving at the gaming house as the sun was setting, as the worst side of London was just taking to the streets. He caroused and rubbed elbows with gamblers and drunkards. They were the only type of people he knew, theirs was the only existence he understood. It was simply not possible for him to conceive of another.

If by some reckless twist of fate Lady Abigail Weston was delivered into his hands, what would he do with her? He was *not* the man for her, and he wouldn't pretend to be.

However, he couldn't abandon her in her carnal quest. He'd promised to help her, and he would, but in the meantime, he had to find a method of dealing with the harsh rush of physical lust she instilled. The strident wanting his association with her induced was becoming hazardous, and it had to abate. He was a grown man, who could and would control his unruly passions, and he could conceive of various methods by which he could sate his desire.

What he required was a hefty dose of the sorts of decadent women to whom he was accustomed. It had been a while since he'd allowed himself to indulge in the pleasures some of them preferred. If nothing else, a few intensive couplings would improve his current bad temperament. With sufficient opportunity, perhaps he could slake these abnormal and unusual sentimental yearnings, as well. By the next meeting with Lady Abigail, he'd have smoothed the edges to where he could proceed to the end with very little suffering or anxiety.

Resolved, he downed his brandy and prepared to leave. Not wanting to confront any customers who might detain him, he sneaked through a side door. Once on the street, he hailed a hackney, and the driver asked for a destination.

There were many sites he could visit for what he sought. A brothel was certainly a possibility, although he wasn't in the mood for any of the professional women of his acquaintance. He craved more than uninspiring sex in exchange for money. He needed an enthusiastic, willing partner, someone wild, shocking, the more ribald the better.

Any number of seedy soirees were currently under way. He knew the locations of all the late gatherings, knew the hostesses, the guests, the types of lewd diversions being offered. After lengthy consideration, he chose his old friend Lady Carrington. She could always be counted upon for a great deal of indecent distraction, and her home was unceasingly occupied by uninhibited, comely, amenable women.

He recited the lady's direction, and several minutes later he was climbing her front steps, a butler accepting his wrap. He strolled through the downstairs rooms, sipping strong Scottish whiskey and murmuring hellos to those clustered in the shadowy corners.

Couples were everywhere, in various stages of intoxication and undress. All were unable to wait for a private chamber, plus there was the added excitement of having others watch. No matter which way he turned, he saw bare breasts, fondling, copulation. In one salon, a naked woman danced on a table while numerous gentlemen sat in a circle, ogling her. In another, a man was reclined on a sofa, a woman balanced over him, sucking his cock. The man's friend knelt behind the woman, fucking her with furious determination.

The carnal atmosphere only served to increase his desire for a tumultuous, mindless sexual tryst. Michael had the right of it: This was the exact cure for what ailed him. With a bit of help from any of the depraved females in attendance, he'd readily vent the turmoil he'd been experiencing in Lady Abigail's company. As he looked around, he realized that this dark world of lust and sin, with these people who could and would commit any despicable act, was what he understood, where he thrived. He belonged here with them, and he couldn't imagine what had possessed him to believe he could fit into the sunny, daytime sphere of a lady such as Abigail Weston.

Certainly he would continue to meet with her, to give her lessons and impart information. He would do it rationally, calmly, carefully. But after . . . after, he would come to a place such as this.

As he finished his second glass of whiskey, he espied Barbara Ritter, a widow and past paramour. He'd stopped bedding her simply because he never dallied with the same lover for any period of time. He belonged to no woman, and an extended affair might have caused her to believe otherwise. Renewing their salacious acquaintance was risky, since it might furnish the wrong impression about his purely sexual interest, but there were obvious benefits, as well. His cock was already stirring at the memory of the forbidden delights in which she regularly engaged.

An added boon, she was tall, buxom, and ebony-haired, the complete opposite of his petite, blond Abby. A worldly, dissolute woman, she grasped—in a manner Lady Abigail never could—how a person could fornicate without strong emotional attachment.

A commoner who had married well to an aging baron, she was lured by the attractions of the night—just as he was. They'd met during the months when her husband had been on his deathbed. While he lay dying, his young, pretty wife had drifted through the maze of London's parties, and she'd gradually allowed herself to be drawn into the city's squalid underside.

Catching her eye was easy. A tip of his glass, a nod, and she was standing next to him. Thankfully, the small talk was minimal. She knew what she wanted, as did he. Holding hands, they maneuvered the stairs, searching through the rooms until they located one that was unoccupied. Quickly, they disrobed and went through the beginning motions.

Happy to let her be in charge, he reclined against the pillows, and she straddled his thighs. Familiar with what he enjoyed, she handled his balls and stroked his cock, using all the wiles at her disposal, which were a formidable amount. Finally, she impaled herself on his rigid member and rode him, her cleft milking him, her large breasts dangling in his face.

Then there was only the sex. Rough and hard and meaningless.

When she finally traveled down his chest to his stomach, then lower, he stared at the ceiling, waiting for that rush of sensation, that blaze of desire, but it never arrived. He held his breath, tensed, ready, longing for the nasty pull of arousal she usually induced, but he was unable to focus on gratification because he was so thoroughly distracted by the lack of feeling the joining generated. When she ultimately closed her lips around him and sucked at him, he absently reached for the back of her head to urge her closer.

If he thought at length about what he was doing, he'd recognize his disgust with himself, his weaknesses, his inability to bond with a woman of refinement, but he didn't choose to dwell on his abundant character deficits. Instead, he centered his musings just on the moment. On hands, and mouths, and tongues, but nothing more.

It was easy to disassociate himself from the room, the behavior, the depraved woman with whom he copulated. None of it truly mattered. The brunette widow, who serviced him so efficiently, gradually faded into the background . . . until . . . she became Abby.

His beautiful Abby was kneeling before him, wanting him and loving him with her sensuous mouth and talented fingers. The fantasy image sizzled to life and spurred his ardor to a previously unexperienced height.

He closed his eyes and let himself go.

SEVEN

Abigail heard his footstep on the stair and nearly staggered with relief. After their last parting, she hadn't known if he'd return. He'd been enraged and perturbed over what they were doing, and his bizarre attitude made her want to laugh aloud. Considering their backgrounds, *she* was the one who should be suffering all the anxiety. Not him. Their change of roles seemed ridiculous.

He grappled with protecting her from herself, but she required no protection. She cherished these encounters, longed for them. For him. Completely overwhelmed, she could concentrate on nothing else. Her world had shrunk to these stolen moments. The dull hours passed in an imprecise haze of monotonous tasks while she brooded away for this single instant when he would walk through the door and their secret assignations would begin anew.

Her entire life was disrupted. She couldn't eat, chat, sleep. Her unendurable nights were a restless litany of tossing and turning, peppered with scattered erotic dreams of James Stevens in various states of undress, of his breath against her skin, of his face buried against her bosom. She would wake in a sweat, her heart pounding, her breasts full and aching and beckoning her toward a release from physical agony that never arrived.

All she could think about was the intimate manner in which he had let her touch the front of his trousers so that she could feel his aroused condition. It was a heady adventure, this initial understanding of the power she held over a man. Who would have guessed that she maintained an ability to excite such a potent, sexual creature?

He had wanted her in the worst way, just as he did his other women, and the knowledge filled her with a strange awe that she could be so fervently desired by one such as

James. She'd never imagined herself as the type of female who could lure a man to desperate carnal heights, and the idea was as exciting as it was frightening, for of a sudden, her body seemed to be possessed with a will of its own, and she had very little say about what direction was taken.

Surprisingly, she'd become this out-of-control, sensual being, and she couldn't change her route and travel back to the person she'd been before. All she could do was hope that James would kiss her again. That he would keep on kissing her and never stop. That the sensations he stirred would grow and spiral until they were beyond her conception.

The door opened, and there he stood, looking handsome, dignified, magnificently virile. He lingered on the threshold, silent and composed, and his stern forbearance gave her pause, but despite his reserved entrance, she couldn't contain her exuberance.

"Hello, James." She smiled warmly, loving the chance to speak his name, and relishing it like a fine wine. "I'm so glad you came. I was so afraid you wouldn't."

Her modest disclosure destroyed his control. Resigned, he shrugged, then flashed his own smile as he held out his hands in welcome. She ran to him, and he began kissing her: her hairline, her forehead, brows, eyes, cheeks.

Finally, finally he found her mouth. Their lips melded, and she was assailed by his indescribable taste. With a flick of the wrist, he removed the ribbon she'd utilized to bind her hair, and his fingers tangled in it, working over and over through the long strands until he wrapped the mass around his fist and used it as leverage to tip her head back.

He intensified the kiss, his tongue dipping inside. She met his with her own, urging him deeper, closer, and he groaned with pleasure. The sound sent a tingling flurry of butterflies coursing through her stomach.

Greatly encouraged, she cradled him in her arms, treasuring the sensation of his robust physique. Her own feminine shape conformed against him perfectly. He was firm where she was soft, flat where she was rounded, and she felt as though she were created for embracing him and no other purpose at all.

They were merged; stomach, thighs, calves forged fast. Her breasts were heavy, the nipples throbbing and extended, and they pressed agonizingly against his chest. Each time he inhaled, they rubbed against him, creating an unbearable friction.

He roamed down, past her waist, to where he kneaded his fingers into her curved bottom, pulling her nearer than she could have imagined. He flexed into her, and she responded in kind, unable to believe the jolt her body received from his erect member pushing against her abdomen.

It was as though a shot of lightning had suddenly pierced her. She sensed a burst of fire in the woman's spot between her legs. The flame roared upward, through her veins, to her nipples, then passed out to her extremities. Yearning to encounter more of the same, she bravely dropped her own hands, landing on the tight cords of muscle across his backside and thighs.

Their hips rocked together. His cock was hard, solid, ready for her, and it occurred to her that, right then, she'd have done anything for him. Removed her clothing. Given up her virginity. Jumped off a cliff! Whatever he might request, she would happily acquiesce—if only he would keep these marvelous sensations escalating one after the next.

There was a definite madness connected to this conduct that made a person quite forget everything that mattered, and she suffered the fleeting realization that this was why young ladies were so heavily chaperoned, watched, and guarded. Others had already learned what she was just discovering: Desire knew no bounds. She could and would please this man in any fashion, with nary a thought or a moment's regret.

He ended their kiss, and she couldn't believe how greatly she immediately missed its absence, or how ardently she craved the instant it would start again. His lovely blue eyes gazed upon her, and they were filled with lust, but also with another sentiment she didn't recognize. Longing, perhaps?

"How do you do this to me?" he queried in a raspy voice. "I've spent the past four days telling myself that I could behave. That I could discipline myself in your presence, and then I have but to see you and all my good intentions fly out the window."

"So . . . you're not angry with me?" she asked.

"Angry? With you?" he asked in reply. "Lord, no. I was upset with myself. I continue to forget why I am here, that you have need of my knowledge and nothing more."

"I find myself forgetting, as well," she admitted.

The torment that had plagued her—that she'd offended him with her brazenness, that she was acting too boldly, that she had pushed him beyond some personal limit—had been torture. Relief flooded through her that her fears had been groundless, and she sagged against his lean body, overwhelmed by the smell of his skin, by the starch and soap in which his shirt had been laundered.

For a long while, he hugged her tightly, so tightly she could scarcely breathe. "I'm terribly enamored of you," he said, "and I can't seem to exercise better judgment."

At his stunning admission, her heart did a desperate flip-flop, and she shut her eyes against the actualities, wanting his words to be true, to be true forever. "That's not such a bad thing, is it?" she inquired.

"Oh, Abby . . ." He buried his face in her hair, then shifted away, slipping his fingers into hers. "Come sit with me?"

Eagerly, she nodded, and he led her to the small sofa. When she commenced to seat herself next to him as she had previously, he reclined against the arm and drew her down until she was stretched out across him and resting between his thighs. She fit neatly into the space, her hip and stomach pressed against his erection, her breasts against his own. His lips hovered inches from hers, a warm sigh sweeping across her cheek and, just when she thought he might kiss her again, he impelled her to relax, and she was snuggled against his shoulder.

Oh, this was sweet! So very sweet! Unable to resist, she kissed against his nape, and in response she earned herself one on the crown of her head. They remained joined as she adjusted to the novel sensation generated by the intimate contact, his hands lazily massaging her back, hair, hip, thigh. Overcome with a vast sense of contentment, she could have kept on in perpetuity. There was nowhere else she wanted to be; no other place that she belonged.

"What are your days like?" she murmured happily.

"My days?"

"Yes, your days. When we're apart, I can't help but ruminate about you."

"You shouldn't."

"I realize that, but I do anyway. I wonder who you're with, where you are, how you've spent your time."

"Boring tidbits, to be sure." A laugh rumbled through his chest, making it rise and fall, and she laid a palm in the center, liking that she could feel his heart beating so slowly and steadily.

"Not to me," she insisted. "It seems as though we're very close, but in fact, I know nothing about you at all, and I would like some substance to round out my imaginings."

"What would you like to know?"

"Let's see . . ." she mused. "How about your home? Where do you reside?"

His hesitation was so prolonged that she decided he wasn't going to answer, or perhaps he didn't wish to tell her. Finally, he said, "I live in a three-story row house here in the theater district." As though he needed to justify the location, he added, "It's convenient for my mother."

"She's an actress?" He stiffened imperceptibly—if she hadn't been in his arms, she might not have noticed—but he seemed to be bracing himself for the cutting remark he expected to follow. When none came, she was rewarded with a kiss against her hair.

"She doesn't take to the stage all that much anymore.

But the theater is in her blood, and she can't leave it alone. She's quite involved at the Chelsey."

"That's where she began her career?"

"Yes"—she could perceive his nod—"she does a little of everything, raising money, directing, and teaching. Occasionally, she acts when there's a part in which she's interested."

"I don't recall that I've ever seen her on the stage, but I hear she was quite something in her day."

"She was," he agreed, chuckling. "She still is."

"What's she like?"

"Oh . . . how does one characterize one's mother?" He pondered his description, then said, "She's extremely dynamic. Talented, tough. Determined and strong-willed."

"Very beautiful?"

"That, too, even after all these years."

"And your home, does your brother abide with the two of you?"

"Yes, and he assists me with the running of our gaming establishment."

"How did you get involved in owning such a business?"

"Our father gave it to us."

Shocked, she reared up to look him in the eye. She couldn't fathom any father buying his children a gambling house, especially Edward Stevens. "Your father? The Earl of Spencer?"

"The very one," James proclaimed. " 'Twas after we returned from France. He hoped that gainful employment might keep me off the streets."

"Did it?"

"Well, in my day, I had acquired a deserved reputation as a *terror*." As he grinned in that mocking way he had, she could just picture how he'd been a young man full of trouble and mischief. He clarified, "My father's family had always owned an interest in it, and he bought out the other two members so that we could have the sole management of the facility. I had just gotten married, and he theorized that it would smooth things over if I had a reliable income, but . . ."

He shifted uncomfortably, gazing across the room, witnessing a replay of old memories. With a shudder, he complained, " 'Tis old history, Abby. I don't like to talk about it."

From the anguish in his voice, it was evident they were poised on the edge of subjects he never shared with others, but she wanted him to share them with her. She felt connected to him as she'd never been with another, and by the very nature of their association, he should be able to tell her any tale. His secrets would readily become her own. After all, to whom could she possibly mention them?

His attempt to avoid discussion of his marriage was highly informative, and though she hated to acknowledge her pettiness, she was privately pleased that his experience had been less than satisfactory. Somehow, she'd started to regard him as her own, and she had difficulty envisioning him linked with another woman, especially a long-deceased wife.

Gently, she prodded, "Your marriage wasn't happy, was it?"

"No," he admitted, shaking his head. "She was very miserable, inconsolable over her fate at having to wed me. She took it out on my mother and Michael. 'Twas dreadful."

"Why did you go through with it?"

"I was young," he said, as if that explained all. "I allowed others to convince me that it was the proper route. My father, mainly, but it turned out to be a frightful decision. I'd never do anything so foolish a second time, no matter the pressure, no matter the cost." Appearing puzzled by his own ardency, he rested his hand on her neck and snuggled her, once again, across his torso, her face burrowed into the crook of his neck. "I can't believe I just confessed so much to you. I never talk about her or that period with anyone."

"I'm glad you confided in me, though." He didn't respond, but she didn't care. She lay still, letting his smell surround her senses, and cherishing the fact that he'd given her such a stunning glimpse into his private affairs. The silence lingered, and she finally revealed, "I met your father the other night."

"Good old Eddy." He snorted disdainfully.

"Gossip has it that the two of you are quite close. Isn't that true? Do you not get along?"

"One does not 'get along' with the Earl of Spencer. One just stands back."

"Is that how you view him? I find him to be extremely pleasant."

"I suppose you would. He can be charming when he wants to be. Unfortunately, some of us aren't graced with regularly witnessing that side of him."

"Did he act badly toward you and your mother? Is that why you dislike him?"

"I don't like him *or* dislike him."

"I can tell that's not true." James's acrimonious opinion of Edward didn't jibe with the funny, overwhelmed gentleman she'd stumbled upon at Caroline's party, and she couldn't make the two versions of Edward Stevens combine into one person. "What did he do to you and your mother that was so horrid?"

"He didn't *do* anything. He's simply very good at walking away from his responsibilities."

"You're overwrought and—"

"One day . . ." he rudely interrupted, "one day, he was there, living in our home and part of our lives, fully involved in our family, and the next, he wasn't. I was five years old, and we moved to France in the middle of the night. I didn't see him or hear from him again until I was nineteen." Without warning, he set her away and rose to his feet, crossed to the sideboard, and poured himself a brandy. Then he sauntered to the window and stared out at the street below, pensively sipping the amber liquid. "I'm not sure how one ever comes to grips with such an event, so spare me your drivel about what a *pleasant* fellow you perceive him to be."

Mortified by how thoroughly she'd distressed him, she grasped that this was exactly the type of debacle she deserved for brashly plunging ahead without respecting the intricacies of the situation. When she'd befriended Edward, she'd imagined there might be consequences, and she was just now discovering what some of them were.

She remained seated but turned to stare at him over her shoulder. "I'm sorry. I didn't intend to disturb you."

He downed the contents of his glass. " 'Tis simply an old wound that seems to have never quite healed. I've spent my life being advised of what a *great* man my father is, and I'm rather tired of it. I don't mean to vent my frustration at you, but I don't need you extolling his virtues to me."

"Please forgive me. I didn't realize he was a painful topic."

"How could he be anything but? He broke my mother's heart. She never recovered."

"What did he do?"

"He married . . . one of your kind."

The insult was expertly delivered, and she caught herself peeking down, checking for flaws, and finding many. His furious regard encompassed none of the good and all of the bad that were represented by her station. "He had to, James. Surely you comprehend the sacrifices his position required him to make."

"He wasn't *required* to marry anyone he didn't wish to marry. He simply felt that Mother wasn't worthy of him. That *we* weren't worthy of him."

"Oh, James . . ." she chided sadly. "Is that what you really believe?"

" 'Tis what I *know*. What I've always known. That's why we fled to the Continent. My mother couldn't stand to stay and watch what he was about to do to the three of us."

From across the room, his eyes bored into hers, and the intensity of his gaze alarmed her. When he spoke again, goose bumps prickled on the backs of her arms.

He said, "I've been thinking about our meetings."

"What about them?" Her heart pounded between her ribs. Would he quit visiting her solely because she'd quizzed him about his family and referred to his father? The idea didn't bear contemplating.

"I have made a commitment to you, that I would tutor you regarding sexual matters. I shall honor my pledge; however, we must contrive some modifications."

His pronouncement fell into the silence like a leaden ball. "What sorts of 'modifications'?"

"We should just go about our lessons. You oughtn't delve into my personal life, and I won't interrogate you as to the details of your day."

"Why can't we learn more about one another?" She sounded as though she were pleading for a few scraps of his attention, but she couldn't desist. "I've never encountered anyone like you before. I want to understand you. You're fascinating to me."

"So?" he barked edgily. "What does your *fascination* have to do with anything? With us? If we meet on the street, will you stop and chat? If I'm with my mother, will you beg an introduction and ask about her latest play? If I'm with my brother, will you tease him about his lack of marital prospects? What exactly is it that you hope to accomplish?"

"I'm merely curious about you," she answered evenly, striving to remain calm, and unable to credit how agitated he'd become over her simple questions. " 'Tis not a crime."

"No, 'tis not," he ultimately agreed. "But to what purpose do you inquire? There can never be anything for us beyond this room."

"I grasp that," she retorted quietly, but was it so terrible to pretend that the reality was otherwise? Like it or no, he was a bright ray of sunshine in her dreary existence who had completely illuminated her world. For a change, she had something to look forward to, and someone to think about. "What can it hurt for us to become better acquainted while we are here together?"

" 'Tis not a question of 'hurt,' Abby," he said more gently. "I simply fear that you are indulging in silly daydreams."

"Why do you find it 'silly' that I would like to be your friend?"

"I suspect you are calling it *friendship,* but you are picturing another image entirely. Perhaps you fancy that I will become so swept up in these encounters that I will marry you, and we will live happily ever after."

His statement was so close to the mark that she could hardly deny it. She'd never been a proficient liar, and she wasn't about to attempt bluffing away her increasing attachment. Secretly, she'd fantasized about proclaiming their relationship around the kingdom, going against the tides of her society, and flouting convention while reaching out and grabbing what she dangerously coveted.

It was ridiculous, girlish wishing, but she couldn't stop herself. She couldn't have defined why she was so positive of the possibilities where he was concerned, but an amour between the two of them seemed to be an eventuality she could make come true.

Now was not the moment to be timid. She gestured about the parlor, indicating the small space and what occurred between them inside it. "Would it be so awful for us to hope for more than this?"

"Oh, Abby . . ." He closed his eyes, her query painful to hear. "What if you had me? What would you do with me?" He ran a distracted hand through his hair. "I already went through this with my bride. She was convinced we would have the most illustrious romance of all time—"

She sharply cut him off. "Don't compare me to her."

"All right, I won't."

"That was unfair of you," she retorted hotly. "You don't know anything about me."

"And *you* don't know anything about me."

"But I want to!"

"No, you don't. Not really. These past few days, you've let some reverie grow regarding my intentions and what they might ultimately prove to be. I take the blame for any capricious plans you're harboring, but you have frightfully miscalculated what I am willing to do for you. You have no conception of the man I am."

"Then tell me," she urged softly.

"I'm trying!" he asserted testily. "For your sake—and mine!—there will be nothing between us but this handful of discussions. Despite how hard I've tried to be different, I am my father's son in all ways." He seemed to deflate with the admission, declaring, "I decline to be held accountable for your tender emotional state, because I'm well aware that I am incapable of revering you with the esteem you deserve. If you expect more from me, you are only deluding yourself, and you will suffer in the end."

He was working so hard to convince her that he was a cad and a bounder, but she refused to assume the worst about him—in spite of the perception he apparently preferred her to carry. "I decline to believe that you're really so callous."

"You must, Abby," he announced. "I am not one of the cultivated swains who sips tea in your polite drawing rooms."

"I understand that about you," she responded, frustrated, irritated. "Perhaps that's why I am so thoroughly attracted to you."

"I'm attracted to you, as well," he admitted, "but I am attracted to *many* women. It is my way. It has *always* been my way. I have many lovers; scores of women welcome me to their beds, where I do unspeakable things with them. I furnish no apologies for my lifestyle, and I shan't endeavor to rationalize or justify it to you. 'Tis simply my fashion to enjoy erotic interludes wherever and whenever they are presented to me."

"It sounds so calculated."

"I seek physical pleasure. Nothing more. Nothing less."

"And your . . . *women* . . ." She could barely utter the word. In the meager amount of time they'd passed together, she'd naively begun to consider him her own man. Though she understood that he was possessed of a strong sexual drive, she'd foolishly concluded that knowing her had brought about some changes in his attitudes and comportment. Oh, how it distressed her to concede how little he cared! While she spent her days pining away for him, very likely she never crossed his mind in return.

"What about them?" he asked.

"What do they think of your indifference?"

"They are sophisticated women, and they accept how the game is played."

"And how is that?"

"I make no commitments to any of them. I shall make none to you."

"I see."

His affirmation was brutal, but luckily, she'd had many years of practice at schooling her facial features. How she'd lingered over impossibilities! A few kisses, an insubstantial quantity of stolen moments, and she'd imagined herself at the commencement of a grand passion. She felt like an idiot.

"I warned you from the beginning"—he was compelled to grind salt into her wounds—"that I could render no promises to you. That still holds true. If we forge ahead with this plan you've concocted, only heartache will result. You would not recover, while I, on the other hand, would casually stroll away without a backward glance to detect how you fared."

She shook her head at her folly. She'd chosen him because of the rumors she'd discerned as to his prowess and his widespread sexual appeal. Women reveled in his free dispensing of favors, worrying not a whit that he harbored no affection toward them in return. When she'd initiated her alliance with him, she'd recognized that she would simply be one in a field of many.

Why, then, was it so devastating when he communicated his propensities so candidly?

He cared about her—she was certain he did!—and she rejected his obstinacy that he was telling the truth about his conduct. He was bent on disparaging himself, and she was incensed by his low opinion. A fine man was hiding under that hard shell, and she yearned to bring him to the fore.

Perhaps he'd never endured an emotional association with a woman, and the idea scared him. Maybe he'd never had a female friend before and was one of those absurd fellows who determined such a relationship to be improbable. More likely, he felt he was being chivalrous, shielding her from herself and her unruly desires, when she was adamant that she needed no guardian.

The blasted man! Deciding he knew the best course without taking her opinion into account! Yet, so long as he persisted, she had no option but to accede to his wishes, or he'd never agree to continue with their meetings, and she couldn't abide the thought that their assignations might be over.

If James walked away, all of her joy would go with him.

"I apologize," she stated, "and I hope you'll forgive me for acting in such a tactless manner."

"Don't apologize for being the person you are. We're oil and water, you and I. We simply don't mix."

"Do you truly believe that?" The question hovered in the air, but she didn't press, and he didn't respond. She rose to face him, her cheeks flushing bright red as she recounted her sins. "I had no right to ask you about your family or to pry into your personal life. I don't know what came over me. I suppose it's this house and the intimacy we share here. I presumed a connection that doesn't exist." She swallowed, chagrined at the tears burning behind her eyes. "I'm sorry."

"Don't be."

"But I've abused you horribly, and I'm not even sure how or why."

" 'Tis my own individual troubles that you've addressed, and I'm simply not comfortable with having them aired. You've done nothing wrong, love."

A soothing balm, the tender endearment flowed over her wounded pride. Had he even realized he'd used it? If he'd recited the word unconsciously, from the heart, perhaps all was not lost.

"How shall we progress?" she queried.

"Just as we'd always proposed. I shall instruct you in those prurient areas about which you are curious, and when you've heard enough, we'll go our separate ways."

Which meant no kisses, no embraces, no lingering touches or smoldering looks. And if there was a hint of regret in his voice that their trysts would proceed so uninspiringly, she had no one to blame but herself.

"As you wish. . . ." She sighed.

"Don't let's fight, Abby," he said so earnestly that another surge of tears inundated her eyes. "I can't bear for you to be unhappy."

"I'm not unhappy," she contended. Just exceedingly disappointed. And horribly deflated, as though she'd just been cheated out of a wonderful prize. Forcing a wan smile, she urged, "Let's have our lesson, shall we?"

EIGHT

James stayed by the window, watching as she settled herself on the sofa. She'd turned her back to him, hiding her sheen of tears. Her slender, sculpted fingers reached for his satchel, and he knew he should seat himself beside her and begin their dialogue, but he couldn't. Considering his emotional and physical condition, proximity was dangerous.

When had this become so difficult? In deciding to assist her, he'd merely intended a diversion from the tedium that reigned in his life, and he'd eagerly enmeshed himself in her deranged scheme. But somewhere along the way, his best-laid plans had gone awry.

Instead, he found himself enchanted by her, caught up in her fantasy, and wondering what it would be like to build a future with her.

Lunacy was quickly overtaking him!

He'd actually spoken to her about his mother and father! Candidly, he'd professed his private opinion regarding his father's behavior, and he'd loudly proclaimed the hurt he'd suffered as a boy that had followed him into adulthood.

Except to his brother, he'd never revealed his innermost thoughts about what his father had done. He'd never discussed his mother's broken heart, one that still lingered twenty-five years later, with another soul. She'd stoically carried on after Edward's abandonment, even though her world had been shattered. They'd all struggled, his mother most grievously, but he'd been so proud of her ability to persevere that he'd guarded her secret well. Yet, with hardly a moment's consideration, he'd confessed all to Abigail Weston.

Beyond all reason, he craved her understanding and longed for her empathy. He *wanted* her to be aware of past events, and his yearning made him appreciate that he had buried many painful memories. Meeting her had caused them to flood to the surface.

Vividly, he remembered the past. There had been the initial confusion when they'd fled to Paris, the melancholy that had descended when he realized that Edward wasn't coming to fetch them home. A pervasive gloom had hovered over their once-joyful household. By his teen years, his distress had transformed to anger and resentment, so that by the time his mother felt strong enough to return to England, he'd been frustrated, acrimonious, hell-bent on trouble and finding it wherever he went.

Of the three of them, he was the only one who had ever sought out the Earl of Spencer. He'd accosted his father outside his gentleman's club, and surprisingly, Edward had been glad to see him. He'd patiently waited while James had hurled his stored-up venom, then he'd proudly escorted his incorrigible son inside for a leisurely meal, where he'd spent hours peppering James with questions about every topic under the sun.

After, they'd developed a strained but workable relationship. They'd gathered occasionally for supper or drinks and, like a starry-eyed supplicant, James had fluttered about on the fringes of his father's life, hoping for bits of Edward's attention—irritated when he received it, enraged when he didn't.

Always, his father inquired about Michael, but Michael refused to communicate with him, claiming that he'd been but three years old when they'd departed, and that he had no recollection of Edward, and thus no need for any belated interference or guidance.

As to their mother . . . Edward Stevens, bastard that he was, had never once asked about her.

While James liked to believe that Edward's renunciation of their small family had had no effect, he'd only been deluding himself. His father's conduct had completely shaped him into the man he'd become. One who formed no attachments, created no bonds. One who distrusted emotional entanglements and eschewed ardent chains.

He'd never allowed himself to care about a woman, never looked farther than where his latest sexual escapade would take him. His defensive walls were high and sturdy and, so far, had done an excellent job of holding others at bay. With no forewarning, Abby had them tumbling down.

The aberrant sensations were frightening, and he couldn't figure out how to deal with them. She was brave enough to acknowledge her developing feelings, but he could not do the same.

Declaring his fondness was pointless. Any proclamation of sentiment would encourage her in her daydreams, so the only manner in which he could proceed was to keep her at arm's length and to advance through their lessons as quickly as possible.

Garnering his courage, he migrated to the sideboard and poured himself another brandy. He sipped it slowly; then, more confident, he studied her. Even as he did so, he was cognizant of how difficult it was going to be to muster his resolve. She was so lovely, so sweet, so pure and enticing, and she adored him with an innocent affection he'd never detected in any of his jaded paramours.

The upset he'd just put her through was well concealed, and he was greatly relieved. If he'd reduced her to tears, she'd have had him blubbering like a babe in his attempts to console her. He hadn't meant to exchange heated words, but he had no practice in dealing with the type of emotional upheaval she stirred.

When she'd mentioned Edward, his initial and total re-action had been rage—rage that she'd met his father, that she liked him, that Edward could delight in her company publicly while he, James, could not—and her brief refer-ence to their encounter brought back in full force all the things that he wished were different.

Lucky for him, she hadn't taken his cruel statements to heart. Though she still appeared quite piqued, he was left with the irrepressible perception that they were naught but an old married couple who had just survived a brief spat. It would serve him right if she got up and stomped out without so much as a by-your-leave, but she wasn't ready to withdraw just yet. He still had occasion to make a few pitiful amends.

She'd retrieved his folder from the table, opening it and sifting through the paintings to find where they'd left off at their previous engagement. From his position across the room, he had a partial view of the sketch with Lily bent across his lap. Abby perused the picture, running her hand over and over the spot where Lily's lips joined his phallus, the depiction keeping her enthralled.

When he could no longer stand her silent reflection, he asked, "What are you thinking?"

She made a derisive sound low in her throat. Her cheeks reddened, her hand stilled, and she impaled him with her eloquent green eyes. "I'm *thinking* that I don't like seeing another woman with her mouth on you."

He was caught unawares. Stunned and—curiously—embarrassed, Barbara Ritter came to mind, accompanied by a troubling collage of the degenerate women with whom he'd lain. He felt unclean and unworthy to remain in Abby's presence and, for the first time in his sorry life, shamed by his behavior, disgusted by his undisciplined desires. Lamely, he offered, "There have been many women, and there always will be."

"Well, I don't imagine I shall ever become accustomed to it." Her gaze held his. "What she's doing to you . . . What do you call it?"

"A French kiss."

"Would a husband obligate his wife to perform this kiss immediately after she began her marital duties?"

"Most likely not. In general, men never expect it of their wives. Others . . . only after extended intimacy, and then on rare occasions."

"Why?"

" 'Tis an exotic technique, usually practiced by the most proficient of females."

"Prostitutes?"

"Not just prostitutes."

"When a woman suckles you in this fashion"—she gestured to Lily's active application—"how does it feel?"

His cock hardened, and she noticed his stimulated condition. Her attention dropped to his groin, remaining there, her intense observation like a physical touch. With incredible effort, he described, "Wet, warm, and tight. 'Tis highly pleasurable."

"Do you require your lovers to give you this French kiss?"

"I have no *requirements* for my lovers," he responded testily, irritated that she could now discuss his sexual proclivities so coldly. "They generally do whatever yields the most gratification. Some appease me with oral copulation. Some don't. It depends. 'Tis not always an agreeable occurrence on the female's part. My cock is large, and when I am in the throes of passion, I'm not gentle."

"I suppose it would be strange. All that thrusting. . . ." She paused, her fingers going to her lips as though she would savor having him there.

"It takes some getting used to. Plus, many do not care for the taste of a man's seed."

"What is its flavor?"

"Indescribable. Like no other."

"I presume it would be hot. Salty."

"So I am told."

"But even if a woman didn't enjoy the taste, she could indulge without proceeding to the very end?"

"Yes, although I am always delighted with those who deliver me to completion in this manner."

"Why is that?"

"I prefer coming inside a woman's body, yet I never empty my seed against a lover's womb. At the moment of fulfillment, I pull away and finish against her stomach or leg."

Her pretty brow furrowed in consternation. "But that way . . . you would never sire any children. . . ."

"Exactly. I will create no children."

"Never?"

She seemed to be asking much more than a simple question about his sexual methods. Weirdly, the inquiry appeared to encompass their own relationship, should it ever proceed that far.

After the havoc produced by his own father's dastardly conduct, he hardly counted himself among the men who should become parents. He had no skill with young ones, no role models as to proper comportment, and no inclination to learn.

"Never," he answered firmly.

"Your decision is very sad, James." She sounded wistful. "Very sad, indeed."

She looked at him with such pity and compassion that he found himself reexamining his resolution. Was he wrong? His mother adamantly contended that he was, that her two sons were her supreme blessing, and that he would miss a huge slice of happiness by avoiding fatherhood.

In the past, he'd always shaken his head at what he considered her naive, maternal musings, but a simple remark from Abby had him doubting a position he'd held forever.

He shifted uncomfortably. How did she manage to prod him until she had him reevaluating every facet of his personality? He didn't want or need all this self-assessment. Damn her, he was fine just the way he was!

"The world can lump along without any progeny of mine," he insisted. Then, gruffly, he ordered, "Look at the next picture."

Without a further contentious exchange, she did as he requested.

In the next painting, he was again reclined on his back, his head relaxed on the arm of the daybed. Lily was stretched out across him, and her bounteous breasts dangled in his face. The tips were firm and elongated, and one of the alluring nubs just brushed his lips. His tongue was visible, the pointed end laving her.

She'd had the most sensitive nipples; the merest touch had always set her squirming, and he'd toyed with her unmercifully that day, driving her to a manic condition while Pierre had grappled with capturing her expression of ecstasy. He'd succeeded well. All these years later, James could still hear her sensual growls of arousal, still sense the steamy surge from her pussy that had saturated his cock and thigh. He could smell her musk, perceive her body's heat.

When Pierre had finally told them they could move about, she'd ridden him like a crazed woman. As she'd battled toward an apex that, at his tender age, he'd not previously confronted with a lover, he'd fucked her enthusiastically, but her level of agitation had been too immense. He hadn't had sufficient hands to appease her, so Pierre had knelt behind her and massaged her, as well, until she'd come in a savage rush.

Just recalling her orgasm, and the one with which he'd followed, elevated his desire to a furious height once again. He'd had so many women since then, but such true rapture proved elusive. The farther he searched, the harder he sought to reclaim the bliss of that early era, the more impossible it was to locate.

Abby sat serenely, overly intrigued by how he manipulated another woman's breast, and he had to reach around his back and physically grab the sideboard to prevent himself from running to her, baring her, and sucking forcefully as his body was commanding.

She noted his intense regard and pulled her eyes from the parchment, retaining his fiery gaze with one of her own. "When you were doing this . . . did you love her?"

"*Love* has never had anything to do with it."

"Did your coupling generate any sentiment on your part?"

"She was a good friend." He shrugged. "Her husband was there, looking on. 'Twas extremely erotic. Extremely stimulating."

"I realize that, but . . ."—she stared at the picture—"but surely you must feel something for the woman."

"No," he admitted. "I need not feel anything at all." And

as he said it, he recognized a distinct absence in his character. The excuses he'd always employed to justify his libidinous behavior failed him, and for a change, he couldn't defend his lewd conduct.

"Can all men proceed to sexual alleviation with a similar indifference?"

"Most."

"So . . . that is why a happily married man could easily visit a whore, or keep a mistress, without any bothersome guilt."

"Yes."

"Which means," she brooded, "that you could readily engage in a bit of love play with me despite your emotions. Or *lack* of them."

"If the spirit moved me," he retorted carefully.

She studied him boldly, her mind working over the possibilities. "No damage would be done to my virginal state, yet I could experience some of what you describe."

"You could," he reflected, "*if* I was willing to risk the consequences, but I've never been a gambling man."

"That's a strange comment from a man who owns a gaming establishment."

His eyes widened in disbelief as her hand went to the collar of her gown. "What are you about, Abigail?"

"I'm not certain."

"You're playing with fire!"

"I know." Her fingers slipped under the edge of the fabric. "And I find that, for once in my life, I don't care."

"I understand naught of what you hope to accomplish, but whatever it is, I'll not help you."

"Are you sure?"

The sleeve of her dress began to descend down her arm, and he gaped in dismay as more and more of her breast was exposed. Their rendezvous had suddenly spiraled into an insane realm! He'd lost control of the situation; he'd lost control of her, and his determination to continue on with his noble, detached course had crumpled to ashes.

"What's come over you?" he gasped.

"Perhaps we can blame it on my spending too much time in your company," she casually remarked, the rim of her bodice now barely covering her nipple, "but I should like to throw caution to the wind. I seek a mindless tryst, with no strings attached and no regard for the outcome."

"I do not."

"Why? A man of your reserve and nonchalance should have no qualms about dabbling with me. Assuredly, you may go about your business when we're finished."

He could think of no greater impossibility! Abby was not the kind of woman with whom one randomly trifled, and any involvement could only lead to disaster. Oh, where would it ever end? And how badly?

"I'll not be responsible for stealing your virginity."

"I'm not asking you to."

"What is it you want from me?" he grumbled in defeat. Rubbing a frustrated hand at the back of his neck, he realized that he needed air, needed space. He had to get away from there, from *her,* but his legs would not transport him to safety. As though he'd sprouted roots, he was anchored to his spot.

"I can't bear the idea that I might hurt you, Abby. I'm fond of you."

"Are you?"

"Yes." And when it appeared that she might argue, he added, "You know it's true."

"I know nothing of the sort," she declared. "I suppose I'll hardly cross your mind after we leave this room."

There was a challenge in her voice, as though she understood more about him than he suspected. She seemed to be intimating that, if their assignation progressed to the next level, he'd never be able to remain aloof upon the conclusion. It was almost as though she was demanding an opportunity to inflict her presence into his heart, fully aware that once she thoroughly ingratiated herself, he'd never be shed of her.

Impatient to advance, the tips of her fingers lingered under the front of her dress, disposed to embrace the final, disastrous step that would bare her breast. Without giving himself an extra second to consider his rash impulse, he hastened to her side and laid his hand atop hers, thwarting her before she could commit herself to her reckless strategy.

He would commence the journey down this improvident path. *He* would make the decision for her. *He* would brook responsibility for the affair's initiation so that, at the termination, when she was bitterly regretting what she'd executed, she could place the entire blame on his sturdy shoulders.

Falling to one knee, they were face-to-face, her expressive, verdant eyes eager with surprise and excitement. The breast she'd come so close to exposing was tantalizing, and he caressed it through the layers of her clothing, massaging in a slow circle. "I want to love your breasts."

"Oh, James . . ." His name escaped on a hiss of breath.

"Let me."

"Yes," she whispered.

He cupped the two exquisite mounds, shaping them, pinching and squeezing the raised crests. At the increased sensation, she started to squirm against the firm cushion of the couch.

Gradually, the arc of his fingers expanded, teasing her neckline, working it fractionally lower until he could see the areolae. With a tug, the bodice dipped and her breasts were free. They were voluminous and round, perfectly shaped, designed for a man's fervid attention. Her skin was creamy white, her nipples rosy and cheerfully begging for a thorough defiling. Powerless to resist, he grasped one of them between his thumb and index finger.

"Your breasts are stunning. As magnificent as I knew they would be." He reached for the other one and gripped it as well, holding both for several long moments, simply allowing her to become accustomed to the intimate touch. As her shoulders relaxed, he applied pressure, perceptibly intensifying it until she was fidgeting against the seat once again.

"I hadn't imagined . . .'Tis so . . . so . . ."

Unable to describe her reaction, she tipped her head back, inhaling deep, while he continued to play. With each additional manipulation, she struggled against the enhanced agitation, grappling for composure. But he didn't want to toy with the cool and collected Lady Abigail; he wanted his Abby hot and writhing and ready for whatever sexual exploit he might wreak upon her next.

"I'm going to suckle at your breast." He applied extra tension to the sensitive peaks, causing her to groan. "Watch me," he advised. "Don't close your eyes."

"I won't."

He stared at her nipples, the anticipation building, then he chose his delectable morsel, leisurely flicking at it before he closed around it and sucked hard. Greedily, he dazzled her, toiling with his tongue, lips, and teeth. Progressively drawn into the undertaking, her hips began to automatically flex in the world's most ancient rhythm, and he lowered a palm and pushed against her mound with the heel of his hand.

He kissed across her chest, tarrying at her cleavage, then he proceeded to the other breast, where he gave it the same fierce courtesy he'd lavished on the first. Once he had it throbbing and swollen, he roughly fondled both breasts, pressing them together so that he freely moved from one to the other until she could barely discern upon which he nursed.

"James, please, stop," she pleaded after a protracted indulgence, but he didn't heed her request. Instead, he augmented her duress, her pleasure and misery multiplying with each flip of his tongue, each wrench of his fingers.

She tried twisting away, but even as she did, the arm she'd kept behind his neck was urging him nearer. Her mind and body were at war, wanting her to travel in different directions in order to achieve contrasted purposes.

"James . . . please . . ." she implored again, more insistently.

"I can't stop," he said breathlessly. "Don't ask me to."

"But this . . ."—her words died in her throat as he rolled

her nipple between his teeth, lightly biting her aggravated, virgin flesh—"'tis more disturbance than a woman should be expected to abide!"

He backed off. Considering how aroused he was, he'd almost arrived at his point of no return. Soon it would become physically impractical to prevent himself from taking her all the way. They either needed to halt immediately or head on to a finale he wasn't entirely convinced he was inclined to impart.

The stronger of the two, she decided for him by leaning back against the couch, but she didn't release him. Her arms went around his shoulders and snuggled him against her chest. He was at eye level with a breast, and it appeared saturated and well tended, and he blew at it, the stream of air causing her to squirm anew, and he chuckled at how generously she responded to his slightest ministration. Since her raw nipples had benefited from the brunt of his concentration, he spared them any further tumult.

Forcing calm, willing his wave of lust to recede, he placed light kisses across her bosom, her neck, nape, shoulder. He traced a path to her mouth, gently making love to it, then proceeding on to her cheeks and forehead. Throughout his exploration, she didn't speak, her eyes stayed closed, but she refused to let him go, sifting her fingers through the thick curls at the back of his hair.

Gradually, her pulse slowed, her hips stilled, and she finally queried, "Are we finished?"

"For now." His fingers roamed across her arms, her thighs. "Are you all right?"

"No," she answered honestly. "I don't believe I am."

He kissed her pert nose; then, sighing with regret, he tucked her aggrieved breasts into the bodice of her dress.

"I feel so wonderful," she said, "but so terrible at the same time."

"That's because we quit before I took you as far as you could go." Her brow wrinkled in question. "Remember? There is a peak of pleasure that one attains."

"We didn't get there?" she inquired with genuine surprise.

"No."

"How could there be more? How does one stand it?"

"With the right person, it just keeps getting better and better." He understood that he was talking about the future assignations they would have. They were so attuned that each meeting would outdistance the next in terms of satisfaction. "My peak comes when I spill my seed."

"You . . . didn't?"

"No," he replied again, but oh, how he'd longed to! His balls were aching, his cock dripping with his sexual juice and awaiting the slightest indication that it could finish what had been so precipitously started. With a half dozen thrusts, he could be relieved of his suffering.

He guided her to the placard of his trousers, and her eyes sparkled with awe when she discovered how enlarged he was. "There is a definite . . . ending . . ." he explained through gritted teeth, barely able to tolerate her touch. " 'Tis much more dramatic. You'd have no doubt if I had discharged my seed."

"But you want me?"

"How could I not?"

She stroked across his front, and he felt like a lad again, equipped to ejaculate at the drop of a hat. When he caught himself seriously contemplating whether he should climax inside his trousers like a callow boy, he hastily removed her hand and raised it to his lips, kissing the middle. "I desire you *too* much. 'Tis painful, right now, for me to withstand your caress."

"Pained . . . yes, that's exactly how I feel. 'Tis not pleasant at all."

He laughed softly. "It will be pleasant. Just not today."

"You can't mean to leave me like this!"

Charmed by her physical distress, he laughed again. "I'm intentionally sending you home edgy and incomplete. When you return on Monday, you'll be ready."

"For what?"

"If you still wish to proceed, I shall show you how orgasm happens for a woman." Boldly, he dropped his palm to her crotch, driving against her through her skirts. "I will slide my fingers under your gown and tease your feminine center. Perhaps I will kiss you there, as well. I will caress you until you reach your peak. The *petit mort*. . . ."

" 'Tis called the *little death*?" She shuddered. "Why such a dreadful name?"

"You'll see."

"What if I . . ." Despite all they'd just endured, she had the grace to blush. "What if I can't achieve this pinnacle?"

"Trust me, love. You are a passionate woman, and I am a skilled, gifted lover. We'll get you there without any problem."

"Are you certain?"

"Never more so. . . ."

He stared into her extraordinary emerald eyes, and she unflinchingly held his gaze. More had occurred than the simple act of his feasting at her breast. They had crossed a bridge, or arrived at a milestone, or rounded a bend, and she regarded him with such a deep, abiding affection that he was shaken to his very core.

Needing to steady his universe, he took both her hands in his own and clasped them tightly. "We're going to stop now, so that we can both think on this."

"I don't need to *think*. This is exactly what I want. *You* are exactly what I want."

"Still," he cautioned, "you must be absolutely sure." Though she insisted verbally that she was prepared to completely capitulate, he wasn't convinced that she actually realized how intimate events would grow to be. Sucking at her breast was one thing. Sucking between her legs was quite another. "If you show up here on Monday, there will be no retreat. . . ."

"I won't change my mind," she pledged. "Why can't we finish now?"

Her smile was so lovely that his breath hitched. How did she do that? Just a look knocked him off balance. "Because," he explained patiently, "we passed so much time conversing that I don't have sufficient opportunity left to love you properly. Besides, you should be hot and bothered for the next four days. When we meet again, your enjoyment—and mine—will be much more profound."

"Cad," she complained prettily. "I hate waiting till Monday."

"It will be here before you know it."

"Easy for you to say. . . ."

"Not hardly." He pressed his provoked phallus against the blunt frame of the sofa, finding little ease and comprehending, disgustedly, that darkness would have him stalking the corridors of Lady Carrington's home, searching for another unfamiliar woman who would deliver only ungratifying relief. To what low level would Abby's esteem plunge if she ever learned what a weak man he truly was in his private hours?

Refusing to peer too closely at his less-than-stellar personal attributes, he changed the subject. "On Monday"—he bent forward and whispered naughtily—"I aim to have your breasts bared for the entire afternoon."

"James!" Her startled brows rose. "As if I would!"

"Naked breasts arouse me," he casually responded without pausing to think how his words sounded to her untried ear. "I enjoy the view with all my lovers."

"Don't expect me to act like your other women," she chided. "And I don't care to have you referring to your past behavior with them or to have you lumping me in the middle of such a vulgar group."

Over the years, he'd had many partners hint at possessive intentions, and he'd always shrugged them off, believing that any woman who allied herself with him was a fool. Yet with Abby, he didn't shy away at the allusion to emotional ownership. Where she was concerned, he would constantly be covering new ground, and he had to be content to see where events would lead him.

Still, old habits were difficult to break, and he heard himself saying crudely, "Get used to it."

"I shan't."

He stood, adjusting his bulging cock and rubbing his sore balls as she watched with avid interest, and he wondered how he would walk down the street in such a severe condition.

"Until Monday, then," he said, but he couldn't make his feet budge. He observed her for a lengthy moment.

"I don't want you to leave," she finally commented.

Her utterance transmitted a minimal amount of fortitude, and he turned toward the door. Best to go while he still had the mettle to depart. But as he reached for the knob, her voice caused him to hesitate, and he glanced over his shoulder.

"James?"

"Yes?" Appearing eminently appeased, she was still casually reposed on the sofa, her hair a mess, her dress askew, her lips swollen and moist, her cheeks flushed.

"Thank you. For everything. . . ."

There was no answer he could bestow. The *pleasure,* such as it was, had been all his. He quickly strode down the stairs before he could choose to remain.

NINE

Abigail rested against the seat of the barouche, letting the sway of the carriage and the clomp of the horses relax her, even as her mind whirled in unceasing circles. Luckily, she was behind the driver and facing backward, so she wasn't forced to smile and wave at the approaching traffic. She could travel along silently, stewing and mulling her predicament without numerous interruptions from the passersby.

It was a perfect spring day for a ride in the park. The sun was shining, the sky overwhelmingly blue, the air crisp in temperature. She could smell fertile earth and the flowers that would soon be sprouting in the various beds, making one think that summer might be just around the corner. Yet she could find no contentment in the balmy weather.

Edward Stevens sat next to her, with his son Charles and Caroline directly across. As she'd deduced from their three previous outings, her decision to accompany the two Stevens gentlemen was a huge mistake. Charles was a fun-loving, charming boy, and Edward a graceful, interesting man, but she winced when either of them glanced in her direction, and she was repeatedly forced to confront the mirror image of James. His resemblance to both his male relatives was uncanny, giving evidence of the strong Stevens bloodline.

Though only half-siblings, Charles and James looked enough alike to be . . . well, brothers. With their dark hair and handsome features, they were a matched pair, the only difference being that Charles was ten years younger, so his face and physique still held a hint of boyishness.

Had Charles ever met James, and if so, what had he thought of his dashing, unrestrained older brother? Did Charles consider him to be, as Abigail did, the most exotic, fascinating, astonishing person ever?

How she wished she could mention his name in the assembled company! James seemed to be a chimera floating above them, overshadowing every word spoken and every idea discussed. Each time Edward or Charles turned his head, she caught herself staring, openmouthed, at the impressions of James she could witness in their every move.

Pondering James—the only theme upon which she cared to dwell—was a mistake, for her traitorous body reacted violently whenever her ramblings strayed his way. Her pulse raced, her cheeks blushed, and she continually shifted against the squab, trying to ferret out a pose in which her clothing didn't seem so tight. She desperately needed to loosen the bindings of her feminine contraptions and shed some of her garments in order to cool her heated skin.

She couldn't prevent herself from remembering the feel of his mouth at her breast, the tug of his lips against her nipple. The action had drawn at something deep inside, at the very center of her womanhood that caused her to ache in new and previously undiscovered sites. The tender tips were aggravated and raw, and despite how soft the chemise she wore, they remained irritatingly enlarged, and they rubbed against her dresses, making her constantly aware of their disturbed condition.

Desire was an interesting emotion, she'd discovered. She'd be utterly content to abstain from food, water, sleep—any sustenance at all—in order to enjoy the physical ecstasy James offered. It couldn't possibly be healthy to crave something this stridently, and she wondered if she just might go mad from such rigorous wanting.

As the days slipped endlessly by, her lust for him should have begun to wane, yet it was growing by leaps and bounds as each passing minute took her nearer to the time when she'd meet with him again.

By his own admission, he'd deliberately put her in this distraught, wretched state. He'd said it would increase her level of anticipation, but as far as she could tell, all he'd done was leave her miserable, uneasy, and downright grouchy from all the disconcerting effects he'd initiated but hadn't seen fit to assuage.

She longed to kill him!

He wasn't the one who had to pass an afternoon and evening with Edward and Charles Stevens. How was she supposed to politely converse with his father and half-brother when she'd gleaned so many of his secrets? No woman of gentle breeding should have to suffer through such torment! She knew how he appeared when he was angry, how his eyes glittered with mischief when he pointed out his bad habits. For pity's sake, but she knew the shape and size of his erection when he was aroused!

The rat! It wasn't fair that he'd left her in such untenable straits, and she couldn't help speculating as to where he was at that very instant, what he was doing and if, by any chance, he might be sustaining some of the same palpable anguish. Oh, how she hoped he was!

But in case he'd been unaffected, she intended to rectify the situation at the earliest opportunity. She planned to learn all he could teach, then she'd practice the wicked techniques on his fabulous, willing torso until he spent every single second of their separate hours pining away as she currently was.

She wasn't certain what she'd expected through her relationship with James, but this yearning was a fire that burned hotter and brighter, recklessly blazing out of control. The intensity of it was now so strong that she imagined lunacy would overtake her in the end. She hoped the caretakers at Bedlam would have an extra bed available when she was ready to check in!

The road curved around the far side of the lake, and Charles saw several of his friends, with young ladies on their arms, feeding the ducks. The driver pulled to a halt, and Caroline and Charles descended to join the boisterous group. Abigail stayed in the barouche with Edward, acting like an aged grandmother long past her prime, who could only watch as the youngsters talked and laughed.

"They're getting on famously," Edward noted of Caroline and Charles as soon as the pair was out of earshot.

"Yes, they certainly are."

"Has Caroline pronounced any sentiments?"

"She says he's very sweet. How about Charles?"

"The same." He smiled and leaned back. "Perhaps we'll wind up as relations before this is concluded."

"Perhaps, we will," she concurred, smiling in return, even though she postulated that an eventual marriage between Caroline and Charles would be the very worst thing that could happen.

Being in such close proximity to the man who had sired James, and who reminded her of him in so many ways, was insanity. If she was forever gazing into his father's eyes, the passion James stirred couldn't possibly abate, her deranged tendencies would never cease, and for the rest of her days she'd forlornly stare at Edward, waiting to catch the occasional glimpse of James that managed to shine through.

Bedlam was drawing nearer every second!

"I feel ancient," Edward remarked wistfully, "as though I'm on the shelf while all of the children court and mingle."

"I was just thinking the same."

"Why don't you join them?" He gestured toward the water. "You don't have to tarry here with me. I rather like my own company; I'm used to it."

"I never could." She was slightly flustered and wasn't sure why. "I'm old enough that I could almost be a mother to some of those boys."

"Abigail, you're only twenty-five," he broached succinctly as he chuckled. Then, much too casually, he inquired, "How come you never married?"

"Good question." She shrugged, cogitating, as she often did anymore, how she'd settled for her present existence.

"What's the matter with your brother that he never located a husband for you?"

" 'Tis not his fault," she answered cautiously. "I never really asked for one."

"I'd always deemed that a grand marriage was what all young ladies desired."

"Previously, I'd have agreed with you. I was engaged once, when I was seventeen, but he passed away shortly after, and then, I don't know . . . I guess the idea never occurred to me." She tried to recall that period, but it seemed so long ago, as though it had never really transpired. "I was happy in the country, raising Caroline, but . . ." How could she explain her increasing discontent and dissatisfaction with every facet of her life?

"But she's grown now, so what about you? What are your plans?" The question was the same one with which Margaret kept prodding her, and it dropped like a blacksmith's anvil into the space separating them. "You've been making the rounds with Caroline. Has some fortunate fellow managed to capture your fancy?"

It was the consummate opportunity to disclose some of the more tame aspects of her goings-on with James. They were totally alone, and from what she'd been able to discern about Edward, she suspected that he would welcome the chance to discuss one of his *other* sons. Yet she couldn't bring herself to allude to James in even the vaguest fashion, and her lack of nerve left her ashamed.

Suddenly Edward lurched forward, narrowing his focus and peering down the road that was filled with horses and all manner of vehicles. He studied the fashionable crowd intensely, obviously searching for someone in particular, but eventually he sprawled back.

"What is it?" she asked gently.

"I thought I saw someone . . . I . . ." Terribly despondent, he shook his head. " 'Tis not important; I'm sure it wasn't he. . . ."

"Of whom do you speak?" Had he espied James? What would it be like to encounter him on the busy thoroughfare? Would they acknowledge one another? Would Edward introduce them? What could she possibly say if they crossed paths in such a public place?

"He is my . . . well . . ." Edward stopped himself.

"You can confide in me," she nudged kindly. "I promise I won't be shocked."

"No"—he carefully assessed her—"I don't imagine you would be." He took a deep breath, then exhaled slowly, his gaze still scanning the crush of people. "I have two other children, besides those I had with my wife."

"I know you do; 'tis hardly a secret." She was immensely relieved that he'd yanked the topic out into the open in such a frank manner. "See?" She grinned and twirled herself back and forth so that he could observe how she'd survived the admission unscathed. "I'm not shocked in the least."

"I'm delighted," he revealed. "I've always had to act as though they don't exist, so I've never been able to talk about them with anyone. But of late, they've been weighing so heavily. . . ."

Abigail was torn. It wasn't appropriate for her to hear any confessions regarding his bastard sons or the mother who had birthed them. Yet she was dying to learn any small tidbit he chose to impart. She relished the prospect of ascertaining more of the factors that had shaped James into such a hard, unattached man.

"Who did you presume that you saw?" she queried.

"Michael," he responded quietly. "I thought I saw Michael."

She couldn't decide if she was glad or disappointed that it hadn't been James. "But you didn't?"

"No. At least, I don't believe so. He's twenty-eight this year, but I've only seen him on a handful of occasions, and then only at a distance." Appearing lonely and melancholy about the entire affair, he sighed mournfully. "I'm sure I'm boring you. This can't be a subject that would hold your interest."

Was he joking? She was hanging on his every word, listening for nuance, probing for hidden meaning. The content was near and dear to her heart, and she felt terrible to be egging him on while he divulged his private miseries, yet she couldn't desist. "Why haven't the two of you become reacquainted?"

He bent forward and rested his elbows on his knees. "He hasn't wanted to meet me, so I decided not to press. My eldest boy, James, says it's because Michael has no memories of me and therefore he sees no reason to get to know me at this late date. I have to admit the idea hurts. It's been giving me some uneasy moments, and I wonder if I made the correct decisions all those years ago. . . ."

He'd edged extremely close to a disclaimer about his decades-long marriage. Abruptly aware of how inappropriate such an outrageous allegation would be, he straightened. "Don't pay any attention to me, Abigail," he announced in a tight tone. "I swear I've turned absolutely maudlin in my old age."

"Recollection is not *maudlin*. You've had any number of diverse adjustments to endure this past year. 'Tis only natural that you'd engage in some self-assessment."

"I suppose you're right," he conceded pensively. "Recently, I've been doing too much ruminating. When Charlie marries, there will be even more transition in store for me."

"Exactly."

Abigail wished she was more experienced at offering consolation and counsel. Altogether, Edward had sired six legitimate children. Four had lived to adulthood. His three girls were married and had been rearing their families for several years. Charles, his heir, was now raised, so Edward would soon be all alone in his rambling Town house with only his reminiscence for company.

How sad that, apparently, he harbored many regrets.

He proclaimed, "I'm not cut out for all this personal upheaval."

"You'll muddle through just fine," she assured him, patting his hand. "No one ever succumbed from a few life changes."

"Maybe I'll be the first," he said in that rueful manner he had, inducing her to chuckle, even as she pondered how odd it was that he and James were so much alike when, evidently, they'd had very little excuse for interaction during James's childhood.

"You've missed your two oldest boys, haven't you?" she asked softly, unable to resist.

"Every day of every year," he admitted with an old sorrow, but as Caroline and Charles were headed their way, he had no further opportunity to expound on the level of his continuing loss.

Abigail's introspection was deluged by a single question: What would James say if he comprehended the true extent of his father's remorse?

Barbara Ritter stood in her bedchamber, staring distractedly through the afternoon sunshine down to the street below as James entered the hansom that would deliver him to his gambling club. Dressed only in a short, transparent robe, she huddled out of sight, concealed from his assessing gaze, should he happen to glance up. The last thing she needed was for him to observe her gawking longingly out the window. He might start wondering if she was obsessing over him, if her emotions had become involved, which they hadn't.

Her passions? Yes, definitely. But her emotions? No.

Still, men were thick creatures, often prone to misconstruing behavior or purpose. If he had the slightest inkling that she carried more than a passing interest in his attentions, he'd be gone—again—in a heartbeat. She wasn't certain why he'd left before, so it had taken a lengthy amount of plotting to bring him back to her bed. Now that he'd returned, she was seriously resolute about keeping him there.

When she'd sent her note around earlier, baldly inviting him to stop by for another spot of daylight bed play, she hadn't counted on him showing, but with James, a woman never knew what he might do. He'd surprised her acutely by knocking on her door. Just remembering his savage, impetuous sex games made her hot all over again. Moisture flooded between her legs, and she began calculating how soon she could lure him to their next rendezvous.

He probably believed that their meeting at Lady Carrington's had been a random encounter, but the truth was that Barbara had been trolling for him for weeks, for months, attempting to force a confrontation. When he'd led her upstairs for those torrid hours of decadent romping, she'd been thrilled and delighted by the prospect of renewed coupling. After the rough display had ended, she'd arrived home only temporarily mollified and recognizing that she would have to use all her wiles to instigate further trysting.

Who would have imagined he'd be tempted so easily? Or so often? Of late, he'd been so randy that he was nearly insatiable. A hastily penned invitation had brought him practically begging for the types of lurid recreation that only she knew how to render.

No other woman could possibly grasp what James desired, what he was truly like, or what he expected from a female. They were two of a kind, and she'd appreciated their affinity from the very first.

The night they'd met, her husband had still been alive—barely—and she'd wandered through the darkness, hunting for the sort of connection that only James Stevens could provide. He was a disgustingly handsome, virile man, who enjoyed extensive carnal release. His sexual mastery, and willingness to engage in the naughty amusements she craved, had enticed her to his side, but his enigmatic disposition caused her to remain.

His selfishness, brooding moods, and lengthy silences drew her like a moth to the flame. She liked his independent ways, his displays of ennui and annoyance with the women who regularly threw themselves into his arms. Those vexatious characteristics implied disturbing needs that exactly matched her own.

She'd initiated a regimen of seduction, one that would tempt him until he was so enamored of her, and so enticed by the disquieting future they could share, that he'd never consider abandoning her again.

Oh, yes, she had definite plans for James Stevens.

Despite how abominably he treated her, his coldness and his truculent disregard kept her interest piqued. He was overbearing, crude, imperturbable, which were the reasons why she cherished him so desperately.

She loathed the idea of possessing some limp man who would come to heel when called. The fickle women of the *ton* could have their boring, castrated males. She wanted James, with his coarse manners and his fuck-me-or-don't attitude. His studied indifference made him all the more exciting, and definitely a heady challenge worth accepting.

In her heart, she perceived that she was different from all his other women, and though he'd told her repeatedly that they had no destiny, she hadn't accepted his opinion regarding their affiliation. She'd had sex with plenty of other men and women, and she understood the lurid diversions available to him. His choices were limited, and in the period when they'd been estranged, he'd wandered through London's private entertainments. She'd heard all the stories: what he'd done and with whom he'd lain. Obviously, he'd chased after the style of tempestuous sex that only she was bold enough to offer, and he hadn't located anything close, so he'd reverted to her.

She was the sole female of his copious paramours who grasped his black side, his solemn personality, his requirements for distance and space. Her background was too much like his own, so she welcomed him with all his flaws intact, for those were the sides of him she liked best.

Always a passionate, vigorous man, for some reason his sexual drives had recently been overwhelming. She was grateful for whatever peculiar events were creating such physical anguish. The amount of carnal appetite he displayed was highly arousing. With her hands, her mouth, her body, she'd given him untold episodes of satisfaction, and thus found her own. Still, when he'd finally decided to depart, she'd sensed that she could have continued on. That nothing would have slaked his raging appetite.

She didn't know what had caused this delirious inferno,

and she didn't *want* to know. She was simply determined to be the one and only woman who extinguished the flame when it burned so hotly.

He would come to her, and her alone, because there was no one else who embraced him completely and without reservation. He belonged with her and always would. There was no other acceptable conclusion. Without fail, she intended to ensure the successful attainment of her wildest dreams.

TEN

"Take off your jacket."

Abigail hesitated. She'd dressed for exactly this moment, understanding that James would hope she'd disrobe for the entire assignation, and she longed to please him. Yet, as she'd already learned where he was concerned, *thinking* boldly and *acting* boldly were two entirely different animals. While she wanted to confidently begin shedding her clothing, she couldn't set her hands to the task.

Her mind frantically searched for the fortitude to bravely strip herself, but her previously mustered courage had definitely deserted her. Her green riding suit contained two pieces: a jacket and a skirt. Underneath, she wore a chemise, drawers, stockings, and slippers. No petticoats, corset, or other feminine contraptions were present to restrict movement or accessibility, so when the outer layer went, he'd be able to see nearly all of her. The idea was exciting and terrifying.

On witnessing her vacillation, he asked, "Is something amiss?"

"No," she asserted.

He'd arrived before she had, and had somehow found a method of entering. Once inside, he'd abandoned the small meeting parlor for the bedchamber, and he'd made himself at home by preparing the room for seduction, with the obvious intent that she'd be unable to resist his rather substantial masculine charms.

The drapes were pulled against the afternoon sky, candles were glowing, a fire burned away the chill. An open bottle of wine and two glasses were set on the table. The bed, menacing and magnetic, called to her from the far wall. The covers had been turned back, and it was shadowed, private, and full of erotic possibilities.

James was lying on the center of the mattress, relaxed and comfortable with the pillows braced behind his head. His long, luscious locks curled nearly to his shoulders. He'd been perusing his portfolio of indecent pictures, although she couldn't see upon which one he tarried, and he tossed the stack aside.

Wearing only a pair of trousers, he appeared too handsome, wicked, dangerous. The pants were stretched tight, the fabric hugging each delectable curve and valley, so she was treated to the sight of much more *man* than she'd counted on viewing.

His broad chest was covered with a thick pile of dark hair. It thinned to a line that ran down the middle of his stomach and dipped under his waistband. He'd loosened the placard, and she could see much farther than she ought as it descended to unknown, tantalizing regions.

Her eyes lingered there, where the dim light and cloth outlined the bulge between his legs. With a thrill of delight, she realized he was aroused, and to her surprise, his member incurred additional swelling just from the heat of her gaze. Exhilarated at successfully exercising her feminine wiles, she moved on, to his muscled thighs, his exposed calves and feet.

He lounged on the bed, in no hurry, letting her look her fill. She visually traveled his length, loitering another good long time on his groin, which caused him to shift uncomfortably, and she couldn't help wondering if this might be the day that she would truly ascertain his nude secrets. How she craved the opportunity to behold him in his altogether!

"Take off your jacket," he repeated.

"I have only my chemise under it," she explained, her cheeks blushing bright red with the admission.

"I know."

"But I'm not certain if I'm ready. . . ."

"I am."

"But I believe I'd like to—"

"No," he said firmly. "I insist on observing your breasts while we talk."

She wanted to shed her clothing. She really, really did, but disrobing was so difficult to contemplate when he was sitting there like a huge cat prepared to pounce. Still, this extra intimacy was what she'd longed for from the moment they'd met, so she latched on to his potent command and used it to bolster her lagging resolve. Trembling, she hastily released the first button, then the second.

"Slower," he ordered. "And watch me while you're undressing."

Deliberately, she lifted her eyes. His hand rested on his chest, and he rubbed it in lazy circles; then, making sure she was paying attention, he lowered it to the placard of his trousers and began leisurely stroking his rigid phallus. "I haven't been able to concentrate on anything but this for days," he admitted. "I've been so hard for you."

Her breath caught; her knees weakened. Her bones had dissolved. Nervously, she advised, "I'm not sure I can proceed."

"You can, and you will," he contended. He nodded to her jacket. "Another button, if you please."

She toyed with the third, then the fourth, and he tensed with anticipation as each additional button slid through its hole. Languidly, she fussed with the final one, stalling in working it free.

Finally, the jacket was hanging open, her chemise visible. Refusing to allow herself any chance for reflection, she reached for the cuffs and tugged at the sleeves. They came off quickly. Her arms and shoulders were suddenly bare, and though the temperature was pleasantly warm, her skin prickled with goose bumps, and her nipples puckered into little buds that pressed frantically against the silk that shielded them. She stared down, and every detail of her breasts was delineated. Nothing was left to his imagination, and she might already have been naked to the waist.

As casually as possible, she strolled to a nearby chair and draped her jacket over the back.

"Put your foot on the chair," he said, "and remove your slipper."

She did as she was told, haphazardly dropping it, and it landed with a soft thud.

"Now the other."

She complied, then turned to face him, her toes feeling strange and exposed, and she curled them into the rug.

"Your skirt."

Her skirt couldn't be discarded in a hurried fashion. The tiny, decorative buttons that her seamstress had painstakingly stitched were dastardly, and as she carefully undid them, she worried about her moderate speed until she dared a glance at James and decided the inconvenience was worth it. He was enamored by each flick of her wrist, so she delayed her pace even more.

Of its own accord, the skirt slid down her hips, swishing as it whisked past her drawers. Though she desperately wished to grab for it to keep it in place, she restrained herself, permitting it to fall to her ankles.

His fierce regard focused on the top of her head, then proceeded languidly, to her face, neck, breasts. Her abdomen, her crotch. To her thighs, knees, and feet. He patted the empty spot next to him on the bed. "Come closer."

She walked to the edge of the mattress. Her throat was dry, her skin hot but cold, and she was shaking, scared, but so excited she could hardly stand.

"Let your hair down," he dictated, and she dislodged the combs and pins. It tumbled across her back in a blond wave, the ends rustling across her hips, and he added, "Run your fingers through it."

She complied. Each time she raised her arms, her breasts lifted and pressed, shifting and reshaping themselves under her chemise, the nipples abrading irritatingly.

"Very nice," he murmured, assessing her to the point of rudeness. Then he decreed, "Your chemise. . . ."

She inhaled sharply. "I would like to . . . I truly would, but—"

"I can see your nipples," he interrupted. His voice was raspy and low. "They're stimulated."

"Yes."

"Would you like me to kiss you there again?"

"You know I would." Heat flared between her legs and moved up her torso, to her bosom, her throat, her cheeks, and she felt on fire, as though she just might ignite.

"Then remove your chemise."

Time seemed to have stopped. The room had grown so silent that she couldn't help speculating if, perhaps, the planet had stilled on its axis. The only sounds were James's ragged breathing and the furious pounding of her pulse in her ears.

Imperceptibly, she reached for the waist of her drawers and drew free the hem of the chemise. Sequentially, she manipulated it upward, baring her stomach, the bottoms of her breasts, the tips, until she dragged it over her shoulders and threw it to the floor.

He didn't speak; his sizzling attention was centered on her chest. His searing scrutiny was so blatant that it produced a savage response in her nipples, causing them to throb with each beat of her heart.

"You have the most fabulous breasts," he said irreverently. "They're simply made for a man like me to appreciate."

He held out his hand, and she grabbed for it like a lifeline and climbed to the mattress. On her knees, she was off balance, and with his swift jerk, she was plunging forward and sprawled across his chest.

Her exposed nipples encountered his torrid skin, and she couldn't do anything but lie stationary while she contemplated the treacherous turmoil the contact instilled. The sensation was too intense, and she buried herself in the crook of his neck, while he idly massaged her back.

"Do you realize the effect you have on me? Feel this," he instructed, and he took her hand and laid it on the front of his trousers. "*This* is what you do to me." His palm was over hers, forcing her to caress him in a sexual rhythm, and he groaned with unrelieved misery. "I've been dying to have you touch me again."

"You're so big . . . so hard. . . ."

"Just for you," he vowed. "Look at me as I dally with you," he urged. "Your pleasure will be so much greater that way." His thumb and finger clasped one of her nipples, gently at first, then with heightened pressure, and she thrashed with uncomfortable expectation.

"James. . . ." She moaned his name.

"This is what you're here for, isn't it?"

"Yes, yes. . . ."

"Then . . . look at me."

He taunted her nipple, pinching and tugging with varying degrees of tension until her own fingers became curious and answered in kind. Tentatively, she twirled through the hair on his chest. It was soft and springy, and she explored until she became courageous enough to inspect the small brown pebble of his nipple.

"Are they sensitive like mine?"

"Very."

"Would you enjoy it if I sucked against them?"

"Always."

Uncertainly, she bent forward and closed her lips around the tiny nub, and the tautness of his body was elevated to a frightening level. He granted her just a few scant seconds of examination before he called a halt.

"Don't do that just now," he warned. He clenched his teeth and closed his eyes, as though willing a terrible suffering to recede. "I can't tolerate any more."

"Why?"

" 'Tis extremely painful for a man to be so cocked for such a lengthy period. Your tender ministrations increase my agony a thousand percent."

"But I'm not ready to stop."

"Maybe another day. . . ." He shuddered with harnessed passion. "I must hold myself in check. If I become too unsettled, I'll have to leave, lest I end up doing something I'll regret." Much too businesslike for her peace of mind, he stated, "Let's chat, shall we?"

"Chat? I don't want to chat!"

"Well, we're going to, my little wildcat." He chuckled.

"You shall have to restrain yourself for a bit while I calm down."

"I've done nothing *but* restrain myself for the past four days!"

"You poor child," he teased, and he flashed her a smile so deadly that she was glad she was reclining when it landed on her. "Just relax and get used to having your skin bared and pressed to mine."

She stretched and shifted over his body, crossing her arms on his chest and balancing her chin on her doubled fists. "Would you at least kiss me?"

He ran his thumb along her bottom lip, but made no effort to narrow the distance between them. Ultimately, he said, "I've been pondering our relationship, and I've decided that our kissing isn't a good idea."

"What?" She bolted upright, no longer caring that her breasts were on display. His comment was the most idiotic she'd ever heard a man utter. Now that she knew what kissing him was like, *kissing* him was all she lived for, all she dreamed about.

"Don't misunderstand," he soothed hastily when he saw the murderous gleam in her eye. "I delight in kissing you, but it makes all this so much more . . . more . . ."

"If you say *personal*, I swear I'll strangle you," she barked nastily. "I'm lying here without my clothes, so things could hardly become more *personal* than this."

"All right, I won't say *personal*. It's just that . . . that . . ." He studied her intently, his gaze steady and true until he finally acknowledged, "When I kiss you, I don't want to ever quit."

"Oh, James," she sighed, "how sweet."

"And when I'm kissing you"—as he attempted to explain his silly decision, he was actually fidgeting, his cheeks flushing red—"I start to think—"

"James?"

"Yes?"

"Don't think."

She leaned forward and initiated a gentle kiss of her own

and, as she'd hoped, he didn't hesitate to kiss her back. His mouth fit hers perfectly, and he lingered until they were both breathless.

"Perhaps I was wrong in my calculations." He gave her a contrite smile. "I'll keep on."

"You'd better."

His sapphire eyes were glowing with a disturbing intensity, and the depth of his estimation alarmed her. If he was beginning to entertain an attachment, if his emotions were becoming engaged, how would she ever hide her own? Their association had to remain cheerful and gay, or her delicate, untried heart would never survive.

"I intend"—she struggled for levity—"that you should kiss me whenever you are so inclined." She wrapped her arms around his neck, eager for more, yet he did nothing but laugh and swat her on the bottom.

"You, madam, are a natural at this." He rolled her off his torso so that she was stretched out along his side. "Have I mentioned that you'll probably be the death of me before we're through?"

"I believe so."

"Well, I mean it."

She batted her lashes, pretending to be a daring coquette. "I'll try to go easy on you."

"Not bloody likely," he muttered. He searched the mattress and found his satchel.

"I don't want to look at pictures," she complained.

"I do." He took her hand and placed it, palm down, on the center of his chest where his aggravated pulse was racing much too fast for a man who was absolutely relaxed. "I need to pace myself. You're not helping."

"I'm hardly going to worry if you're disturbed; I haven't been comfortable in days, and I've longed to kill you."

"I was hoping you were hot and bothered."

"I was, you cad!"

He tapped a playful finger against the tip of her nose, then sobered and pulled her close. "I'm serious, Abby. 'Tis difficult to explain, but a man can arrive at a point of stimulation from which he can't back away, and if I'm overly excited, I'll have to depart long before either of us is ready for me to go."

His admonition was earnest, his concern for her welfare clearly apparent, and she could only agree to be more amenable. "I'll behave myself."

"That's my girl. . . ."

"But I don't have to like it."

"No, love, you don't."

Distractedly, he flipped through the pile of drawings, past the nude renderings of himself and Lily in their various sexual poses. When he paused, she inspected the parchment he'd selected and wondered what she was seeing. It appeared to be some type of exotic flower. There was a pink center and what seemed to be petals. "What is it?"

" 'Tis the spot between a woman's legs. Her privates."

Her breasts swelled; her nipples grew rigid. She stared, then stared some more at the strange depiction. Finally, she traced across it. "This is Lily?"

"Yes, but it could be most any woman." His hand locked on hers, and he guided her path. "These are the lips that protect the opening. This is the cleft where a man inserts his cock. A woman's maidenhead is hidden past the folds. Here"—he used the tip of her index finger to touch a small nub of darker skin at the top—"this is the clit. Or clitoris. 'Tis the feminine pleasure center. When a man fondles it or licks against it in just the appropriate fashion, she reaches her peak—"

"The *petit mort*."

"Yes. I'm going to show you today how it can be. If that is still your desire."

He turned to the next picture. Lily had reclined, her legs splayed wide. James knelt between them, his mouth and tongue on her. One of his hands was at her breast, pinching the extended end. Her back was arched, her fingers frantically gripping the edges of the daybed. Eyes closed, lips parted, there was an expression of pure bliss upon her face.

When James had first described this kind of oral animation, she hadn't been able to imagine it, and she certainly hadn't been able to envision it as an agreeable occurrence for either party. Yet, when she saw how well the artist had captured the physical tumult, it was easy to understand why a man and woman would engage in such an act.

Their enjoyment was readily conspicuous, and surprisingly, observing the two of them inflamed her. At her womanly core, she felt sticky and moist in a manner she now associated with rising lust.

She wanted this, what Lily had encountered with James; she wanted it desperately, with an enthusiasm that went beyond rhyme or reason. As with all the previous occasions she'd reviewed the drawings, she could shut her eyes and become the female in James's arms, and she craved the opportunity to endure Lily's obvious rapture. Even if it meant James would do something as shocking as *kiss* her scandalously, she had to know what the experience was like.

"Show me," she whispered.

"Gladly."

With a toss of his wrist, the collection of illustrations was gone. He burrowed into the pillows and hauled her over him. His legs wrapped around her own, his feet hooking behind her calves and locking her in place. The position forced her to spread and to directly expose herself to his erect phallus.

"I'm going to make love to your breasts," he announced as they dangled directly over his eager, waiting mouth, "until I have you begging me to cease."

"Never!" she insisted. "I'll never ask you to stop—"

Her breath left her lungs in a vicious *swoosh* as his rabid tongue deftly pulled her far inside. Nibbling, trifling, biting, he sucked greedily, and he stayed until the nipple was swollen and raw, continuing on far past the point of comfort.

Just when she decided she could bear no more, he shifted to the other nipple, giving it the same drastic attention. When he had it crimson and distended, he migrated back and forth between the two, using his fingers to stroke and caress until he had her squirming and writhing.

Her inner cleft wept, her womb stirred, and her carefully ingrained inhibitions detached, then fled, causing her to wish they could create a babe together. Her entire being cried out with the need, the feeling so intense that only a full-blown coupling would suffice.

Perilous, atrocious thoughts, she knew, but she cared not. At that moment, she'd have let him do anything to her, and happily joined him in the doing.

As though her body recognized the direction she must travel, her hips flexed, hoping to welcome him to her interior, though clothing barred his route. Slowly at first, then more vigorously, her pelvis drove against his, and she could relish every inch of his rigid cock, and she found herself deliriously anxious for the ecstasy he'd promised would come next.

Down below, he was busy, untying the ribbon at the waist of her drawers, then slipping inside. He feathered across her abdomen, and her stomach muscles clenched as he tangled in the cushion of hair that shielded her privates. She was wet, slick, and for a few minutes he simply rested his palm, cupping her and letting her acclimate to his familiar fondling.

As she mellowed, he slid into the folds, and one long, slender finger discovered her mysterious path. Another joined it, and she bowed up off the bed, but he held her immobile, allowing her no liberation from the brutal sensation he inflicted.

"Feel it, love," he murmured. He stroked back and forth, and her hips perfectly matched the age-old rhythm. She was melting, the flood from her center dripping onto his hand and across her thighs.

The tempo magnified. A third finger merged with the first two, and she wailed aloud at the startling maneuver. His thumb crept to the nub of her sex and sketched deliberate, piercing circles. She jumped from the impact of it, but James had her pinned down, so there was no escaping his barbaric torment.

A strange pressure started to build deep inside, radiating out across her stomach and chest, shooting to her extremities. Her breasts were rock-hard, her nipples beyond sensation, her flesh tensed, her fingers grasping the bedcovers, her toes twisted into the mattress. She seemed to be standing at the brink of a cliff, geared to leap into space.

" 'Tis time, Abby," James advised. "Let yourself go."

With that, he increased his demands at her nipple, sucking forcefully, and the extra bit of stress pushed her over the precipice to which he'd led her. She recklessly vaulted over the crevasse that beckoned, then she was falling, shattered and flying free and unimpeded across the universe. From somewhere far off, she heard a voice crying out with an extraordinary sort of joy, and in a hazy glimmer of perception, she realized it was her own.

The surge of pleasure went on and on, until gradually, it abated. She reassembled, her muscles calmed, her frantic breathing diminished, and she was once again within the small bedchamber, cradled in James's arms. As though he knew she couldn't tolerate any more handling, he'd extracted his mouth from her breast and his hand from her genitalia. His damp fingers just grazed her lower abdomen.

She hoped he would say something, but he didn't. He simply looked at her; then, almost against his wishes, he bent down and kissed her. It was tame, almost chaste, and she kissed him in return, as she concluded that this quiet interlude following the excess of excitement was more wonderful than the raucous act itself.

Eventually, he pulled away, but he was gazing at her with an abiding fondness, almost as though he profoundly cared. Tears surged to her eyes and a few dribbled down her cheek. The aftermath was much more stirring than she'd supposed, much more special than a person could ever appreciate without having experienced it.

She was severely embarrassed by her show of emotion. Her innocence was humiliatingly conspicuous, for surely none of his other women would carry on so, and she was terrified that her bald display of sentiment would irritate him. Lest he storm out in a huff, she struggled to get her careening passions under control.

Offering him a watery half smile, she tried for lightness. "I'm sorry," she asserted. "You must think me a complete ninny." But as she cautiously met his eye, she saw only affection and something that had to be very close to love and, if she didn't know better, a hint of male pride that he'd reduced her to such a disconcerted state.

"I don't mind," he insisted. "All of this is very new to you. It can be overwhelming." He gently kissed her lips again, then raised one of the covers and dabbed at her cheeks, wiping away the tears that had managed to escape, then he nestled her against his chest.

With her ear pressed tightly, she listened to the steady beating of his heart, the sound soothing her tattered nerves. If she'd had any previous doubts, she had none now: She loved him, heart and soul, and always would.

CHAPTER

ELEVEN

James held Abigail in his arms, while he struggled with the intimacy of the moment. Something had happened between them during the intense journey to her first orgasm, though he wasn't quite sure what. From the way she was staring at him, her eyes wide with wonder and serenity and some other indefinable emotion that looked very much like *love,* he could tell that she sensed it, too.

From the beginning, he'd been blatantly, masculinely aware of his physical attraction to her. But apparently he was forming a deep romantic affinity, as well. He'd imprudently believed that he could manage the assignations by having them proceed on a superficial basis. That he could merely pronounce his commands—to disrobe, to let her hair down, to bare her superb breasts—and then nonchalantly watch all, an indifferent voyeur and teacher. Little had he understood how unfeasible it would be to travel the aloof course he'd charted.

As he'd lain on the bed, immobile and apart, he'd been forced to recognize the flaw in his plan. In all his days, he'd never witnessed a sight as erotic as Abby stripping herself for his carnal perusal.

Throughout the years, he'd experienced the most arousing instances of which any man could possibly imagine. But nothing compared to Abby's blending of bravado and hesitation. Virgin and temptress, innocent yet adept, she'd casually and valiantly—yet timidly—exposed herself until he'd grown hard as stone, provoked past comprehension, needing and wanting her beyond logic or reason.

How he'd disciplined his impulses sufficiently to keep from tearing off her drawers and stealing her maidenhood was a mystery. They'd certainly come far enough to consider her virtue as completely destroyed. The knowledge was a lodestone around his neck, one he could hardly carry.

By allowing herself to go to completion, she'd given him her absolute faith and confidence, assured that he would lead her safely through the scary path of initial passion. As he'd suspected, she was a sensual woman, one who was unafraid of her burgeoning lust. She was eager to learn, and with a minimum of practice, her awe and delight would turn to a feminine ability that she would wield with devastating effect. Yet he couldn't conceive of a future where she might take the skills she'd garnered and use them with another man, a lover, a husband. The very idea was unthinkable.

In the past, he'd always stridently insisted on no strings in his relationships, but after a handful of trysts with Abby, he was totally bound to her in a manner he'd never visualized. Though he hadn't perceived it about himself, he yearned for the completion and connection that he'd only ever felt with her. He caught himself fantasizing as to what it would be like to have a true wife, a family, a home, children. He'd convinced himself that he wanted no ties, but now familial attachment—to Abby—seemed to be not only a worthwhile goal, but a happenstance he couldn't live without.

An ache began in the center of his chest and worked outward. Stunned to the core, he acknowledged that he . . . he . . . *loved* her. That had to be it. This overpowering pathos to cherish and protect, coupled with his unceasing thoughts of her, his inability to sleep, his disrupted dreams, his frantic, raging lasciviousness made him decide that *love* was the only explanation.

As he'd never endured anything close, he was amused, bewildered, and apprehensive. Previously, his foremost reaction to any sort of developing entanglement was to flee at the earliest opportunity, to run fast and furiously without ever glancing back.

Astonishingly, for the first time, he didn't wish to depart; he longed to remain. Like the most immature boy, he craved the opportunity to confess his undying devotion, to shower her with endearments, gifts, tenderness. Mawkish words were poised on the tip of his tongue, begging for the chance to spew forth so that he could make a great fool of himself. For if he spoke of love, what then?

In her naïveté, she'd probably profess the same, and there they'd be, in a coil of ardor and emotion from which there seemed no logical retreat.

As though conscious of his weighty distress, she asked, "Are you all right?"

He hated that she read him so effortlessly, that she noticed so much about him, because such inherent enlightenment came from a strong, abiding regard of the type he shared solely with his mother and brother. They were the only two people with whom he'd ever been close, and they were apt to uncover his thoughts before he grasped them himself, and he was discomfited to have her doing it, too.

"Yes," he lied. "I was merely wondering how you're feeling."

"Rather overwhelmed."

"I expect you are." He smiled, relishing the way she relaxed against him after such a short association, her level of comfort far out of proportion to what it should be. " 'Tis difficult to describe what occurs."

"I can see that now." She stretched and purred like a contented kitten.

"And as you grow accustomed to my touch, the passion will overtake you quicker and easier." Suddenly he was terrified that, if he wasn't careful, he'd start babbling like a love-struck moron, unable to stop himself from confessing how different this affair was for him, how much she varied from his past paramours, how much he treasured those contrasts.

He didn't want to talk! He didn't want to discuss what had just transpired! He simply wanted to purge himself of these inexplicable urges and wrongful impulses.

So he kissed her. Madly. Passionately. His lips, tongue, teeth, sparred with hers in a torrid dance that frazzled his intellect and stretched his tattered nerves to the breaking point. He couldn't help but hope that if he persisted long enough, thoroughly enough, some of these disturbing responses would abate.

While he played with her mouth, her hands were in his hair, on his shoulders, down his back, until she boldly found his buttocks and spurred him closer. He burned with an out-of-control fire, as his hips began thrusting, and their attempts at joining were so furious he could barely discern that fabric was serving as a barrier.

He set himself to her breasts, fondling and pinching at the swollen, raw nipples until she was panting and writhing anew, then he burrowed under her chin and traced a sizzling trail down her neck, her bosom, until he was sucking against her once more.

"James . . ." She sighed on a ragged breath. "James . . . no, I can't go there again."

"You *will*, just for me," he declared, his own breathing unsteady, his voice sounding as though it belonged to someone else.

His lips closed over the extended tip, and her back arched, even as her legs were spreading to welcome him. He accepted her invitation, sinking his fingers to her moist folds, and as he continued to labor at her breasts, he tugged her drawers down her thighs, over her ankles.

Finally, she was naked, and he scorchingly scrutinized every luscious detail.

Her skin was creamy smooth, her stomach flat, her shape curvaceously tempting, the hair decorating her mound a cushy pile of blond. She was flawless, radiant, enchanting, and for now she was his and his alone, to do with as he pleased.

He moved over her, covering her with his body. "You are so beautiful," he murmured through gritted teeth. "Made for fucking. Made for *me*. God, I want you. . . ."

At a perilous crossroads, he desperately needed to focus on something besides his heedless drive for alleviation at all costs.

He edged his cock away from the cushion of her sex,

and he kissed down her stomach, flicking into her navel, along the tender, lower part of her abdomen. Her stomach muscles clenched with each movement. Then his enthusiastic tongue found her pussy, and he dipped inside, parting her, sampling her wet, blazing center.

"James, I can't. . . . I'm not ready. . . ." She tried to protest, but her body recognized what it craved, and her legs widened farther.

He paused, raising up from his precarious perch. "You trust me, don't you?"

"You know I do."

"Then lie back and close your eyes. Don't think!" He threw her earlier command back at her. "Just feel." Refusing to be denied, he licked across her clit, slowly and scrupulously torturing her with every blasted second of the outrageous caress.

"Oh, my Lord. . . ." She fell against the pillows. Her fingers clasped the bedcovers, as he buried himself in the sweet haven.

She smelled like heaven; she tasted better. Her individual musk was an aroma that cast its wily spell, an irresistible bewitchment that only he could detect. He meticulously explored, examining, experimenting, revering, probing her inner depths until her desire flared once again, spiraling in her quest for surcease from torment.

Resolved to show no mercy, he tunneled his hands under her knees and reached for her breasts, manipulating them roughly while his tongue settled on her, the force of his contact burgeoning in proportion to how strenuously she grappled for release. When he had her entire being crying out for emancipation from anguish, he sucked at her clit, instantly throwing her into her second orgasm.

From the cry that erupted, and the tension that coursed through her, it was obviously ten times more powerful than the first. She fought to escape the conflagration, but he had her pinned in place, luxuriating in the chance to ride out the storm with her.

Gradually, the potent sensations relented, her muscles

relaxed, she eased against the mattress, and he kissed up her stomach, her cleavage, until he was stretched out along her side.

"How do you do that?" she asked, gasping.

Teasingly, he inquired, "I take it you're satisfied with my performance?"

"I'm not saying." She elbowed him in the ribs. "Not when you're already much too sure of yourself in these situations."

"I'm very good at what I do."

"Oh, you arrogant man!" she scolded, but she was laughing. She shifted around. "If you ever decide to indulge yourself in such a fashion again, and I am mad enough to contend I don't want you to, I expect you to ignore me. I demand that you have your way with me."

"As you wish, my dear lady."

Daringly, she took his hand and placed it, palm down, between her breasts, where even now, long after the event had ended, he could still sense her elevated pulse. "My heart may quit beating."

"I doubt that." He chuckled. "Only the very aged, or infirm, ever expire from carnal joy."

She made as if to sit up, but her limbs wouldn't cooperate. "My bones have turned to mush. I can't move."

"You don't have to." He turned her and spooned himself along her backside, one arm under her head, the other across her waist. "Just rest for a few minutes."

Being cruel without realizing it, she cuddled her shapely ass against his groin, and his erect phallus cried out in misery. Holding her tightly, he wallowed in a single, languid flex against the cleft of her bottom. Then he clenched his teeth and strove to focus his mind on somewhere far away.

"You're still hard." She sounded surprised.

"Very much so." She endeavored to roll over, but he wouldn't let her. In his stressed condition, he couldn't bear any searching assessment.

After a lengthy silence, she said, "This wasn't very enjoyable for you, was it?"

A laugh rumbled from deep in his chest. "Love," he murmured in her ear, "if it had been any more *enjoyable,* I'd have died from the doing."

"But you—"

"Ssh," he quieted her. " 'Tis no matter."

" 'Tis to me."

She finally had her way, rotating just enough to look him in the eye. As he'd suspected, her astute appraisal made him feel like a deer trapped in the carriage lamp. Too much bald emotion showed on his face.

Solemnly, she stated, "I don't like that your experience was distinct from mine. You gave me so much gratification, but I gave you none in return."

"*My* gratification came from yours."

"But you would have liked it more if you'd spilled your seed. Am I correct?"

"I'm fine, Abby," he lied, even as his cock throbbed, his balls ached.

"I'd like to learn how to please you," she said earnestly. "You could teach me. There must be some method of bringing you comfort. . . ."

He stole a quick kiss then returned her to her side. "We'll talk about it."

"Maybe at our next meeting?"

"Perhaps. . . ." He intentionally let the discussion die away. While he would love nothing more to be in her hands, in her mouth, he simply didn't know what might happen if he dropped his trousers. Without a doubt, he'd come like an eager lad, but was she ready for such an event? Was he?

"I'm so tired. . . ." She stifled a yawn.

"Close your eyes. I'll watch the clock."

"I need to be home by five."

"Plenty of time. I'll wake you."

"Promise?" she asked, but sleep was promptly taking her.

"Promise . . ." he whispered.

He cradled her loosely, kissing her shoulder while stroking leisurely up and down her hip. With the ebb of passion, the air had cooled, and he pulled one of the blankets over them, wrapping them together in a warm cocoon. Completely at ease, she nestled closer, and his untended, inflated phallus reacted urgently.

Poor fellow, he reflected. There'd be no relief in this room. *But later...*

Instantly he suffered his usual wave of loathing. How could he contemplate his lurid midnight wanderings while she rested in his arms? But considering his unrelieved predicament, what other choice did he have but to seek out some type of mitigation? Quite frankly, he couldn't carry on in the plagued condition she readily inspired.

Declining to dwell on the negative, he denied himself any opportunity to ruminate on his disgusting character—or lack of it—switching instead to the miraculousness of the present. He was holding her while she slumbered!

As he listened to her slow, steady breathing, he endeavored to recall if he'd ever lain next to a sleeping woman before. Never with his young wife, certainly. She had insisted on separate bedrooms, and he'd eagerly agreed. The few occasions he'd visited her for marital intercourse, he'd left immediately after, longing to be gone as much as she desired his absence. With his host of other lovers, he always departed shortly after the sexual games had ended merely because he refused to impart the wrong impression by generating the type of intimacy that sleeping together would prompt.

So . . . holding a sleeping woman—make that a sleeping *Abby*—was a novel experience, one that he was hastily discovering to be most enchanting. She smelled like flowers and soap, like sweat and sex, and he toyed with the soft strands of her hair, the smooth expanse of her naked skin.

She stirred and mumbled something that sounded very much like, ". . . love you, James . . ."

Though he wasn't entirely certain that was what she'd said, he pretended it was. At her drowsy words, his heartbeat surged with excitement, and he kissed behind her neck as he mouthed a response she could never hear. "Love you, too, Abby."

Much too swiftly, the hour of five approached, and he could tarry no longer. While he wished he could awaken her with languid embraces, he was still overly titillated, and if he attempted any bed play, they'd never manage to leave on time. With the greatest effort, he forced himself to his feet, and when she sensed his exit, a pretty frown wrinkled her brow.

Already, he mused, *she's used to lying next to me.* The perception was as disturbing as it was exhilarating. How he yearned for the freedom to share a bed with her whenever the spirit moved him!

Even as the disgraceful idea spiraled through his head, he was shaking it away. What foolishness was overtaking him? He had to get a handle on all these fractious flights of fancy before they caused him to do something reckless, something dangerous.

Silently, he dressed, then tiptoed to the bed and eased down beside her. "Abby . . ." he called, but he had to speak her name over and over before she roused.

"Oh, I was sound asleep. . . ." Her gaze settled on him, fully clothed and prepared to go. "Time already?"

"Yes, love." She stretched, and the blanket fell to her waist. Her blond hair was scattered across the pillows, her nipples were beaded into taut peaks, her breasts were marked with abrasions from the stubble of his beard. All in all, she appeared to have been very well loved.

"I don't want to leave just yet."

Neither do I, he brooded, but he bit his tongue to keep from saying so. No use lingering. "You mustn't be late, or others will wonder where you've been."

"I suppose," she said dejectedly.

Without the least hint of modesty, she sat up and tossed the covers aside, swinging her legs over the edge. Strange, but it seemed as though they'd participated in this kind of *moment after* a thousand times before. There was no reason for embarrassment or reticence, and surprisingly, he suffered no urge to rush out the door as he usually did after spending an afternoon with a lover. Despite the risks, he appreciated the chance to dawdle.

Lifting her hands high, she groaned as her sore muscles protested. The sight of her—breasts swinging, back arched—was more than one mortal man should be required to behold. His abused phallus refilled and became painfully erect once again.

"Let's get you arranged," he said, preferring to have her various charms thoroughly hidden before she drove him mad.

"Where are my things?" She looked lost and confused, much like a young child just awakened from a nap.

Oh, but she was lovely. Too lovely for the likes of him. He searched through the blankets and found her drawers. "Here," he said, passing them to her.

She remained unmoving, then smiled up at him and chuckled. "You've cast a spell over me, Mr. Stevens. My arms won't do what I tell them."

"I'll assist you." He knelt before her and slipped the underwear over her toes. "Up you go," he ordered, helping her to stand. He tugged them to her hips, then tied the string at the front, but not without pausing to kiss her stomach.

She rifled her fingers through his hair, and it was such a familiar, loving gesture that he glanced up into her eyes, startled at the depth of affection and adoration he observed. For once, he didn't shy away; he let her devotion wash over him like a gentle rain, then he forced the tenderness to conclude by reaching for her chemise.

Stockings and garters were next, and as he secured them, he queried, "Are all your undergarments white in color?"

"Yes."

"Who sews them?" She blushed at the impertinent question, which was absurd in light of what they'd just accomplished.

"A woman in the village back home."

"The tone is too pale on you."

As she'd never previously had occasion to undress for

a man, he was an utter cad to be complaining about what she was wearing under her clothes, especially when she'd had no prior reason for worrying about seductive disrobing. From what he'd viewed so far, her unmentionables were well crafted and attractive enough in a drab, functional sort of way, but when they were alone, he intended that she be at her most captivating. After a little practice, she'd begin to comprehend just how refreshing the appropriate intimate apparel could be.

"Your skin demands shades that are more striking. That will enhance your hair and eyes. Dark green. Bright red. Perhaps black. I'll think on it and order some things for you. Expect a package."

"James Stevens! Absolutely not! I'll not have you sending me undergarments!"

"No one will know," he asserted, "and I'm afraid I'm going to insist."

She gave him a hard stare. "You certainly can be bossy, and I'm not at all sure I like it. Besides, why are you so determined to shower me with new underwear?"

He chuckled and ran a thumb across her bottom lip. "Simply because it would make me happy."

"Oh. . . ."

"You have the build for the most scandalous attire, so you should outfit yourself in the most provocative styles."

She placed an affectionate hand on his cheek, then sighed, giving in, accepting his guidance in the matter. "As you wish. I shall anticipate receiving something quite shocking."

He assisted her with the remainder of her ensemble, watching and rendering aid as he'd never done with another lover, for he'd never previously had the inclination. Finally, she was ready. Only then did the appointment become awkward, for neither of them could bear to part. Just that quickly, just that easily, they'd grown used to each other's company. Separation was inconceivable, the stretch of time till their next meeting looming like an eternity.

Abby stared at him for a long moment, then admitted, "I'll miss you."

He prevented himself from responding inanely by smiling and stealing a swift kiss. "The time will pass rapidly"—although he hardly believed it would. He was already wondering how he'd fill his days. *And* his nights.

"I've been thinking . . ." she said.

Though she'd started assuredly, she couldn't complete the sentence, so he nudged her a tad. "About what?"

"Well, we're scheduled to meet again on Thursday, but on Friday . . ."

"What about Friday?" Hope surged to the fore.

"My family will be out of Town. They're leaving around noon, and they won't be back until Saturday evening. There's a party to attend just out of the city—some acquaintance of Jerald's—but I'm not going, so . . ."

"You could get away," he finished for her. "We could spend the entire night together."

"Yes."

He felt like a man who had fallen overboard and was about to be rescued. Wasn't this what he'd coveted? An occasion where he could have her, guide her, teach her? Love her? But even as she threw him a rope, his more rational side was imploring caution. One of them had to keep their teeming relationship under control. He couldn't discipline himself for that many uninterrupted hours, so she'd very likely wind up surrendering her virginity.

Did she care? Did he?

He stepped to her and cradled her face in his hands. "Do you comprehend what you're actually suggesting?"

"Yes. I've not been able to contemplate any other topic."

"If we engaged in such a lengthy tryst, my masculine drives would eventually have to be assuaged."

"I understand. Especially after today"—she placed her fingers on the front of his trousers, where he was still rockhard—" 'tis what I crave above all else."

"Are you certain?"

She raised up and brushed a kiss across his lips. "More certain than I've ever been about anything."

He studied her, searching for qualms or reservations, but he detected none. She was a woman full-grown, twenty-five years of age. Surely she could make this type of informed decision. Who was he to say nay?

With deliberate intent, he linked his fingers with hers and squeezed tight. "Until Friday, love."

"Until Friday."

He grinned, and she grinned, too. Like two smitten half-wits, they stared into each other's eyes. The air was charged with sexual tension, but also with joy and anticipation of what was to come. It would be a miraculous rendezvous, brimming with wonderment, and his black heart leapt with something approaching delight.

"Now . . . off with you," he ultimately said, already regretting the long wait that he'd have to endure.

"Good-bye," she murmured, taking another quick kiss. Then, like Cinderella at the ball, she peeked at the clock, and she gasped in dismay at seeing how late it was. She fled down the stairs so abruptly that he wouldn't have been surprised to find a glass slipper left behind.

He listened as the door opened and closed, then he walked to the parlor and peered out the curtains, hoping to catch a final glimpse of her on the street as she hailed a cab. But she'd vanished, so he returned to the bedroom, lingering while he gathered his belongings. He tarried there, where he sensed her presence so strongly. Then he departed as well. Counting the minutes. Counting the hours. Counting the days.

TWELVE

Barbara pushed a comb in place, secured her hat on her head, then stepped to the door of the exquisitely appointed fitting room. She turned the knob and made to leave, but not before sneaking a final glance at the flowered wallpaper, the matching chairs that appeared too dainty to sit upon, the brass hooks and mirror frames that some poor ninny polished to an outrageous shine.

Madame LaFarge, London's most popular dressmaker, definitely knew how to cater to her wealthy clientele, and Barbara thanked her lucky stars that she was now included in that group. Although certainly not the wealthiest of women, she wasn't poor, either. Her deceased husband had been a man of some means, and she'd inherited plenty, and she relished the fact that she could shop where she liked, dress as she desired, and spend money without counting every last farthing.

After growing up with a father who was prone to excessive drinking, gambling, and carousing, she understood what it was like to be penniless, to have no food on the table, no cash for the rent, well-off one day, but on the streets the next. With the ultimate loathing, she'd watched him fritter their lives away, so she'd struggled and scrounged, pulling herself from the very bottom and working herself up to . . . well, not the top, but she could definitely see it from where she resided.

Using her wits, youth, and beauty, she'd deliberately set after the old fool who'd married her. He'd given her everything she'd ever needed: security, funds, status, but most importantly, freedom. His death had been a blessed event, and she'd only had to wait for it a handful of years.

In the process, she'd learned that she was tough, determined, willful, and she never failed. When she focused on a goal, she never relented until the object she craved was within her grasp. She could be merciless, ruthless, in attaining her objectives, and Lord help anyone who stood in her path, because in the end, she always got what she wanted.

Consider James Stevens, for instance. With no advance warning, he'd left her, and for months after their split, she'd bided her time, patiently plotting and scheming on how she'd win him back. Now a bit of luck, coupled with an excess of preparation, had him returned, and she meant to keep him.

Taking a last assessment of the gilded salon, she walked into the hall, where she passed by the other fitting rooms on her way to the front. Some of London's most famous and infamous ladies were sheltered behind those doors, and Barbara couldn't prevent a feral smile from crossing her lips. So many of them had vied for James's affection, his wandering attention, his riches, his body, his bedroom skills. But she, and she alone, had triumphed.

He came to her regularly, three and four times a week, always urgent, always ready, spilling himself over and over like a lad of thirteen. Possessively, she grinned. There wasn't a female in all of England but herself who could effectively satisfy him when he was in such a state.

Just remembering their previous night's sexual play had her reddening, and she paused in the middle of the hallway to fan her flaming cheeks. A man like James could do that to a woman, could cause her to forget herself, her surroundings, her position.

Lest someone observe her woolgathering, she started to move on when she heard a familiar male voice speaking from the adjacent chamber. Instantly she recognized it as belonging to James.

What was he doing here?

Shopping was the obvious answer, but for what? For whom?

With an informed certainty, she knew that there was currently no other lover in his life. During the small hours of the night, when he was inclined to roam, she had his home and his club watched. He no longer sought out any other women.

It was risky to eavesdrop; dangerous, too. If she should be detected, James would be furious, but she absolutely *had* to discover what he was about. Even as she sidled nearer, she was practicing the innocent explanations she'd provide should her presence be revealed.

To her great delight, the door was ajar just the slightest fraction. She could see inside! James's hands were visible. He was holding a bolt of shiny black cloth and warmly running his fingers across the smooth nap.

"I believe I'll get this one," he was saying. "And the green."

"How about the red?" a woman asked in a husky French accent. "Very sexy, *non*?"

Barbara's eyes widened in shock as she realized that James was privately secluded with Madame LaFarge. Despite her extensive staff, the modiste had deigned to wait on him herself!

The distinguished couturiere was so celebrated that she rarely interacted with the clientele. Only a special circumstance would have her showing fabric samples to a gentleman. If the customer was renowned, an old friend, or the order required extreme discretion—which Madame possessed in abundance—she would handle the matter personally.

Why was she pandering to James? Evidently, an important event was occurring. How lucky to have the chance to ascertain what it was, and the shrewdness to use the information to best advantage.

There was a silence, then James muttered, "Ah, hell . . . I can't decide. Give me outfits in all eight colors."

"Magnifique!" Madame crowed, growling lustily. "Your friend . . . she will look very naughty in my tiny creations."

"I'm hoping." James grinned and commented in a flurry of French, which Barbara didn't understand, then he made a gesture that was blocked from her view, but whatever it was, Madame laughed with unbridled glee. He said, "Just promise me that at least one item will be delivered by Friday morning."

"I will have the first ensemble done by Thursday, *mon ami*. Would you like to have it modeled before it is sent?"

"No, *chère*," he replied familiarly. "I trust you to design something perfectly scandalous."

"*Oui!* Just for you, my Jamie." She paused, then added, "I am thinking that I will begin with the black. . . ."

"Ooh, I do *love* black," he murmured, his tone oozing carnal promise.

They were both laughing as Barbara tiptoed away, her heart racing with excitement.

James was buying her lingerie! As a gift!

He never had before, not for her or any of his other paramours. She'd extensively researched his past and had dug up all there was to know about James Stevens. He did *not* shower his women with presents, not even in good-bye when he was breaking off an association.

Surely this was a monumental leap forward in their relationship! Although she cautioned herself not to be overly confident, she couldn't help preening. The past few weeks, James had been remarkably amorous when they were together. She couldn't point to any one thing she might have said or done to have brought about the change in her condition, but she wasn't about to dissect the reasons behind her good fortune. Whatever had happened, she intended to ensure that he never regretted his decision.

She exited onto the wet street and hailed a cab, already planning how she'd endeavor to look surprised when the package from Madame's shop arrived.

Caroline Weston strolled along the pathway through the garden behind her brother's Town house. It was too early in the season for many of the plants to be blooming, so vegetation was scarce, and there wasn't nearly enough foliage to hide her furtive trip to the gazebo.

The temperature was frigid, and she shivered. She'd

stealthily slipped outside without a cloak because, if she'd grabbed one, someone would have noted her behavior and questioned her. There was a light mist falling, yet she couldn't let it dampen her clothes. How would she explain it?

She sneaked a surreptitious glance over her shoulder, back toward the house. No one had witnessed her escape. Everyone was too busy with the last-minute preparations for their brief jaunt to the country, but just in case she was found to be missing, she needed to appear nonchalant, as though she'd just stepped out for a spot of fresh air.

Which she had, although she was certainly hoping that she'd encounter Charles Stevens along the way. The previous evening, Charles had whispered of his desire for a secret rendezvous, and Caroline had readily agreed. She was bearing an immense risk by meeting him, but for pity's sake, it was the middle of the morning, in her brother's yard. Surely the consequences couldn't be too terrible if they were observed.

What a tedious affair this was, having all these intrusive chaperones and guardians! She was never alone! Not that she ever had been in the past, but for the first time ever, she didn't want anyone following her about. There wasn't a single second where she and Charles could be by themselves. She was madly in love with him—at least, she thought she was—but how was she to know with any conviction? They were hardly permitted to converse, and never afforded any privacy where they might disclose deeper feelings. The situation was so frustrating!

He was absolutely the most handsome young man she'd ever encountered, but he was also sweet, witty, and a joy to be around. Always cheerful, always gay, it was impossible to be in his presence and not be delighted with the day's prospects. Though it had only been a matter of weeks, she felt as if they'd been acquainted forever. They were so close in temperament that each could guess what the other was thinking. While standing together at a ball or in a supper line, all he had to do was gaze at her, raise a brow, and she could read his mind. They were that attuned to one another.

When he stared at her with those gorgeous brown eyes and confessed how much he'd pined for her while they were apart, she dissolved. His beguiling voice, broad shoulders, and lanky build stirred her insides until she yearned to throw herself into his arms and let him do all those things about which she fantasized—which were few in number.

Her imagination was vivid, but not *that* vivid. Some acts were simply beyond her discernment. She was aware that physical episodes transpired between men and women, and Abigail kept insisting she'd explain all when the opportunity was ripe, but curiously, the nearer Caroline grew to Charles, the less inclined she was to wait for Abigail to get on with it. She craved firsthand knowledge, and she craved it straightaway.

Her marriage would be carefully arranged, but in spite of the strictures under which it would come to pass, she refused to settle for a boring half-life. Love, passion, and friendship with her husband were her lofty goals. Abigail contended it was possible to have it all, and Caroline adamantly believed her. Yet, while she was beginning to perceive that Charles was everything she'd ever dreamed of finding in a man, how was she to determine if she was correct in her assessment?

She'd never enjoyed a man's exclusive company. Had never held a man's hand. Had never ambled in the moonlight or been passionately kissed.

But she certainly wanted to be! Oh, how she wanted. Starting now.

With vast trepidation, she advanced toward the entrance to the gazebo, taking great pains not to hasten, even though she was eager to rush up the steps. Margaret would suffer an apoplexy if she uncovered Caroline's antics, and the older woman's distress would be so enormous that she'd probably harangue poor Jerald until he suffered one, too. If Caroline pushed the pair of them into a conflagration, she'd very likely never be allowed to see Charles again.

Just then, she heard him calling her name, and she experienced such a pang of gladness and relief that her worries about Margaret, about proper comportment and decorum, flew out the window. She abandoned all caution and raced up the stairs to where he was smiling and waiting with open arms.

Without pausing to identify the most prudent course, she ran to him and was fiercely enfolded in a tight hug. Not inclined to scrimp on pleasure, she hugged him in return, and as her body extended out the length of his, she was lambasted by the most astonishing sensations.

Her nose was pressed against his shirt, and she was overwhelmed by masculine aromas of brandy, tobacco, and horses. She breathed deeply, wanting to imprint the sensory stimulation into her consciousness so she would never forget. As she inhaled, her ribs expanded and her breasts brushed his chest. Strangely, her breasts seemed fuller and heavier, and her nipples were suddenly poking at her corset, abrading and irritating her in a fashion she'd never noticed before.

"I feared you weren't coming," he whispered into her ear.

"Margaret was in a high dudgeon." She whispered, as well. Who knew how far their voices might carry? "Until just now, I had no opportunity. As it is, I can only tarry a moment."

"When are you leaving?"

"Just as soon as the final bag is loaded."

There was a bench directly behind him, and he sat back, spread his thighs, and pulled her down to perch on his lap. Another tug, and she was lying across his chest, a breast and nipple now naughtily connected, and the feeling was so wonderful that she could barely restrain herself from rubbing up against him like a stretching cat.

"I don't want you to go away. Not even for a day," he said fervently. "I can't stand the idea of your being out of Town."

"Abigail is staying here. I don't understand why they

won't let me stay with her. . . ." She trailed off as she realized he was staring at her with an open regard that was so unwavering it was almost frightening. "What is it?" she couldn't refrain from asking.

"I . . . I know we've only been acquainted for a short while. . . ."

He hesitated, and her pulse pounded. Was he about to make a declaration of intent? Encouraged, she finished the thought for him. "Yet I feel as if we've been friends for a very, very long time."

"I was about to express the very same!"

He shifted uncomfortably, cleared his throat, straightened his cravat, prevaricating for so long, and causing her anticipation to inflate to such a height, that she wanted to shake him in order to pry loose his next statement. What would it be?

Finally, he inquired, "Would you marry me?"

Calm as you please! He'd popped the question! Her breath escaped in a hard surge of air. "Oh . . . oh, my," she babbled. "Yes . . . I'd like that very much."

Her hands were shaking, and he wrapped them in his own, sharing his strength and warmth. "I'm very thrilled."

"So am I." He placed a chaste kiss on her forehead, but it was a far cry from what she truly fancied. Still, she forced herself to remain composed lest she react like a wanton.

"I must speak with your brother. Have you any idea of what he might say?"

"He's agreed to let me make my own choice."

"A wise, wise man," he said, chuckling. "Dare I hope that my name might be mentioned in your conversations?"

"Absolutely."

"In addition, I'll need to discuss this with my father."

She stiffened, unexpectedly panicked. The earl mightn't care for her to be Charles's choice. Charles would be marrying to provide an heir and to protect the title, so the earl's opinion counted more than anyone's. If he considered another girl better suited, she'd just die! Never before had she been lacking in self-confidence, but all at once her entire future was on the line. "Will he be amenable?" she queried prudently.

Charles patted her hand. "He'll be delighted."

"Are you sure?"

"How could he not love you?"

"Oh, Charlie . . ." At his tender words, she glowed with adoration. "I'm so dreadfully happy."

"Good," he declared, "and you shall only grow more content in the years to come. I swear it to you."

He closed the distance between them and gently kissed her on the mouth. His lips were soft and warm, and her heart thundered so loudly that she was certain he could hear it. Shamefully, she was eager for the moment to become much more torrid, and she readily conceded that such modest embraces would never suffice. The man simply inspired all manner of passion.

Like it or no, she and her sister were having their little *talk*. And soon!

"You'd best be getting back," he urged as he ended the sweet moment, "before someone misses you."

"I suppose," she said dejectedly, and she rose to her feet just as a depressing thought occurred to her. "I just remembered . . . Jerald will be gone for the next three weeks! Margaret and I are returning tomorrow, but he has business in Surrey, so he's staying on. You won't be able to speak with him for an eternity."

"That's all right. We have plenty of time." He stood, too. "I'll discuss our agreement with Father so that everything's arranged with him, but in the meantime, we should probably keep our decision a secret until Jerald gives us his permission."

"Silence will be extremely difficult. I yearn to shout the news to the entire world."

"As do I." Shockingly, he bent down and nibbled against her neck. Her skin prickled, and she blushed furiously, but just then a strangled sort of birdcall arose from the terrace, and he whirled around. "What the devil is that?"

"My maid." She glanced through the latticework toward

the house, and the servant was leaning against the balustrade, scanning the lawns. " 'Tis our signal. Margaret must be looking for me." She hurried to the stairs, but turned for a final good-bye, and as she did, Charles swept her into his arms, bestowing an ardent kiss—the kind she'd always longed to receive. It was urgent and invasive; he toyed with her mouth, and his hands stroked up and down her back, once even landing on her bottom! He groaned with his desire for her, and the sound unleashed a flurry of mad butterflies that swirled through her stomach.

Her maid whistled again, more frantically, and regretfully their lips separated.

"I must go," she asserted, nervous and disappointed. She wanted to kiss him again, to continue kissing him until . . . Well, she didn't understand what *until* would entail, but her body unmistakably recognized the appropriate direction. She was aching and disturbed in ways she'd never been previously, and with extreme clarity, she grasped that Charles would be able to ease her distress in a manly fashion she couldn't define.

"Will you be in church on Sunday?" he asked.

"Definitely."

"Sit where I can see you."

"I will," she promised, then she was away.

She traveled through the garden, walking sedately as she'd been taught, even though her flesh was screaming with an overload of sensation. With a practiced patience and control, she waltzed up the steps to the terrace and slipped in the rear door. As she passed her maid, the girl whispered, "Lady Margaret was asking for you."

"Thank you," she mouthed in reply.

Passing a mirror, she took a peek. Her nose was red, mist glistened in her hair, goose bumps riddled her arms. Other than those small catastrophes, she was in one piece. She looked cold, but not undone.

As she approached the front parlor, Margaret huffed into the hall. "Where have you been?" she snapped.

"I decided some fresh air would be beneficial. You recall

how I hate riding in the coach." It was the perfect lie. As a child, she'd often gotten motion sickness from the rocking.

"We are ready to depart. Go make your *au revoir* to your sister."

"I shall."

"Don't dawdle."

"I won't, Margaret."

Relieved by the brief respite, she headed for the stairs, while wishing fervently that she could remain in London with Abigail. At the best of times, Margaret was unpleasant, but trapped in an enclosed carriage, she was categorically impossible. Caroline never minded Jerald—as it was, she hardly ever saw her older brother—but Margaret was a different matter entirely. As was his detached custom, Jerald at least *tried* to be pleasant, but Margaret went out of her way to be annoying.

She reached the top landing and made for Abigail's room, disheartened that she couldn't spill her grand secret to someone. Especially Abigail. This was the greatest day of her entire life! She was promised! But Charles had the right of it. She couldn't gamble by confiding in a single soul.

Abigail was a wonderful person, but she could also be extremely conservative. Caroline had wrongfully sneaked off with Charles, and Abigail might not like learning of it. She might tell Jerald, then Jerald would tell Margaret, and how it would go from there was anyone's guess. With her marital status about to be resolved, Caroline couldn't risk creating an uproar.

She knocked on Abigail's door but didn't receive an answer. Assured that her sister was inside, she entered. A quick scan of the premises indicated that Abigail wasn't present, but on her bed were two boxes with Madame LaFarge's distinctive logotype on the front. The lids had been removed, the contents rifled through, and she looked in the first one to see what Abigail had received from the eminent dressmaker.

Unequivocally surprised, she stumbled upon a one-piece undergarment, the likes of which she'd never previously confronted. It had two narrow shoulder straps, and it attached at the crotch with three small buttons. The color was shiny and seemed dark black, but when she slipped her hand under the fabric, it was nearly transparent. There were bosom cups, but they were extremely low-cut. Lacing down the center could be untied to the waist.

She picked it up and turned it back and forth. It was skimpy, and it wouldn't cover anything a woman needed to keep covered. If Abigail were to don the scandalous costume, she'd be prancing around naked under her clothing, and Caroline couldn't help pondering the purpose to be served by such a sordid ensemble.

Unless Abigail had a man who would . . .

The notion burst out of nowhere, and it was so outrageous that she couldn't possibly conjure a means of finishing it. Some thoroughly feminine part of her discerned that the scant speck of silk was exactly the thing a man would enjoy for some sort of passionate activity. There couldn't be any other reason to wear it.

Apparently, there were major events transpiring in Abigail's life of which all in the household were grossly unaware.

Wouldn't Margaret just expire if she knew!

Intrigued, she dug through the box. Underneath was a gauzy robe that would only fall to midthigh, black garters, black stockings, and two black shoes with very high heels. Her gaze shifted to the other box, and she saw red . . . a red mini-robe, red stockings, red garters and shoes. Whatever costume had been there was gone.

"My, my . . ." Caroline muttered.

In the adjoining dressing room, Abigail was moving about, and like the worst voyeur, Caroline tiptoed to the door and peeped through the crack.

Abigail dawdled in front of the mirror, studying her reflection. Fully dressed, but holding the bright red garment against her torso, she was swaying as though dancing to an unheard tune. Clearly, she was picturing how the apparel would appear once she had it on.

Like the black contraption on the bed, the garment was meant to tantalize and seduce. Two pieces instead of one, the top was a cupped affair with a single string of lace in the middle to bind it together—or let it fall open. The bottom was an inadequate swatch of crimson, a sort of pantalet, that would leave a woman's privates completely exposed.

If Abigail had been modeling the frippery, her entire midriff and backside would have been bared!

Lost in her reverie, Abigail twirled around, and abruptly, the two sisters were face-to-face. They regarded each other silently, both flushing with embarrassment. Caroline *knew* why she was chagrined: She'd been caught snooping. But she wasn't sure why Abigail was so abashed unless her suspicions were correct. Perhaps there *was* a man in Abigail's life.

"I'd thought you'd departed without a good-bye," Abigail said pleasantly, as though Caroline hadn't witnessed any untoward behavior. She dropped the red outfit to her side, not attempting to hide it, but plainly not intending to allow Caroline a close assessment.

"I came to do just that," Caroline responded, trying to act as nonplussed as her older sibling. Casually, Abigail proceeded out of the dressing room and into the bedchamber, where she put the red ensemble into its box with the other scarlet-colored items and replaced the lid. She covered the black items, as well.

"Is Margaret ready?" Abigail inquired.

"She says she is," Caroline indicated, and they both stifled a giggle. Their sister-in-law was a master at delay.

Then a jarring quiet descended, and Caroline struggled to tactfully break it, ultimately deciding to blurt out the question to which she was now dying to have an answer. "Abigail . . . are you involved with someone?"

"What?" Abigail gasped.

There was such a glimmer of alarm in her eye that Caroline knew, without a doubt, that she'd hit on the truth, despite what Abigail's rejoinder might be. "Well, my goodness," Caroline pointed out cautiously, "look at these undergarments you've ordered from Madame LaFarge."

"Oh, those. . . ." Abigail scoffed, gesturing toward the bed as though they were of no import. "They're just a spot of foolishness. I let Madame convince me to purchase them when I was at her shop." She walked to her vanity and began fidgeting, rearranging her brushes. "They're quite unsuitable. I believe I'll return them."

Caroline might have bought the lie if she hadn't caught a glimpse of Abigail's manic joy that was hastily replaced by misery and despair. "You can tell me who he is," she implored quietly.

" 'Tis no one," Abigail maintained. "Truly."

"Is it Edward Stevens? Is that why you're afraid to say?"

Abigail forced a laugh. "Whatever would make you think so?"

"People have been noticing the two of you together. There's been gossip. Even Margaret's commented. . . ."

"That's downright silly. We're friends, nothing more."

"Then what gentleman has you so enamored that you're dancing in the closet with your underwear?"

For a moment, just one, Abigail flashed an expression of such unbridled hopelessness that Caroline was sure she was going to admit all. Whatever was weighing on her sister's mind appeared to be a heavy burden that she would gladly unload.

But just as abruptly as the moment came, it vanished as she pasted her customary serene smile on her face. "Really, Caroline! As if I could keep some *man* a secret from all of you! Even if I wished to commit such an atrocious act, how would I go about it?" She sauntered toward the door and advanced into the hall, effectively preventing any further discussion. "Your imagination is playing rather wonderful tricks. Let's go down, shall we?"

Left alone in Abigail's room, all Caroline could do was follow.

THIRTEEN

Abigail lounged on the bed, leaned against the pillows, and awaited James. As he had done previously, she'd staged the room for seduction. Candles burned, and a fire sizzled in the grate. Outside, a cold drizzle was falling, and the drops splattered at the windowpanes. Inside, all was warm, cozy, and snug, a welcoming lovers' nest filled with fine wine, scrumptious treats, and an eager, willing woman.

She'd chosen the black ensemble for their encounter, and before reclining, she'd taken a prolonged evaluation in the mirror. James had been wise, she'd readily decided, in asking her to wear the scandalous attire.

Just from staring at her reflection, she'd become unsettled and excited. James hadn't even joined her as yet, and the intriguing costume was working magically, augmenting her level of agitation and anticipation, and she couldn't help but contemplate how much extra delight the carnal apparel would bring to their assignation.

She ran a hand across her scantily covered breast and stomach, letting it rest on her naked thigh. The material clung to her like a second skin, and she adored how it slithered across and cooled her heated surfaces. She couldn't wait to see his expression when he espied her in the slinky garment, or to feel his fingers skimming across it, gliding underneath and down.

In their haste to depart after the prior meeting, he'd left his precious portfolio of risqué pictures, and she balanced the stack on her lap, casually scanning the renderings. During their sexual lessons, she never had enough time to peruse the paintings, and she flipped to the nude of James, assessing his hairy chest, his erect cock, and the manner in which Lily so affectionately tended him. At the thought that today would be the day she'd finally be allowed to do the same, her entire body tingled.

She skimmed the picture, then hastened on to the one where Lily was servicing him with her mouth. One of his hands was at the back of her neck, guiding her. The artist, Pierre, had truly been a master at depicting profound emotion, for James's enjoyment of the event was excessively manifest. He gazed at Lily, monitoring her ministrations with an incredible expectancy.

Abigail traced the spot where James's phallus met Lily's ruby lips, and she stifled a groan. She hated viewing James with another woman, but even as she despised the sight, she was fascinated and unduly stimulated. Disgusted with herself, she couldn't quit staring, wondering how it had felt—to Lily, to James—and hoping she would have the chance to experience some of the same undeniable pleasure.

Though James wasn't with her as she would have liked, she wanted to discover what naughty adventures lay ahead for the pair, so she accelerated past the portion they'd surveyed together. Past where James suckled Lily's breasts, past where Lily's privates were detailed, past where James was positioned between her legs and savoring her with his tongue.

One at a time, she pitched the individual parchments on the mattress until she was surrounded by a sea of lewd drawings. Inevitably, she arrived at new territory, and she received her first true inkling of what marital intercourse entailed.

Lily was lying down, her knees wide, and like a conquering hero of old, James crouched between her spread thighs, tightly gripping her hips, ready to plunder. Lily stared at him possessively, with feminine approval and admiration, as though daring him to proceed. James scrutinized her in return, pompous and sure of himself and his purpose.

Inflamed, Abigail flipped the portrait onto the bed, then gazed at the next.

The lovers had switched positions. James was now on

the bottom, Lily on the top. She was straddling his groin,
riding him much as one would a horse. In pure anguish,
her palms were on her buttocks, her shoulders thrown back,
and the position thrust her large breasts forward. James
cupped them, his thumbs on the elongated nipples.

As long as she could stand to, she let the image wash
over her and through her, but try as she might to will away
the representation, she couldn't get beyond the fact that she
was watching him as he made love to another woman. The
exhibition was ominously arousing in a fashion that acutely
bothered her, and she wanted to cast the illustration aside
but couldn't.

His perpetual search for mindless liaisons was a facet of
James's personality that she couldn't abide, yet she had to
understand it if she was to ever really know him. It hurt
her to think that his life of dissipation led him to consort
so aimlessly with any woman who gave the slightest indication that she was interested—in Lily's case, a friend's
wife. Perhaps she was only fooling herself, but she refused
to believe that he actually preferred the insensitive couplings in which he so regularly engaged.

Miserably, she continued on, only to find the couple in
another pose. How many ways could the sexual act be con-
summated? Apparently, there were at least three!

The vigor of the joining had increased, the lovers nearing the conclusion. Lily was on her hands and knees, much
like an animal. Her head was hanging, her forehead pressed
into the pillows, and she bit against her bottom lip as her
bountiful breasts swung unimpeded, her enormous nipples
brushing the sofa cushion.

James was rutting on her from behind, his slender fingers
stark against her skin. He was perched at her entrance, his
erect rod slick and wet. Though the picture was motionless,
it was easy to imagine him thrusting, working at her mer-
cilessly, taking what he needed, and in return giving her all
she could handle and more. His demeanor was bleak with
a beautiful sort of desperation, his body stressed, zealous,
exultant.

Brimming with regret, she tossed away the remainder of the paintings, suddenly feeling very sorry for James. He was supposed to be the expert on men and women and their antics, but she was convinced that the kinds of things he was doing with Lily should only happen between two people who were in love. The sins of the flesh were too dramatic, personal, and overwhelming to be committed so casually.

Then and there, she resolved that their physical engagements would become events he could recall with comfort and joy. When they separated for good, she wanted him to carry fond memories of their affair, perhaps to recollect it as the one and only time he had been truly treasured by his paramour. She couldn't bear it if, in the end, he dumped her in with all the others with whom he'd fornicated. In actuality, she couldn't stand to contemplate the future at all, to hypothesize over the nameless scores of women he would ultimately seduce after her, or to imagine how she might be perceived during his periods of reminiscing.

Belowstairs, noise erupted. He had arrived!

Chaotically, she grabbed the scattered pictures and stuffed them into the satchel, then she struggled to pull herself together, smoothing her features, burying her worries. Instinctively, she fathomed that he had come for an evening of spontaneous sexual play, and he wouldn't be disposed to witness any emotional upset. He'd already made it clear, on numerous occasions, that he didn't wish to be reminded of extraneous issues. Not his father, or his family, or their lives outside this room.

If she raised the topic of his lifestyle, he'd protest her intrusion of his privacy while insisting, as he seemed wont to do, that he couldn't be expected to act any differently since he was lacking in morality and reveled in debauchery. Should she prod too deeply, he might depart, and her enchanted night would be ruined, a catastrophe for which she'd never forgive herself, so her concerns had to remain her own.

The door to the bedchamber opened, and James stepped

through. He brought a wave of frigid air with him. With a wifelike attention to detail, she noticed that he'd shed his outer garments, that his clothes were dry, but his hair was damp, and she could smell the rain on his skin. She thought to go to him, to tend him while he dried in front of the hearth, but as she started to rise, he stopped her.

"Don't move," he said, his voice husky with desire. "Let me look at you."

He approached the foot of the bed. Beginning at her feet, at the black shoes, he traveled visually, evaluating her stockings, her garters, her bare thighs. He lingered at the V between her legs, then proceeded up her stomach, her ribs, to her breasts, pausing at her nipples. He gave each one his undivided attention, tarrying while they hardened, peaked, commenced aching. Only then did he continue. To her bosom, her neck, her mouth. As his astute gaze finally settled on her own, he hesitated. His eyes narrowed.

"What's amiss?" he asked, repeating the same question he'd posed once before upon entering.

Despite how carefully she'd schooled her swing of emotion, he knew her too well. He could read her moods as no other ever had, and she was gratified but unnerved. How could she play at being casual when he had pushed the discussion to the next level before she realized what was occurring?

"Nothing," she fibbed. "I was just thinking about you." She amended, "Waiting for you."

He focused on the leather envelope beside her on the mattress. "You were reviewing the pictures."

"Yes."

"They disturbed you?"

"Not overly much."

Rounding the bed, he sat next to her, his weight causing it to sink and her torso to shift toward him. He braced his hands on either side of her. "You shouldn't ever lie to me," he said fervently. "I can tell when you are." Closing the distance, he gifted her with a chaste kiss, then he pulled away and reached for the satchel. "Let's examine whatever it is that has you so troubled."

She couldn't tolerate a second perusal of his interactions with Lily, so she placed her hand over his, stilling his attempt to open it. "I can't look at any more. I don't like seeing you . . ." She hesitated. No matter what type of excuse she provided, it would sound overly possessive.

"With another woman?" He finished for her.

"Exactly. I don't like it at all."

"I'm glad," he said softly, greatly surprising her. He bestowed a second sweet kiss, then wrapped his arms around her and reposed her across his chest. "Lily was my friend, but the things I did with her . . . they didn't mean anything. 'Tis just a man's way. 'Twas her way, as well."

"But that's what I don't like about it," she explained. "I don't like knowing that you can engage in sexual games with her—with any other female—but then do the same with me as though I'm personally of no import to you."

"Oh, love. . . ." He chuckled and stole another kiss. "Is that what you believe I'm doing?"

"Yes," she whispered, "and it makes me afraid."

"I care for you, Abby," he vowed gently. "That's why all of this is so dangerous; why I've worked to slow the process. Because I can't determine how it shall come to a worthwhile end. When I'm with you, I . . . I . . ."

He couldn't complete his frank comment, but she'd heard enough. Enough to hope. Enough to dream. Enough to love him all the more. Even if he never found the courage to admit deep feelings, she had an ample amount to go around.

She rested her palm against his cheek. He'd just shaved, and his skin was sleek and soft, still cool from his journey to be with her. "Show me what you mean."

"With pleasure."

Instantly alight with excitement, he kissed her deliberately, and, as always happened between them, the fire quickly ignited. Not breaking contact, he eased her against the pillows, and he came over her, covering her with his

weight and the rough fabric of his clothes. He ducked under
her chin and nibbled her throat.

Unexpectedly sounding shy and embarrassed, he said,
"Thank you for wearing my gift."

There was a wistful tone in his voice, and she couldn't
get past the notion that he'd sent the lingerie to prove to
himself that she'd refuse it. "I love it," she replied. "How
could I not?"

As a response, he rooted under her neck again. "You're
so beautiful in it. As beautiful as I knew you would be."

He rolled onto his back, taking her with him so that she
was stretched out on top of him, her breasts over his face.
He grasped them, milking them, squeezing the stiff tips.
With minimal effort, he had her squirming. Shifting her
higher, he brought a nipple to his mouth, and he suckled
her through the silk. Teeth, tongue, and cloth combined to
torture her.

As he played with her firm nipples, he stroked up and
down her back, and she initiated some maneuvers of her
own. Following his lead, she imitated how he touched her,
held her, cherished her.

Tentative at first, she petted and nuzzled, and he was
responsive to whatever she tried. His reactions guided her,
and she quickly discerned that it was easy to tell what he
liked best from how ardently he tensed, moaned, or hugged
her tighter.

Deciding that he had on too many articles of clothing,
she pulled away and balanced on her haunches, tarrying as
long as possible, letting the anticipation build as she slowly
undid the buttons and tugged at his shirttail. He laid against
the pillows, observing, enjoying her leisurely attention, rubbing her thighs, caressing her stomach, her ribs, her breasts.
His fingers were never still, always busy with some tactile
endeavor.

Hers never remained stationary, either. Undressing him
as one might a child, she struggled with the long hem, the
cuff links, until she was finally able to draw the shirt off
his arms. His magnificent chest was splendidly arrayed, and

she explored meticulously, discovering peaks and valleys, till she was familiar with every inch.

Enticed by his flat brown nipples, she flicked a nail across one, and it pebbled into a small, firm bud, so she pinched it, unable to believe how she instantly had him writhing.

"You like that, don't you?"

"Very much." His jaw tight, he bit off an oath as she captured the other and began manipulating them both, much as he did to her own.

She studied him carefully, gauging his responses, until ultimately she bent down and sucked one of the taut nubs into her mouth. As her teeth closed around it and she nipped lightly, she was rewarded by the vicious hiss of his breath escaping. He urged her closer, holding her there while she delighted in his tang, his smell, his pleasure.

What a marvelous thing this was—this loving! To think that she'd denied herself this unrelenting delight for so many years! But she hadn't understood . . . no one had told her. . . . Then again, she hadn't met James, either. He was the one who inspired this evolving passion. What a joy! To chance upon him! To share these particular pieces of herself!

She kissed down his chest and stomach, leisurely delving into his navel, then . . . she was at his trousers. Migrating lower, she burrowed against the placard, the bumpy mound, the rounded sacs, etching patterns across the crest, constricting the fabric to get a better outline.

Her fingers went to the top button, but before she could snap it loose, his hand topped hers, stilling the motion, and she gazed up into his handsome face.

"Are you certain?" he asked, subtly reminding her that when the initial one came undone, they would all go.

"I am."

He elevated himself and brushed a thumb across her bottom lip. "Once my trousers are open, I may not be able to control what transpires. I'll try, but—"

She cut him off. "Don't restrain yourself on my account.

I want to experience all, James. That's why I'm here."

"I'm afraid that you don't realize . . . that . . . well . . ." He vacillated, then added, "Until we're finished, you can't possibly grasp all that you'll be giving me, and then we can't change it or fix it."

"I'm a grown woman. I can make my own decision about how to proceed."

"I appreciate that. I would just hate for you to have any regrets once it's over."

"No matter what we do together, I could never have any regrets."

For a long, telling moment, he regarded her, assessing the level of her resolve and, apparently, deciding it sufficient. He released the upper button himself, by the act, granting permission. In agony, he propped the pillows under his head so that he could observe. Though he endeavored to appear uninvolved and unmoved, he seemed brittle as glass, fragile and breakable, as though he could be readily shattered into a thousand pieces.

Kneeling at his center, she languidly worked at the buttons, wanting this expectation to continue on forever. Finally, the bottom one was free, the fabric loose around his lanky hips. She sat paralyzed, not certain what to do next.

Sensing her consternation, he took her hand and slipped it inside. "Caress me," he said. "Like this." With his fingers gripping hers, he curled them around his shaft.

"Oh, my . . ." she managed at perceiving his immense size. He was so big that her fist was scarcely able to surround him. The outer skin was hot, smooth, and pliant, but underneath, he was hard as steel. His pulse was thumping into her hand, and the exotic sensation surged through her palm, up her arm, and into her chest, where his heartbeat connected to her own so that the two separate organs throbbed together in the same heightened rhythm.

Unable to bear the suspense, she shoved the material away, wanting to see, needing to see, and as he was unveiled, she determined that no painting could have accurately portrayed how he would really appear.

His cock was an abnormal creature. Attenuated, large, solid, covered with palpitating, ropy veins, it reached out toward her, reacted immediately to her slightest handling, yearned for manipulation as though it were a thing alive.

"Stroke me," he commanded, and he guided her in the tempo until she adopted it as her own. "Squeeze me, too. Gently in the beginning, then more strongly as we progress. And the end . . ."—his breath caught as she flicked her finger over the agitated, extended tip—"is the most sensitive part. Brush across it every time. I'll obtain the most stimulation that way."

Still hovering amid his thighs, she massaged him for a protracted period, testing different speeds, different pressures. He bravely withstood it all, gradually growing more strained. The opening at the crown started to ooze a clear fluid, and she halted. "Is this your seed?"

"No." His voice was hoarse, strained with exertion. " 'Tis simply moisture, informing you that my seed is close."

Excited by the news and ecstatic over the prospect, she leaned down and did what she'd longed to do since she'd first seen those stunning pictures of Lily. Starting at the base, she ran her tongue along his length, finishing at the wet apex, where she licked away all his juice, but more came to replace it. Powerless to resist, she closed over him, and he tasted like heat and salt and sweat.

He valiantly strove to remain stationary, but immobility was impossible, and he steadied her, then flexed, offering her just the blunt extremity, then more and more. She eagerly took what he imparted, intrigued by the strange display of physicality. There was something extremely satisfying about having him at her mercy in this fashion. What authority she wielded! It seemed that time was at a standstill, that nothing else mattered but this: her mouth on his cock.

She moved her attention to his soft, dangling sacs. They were two compact balls, layered with silky skin more delicate than her own, and she cradled them, administering to them while her lips and tongue continued on his shaft.

Without warning, James grabbed her and yanked her to the side. A fine sheen of perspiration glistened on his abdomen and chest; his heart thundered so furiously that she could see it vibrating against his ribs. Obviously, he demanded immediate surcease, but her entire world had shrunk to the intense carnal torment she'd been inflicting, and she didn't want to stop. She reached for his cock again, but he swatted her away.

"Wait, Abby!" His tone was stressed and forced, but she paid him no heed as she licked his length once again, reveling in how his cock jumped and swelled. He cursed, pulling her into his arms, and he buried his face at her nape. "Your first time, I wanted it to be . . ." He halted, groaning, sounding in pain. "Oh . . . I can't hold off any longer!"

"Then don't . . ." she answered. His body was behaving much as her own had when he'd brought her to sexual release. He was so close to completion, yet she hadn't grasped how well she'd accomplished her task. Apparently, she'd shattered his precious self-restraint. As he'd lain there, viewing her stoically and scrupulously, he hadn't been nearly as unaffected as he'd attempted to appear.

"Fuck me," he said crudely. "Fuck me with your hand." He urgently seized it and clutched it around his burning phallus.

After only a half dozen caresses, his hips thrust strenuously, and he emitted a haunting moan that reverberated through her skin and bones. A mysterious liquid heat spread across his stomach, and he hugged her so frantically that she feared he might break one of her ribs if he didn't relax. Just as she could endure no more of the forceful pressure, his muscles eased, his grip lessened, his flesh slackened.

Silently, he held her, kissing up her chest and neck until he encountered her eager lips. Tenderly, he made love to her mouth, and she accepted his tongue and cherished it with her own. When they eventually separated, they lay side by side, their breath mingling, their hearts beating at a singular rate. He gazed at her with a searing look of affection.

Near to love, she thought, but with such a man, who could know?

"I didn't hurt you, did I?" he asked.

"No," she said quietly, reveling in a kiss of her own.

"I'm so attracted to you . . . You make me so aroused . . ."

He couldn't complete whatever it was he was attempting to say, or perhaps there were no words to convey his true feelings. As for herself, absolutely nothing could have prepared her for how private this moment was. She extended a finger and drew a circle on his stomach, exploring the steamy pile of moisture, then she rested her palm across it, letting its sticky essence glue her hand to his abdomen.

"This is your seed?"

"Yes."

She twirled her finger through it, then placed the tiniest amount on her tongue. The flavor was unique. Like heat and salt and him.

"What do you think?" he queried.

"Delicious," she responded, and he chuckled, but the short laugh drifted away and silence ensued once again.

Peculiarly, he seemed altered, apparently overly affected by the intimacy he'd allowed himself to undergo with her. He looked young and innocent, and although it was difficult to believe of a man with his wealth of life experiences, he appeared extremely vulnerable, as though he'd exposed himself in ways he'd never intended.

"I'm so glad you showed me," she said.

He gifted her with one of those smiles she was quickly coming to realize she couldn't live without. "I didn't have much choice," he replied. "You, my dear, are deadly."

She acknowledged the compliment in the teasing vein in which it was dispensed, but as they lingered together, the closeness grew again. Studying his eyes, peering to his very core, she recognized what had changed. His smoldering anger and imposed distance had vanished. It was almost as if the simple act of baring himself were an admission—of his emotional state? of his need for her? of his acceptance of their relationship?—that he could not make aloud.

The opportunity seemed ripe to speak candidly. At that instant, she could say anything, and he wouldn't mind, so she boldly forged ahead. "If you had been inside me, we might have created a babe."

He laid his hand on her abdomen, clearly imagining what it would be like to have his child nestled there.

"Would carrying my babe make you happy?" he inquired.

"Very much. I would like to give you a son. One who would be produced like this . . . with so much joy and . . ."—she almost said *love* but caught herself and modified it to, "gladness. He would be such a special child. I just know it. . . ."

She felt bereft, as if the child had been within their grasp but lost somehow because the two of them couldn't detect the appropriate path. Tears came, and one plopped over the edge and trailed down her cheek. He caught it with his thumb and licked it away, then he cradled her face and kissed both her eyelids.

"Don't cry, love," he murmured. "Some things were never meant to be."

"But that doesn't mean"—she swallowed in order to keep her careening emotions in check—"that I have to stop wishing."

"No, it doesn't," he agreed, and he sighed as he snuggled her close and held her safe in the cradle of his arms.

FOURTEEN

James walked behind the screen that was discreetly positioned on the other side of the room. There was a basin, a pitcher of water, and a cloth. He dipped the cloth and swirled it in the water, then went back to where Abby was snuggled on the bed. Just from viewing her there, stretching and purring, he began to grow hard once more.

He hadn't meant to spew himself across his stomach; he hadn't wanted her first encounter with male lust to be in such a fashion. In fact, when he'd arrived, he'd hoped that he wouldn't do anything at all, that his actual participation would be minimal other than to give her pleasure, but as always happened while in her presence, he simply couldn't resist the spiral of desire. As she'd knelt before him, wearing the erotic black clothing he'd selected, as she'd toyed with him, deftly using her hands and mouth, a wave of unmanageable passion had swept him away.

Though his orgasm had relieved some of the sexual pressure, she titillated his senses as no woman ever had, and he couldn't stop himself from coveting her again so soon. If he continued at this level of stimulation all night, what would his condition be come the morn? Would this rampant arousal never abate?

"Are you feeling all right?" she queried, much like an accomplished courtesan who had spent years satisfying one lover after the next.

"Much better." He'd been worried that she'd be troubled or disgusted at enduring his end of things, yet she seemed to have weathered it well. As she was a novice at love games, he'd intended to practice patience, but events had progressed much more rapidly than he'd planned. "I become so provoked when I'm around you that I can't control myself. Hopefully, the release I just enjoyed will keep me from behaving like an ogre."

"You *are* grumpy when you're in a carnal situation."

She was so quick to notice the smallest tidbits! " 'Tis a manly problem. Unrelieved sexual tension can be . . . distressing."

"Well, it leaves *you* downright cantankerous." She appeared luscious, ripe, and ready for whatever was next. "And I have to tell you that I don't care for your bad humors at all, so you must allow me to ease your *distress* whenever it arises."

"You didn't find my . . . discharge . . . upsetting?"

"Not in the least. Why? Do some women?"

"On occasion. Those with less experience can be . . . shall we say . . . overwhelmed?"

"Not me, apparently." She licked her lips like a contented cat. "I particularly liked having you in my mouth."

He groaned and rubbed at his promptly inflating erection. He'd created a monster! "My lady," he offered gallantly, "my body is at your disposal."

"Does that mean I'm to be treated to an encore performance?" She was eager as a young child who'd just spied her favorite candy.

He chuckled. "As many times as I am able."

The libidinous look she flashed was worth all the uncertainty. He reached for her hand and conscientiously swabbed all traces of his seed. Then he cleaned himself. Through it all, she watched attentively, and as he grasped his cock and started to wash, she scooted to the edge of the bed.

"Let me do that." She took the cloth and sponged him, which of course caused him to swell further, filling her hand completely. "You are so beautiful," she said, smiling up at him, the devotion clear in those enchanting green eyes. "I love seeing you like this."

She finished, then dropped the cloth to the floor and nuzzled her face in the rough pile of hair around his cock and balls. He stood still, staring down at her, and he couldn't help but wander back to her admission that she fancied making a babe with him.

Always in the past, he'd coupled for the sake of physical alleviation, never fretting overly much about his partners. In light of the type of women with whom he consorted, he had no illusions: His obvious ennui was part of his allure. They were fascinated by his lack of regard, and they welcomed him to their beds for many reasons: to be able to brag that they had, to determine what it was like, or to gossip with others about what they'd done. He consented merely for the relief it brought, but also because it as an interesting way to pass his leisure hours.

Never had he contemplated having children with any of them! None had ever stirred paternal impulses. Even during his most aggressive, intense encounters, he'd never fornicated out of some deep-rooted aspiration for a child. He was always prudent, refusing to procreate or to wind up joined to one of his lovers through such sloppy attention to detail.

But when Abby had mentioned a babe . . . her declaration had instigated a whirl of dangerous ideas.

A babe! With her! Some ancient, primal element cried out that *impregnation* was exactly what he should be striving to achieve. No longer could he initiate bed play just for sport; there was a definite goal attached to the feat of mating. She had to carry his babe!

With an insane craving, he wished to hold her down, and fuck her until she was so saturated with his seed that there could be no other result. The concept was feral, savage, insurgent, and he couldn't risk shedding any more apparel, because he would definitely make love to her, and for once he didn't know if he'd be able to pull away at the conclusion.

For the first time in his life, he *wanted* with a desperation that was as amazing as it was disconcerting. He daren't close his eyes, because when he did, he saw visions of small children. Of adorable little girls, with Abby's blond hair and sweet disposition. Of rough-and-tumble boys, with

his lanky build and overbearing attitude. He could picture
them as clearly as if they were playing alongside the bed.

This yearning was terrible and menacing, but even as he
thought so, and even as he understood that he had to fight
against it and whatever outrageous exploits it might cause
him to commit, she was removing the remainder of his
attire and he was helping her. His boots, stockings, trousers.
With the loss of each item, he allowed her to pet and fondle,
while suffering through her virginal oohs and aahs. But
there was nothing innocent about her behavior; she was a
female bent on seduction, and she knew precisely how to
go about it.

As the last piece of clothing was shucked away, she fell
back onto the bed, and he went with her, his body enthusiastic, his mind resistant. Yet, as he stretched out and
folded his arms around her, he couldn't muster the reserve
or the detachment he always used during his erotic liaisons.
He simply longed for the moment too badly, and surprisingly, not just the act itself. If they did nothing else but lie
together, kissing and talking, he would travel home in the
morning a perfectly happy man.

"I must ask you a question," she said. "Promise me that
you won't be angry."

"You can ask me anything, Abby," he attested. "Surely
you realize that."

"Yes, but this is personal, and you told me not to inquire. . . ."

Had he really?

Yes, at the outset, when he'd been so disturbed by his
indescribable emotions where she was concerned that he
hadn't known how else to respond. Distance had always
been the method he'd used with his paramours, but with
Abby he couldn't pretend disinterest. Pathetically, he was
regularly trolling for news about her, and his conduct had
gotten so pitiable that, at his club, he frequently caroused
the gaming rooms, hanging on the fringe of Jerald Weston
and his acquaintances whenever Jerald was out bingeing
and whoring.

While he rarely heard Abby's name, at the slightest reference he felt like a starving dog who'd been tossed a bone. Even though he insisted they not share individual information, in all actuality, it was imperative that he ascertain everything about her, down to the smallest particulars.

But to what end? came the constant question, and for a change, he chased it away. On this one, special occasion, he wouldn't let irrelevant concerns infringe on how he should deal with her. What Abby preferred to learn, he would disclose.

"I'm sorry I said that," he murmured. "Ask away."

"I was wondering about your half-brother, Charles. Have you ever met him?"

"No." He hid his surprise well. He'd expected something about his father. Perhaps his mother or Michael. The club. Their home. "I was never allowed to," he added with more bitterness than he intended.

Charles Stevens, the *other* son who had received all—a life with their father and all the respect and acclaim that went with it—had been a constant thorn over the years, irritatingly jabbing during those inopportune instances when James had been foolish enough to lament over the unfair state of the world.

He bore the boy no ill will; he simply never reflected upon him, because his existence was proof of the kind of man Edward Stevens was and all the ways he had failed James's tiny family.

"I was so hoping," Abby was commenting, "that you had some opinion of him."

"Why?" He was unable to prevent a flare of curiosity.

"He's been courting my sister, Caroline, and she's quite taken with him."

"They might marry?"

" 'Tis certainly possible, and I'd like to discover more about his character before it progresses."

James shifted to his back, his arm around her shoulder, and the move enabled him to keep her close while staring at the ceiling, rather than into her eyes.

The report was extremely disconcerting, and he remembered a street urchin he'd seen once. The lad had been standing in front of a bakery and gazing inside at the displays of treats, though he recognized that he could never have any of them.

James now comprehended exactly how the boy had felt.

With a fierce surge of resentment, he unexpectedly hated Charles Stevens, this half-brother of wealth and privilege to whom he'd never been introduced. Why should Charles have so much, when James and Michael had never had anything at all? Charles could woo and wed one of Jerald Weston's sisters, but James had to clandestinely meet with the other. If they were detected, her life would be over, simply because of the accidents of birth. They couldn't even utter *hello* to one another if they passed on the street.

For a long while, he perused a crack in the plasterwork as he forced his rancorous musings to diminish. His skewed relationship with Edward and Charles had never bothered him overly much, but since he'd launched his affair with Abby, he couldn't abide these societal strictures that declared him not good enough for her. The knowledge dredged up other old hurts that usually remained buried, namely the loss and abandonment he continued to suffer since that night, ages ago, when his mother had awakened him so they could flee to Paris.

He was thirty years old, a grown man with a thriving business, a fine residence, and a substantial, steady income, yet the deeply hidden wounds still occasionally oozed as though they had just been inflicted.

Intuiting his anguish, Abby massaged over his heart as though she perceived precisely where it ached. "Why does it upset you so much to talk about Charles? About your father?"

"Old history, Abby," he prevaricated, but she refused to be put off.

She shifted until she was lying on top of him, covering him with her body, but he had the sense that she was also shielding him with her strength and love. "Can you tell me about it?"

He persisted in searching the ceiling as he explained, "When I was young, I worshiped Edward. He was the grandest, most wonderful father any boy could possibly have. He was so dashing . . . bigger than life. . . ." He narrowed his eyes, recalling that distant time. "When we were living in Paris, I was so sure he'd come for us. For years . . . for years! . . . I sneaked to my mother's bedroom first thing every morning and peeked inside, thinking it would be the day that he'd arrived to take us home. . . ."

Pausing, he chuckled at his sudden nostalgic accounting. He couldn't believe he'd admitted so much, and he shook his head. "Lord, I'd completely forgotten I used to do that. I looked for him until I was twelve or thirteen years old. . . ."

"What made you quit?" she urged wistfully.

"I started looking at girls instead." She nudged him in the ribs, and he hugged her closer. " 'Twas more fun than pining away."

"Your father harbors a great degree of remorse about all that transpired."

" 'Tis easy for him to claim as much now." He sounded petty and resentful but was unable to stop himself. "Did he say so?"

"Yes." She nodded. "Numerous times. He terribly regrets that he hasn't become reacquainted with Michael."

"He has plenty of other children. Why would Michael be so important?"

"All his children are special to him." Kindly, she maintained, "Even the ones he left behind."

"He's always had a funny way of showing it, then." Sitting up, he strolled across the room to the food and wine she'd brought. He was naked, and she shrewdly observed him as he walked about, and he appreciated the feel of her eyes, her avid curiosity, her dearth of virginal inhibitions.

"Have you ever talked to your mother about their split?"

"On many occasions. Why?" He nibbled on some cheese and poured himself a glass of wine.

"I'm just interested. I know you don't like your father, but—"

"I never said that," he interrupted. " 'Tis difficult between us. There are too many unresolved issues."

"My mistake." She patted the empty space beside her, with her gesture encouraging him to return, and he came willingly, even though she insisted on airing all these difficult topics. " 'Tis just that I've socialized extensively with Edward of late, and he doesn't seem the type who would do something nefarious to your mother or you boys." She took the wine and held it while he settled next to her.

Like old married folks, he thought. *We've adjusted to sharing the same bed.*

"I was just speculating," she stated, "as to your mother's opinion of him."

"She's always remained fond. And loyal. I've never heard a bad word out of her mouth." He shifted about, searching for a comfortable spot, but with all this candid discussion, there wasn't one to be had. "Actually, we rarely speak of him. It always hurt her, so early on, Michael and I decided to never mention his name."

"What did your mother think of that?"

"I don't know . . ." he claimed pensively, striving to recollect. "In the beginning, she was so distressed herself that she didn't notice. Later, I believe she convinced herself that his absence had simply made us quit missing him."

"How very sad. For all of you."

She sighed so sentimentally that a lump formed in his throat, the emotion of it all abruptly choking him. It had been sad, indeed tragic, but he'd spent so many years being angry that he hadn't grasped how much sorrow they'd all endured, as well. The comprehension was a heavy weight, and it filled the room, pressing down on him and inundating him in a landslide of old reminiscence and acrid retrospection.

He didn't want to waste one second of their precious

rendezvous being deluged by prior events. It was over. Done. The past couldn't be changed or amended, but the familiar torments and longings were near the surface, and he couldn't stand to endure them alone. He yearned to have Abby tend them for a brief while so that, he hoped by daybreak, they'd be less excruciating, less able to still inflict damage.

He held the goblet of wine to her lips, helping her to take a sip, then he set it on the table next to the bed. As he turned back, she opened her arms and held him tight. Almost gratefully, he latched on to her, embedding his face in her hair, inhaling and letting the heat and fragrance of her skin soothe him.

"I've upset you again," she murmured, kissing against his neck and chest.

"No, I'm not upset. Not with you anyway. 'Tis just difficult, sometimes, to ponder my childhood."

"I hate that you're suffering," she said softly. "Let me comfort you."

Previously, he'd never lain with a woman in order to achieve contentment. Assuredly, he couldn't recollect a single assignation when he'd desired more than the temporary relief he'd find through orgasm. He was about to have sex with a woman he loved, and the insight frightened him. This unique, singular event had to be unequaled by any other she might have later on in her life.

To fuck and love at the same moment! How odd that he'd never imagined it possible before.

He began by kissing her, simply because she treasured it so much. In the past, he'd never been overly keen on kissing, always more intent on getting down to business, and his jaded, sophisticated lovers hadn't minded. They, too, were eager for the more straightforward aspects of coupling. Time had often been a factor. Location, as well. Considering the sorts of places he'd engaged in carnal relations—coaches, closets, stairwells—kissing hadn't normally been at the forefront of what he'd been trying to accomplish.

With Abby, he was discovering an entirely different method of making love. There was pleasure to be gained in seeing her happy, in reveling in her company, in experiencing the leisurely, progressive changes that warmed and relaxed her as he readied her for what was to come.

This was new territory, this exposing of all these layers of passion, of the miniature delights available with the right woman, and he almost felt like a virgin himself. Why had he never sought out the minor joys, instead of pursuing only the end result? The route, he was finding, was just as delectable as the final destination.

"You have the most kissable mouth," he said as he eventually pulled away.

"Do you think so?" She blushed prettily and smiled.

"Yes, I do." For good measure, he kissed her nose, her cheek, her forehead, too.

"I feel the same about yours," she acceded, "but since you're the only man I've ever kissed, I'm hardly much of a judge, so don't let it go to your head."

"I'll try not to," he said wryly, "and don't you dare hie off, searching for comparisons." The statement was light and teasing, as he'd meant it to be, but he amazed himself with the possessive remark. He'd never cared what one of his lovers did or didn't do with others. Their extraneous conduct simply hadn't mattered. "I don't want your lips touching anyone's but mine."

"I'm not sure I can control myself." She batted her lashes in mock play.

"You'd better," he responded, swatting her on the rear. It was so easy, being with her. When she wasn't working to shape him into a better man, she was funny and carefree, and though she was blatantly aware of his worst traits, she was willing to accept him—flaws and all.

A major concession on her part!

"I've never been much of a one for kissing," he admitted, nuzzling under her neck and across her bosom.

"You're joking! With all the women you've had?"

"I didn't know it could be so pleasant."

Dubiously, she studied him. "Until you met me?"

"Yes."

Disbelieving, she grumbled low in her throat. "I can't tell when you're serious and when you're not."

" 'Tis true, love." To prove his point, he kissed her long and thoroughly, not easing up until she was panting and writhing beneath him. "I enjoy kissing you very, very much."

"I'm finding that I like it very much, as well, so I insist that you kiss me whenever the mood strikes you."

"That, my lady, shall never be a difficult task."

The light banter trailed away, and he lay there, half on top of her, half off, connected from shoulders to toes. His palm massaged her breast, his thigh lazed on her mound, his foot tickled her knee and calf. She was caressing him, and already he was wondering how he'd ever survived without her hot hands on his fevered skin. He needed her touch as he needed the very air he breathed!

He ached to brand her, to mark her with this night of ardor. Though it was wrong, and he knew it to be, he *had* to be the one to relieve her of her maidenhood. No matter where she ended up, or with whom, he wanted her to always remember that he had been the first. "I want to make love to you. In all ways, I want to make you mine."

"Oh, James . . ." she said kindly, resting a loving hand on his cheek, "I am yours in all ways. Surely, you realize that?"

His heart swelled, his body surged with desire. He came over her, covering her, pressing her down, taking her with his lips, his tongue, his teeth. He moved to her neck, chest, breasts. The fabric of her outfit was still damp from where he'd suckled earlier. He slowly untied the lace at the front, baring pale, creamy flesh that was stark and arousing against the dark black. Dipping under the edge, he hunted until he found her nipple. Free of silk, skin to skin, he nipped and played.

He took the other breast. Laving it. Milking it. Squeezing and sucking until, of their own accord, her legs widened. Her feet went around his thighs to hook behind his legs, anchoring him closer. Her cleft was exposed, shielded only by the black, and his cock stroked along it. The shiny material was tantalizingly cool, yet heated. The cloth was moistened, her desire seeping through the thin layer, imploring its removal.

"Touch me there," she pleaded. "As you did before. . . ."

With one finger, he slid under the hem, detected her core, glided inside. She was slick and saturated, dripping. "Like this?" he asked.

"Yes . . ." she groaned.

"And like this?" he asked again, two more fingers joining the first.

"James, please . . ."

He flicked across her clit. "Come for me," he ordered. "Come now." And she did, rushing into his hand, tensing as she cried out his name and squirmed in ecstasy. When she finally returned to him, he had the buttons opened on the bottom of her pantie, her privates revealed for his inspection. Her sex was weeping, her lips swollen, her curly hairs wet and slippery.

Kneeling between her smooth thighs, he bent forward and licked at her love juice, implanting it on his lips, permanently embedding her taste. He toyed with her until she was twisting and turning anew. She was distended, raw, unduly stimulated from the aftereffects of her initial orgasm, but he didn't care. He fucked her with his tongue, feeling her tension grow, her torso tightening, her cleft condensing.

He went to her clit, sucking at her. The tiny bud was already enlarged and anxious for his renewed thoroughness.

"No, James." Her agony was readily apparent. " 'Tis too soon . . . I couldn't possibly . . ."

" 'Tis *never* too soon to do it again," he asserted. He rose, reaching for her hips, centering himself. His hand on his erect cock, he placed the tip in her dampened folds.

"Look at me!" he commanded.

"I'm not ready," she declared, appearing apprehensive,

but he refused to give her the opportunity to change her mind. They were too far along, and he'd warned her. It had been her decision to play with this fire, and there could be no going back. He would have her!

"But you *are* ready, love," he advised gently, firmly. He pushed in the blunt end. Pushed farther. Partially buried, at her barrier, the slightest forward movement would have him immersed to the hilt. He paused, draped her legs over his thighs.

"I'm frightened . . . of a sudden. . . ."

"Don't be. I'll be with you. . . ." He steadied her as sweat pooled on his brow. "Look at me," he repeated fiercely. "Keep looking at me." With that, he flexed and entered, and her cleft was so eager for him that he hardly sensed the tear, yet she strained furiously against the turbulent invasion. Her back bowed up off the bed; tears pooled at the corners of her eyes.

"It hurts," she whispered.

"Just for a moment. 'Twill abate directly."

He settled his weight, covering her again, sheathed in her narrow tunnel. Her virgin's blood and sexual flux conspired to produce an ocean of sizzling sensation. His cock floated in it, was scalded by it, begging to thrust, but he restrained himself, holding her and kissing her. Delectably, tenderly. She tasted like wine and his semen, and he molded his lips to hers so she could experience the musky tang of her sex mingled with his own.

Gradually, she accepted him. She mellowed, and her arms came around him, her fingers caressing up and down his back, his signal to recommence.

"This is our dance, my lady." He pushed in as far as he could go, pulled out, pushed in. "Let me show you the steps."

He was not solicitous of her virginal state. Probing, exploring, never sinking as deep as he needed to be, he simply could not get close enough, and she had to understand, from the very first, that this was how it would always be between them.

They would never have the soft intercourse of new lovers, the tepid joinings, the lackluster connection or half interest in fulfillment. There would only ever be this frantic, maddening drive to completion, this desperate search for culmination that, upon release, would leave them hungry for more.

He pounded into her, his thighs slapping against her, his hips meeting hers with a frenzied desperation. They were sweating, hearts pounding, breathing labored, muscles taut, winging toward their mutual goal. He reached between them and rifled his thumb across her.

" 'Tis too much, James . . ." She arched into his hand, her interior walls clenching around him. ". . . too much . . ."

"Yes . . . too much," he agreed. "Always too much with you." She was at the edge; so was he. "Follow me, love," he implored. "Come now. . . ." With his torturing of her nipple, her clit, she exploded into the heavens.

"James . . ." she called from a long distance. Her tight pussy was luring his seed, and it swelled to the crest in a blistering torrent, so he plunged once, again, again, then, using every ounce of his fortitude, he jerked away and spilled himself on her abdomen, his scorching come washing over her sweltering skin.

He collapsed onto her, his semen a sticky residue binding them together. The air was heavy with the aroma of sweat and sex and, as his arms went around her, her shoulders were shaking, the heat of her tears seared his chest.

"Why are you crying, love?" he asked, sampling them, kissing them away.

She was gazing up at him in awe. " 'Twas just so beautiful. I didn't know. . . ."

"No, you couldn't." He smiled and rolled to the side, cuddling her close. "Ssh . . .'tis all right," he crooned. Comforting a distraught woman for the first time, he noted it to be an extraordinary circumstance.

"Hold me close," she entreated. "Don't let go."

"I won't," he avowed. "I'll never let go."

*   *   *

Barbara stirred on the rigid seat of her rented hansom, rubbing at the small of her back. The lengthy night of patient observation had taken its toll, and there was no comfort to be had. She didn't have a timepiece with her so she could only guess at the hour, but with the sun so high in the sky, and commerce so fully under way, it had to be nearing nine o'clock.

Outside, the horse shook itself, rattling the carriage, and the driver murmured something to the pitiful animal. The beast was ready for the warmth of his barn, but the driver wouldn't leave until Barbara gave the word. With the money she'd slipped him earlier, he'd said he'd be happy to tarry till Christmas if need be.

She peeked toward the anonymous row house down the block. It was nondescript, no better, worse, or different than any of the others, so nothing about it provided any indication of who lived there, but if she was forced to remain for days—for weeks—she would learn the identity of the woman who was sheltered inside with James.

The previous day, she'd fussed and stewed, wondering why Madame LaFarge was late with her gift. In case James had deigned to visit, Barbara had wanted to be wearing the garment. But as the hours had passed, she'd finally comprehended that she'd been played for a fool. Clearly, there would be no delivery from the modiste, no present from James made especially for her.

Like a silly schoolgirl, she'd stood in LaFarge's shop, so enamored with her personal success where James was concerned that she'd never imagined he could have a second lover about whom she wasn't aware.

Once the shock had worn off, she'd regrouped. She'd begun by journeying to his club, lingering outside until she observed him sneaking out the back. So intent was he on his amorous rendezvous that he'd never so much as looked over his shoulder, so the driver had easily tailed him to his destination.

After he'd covertly slipped inside, she'd hoped to also catch a glimpse of the woman who would join him, but

when no one arrived, she gradually realized that his lover
was already closeted with him, so Barbara had determined
to wait them out. Torturing herself, she'd sat in the cold,
dark coach, watching as a lamp was lit in an upstairs bedroom, as an occasional shadow passed the window. The
torment had grown worse when the lamp had been blown
out and James hadn't departed. The understanding that he
was to spend the entire night with this unknown paramour,
this adversary who vied for his attention, had caused her to
simmer with hatred.

He had another woman! The blackguard!

Whoever she was, Barbara was seething. James had been
cuddled with her now for a good share of sixteen hours!
He'd come to her in the late afternoon, fucked her copi-
ously, slept with her, and, by allowing her to pass the dawn
in his arms, he'd favored her with that most precious of
moments, the one Barbara had always intended to reserve
for herself alone.

Some other nameless, faceless woman had awakened by
his side!

He had never slept with a woman before; Barbara knew
this with absolute certainty. When he stooped to selecting
a lover, they went to *her* bed—never his own—they
fucked, he went home. If his partner so much as raised the
topic of his remaining, he was *never* interested, and any
woman stupid enough to press never saw him again.

Which only meant one thing: He had formed a dangerous attachment. It was a condition Barbara simply couldn't
tolerate.

"But who?" she muttered to herself, tapping a manicured
nail against the cheap leather seat. "Who could it be?"

Suddenly the door to the house opened and James
walked out, looking freshly groomed and neatly attired,
with no visible hint that he'd just endured hours of significant debauchery. Only the light in his eyes and the spring
in his step gave him away. The bastard was fairly skipping
with joy.

He proceeded down the three stairs, ready to hurry away,

but not before stopping to gaze longingly toward the upper window. His unseen partner was hiding behind the drapes, and James actually had the audacity to kiss his fingertips, then send it sailing in the direction of his new darling. At witnessing the sight, Barbara's rage was so great that she had to grip the squab, lest she jump out and accost the two of them.

Patience, she counseled. Patience and planning would see her triumphant in the end.

James left, but she didn't need to follow. She already knew how he spent his days. He'd return to the house he shared with his whore of a mother and his sleazy, wayward brother. There, he'd doze for a few hours, then he'd make his way to his club, where he'd count the previous evening's receipts.

Now she need only learn how he truly spent his nights—when he didn't spend them with her.

Many minutes later, the door opened again, and a woman emerged. Slender, petite, blond, she was dressed expensively in a fine wool cloak and fancy slippers. She fiddled with the key in the lock; then, as luck would have it, she turned toward the street. The idiotic female had her hood down, and she glanced up toward the mist that was falling. Smiling, inhaling the fresh air, she had an expression of pure bliss on her face.

Barbara stared in shock, then started to laugh. Hard, then harder.

"Abigail Weston!" she hissed. So . . . the straitlaced, boring spinster had taken a lover.

Barbara thought of Abigail's pompous, self-righteous brother, Jerald, with his prissy public manners and private sexual oddities. Of his wife, Margaret, with her holier-than-thou attitudes and preachy morals. Of the younger Weston sister, Caroline, the pristine little virgin who would make the grandest match of the year.

This was too good to be true!

Under all their lofty, exalted noses, Abigail was carrying on with the most despicable, deplorable of men. A thousand questions flew into her mind: How had they met? How had they become involved? How had this dragged on?

Even as the queries rushed past, she shook them off. None of Abigail's recent association with James mattered a whit. Only the future counted—the one she wouldn't have with him, for Barbara wouldn't permit some simpering noblewoman to ruin her chances.

What would Jerald and Margaret think once they discovered what was happening? And what would be the most delightful method of telling them?

She tapped on the roof, ready for home, where she could formulate Abigail's downfall over a hot bath.

FIFTEEN

Abigail walked through the doors of the theater house, clutching Edward Stevens's arm. The Saturday night crowd of patrons was so tightly packed into the small entrance that, if she let go, she was afraid they would become separated. Across the foyer, she could see the stairs leading up to the box seats, but being a petite person, she didn't know if she could successfully maneuver the route by herself.

She glanced over her shoulder. Charles and Caroline had been right behind them, but already they were divided by a wall of people. Through several pairs of legs, she could just make out the pink flounce on her sister's skirt. Charles was a responsible young man, however, so he'd escort Caroline safely through the crush, and they'd eventually be reunited, although Abigail could barely stand the thought of the coming sequestration in Edward's box. She was desperate for some privacy!

Had it only been a few hours earlier that she'd been with James? The difference between that private encounter and this unrestricted public spectacle was so striking that she almost couldn't believe the magical rendezvous had truly happened.

Yet it had, and she couldn't find the temerity to be sorry. Such delirious joy was meant to be indulged. She ached to shout her rapture to the world, instead of ruminating in this stifling, suffocating stillness. If she didn't soon give voice to her exhilaration, she just might shatter into a thousand tiny pieces.

Couldn't everyone tell? How could they all gaze upon her and not perceive the changes?

Caroline had nearly stumbled upon her secret the prior morning, as Abigail had been reveling in the look and feel of the undergarments James had sent. Oh, how she'd been dying to confess her relationship with James. She was no longer an unlovable woman, a spinster, a sister, a boring female with no distinguishable life of her own.

She had been created for one purpose and one purpose alone—to love James—and she didn't want to think about anything else, or talk about anything else or do anything else but sit in her room and reminisce about the glories that had been unearthed in their hideaway.

When this last-minute invitation had arrived from Charles, asking them to attend the new play that was all the rage, how she'd yearned to stay at home. With all the excitement of a woman headed for the gallows, she'd primped and preened, preparing her person and calming her mind, but nothing could focus her on the evening of gregarious entertainment.

She had been with James! In every way imaginable, he had claimed her and taken her for his own! How could she be expected to perform these ludicrous civic functions when her entire life had been so completely disordered?

She could still smell him on her skin, taste him on her tongue, feel the whisper of his lips against her mouth, her breasts. Bruised and sore, she had scratches across her stomach, and nipples that were suckled raw, the tender skin inside her thighs abraded by his rough beard. Her cleft was in the worst condition, the delicate, virginal area having received James's undivided, strenuous attention for untold numbers of couplings. With muscles cramped from all that arching and straining, several body parts cried out in agony whenever she stirred, reminding her, over and over again, of her wanton, decadent behavior.

How gratifying the experience had been! He'd incited her to the pinnacle of passion—with his hands, his tongue, his phallus—so perfectly, totally, and on so many occasions. Turning her and riding her, using, teaching, caring, he'd overwhelmed her with his body, his character, his adoration. The best episode had occurred early in the morning, when she'd wakened him slowly, toying with him and employing all the techniques he'd managed to impart. As he'd finally entered her, she'd been painfully inflamed, and he'd moved languidly and sweetly, the emotion flaring between them so powerfully that they'd both had tears in their eyes at the conclusion.

What was she going to do?

She abhorred all these people who insisted on socializing! Their inane chatter was driving her mad! She'd like to snap her fingers and make them disappear so that she could be alone with her thoughts and memories.

Her mind drifted back to the current task—proceeding through the crowd—and they were temporarily stalled. A large man was blocking their path, and in order to move around him, Edward shifted them to the side. Where ... they came face-to-face with James.

She inhaled sharply. In surprise. In joy. In fear.

He was immaculately attired in dress blacks, a snowy white shirt, with perfectly tied cravat. His hair had been swept off his forehead, leaving his stark beauty plain for all to witness. They stood so closely that her skirts tangled about his legs and shoes. She could behold the gold flecks in his eyes, a spot where he'd nicked himself shaving. There, just below his collar, was the edge of a bite mark she'd dispensed.

Her pulse was pounding, her breathing suddenly ragged. She'd never expected to meet him here! Like this!

Terrified by what he might say or do, she frantically searched for the proper method of handling the situation. Not by even the smallest hint of a smile could she give any indication that she knew him. She cast about for a solution, but her astonishment and panic were so great that she couldn't find one.

At the same time, he was flashing her an angry stare, daring her to acknowledge their acquaintance, to tip her head, to endorse him in any slight fashion at all, but, coward that she was, she frankly couldn't react. She responded as she'd been taught: She pasted a smooth expression of disinterest on her face, pretending indifference to the man in front of her.

He hesitated, offering her an extra chance. And an extra one after that. Waiting . . . waiting . . . waiting . . . for some tiny sign of recognition that didn't appear.

Never more ashamed, she failed his test, remaining silent and serene at his father's side, on his father's arm, understanding how deeply she was hurting him, how piercing the wound, how dreadfully disgraceful her uncivil comportment.

She loved this man! But she could not, and would not, reveal her connection to him by so much as the flicker of an eyelash. Then and there, she wished that she would fall dead. That the heavens would open and suck her up. For surely her life had just ended.

James's eyes widened minimally, with that lucid motion communicating his disappointment in her, his distress over her repudiation, the degradation he felt by her disavowal.

Quick as a heartbeat, his torment melded into fury, and he aimed it at his father.

Standing, they were of equal height, exact copies of one another. Handsome, influential, and dynamic, there was a strange current of energy flowing between them. Palpable dislike coming from James. Powerful affection coming from Edward.

"James . . ." Edward said pleasantly. "How nice to see you. What brings you out?"

"Since you never show your face at the Chelsey, I could ask you the same," James replied. "Of course, you'd have no way of knowing. . . ."

"Knowing what?" Edward inquired, his interest in James evident.

"Mother is taking to the stage tonight."

Abigail was certain she was the only one who could sense Edward's reaction. A faint shudder traveled through his body, and his hand squeezed hers so tightly that she thought he might break bones, but other than that, he presented no outward sign that the news had had any effect. "How wonderful," he said cordially. "I look forward to it. What role is she playing?"

"The lead. The regular actress fell ill, so Mother had to fill in." James obviously relished how those closest were turning to eavesdrop on the juicy confrontation. " 'Tis the part of the *wronged* woman. I'm sure you'll be able to recognize her."

Edward sighed, once, sadly—this was a tedious, ongoing argument—then he pulled himself together and beamed with approval. "She'll be fabulous. As always."

With an exceptionally malicious glare in Abigail's direction, James rotated slightly, imparting a view she'd not previously enjoyed.

A woman accompanied him!

She was tall, dark-haired, clothed in a fabulous red gown that was low-cut to highlight her splendid bosom and slender waist. Regrettably, she was incredibly beautiful, but what had Abigail expected? The striking belle was exactly the sort Abigail conjectured James consorting with—whenever she could bear to dwell on such a depressing topic.

"Eddy"—James placed particular emphasis on the nickname, as though desiring that those around them be shocked by the salutation—"may I present my companion, Barbara Ritter, Lady Newton."

The woman stepped forward to pay her respects to the earl, but not before pausing imperceptibly in front of Abigail to display a look of hatred so virulent that Abigail felt as if she'd been slapped. She actually jerked back as though contact had been made, but as the other woman said hello to Edward, she wore a lovely smile and was the absolute picture of pleasantry and decorum. The strange sensation of loathing passed, and Abigail wrote it off to the stress of the encounter.

Lady Newton graciously curtsied to Edward and demurely addressed him, sounding sweet and soft-spoken, but as she straightened, Abigail could perceive Edward's distaste. He appeared to know her—or know *of* her—and he caustically assessed both her and James until his regard nearly reached the point of rudeness. Clearly, he was pondering his son, his conduct, his choice of associate, but he was unable, just as Abigail was, to utter what he was really thinking.

"And who is your pretty *young* friend?" James inquired, showering Abigail with his livid gaze. "I had heard you were seeing someone. That wedding bells might be in your future. Is she to be my new *mum*?"

"James!" Edward exclaimed, mortified and exasperated. He moved slightly, watching James out of the corner of his eye as though his willful son might do something rash if he wasn't observed carefully. "I apologize, Abigail."

"No apology is necessary, Lord Spencer." Two bright spots of embarrassment colored her cheeks, and she opened her fan, hoping to cool herself, but there was no air left in the room. "But your colleague appears upset," she added politely. "Perhaps it would help if we were introduced."

"Yes, *Lord* Spencer," James agreed, plainly taunting his father, his own cheeks marred scarlet, his eyes glittering with bitterness, "do let us be introduced."

Edward took a long, slow breath. The entire world braced for his decision, and finally he said quietly to Abigail, "No, I'm sorry, dear. You may not be."

Had there ever been a more vicious, more heinous cut direct made in all of history?

The earl's statement rang like a death knell, killing all three of them. Edward sagged a little, some of the vitality flowing out of him. Abigail flinched as if she'd just been impaled with a sharp, hot knife. Her agony was bleeding from every pore, and the voyeuristic group surrounding her, packed elbow to elbow, was able to analyze her terrible sins as they coursed across the floor. Yet, horridly as she'd been run through and exposed, James's injury was far worse.

Their outrageous behavior toward him was more than just a blow to his pride, although it had been forceful and apparent. Edward's refusal to present him dug much deeper, shattering illusions, slaying dreams, ruining expectations, obliterating love. Finally and forever.

James! I'm sorry. I'm so sorry, she longed to shout. But

still, to her undying shame, she said nothing. She did nothing.

He chuckled malevolently, expecting nothing more from either of them, and Abigail shivered with uneasiness at what the showdown would mean for him.

Wanting to exit the wretched scene, she cast about seeking escape, just as Charles and Caroline approached. Not aware of what was unfolding, they strode into the circle that encompassed James and his paramour. The onlookers, bent on determining how delectable the occasion would become, were more than happy to let them close.

"What is it?" Charles asked at witnessing the tense confrontation. His gaze roved and settled on James, and he stiffened as instant recognition dawned. "James . . ." He murmured the name and stared up at his older half-brother with something bordering on hero worship. Echoing the question Abigail had raised only moments earlier, he beseeched, "Father . . . may I be introduced?"

Horridly torn, Edward looked back and forth at his remarkable sons, then at Abigail and Caroline, but their innocent, eminent female presence precluded any family reconciliation. Edward simply daren't proceed when James was such an inappropriate person for the two women to meet. A cataclysmic mien—a combination of ancient pain, grief, and disappointment—seemed to envelop Edward as he publicly denied his eldest son for the second time in a matter of minutes. "No, Charles, I'm sorry."

"Father—" Charles started to protest, but Edward interrupted.

"Not now," he said calmly. "Please escort the Ladies Weston to our box."

"But I want to—" Charles tried again.

"Do it immediately, Charles."

The authority in Edward's tone brooked no argument, and his youngest son grudgingly obeyed. Caroline's hand was still in the crook of his arm, and he held out the other for Abigail. She wavered, wanting to say something, *anything,* but she couldn't conceive of what it might be. Ed-

ward and James seemed as though they might come to
blows, and she wished she could diffuse the situation, but
this was an old war, one in which she couldn't choose sides,
because she didn't understand who was the enemy or what
were the issues over which they were fighting. She only
knew that there could be no winner.

Charles proceeded toward the stairs, and the assembly
parted to allow them passage. As she moved by James, she
visually begged him to take a quick peek in her direction
so that he could behold her unspoken apology, but he kept
his gaze firmly locked on his father's. Any comment from
her would only provide more fodder for the gossip mill, so
she carried on.

As though they were members of a funeral procession,
they ascended the narrow steps, then slipped through the
curtain to their box. Like mechanical dolls she'd once seen
at a museum, they transferred about and silently selected
their seats. In the adjoining boxes, the incident was already
being dissected. People were discreetly pointing and laughing behind their hands. The entire audience seemed to be
staring at them, yet they sat proudly, their heads held high.

The strain was so profound that Abigail thought she
might start screaming, but there was no means available for
alleviating the tension. She couldn't mention what had transpired to either of her two companions. Since she wasn't
supposed to know of James, or his sordid background, she
could hardly begin conversing about him as though they
were familiar.

From Charles's reaction in the lobby, he was evidently
aware of who James was, but he could never be so crass
as to raise the issue of a bastard brother—his father's ultimate misdeed—in front of a young lady he wished to
marry. In their bizarre world, James didn't exist.

Caroline was the most perplexed, remaining straight and
rigid in her chair, while pretending to be fascinated by the
pit and the wave of commoners who were packing the rows.

Eventually, when Charles espied an aunt and two cous-
ins across the way, Abigail heartily gave her blessing for

the visit that allowed the younger pair to depart. She was left in solitude, and shortly, Charles and Caroline joined the opposite box.

As she watched, they huddled, whispering intimately, and from their positions it was obvious they'd grown much closer than anyone suspected. Charles appeared to be explaining the deadly undercurrents that had swirled belowstairs, which only emphasized how intimate their association had become. Abigail was quite certain they were holding hands in the shadows, the confidential gesture hidden underneath Caroline's full skirts.

Would they wed? They made for a merry, elegant couple, and viewing their bond made her pitifully jealous. With her own disgraced heart breaking into tiny pieces, she couldn't abide their conspicuous connection. Tears stung at her eyes.

Where was Edward? Why didn't he come? Was he still with James? Were they arguing?

If she'd had any idea of their whereabouts, she'd have gone in search of them. She couldn't stand to think of them clashing when she was the cause. Her despicable comportment had created the entire mess, and poor Edward had been left to sort it out when he had no clue as to what had precipitated the calamity. James was in a state, so there'd be no reasoning with him. He needed to lash out, and Edward was the easy target, so he'd unleash his wrath regardless of whether his father deserved it or not.

She hoped Edward would be strong enough to weather James's harsh words. They had a tenuous relationship at best, and Abigail would never forgive herself if she was the one to destroy what little affection they shared.

Caroline and Charles tipped their heads together, and Caroline murmured soothingly. Abigail couldn't bear it. She had to escape from the snoopy, gawking neighbors in the surrounding boxes, from Caroline's overt displays of fond empathy, so she slipped into the hall, whispered to an usher, and received directions to the ladies' retiring room.

Yearning for the opportunity to regroup, she hastened to

the haven. Inside, she advanced to the mirror, pretending to check her coiffure, when to her horror she realized that she was sequestered in the small space with James's paramour, Lady Newton.

As Abigail studied Lady Newton in the polished glass, she was graced, once again, with an unmistakable glint of hostility, but the other woman hastily covered it with a congenial smile. Still, Abigail knew she hadn't invented her unease this time. For some reason, Barbara Ritter despised her, and she couldn't help but suffer the impression that the woman was a dangerous adversary.

"They haven't returned?" Lady Newton asked, not even pretending that Abigail didn't understand of whom she spoke.

"No," Abigail replied haltingly. She couldn't tolerate this unknown, rancorous person, but she was completely at a loss as to how she might execute a graceful exit. And though she didn't want to chat, she couldn't help inquiring, "Where did they go?"

"The earl suggested they step outside where they could have a bit of privacy." She primped at her hair. Appearing bored, she queried, "You *do* know how they're related, don't you?"

"Well, yes," Abigail answered hesitantly, not wanting to reveal too much unexplainable knowledge. "I had heard that James is the earl's son. From a previous affair."

"I just *love* it when they fight. James is always such a tiger in my bed after they've had a good row." She checked her reflection again, and the venomous gleam was back. "He was quite potent this afternoon, before he'd even seen his dear old da, so I can't begin to guess what he'll be like later. I'll hardly be able to keep up—"

"Excuse me?" Abigail's bones seemed to have crystallized; she'd been turned to stone. Surely her ears had deceived her. She'd lain with James this morning. He couldn't have been with this . . . this creature in the afternoon!

"Have I offended you?" Lady Newton casually assessed Abigail's patent distress. She laughed coyly. "Oh, please tell me you're not some squeamish miss. The earl will never remain intrigued with that kind of prudish behavior."

"What?" Abigail couldn't form a single coherent comment. James had gone to this woman's bed? Only hours after they'd ended their own night of blissful passion?

"I must admit that I'm quite well acquainted with Edward Stevens. Like father, like son, as they say." Lady Newton winked. "Edward likes his women a tad on the wild side. Just like James does."

"You believe that the earl and I . . . that he and I . . ." In front of this hideous woman, she couldn't even contradict the shocking sexual allegation.

"Dearie, we're both grown-ups. You don't have to deny it to me. I'm *extremely* friendly with the Stevens men. Why . . . once you marry Edward, and I marry James, you and I will be . . ."—she raised her brows—"family. . . ."

"You and James are marrying?" These were the most appalling tidings she'd ever received, and considering everything else that had already occurred that evening, it was more than she could endure.

"Of course," Lady Newton said, definitely smirking. "We've been planning it for months. Hadn't you heard?"

"No." Abigail felt sick.

"We've been rather quiet about it, but that's why I'm in such an excellent position to offer you solid advice. If you're expecting to snag the earl, you'll listen to me. You may get a ring on your finger, but you'll never keep him in your bed by acting all prim and proper." She dabbed at her lips with a rouge stick. "Take James, for instance. He just adores the chance to seduce an innocent female. There's nothing he relishes more. He dallies, he lures, he entices. And eventually"—she shrugged, unconcerned—"he fucks, but he always comes back to me when he's through. Do you know why?"

"Why?" Abigail choked.

"Because he detests inexperience. Bumbling virgins are fun, but over the long haul, he likes a woman such as myself. One who comprehends what he truly needs. He's no different from any other man: He fancies the chase, but once the girl is caught . . ." She shrugged again. "The rascal has had me at my wits' end all this month over his latest conquest. But yesterday, he finally bedded her. Thank God that's over! All afternoon he was beside himself, crowing about how well it had gone—I have to listen to the details; can you believe it?"

James had discussed her, and what they'd done, with this vile individual? "You're joking. . . ."

"No, I'm not. The bastard was preening like the biggest cock in the barnyard. I actually felt sorry for the poor child. They all fall in love with him, and he doesn't even have the good grace to let them down easily. But then he's ready for a *real* woman." She shuddered with delight and anticipation. "After this skirmish with the earl, I can't conceive of what he'll demand of me tonight. What do you suppose put him in such a state that he—"

"I have to go." Abigail lurched out to the hall and somehow stumbled down the corridor. Her vision was failing, everything was dark; she was blindly floundering through a tunnel. Her heart was beating so hard that she wondered if it might burst out of her chest.

It couldn't be true! It simply couldn't be!

In grave despair, she blundered into Edward's box, relieved to come upon him calmly sitting by himself as though nothing untoward had transpired. Wanting only to flee, to rush home and crawl into the safety of her own bed, she scooted next to him just as the curtains parted and a man emerged to announce that the leading lady for that evening's performance would be none other than the incredible Angela Ford. He took a quick bow and retreated.

The gathering was quiet for several seconds as the proclamation sunk in. Then the news buzzed through the auditorium like wildfire, several men called out, and the place burst into uncontrolled applause. A testament to her fame and popularity—all these years after she'd abandoned her position at center stage—the ovation was still continuing as the curtains opened. The patrons' rapt attention was centered on the actress standing off to the side and sniffing flowers next to a rose-covered trellis.

A great beauty, she was willowy yet voluptuous, and she hovered patiently until everyone watched her, then her stunning blue eyes swept across the audience. In a flirtatious gesture, she tossed her glorious mane of blond hair over her shoulder, exposing her magnificent bosom and earning herself dozens of whistles. Portraying an eighteen-year-old girl, she was so marvelously talented that if Abigail hadn't known Mrs. Ford's age to be in the fifties, she could have easily mistaken her for a comely lass awaiting her first swain.

As her fans recognized her, the theater erupted in applause a second time, and Abigail leaned close to Edward, over the din asking if they could leave.

With his usual acute assessment, he noticed her disheveled plight. "Are you upset?"

"No. I'd just like to go. If it wouldn't be too much of a bother."

Edward took her hand in his own; her skin was chilled and clammy. "This is all James's fault, isn't it? I'd like to wring his neck! The way he behaves sometimes . . . I don't understand him at all."

" 'Twasn't James," she insisted, looking down at her lap as she lied. "It might be something I ate for supper. I'm unwell."

He regarded her scrupulously, obviously identifying the fabrication for what it was. "I'm sorry for the things he said. I hadn't realized his conduct would distress you so. If it's any consolation, I ordered him home—like the naughty boy he is. I've told him—repeatedly—that he oughtn't be out in Polite Society if he can't discipline himself."

"Oh, Edward . . ." She sighed. Considering James's mixed sentiments, she couldn't think of any worse criticism his father could possibly have leveled. "Please . . . could we just call it a night?"

But his attention was already directed back to the stage.

To Angela Ford, the reputed grand love of his life, with whom he'd fraternized, shocked, reveled, and, as a much younger man, created two sons. He was so focused on her that he was hardly aware of Abigail's presence any longer.

Finally, he wrenched himself away from the action. "Can you bear with me for a short while? After what happened downstairs, everyone is watching us. If I leave now, they'll all infer that it's because Angela has taken the stage. I'd never embarrass her so terribly."

Her own distress was so enormous that she hadn't contemplated how anyone else might be affected by the atrocious events. She'd caused enough trouble for one evening, for one lifetime, and she'd remain with Edward until Hades froze over if that's what he requested of her. "I understand," she murmured. "I don't mind waiting."

"We can slip out after the first act," he said, sounding like an eager schoolboy. "If that's what you still want. . . ."

His tentative joy at seeing Mrs. Ford was so great that Abigail didn't have the heart to demand departure. Despite her own misery, she'd already wreaked plenty of havoc on the Stevens family. She'd inflict no more suffering. "We can stay as long as you'd like."

His reprieve granted, his fierce concentration shifted back to the funny, sexy, gifted woman on the stage who had the spectators bristling with continual laughter. A few minutes later, when Abigail dared glance his way again, quiet tears were rolling down his cheeks.

SIXTEEN

Edward sat in the rented, unpleasant carriage, ignoring the lingering aromas, all of which he was trying hard *not* to identify. The horse shook itself, and the cheaply built conveyance rattled at the seams, making him realize that he needed to either get out or travel on.

He'd been parked in front of Angela's house for the past half hour, too anxious to depart, too cowardly to bang her knocker. For that very reason, he hadn't brought his own coach. Lest he never find the necessary resolve to follow through, he hadn't wanted to be seen in her neighborhood. So he'd hired a cab, and now he tarried, minute after agonizing minute, while wondering what would happen if he forged ahead. Would she welcome him inside or, more likely, would she slam the door in his face? Regretfully, he couldn't decide which outcome would be worse.

The three-story row house, tucked in along the narrow lane with scores of others that were nearly exact copies, was a cozy, comfortable abode, just the type of place he'd always imagined Angela would select for herself. Only three blocks from the theater, a few more from James's and Michael's gaming house, it was conveniently located and set smack in the middle of all the hustle and bustle he used to share with her when they were so young, so foolish, and so madly in love.

Their world had been exciting, enchanting, filled with gaiety and pleasure, their home always overflowing with her friends and coworkers—of whom she'd had so many. People constantly gathered around her. She had a sparkle and charisma that made you long to be close, to bask in her glow and energy, to have some of her attention focused in your direction.

James had acquired her natural flare, and, from what

he'd gathered, Michael had received a healthy dose of it, too. While they were both handsome lads, endowed with his height, masculine physique, and intellect, he had no illusions about why they were so sought-after by those who occupied their demimonde. It was their inheriting of Angela's seductiveness that had turned them into the forceful, admirable men they had grown to be.

Women flocked to their sides, aspiring toward liaisons and more. Men clamored to be their associates, their partners. It was simply impossible to be in the same room with one of them and not be drawn in. They both maintained a heavy measure of Angela's allure, and as he himself had learned from the first, her enticement was irresistible.

Oh, what a lucky, unlucky man he was! To have sired such magnificent, strapping sons! But to have witnessed only the smallest part of their development, so that now, watching them from afar, all he could do was lament over what might have been.

What was he going to do about James? After their quarrel the previous night, with all of fashionable London looking on, he didn't know what would become of their intermittent, strained relationship. If they never spoke again, he wouldn't be surprised. James was so regularly angry, either unwilling or unable to forgive the sins of the past, and with their latest exchange of bitter words, Edward saw little chance of them ever gaining any ground.

Throughout the last decade, he'd endeavored unsuccessfully to be James's friend, and an occasional father figure, even though James stridently insisted he didn't need one, but it was too difficult to pretend they were anything more than strangers feigning an affection James plainly didn't feel. Edward was unsure of what had transpired in James's early years to make him so virulent in his dislike. No matter what Edward attempted, he was unable to bridge their gaps.

To be loathed by his oldest son was burden enough, but his second son appeared to despise him, as well, creating a load that was doubly cumbrous to bear. Michael obviously harbored an intense antipathy of his own that he couldn't—or wouldn't—put aside.

What a mess he'd created, by forsaking his children, by severing his connection with Angela. At the time, it had seemed the only appropriate and logical step, but who could recognize the proper course at such a young age? He'd been little more than a child himself and incapable of foreseeing the unending sorrow and distress his flip decision would cause. His behavior toward the three of them remained a brewing cauldron of guilt and shame that he couldn't tamp down.

"Oh, Angie," he whispered, sending his lingering affection winging to her doorstep. His transgressions were weighing heavily, and he felt such a tremendous desire to atone. Especially after fighting with James again, he desperately desired the opportunity to confer with her, to share some of his anguish, for she was the only person to whom he could go with his worries and discouragement.

But if he approached her, what would she say? Would they be able to take up again, just like the old days? She'd been his only constant, the other half of a whole, the part that was missing. Would that still be true? Or, would he only become further disheartened because, just as with his sons, too many wounds had been inflicted that could not be healed?

From the very first moment he'd laid eyes upon her, he'd been smitten. Over the intervening months, and the handful of too-short years, his ardor had bloomed into a full-fledged love that, apparently, had endured through the twenty-five years in which they'd been separated. He'd tried to deny it, tried to tell himself that he'd built a good and solid life without her and their sons. That he'd moved on—as had she—and it had all turned out for the best.

But he didn't really believe it.

He still vividly remembered every aspect of that long-ago Wednesday when he'd returned to London, only to discover that his small family had vanished without a trace. Upon the death of his older brother, Edward had become the earl and thus required to marry. In her head, Angela had rationalized his newly earned responsibility, but in her heart, she'd never come to terms with it.

She'd firmly declared that she couldn't stay to watch, but he hadn't listened to her blaring insistence that she would leave England. He'd never taken her anguish seriously, never aided her in her efforts to find a workable solution. Naively, he'd simply assumed her love was so vast that she would never go.

Many months later, after an extensive investigation, he'd learned their whereabouts, and he'd initially planned to rush to Paris to bring them home, but he'd listened to older—seemingly wiser—counsel. From his uncles. From his father's associates.

With his wedding only weeks away, they had argued, what was to be gained? Why inflict the humiliation on his bride, especially when he would have presently sired his heir? They'd maintained that Angela and the boys were better off away; that they had been naught but a youthful indiscretion. With his destiny at hand, they'd contended, he'd grown beyond illicit relationships and bastard children. The opportunity was ripe to establish himself as a man of consequence among his peers.

Disgustingly, he'd let them convince him to do nothing—a failure to act that had haunted him now for nearly three decades. Because deep in his soul, his great love for Angela had not been immature or wrong. Despite the fact that he'd never married her, he'd considered her to be his wife in every way, and he'd never deemed his children to be illegitimate. They'd been born to devoted parents, wanted and adored, an immense joy.

To his undying shame, his sole response had been to set up a trust account for her. His solicitors had contacted her, and then he'd waited impatiently for news that she'd extracted some of the funds he'd so callously imparted, but she never had. Never so much as a single farthing, and he was compelled to confront the fact, on a daily basis, that they'd gotten along perfectly fine without him. His tough, capable family, the one he'd produced with such delight and impetuosity, hadn't really needed him. It was a bitter tonic to swallow.

Over the years, he'd kept tabs on them, uncovering the details of how they were faring, and of course acquaintances were ever eager to mention when they'd seen her on the stage in Paris. She'd flourished there beyond her wildest dreams, so it had been a wonderful shock and surprise to find out that she had returned to London. But he'd been married, raising his other children, so he'd never visited her, but he'd immediately sought to correct some of his earlier misdeeds.

He'd attempted to establish an association with James, which had never been easy. The boy remembered too little of the fondness that had once bound them together. Yet he was a dutiful and loyal son, a hard worker, who was bright and energetic. Edward had given him the gaming house, knowing that James would thrive at the business, that he'd earn a lot of money, and that he would judiciously use it to care for Angela.

His financial support of his mother had allowed her to continue her acting without the stress over her income. Her passion for the theater had never diminished, and she was as involved as ever, able now to do it for fun instead of as a method for putting food on their table.

Watching her the previous night . . . as she'd captivated and vamped, twirled and floated across the stage . . . That voice! Those eyes! It was as though not a day had passed since he'd last seen her, and he couldn't fathom why he'd delayed so long in dropping by.

What would she say, he tortured himself for the hundredth time, *if she opened the door and saw me standing there?*

Tired of debating over what the answer would be, he forced himself from the carriage and sent the driver on his way. Resolutely, he marched down the block, then climbed the steps. With a shaking hand, he rapped loudly. No sounds emerged, so he knocked again and was rewarded by footsteps. A lock grated, a handle rotated, a door swung back, and . . .

There she was, every bit as vibrant and lovely as he recalled. Her hair had some added strands of silver, and there were a few wrinkles around her beautiful eyes and mouth, but to his uncritical eye, she was as stunning as she'd been on the morning they'd met when she'd been just a seventeen-year-old girl, a struggling, unknown, talented actress with big plans and high hopes, and a zest for living he'd never found matched in another.

"Eddy?" She smiled in that ravishing manner she had. "Is it really you?"

"Yes, Angie." He paused, suddenly shy as a green lad with his first crush. "May I come in?"

"I thought you'd never ask."

She stepped aside to allow him entrance, then closed the door and gave him a tight hug and, easy as that, it was as though he'd never been gone a single day.

Michael walked slowly toward their house, relieved when he viewed their stoop. He stunk like the dockside tavern where he'd finally located James. Retrieving his older brother from the place had been difficult, however, so he was covered with grime, his jacket sleeve ripped, his shirt-front speckled with some unlucky fellow's blood. His fingers ached from the punches he'd thrown, and his ribs hurt where he'd caught several blows. He yearned for a hot bath, then he would fall into bed for a few hours of mindless oblivion before he had to be back at the club for the beginning of the evening of play.

James was lagging somewhere behind, but Michael refused to look over his shoulder to see if his incorrigible sibling was following. At the moment, James could stumble off the face of the earth and Michael wouldn't care overly much about the loss.

The Saturday night debacle at the theater had dispatched customers and acquaintances to the gaming house, eager to relay all the sordid particulars. That James had had a public encounter with Edward Stevens was bad enough, but that he'd aired so much of their family's private business in such a common fashion was unforgivable. Their continuing conflict with Edward was nobody's affair, especially not those toplofty bastards—the lowlifes and slackers of High Society—that Stevens called his peers.

James was the only person who grasped how deeply Michael loathed their father, for the simple reason that James had also survived Edward's abandonment. Though Michael always insisted he didn't recall Edward from their childhood, he was lying. He had several precious and distinct memories of the father whom he had loved beyond imagining, which only served to increase his current level of disregard for the man.

James knew—he knew!—how horribly upsetting any sort of altercation would be, yet he had forged ahead and involved himself in a spat. Michael's opinion was that they should keep Edward Stevens out of their lives, proceeding as though they had no father. After all, it was what Edward had intended, yet James persisted in imposing the blackguard into their peaceful existence at every turn.

Michael didn't know what Edward had privately said to James after they'd removed themselves from all those gawking onlookers in the theater lobby, but whatever his comments, they had sent James into an appalling decline. When he hadn't returned to the club Saturday night, Michael hadn't worried. Sunday morning hadn't caused much concern, either. But as Sunday night had approached and there had been no word, Michael had begun to fret, and he'd dispersed several of their most discreet employees onto the dark streets, but James hadn't been at any of his usual haunts.

It had taken most of Monday to ferret him out. Drunk and raging, he'd been wagering at a seedy tavern notorious for its despicable clientele and the disgusting pastimes that were practiced in the back rooms. With a whore on his lap, and having lost several thousand pounds to an Italian sea captain who was probably cheating, he had refused to vacate the premises, and his fellow gamblers hadn't been content to see him go until his debts were squared. With assistance from the three employees who'd accompanied him—and none from his brother—Michael had forcibly dragged James out, even as he wondered why he didn't just leave James to his own devices.

All the while, he couldn't help pondering what had really happened to James. His brother had suffered through previous antagonistic disagreements with Edward, too many to count, so his condition had been far beyond that which Edward's reprimand would have induced. Something else was eating at him, something that had him delirious with frustration and completely out of control.

It was the woman's fault, Michael suspected. That Abigail Weston. Since the theater debacle, the bloody female had dared to relay five unsigned messages for James to the club. Though they contained no signature, Michael was well aware of who had authored them. In each, she begged and pleaded with James for a rendezvous.

James continued to fabricate and lie, but Michael had worked out the truth: James was involved with her, yet she was prancing about London on Edward's arm and rumored to be his new lady love. Without a doubt, she was the underlying explanation for James's recent breakdown, and Michael planned to deal with her as soon as he could get his brother into some kind of stable situation.

If the blasted woman didn't have the good sense to leave James alone, Michael intended to see to it that she recognized the error of her ways. No way in hell was his mother going to endure a repeated calamity like the occasion when James had married his spoiled little *ton* princess. There were numerous methods Michael could devise to ensure that Lady Abigail listened to reason, and he would try all of them until he achieved his goal. The idiotic noblewoman needed to scurry back to her ivory tower before her irresponsible behavior perpetuated any more chaos.

Overly fatigued, frightened for his brother, craving solitude, he stuck his key in the lock and entered the foyer. It was strange to be home so late in the day; if his mother was still about, she'd certainly be amazed to see him. By this hour, he was always at work, setting up the cash drawers, or checking the liquor inventory, or doing any of the dozens of chores that were required before the crowd of wealthy patrons overwhelmed them.

Not wishing to worry her unduly, he hadn't told her that James had run off, or that he'd been retrieved from one of his unacceptable circumstances, yet her elder son was about to blunder in sporting a black eye, fat lip, torn clothing, and reeking of cheap perfume and stale liquor. Their dear mother could put up with a lot, but even *she* had her limits, and she had to be warned of James's plight.

One of the servants scurried for his things, then he started up the stairs. Down the hall in the dining room, his mother was chattering gaily, and the sound lifted his lagging spirits, although he was curious as to who was visiting. He was hardly prepared to meet with guests.

Still, he had to speak with her before James's undesirable arrival. Thinking to catch her eye, he tiptoed to the door and peeked inside, and the sight that greeted him froze the blood in his veins.

Edward Stevens! The cad was sitting in the chair at the head of the table as though he belonged there! He wore one of James's robes and nothing else. The robe was open, his chest bared, and Michael felt foolish as his first cogent thought was that his father appeared older than he ought; his chest hair was gray with only a small sprinkling of the brown it had once been.

Angela was perched on his lap, clothed only in a robe herself. It, too, was parted, her cleavage and most of her breasts were visible. Her long hair was brushed out and hanging down her back. Her bosom was pressed against him, and she dangled a strawberry for him while he playfully took tiny bites.

They looked to be exactly what they were: a pair of lovers who had just enjoyed some rather extensive bed play. They were rumpled and mussed, smiling, and staring into each other's eyes with such glowing affection that he was terrified and disgusted.

He had no idea how many paramours his mother had had over the years; though he suspected there had been a few. She always had male friends, but her sex life was her own business, so he'd never inquired as to the depth of her relationship with any of them. Certainly he'd never before caught any of them sneaking out of her bed, and he'd never had to face any of them across his breakfast table!

For it to have occurred now, on this ghastly afternoon! With this man of all men! What game did Stevens play, that he risked breaching the sanctity of their home? They didn't need him; they didn't want him! After all he'd done, he had an incredible amount of gall to speak with Angela, let alone tup her!

Angela reached for a glass of champagne and tipped it to Edward's lips. He drank, then steadied the glass as she sipped from the same spot on the rim. They were giggling, stealing kisses, and whispering like besotted newlyweds.

Trembling with rage, he burst into the room and hissed, "Get your filthy paws off of her!"

They jumped at being startled but didn't move apart, as though they were already so completely connected that nothing could divide them.

"Michael," Angela chided, but she was laughing as she said his name, "you scared the life out of me." Then she realized her untenable state and tugged at the lapels of her robe. "Oh, my"—she blushed like an innocent lass—"this is so embarrassing. I hadn't expected either of you boys to be about. . . ."

Edward straightened in the chair as she closed the front of his robe, as well. He kept a proprietary hand on her waist, murmured something in her ear, and she bit back another giggle. He was blushing, too, but showed no remorse for his lewd, outrageous conduct.

"Hello, Michael," he said.

He flashed a smile of such genuine affection that Michael burned with fury. How dare he come here! How dare he do this! "Get away from him, Mother," he decreed, but she didn't comply, so he yelled, "I said, get away from him!"

"I can't believe you are ordering me about," she reproached. "I swear, your manners have flown out the window!"

He turned his furious regard to Edward and bellowed, "Let her go!"

When neither of them paid any attention to his dictate, he stormed around the table, grabbed his mother's arm, yanked her to her feet, and pulled her off of him.

"Michael!" his father scolded, rising. His chair toppled over. "Don't treat your mother so."

Michael felt as if he'd gone mad. In his entire life, he'd never raised his voice to his mother. He'd assuredly never manhandled her! But his distress at seeing her with Edward was so immense that some sort of crazed animal seemed to have inhabited his body. "Don't speak to me about my mother." His tone was cold and deadly. "She is none of your concern. *I* am none of your concern."

"Calm down, son," Edward gently remarked.

To be hailed as *son* by this man was more than he could abide. He stepped forward and seized Edward by the front of James's robe, shaking him once, then pushing him against the wall. "I have no father, and I am not your son."

"Michael!" his mother retorted sharply. "Apologize this instant!"

"I will not!"

Then she did the very worst thing he could possibly imagine: She turned to Edward and burrowed herself against his side. His arm came protectively across her shoulders, and he hugged her close. Their mutual response appeared to be a betrayal—of himself and James, of the family they'd sustained on their own without any of Edward's assistance.

"Well, if you won't apologize," she berated him, "I'll certainly do it for you." She gazed tenderly at Edward. "I didn't rear him up to act so abominably."

"I know you didn't," Edward said, smirking as though they shared a secret joke, then he applied his angry concentration to Michael. "Your mother and I wish to discuss several matters with you. But I won't allow you to hurt her, so I ask that you cool down. We'll proceed as rational adults, or not at all."

Michael had no intention of talking with Edward Stevens. He couldn't conceive of a single topic the man could possibly address that would be worth hearing, so he did not meet Edward's challenging glare. Instead, he focused on Angela. "Mother, go to your room."

"Oh, for pity's sake," she grumbled. "I will not! You're acting like a petulant, willful child. Is this the kind of person you want your father to suppose you are?"

"I don't care what he thinks of me!" Michael roared. His world was tipping upside down, and he was rapidly losing his balance. "Will you allow him to do this to you again?"

"Do what?" she queried irately in return. "He didn't *do* anything before."

"He used you," Michael shouted. "He toyed with you, just as he's toying with you now, and he'll break your heart a second time. He's to be married soon! To another one of those girls. Don't you want more from life than to play his whore while he scurries home at night to snuggle with his own kind? Have you no pride?"

Angela promptly slapped him as hard as she could. As she'd never struck him before, not with so much as a swat on the bottom when he was a lad, it was an astonishing moment for both of them. Tears welled to her beautiful blue eyes, and she covered her mouth. "Oh, Michael . . ." she implored. "I'm so sorry. Forgive me—"

"Don't beg his pardon when he's behaving so contemptibly," Edward cut in. "If you hadn't slapped him, I would have." He cradled her more tightly in the circle of his arms. Already they'd transformed themselves into one unit. They were of like mind, separate and distinct from their son, and Edward shifted her so that she was behind his body and shielded from Michael's wrath. "Your mother and I have decided to marry."

Michael shook his head in dismay, taking a step back, then another. "No . . . you can't mean it."

" 'Tis true, Michael," Angela said. "We should have done it years ago . . ."

"So we're doing it now." Edward finished the thought for her.

"This can't be happening. . . ." Michael was choking on his denial. "Please tell me it's not true." But from Angela's compassionate demeanor, he knew it was.

"I didn't intend for you to find out like this. . . ." She held out her hand in entreaty, but he stared at it as though it were a venomous snake.

Just then, James entered, but Angela was so enamored with Edward that she didn't so much as notice his dishevelment.

On observing the frozen tableau and Michael's startled expression, James's gaze settled on his father. "Why are you here?"

Before either of his parents could answer, Michael said crudely, "The bastard crept in here while we were out and crawled into her bed like the vermin he is." He snorted with derision. "He claims that he's going to marry her this time."

"Aren't we lucky?" James murmured. He assessed his parents, their state of undress, the gleam in their eyes, the patent admiration, and the evidence of what they'd been about for the past two days was unmistakable. In disgust, he commanded his father, "Get out."

"I don't recall asking him to leave," Angela admonished furiously.

"Perhaps I should," Edward remarked placatingly, but to Angela, not to James. Appearing forlorn, but love-struck, he regarded her adoringly. "We can hash this out when we're all more calm."

"No," she replied. "This is *my* home. You don't go unless I request it."

"Weren't you listening, Eddy?" James menaced. "You're not welcome here."

"Oh, but he is," Angela announced firmly, "and he shall be."

"Never," James asserted. "Not in this house where he caused so much heartache and pain."

"Is this my house or isn't it, James?" Angela pressed. There was a long, charged silence, and she added, "You always maintained that you bought it for me, so I consider it mine, and I say he stays."

"Mother . . ." James pleaded softly, "don't do this to Michael and me. Don't do it to yourself."

"Then don't force me to choose between you. My decision is already made, and I don't think you'll care for it."

"You don't *need* him in your life."

"Oh, but I do, James. You know I do. I want to be happy. 'Tis all I've ever wanted." She waited an eternity for some tiny signal of his acceptance of her life-altering decision, but none came. Both her sons were too set against their father, too adamant in their feelings. Finally, her disappointment and indignation gravely apparent, she shrugged sadly. "All right, then. I'll begin packing—"

"No . . ." James breathed, aghast and perturbed.

"Come, darling," she said to Edward, and she linked their fingers. Together, they headed for the door.

"Mother, you can't do this!" James persisted. "I won't let you."

" 'Tis not up to you," she declared.

They kept walking, and as they passed, Edward laid a sympathetic hand on James's shoulder. "I'm sorry," he admitted, "for what occurred between us on Saturday night. I was upset and overwrought, and I didn't mean what I said. Please stop by my club tomorrow so we can talk about it."

James shook off the unwelcomed touch. "Leave me be."

With a collective sigh, their parents continued on, and at the last moment Angela noted over her shoulder, "Should you wish to contact me, I'll be staying at the Carlysle. Just until everything is finalized. . . ."

She closed the door with a resounding click, her exit perfectly timed to be fabulous, as always.

In the absolute quiet that followed, Michael whirled on James. In some manner—he wasn't certain how or why—this was all James's fault. His brother opened his mouth to speak, but Michael stared him down with such rancor that no words emerged. "Don't you say a bloody thing to me."

He lifted a vase off the sideboard, threw the flowers onto the floor, then flung it against the fireplace, where it shattered into dozens of pieces. Because he felt so much better after, he stalked around the table, removing all the china and stemware and tossing it, as well. Frantically, he hurled every breakable object in the room until, from the middle of a mountain of broken glass, his breathing labored, his heart breaking, he decided that he could do no more damage.

Unable to hide the flood of blistering, tumultuous tears, he hurried for the door. James, who had observed his frenzy with tolerant reticence, reached out to stop him, but Michael raced past.

"Michael . . . wait . . ." James called. "Don't go."

But he kept on, down the hall, down the stairs, out to the street. Running. Running as fast as he could.

SEVENTEEN

With a trembling hand, Abigail knocked at the door of James's home. As it was late in the day, he was at work, preparing for the night ahead, but she hadn't come to see him. Not that she hadn't considered it, but if he'd learned she was waiting on his front step, he'd not have allowed her in.

Most likely, his residential servants were as efficient as the ones he employed at his club. There, his competent staff had regularly prevented her entrance until, on her fourth attempt, one gentleman had kindly, but bluntly, told her that they had standing orders—from James Stevens himself— to turn her away.

It had been nearly two weeks since their ghastly encounter at the theater. She'd sent him so many notes, begging for a meeting, but they had been all for naught. He'd answered with silence.

Each Monday and Thursday afternoon, she'd gone to their secret hideaway, hoping he'd show. Even if it was anger that motivated him, she'd not have minded, for she absolutely had to speak with him. Assuredly, she needed to apologize for her abominable behavior, but more than anything, she was frantic to ask him about Lady Newton and what his offensive paramour had said.

She had to learn the truth! The woman's words were tormenting her. During the never-ending days and nights that now stretched endlessly together without James, Barbara Ritter's hateful diatribe was an unceasing litany that rampaged on and on until Abigail had begun to imagine that she just might go mad from listening to it.

Had James, by bedding her, simply been playing some sort of evil, wicked game? Had it been a crude sham on his part? She refused to believe it; she would *not* believe it until she could confront him face-to-face.

The door opened, and a servant rudely glared at her. She was a sight, in her dark clothing and cloak, with no coach or escort and dusk approaching.

"May I help you?" the man inquired.

"I would like to speak with Mrs. Angela Ford."

"I don't think she's receiving visitors. Have you a card?"

"No . . . I . . ."

The retainer *tsk*ed at this appalling breach of good manners. "Then, madam, I am quite confident that she is *not* at home," and he commenced closing the door in her face.

"But this will only take a moment." She added, "Please. . . ."

She sounded desperate, and she was. At her wits' end, she could conjure no other means of proceeding. James deeply loved and respected his mother, so Abigail intended to inappropriately impose on Mrs. Ford, requesting that she convince James to attend a final meeting. A last rendezvous would allow Abigail to make verbal amends and to raise the questions that had been driving her insane, and thus she hoped to ease her guilty conscience and her aggrieved heart.

From behind the stoic houseman came a husky, full-bodied female voice, and Abigail instantly recognized it as that of Mrs. Ford.

"Who is it, Arthur?" she asked.

" 'Tis a visitor, ma'am. With no card of introduction, so I don't know her name." He blocked Mrs. Ford with the door, but he glanced out, giving Abigail a chance to reveal herself, but she declined with a quick shake of her head.

"I'll handle it," Mrs. Ford said.

"If you're sure?" Arthur looked overly worried, as though Abigail might do something nefarious to his employer if admitted inside.

"I'm fine, Arthur. Truly." She stepped into view, and the servant retreated as she called to his departing back, "There are two boxes in the back bedchamber. Could you fetch them down for me?"

As she focused her attention on Abigail, Abigail was impaled by those intense sapphire eyes, and she suffered a hasty intake of breath. At the theater, in wig and makeup, it had been difficult to discern her resemblance to James, but up close, their similarities were uncanny. She was just as striking as her handsome, seductive son. More so, if that was possible.

Taller than Abigail, she was lithe yet buxom, a stunning beauty trying to hide her appeal in homemaker's drab clothing, which was laughable. Angela Ford's charisma was simply too blatant to disguise in a gray dress, white apron, and conservative chignon. She appeared ready to burst out of her plain costume in order to reveal the majestic person concealed underneath.

"Thank you for agreeing to see me," Abigail said.

"Are you here about James? Or Michael?" she queried without preamble. "If you're wanting one of them, Michael is out of Town, and James is temporarily staying at their club."

"I didn't know . . ." Abigail murmured, disturbed by this turn of events.

" 'Tis a long story," Mrs. Ford remarked, gesturing dramatically as though she'd love nothing more than to tell it then and there. "But let's get you off the stoop, shall we? You obviously desire a discreet discussion, so we hardly need all the neighbors gawking."

Mr.. Ford flashed a confident, knowing smile, so radiant and full of dazzle that Abigail was temporarily paralyzed by it, but she shook herself into action as the other woman disappeared into the house, and she had to follow or lose her opportunity.

They entered a parlor on the second floor, and Mrs. Ford seated herself on a large sofa, directing Abigail to the one across. Abigail went through the motions, taking extra time in adjusting her skirts, while in reality, she was furtively surveying the well-appointed chamber. James lived here, passed his private hours here! He probably enjoyed that chair by the window, threw a log on that hearth. She savored the moment, wanting to imprint every color, shape, and image so that she'd remember all the details after she left.

It was clearly a pleasantly decorated residence, designed for use by a robust family. The drapes and rugs were brightly done in reds and greens, the furniture overstuffed and comfortable. The walls were covered with outstanding watercolors of Paris street corners, and Abigail suffered a sharp pang wondering if they'd been painted by James's friend Pierre, who had created his notorious collection of erotic pictures. She was dying to sneak a peek at the artist's signature, but she restrained herself, forcing herself to concentrate on her task.

In one corner, there were several shipping crates. Household belongings were haphazardly dumped inside. On observing Abigail's curiosity, Mrs. Ford breezily explained, "I'm moving out."

"You're what?" Abigail wasn't certain she'd heard correctly. She sagged a little, not understanding why, but something about the deed seemed wrong.

"Moving," Mrs. Ford repeated. "I've had a huge disagreement with my sons, so I'm abandoning them. But I'm sure they'll survive without me." A servant came by with a refreshment tray. Mrs. Ford glanced at Abigail, but Abigail was too nervous to consider any sustenance, and the maid retired from the room. When they were alone once more, Mrs. Ford faced Abigail.

"All right, let's have it," she said. "Is it James or Michael?"

"James," Abigail replied.

"Are you in the family way?" Mrs. Ford questioned bluntly.

Abigail gasped, her cheeks coloring to a flaming scarlet. In deciding to call, it had never occurred to her that James's mother might form such a low opinion.

As she stumbled for a response, Mrs. Ford continued.

"Because if you are, I'm not sure what I could do about it. James is a grown man, and my opinion holds very little sway with him. Besides, he wed previously after a dalliance, and it was quite horrid for him. I wouldn't demand that he endure such a fate again, and I'd definitely never pressure him to marry someone he didn't love."

"I'm carrying no babe," Abigail assured her, though a part of her wished her visit were about that very subject. She could fathom no greater miracle than to be increasing with James's child.

"Well, then," Mrs. Ford mused in her succinct fashion, "what brings you here?"

"James is a friend of mine."

Mrs. Ford raised a dubious brow. "Really? I wasn't aware that he had any female *friends*. I'm quite confident that he intends another purpose entirely for his feminine companions."

"Be that as it may," Abigail pressed ahead, "he is a close friend. Perhaps the best I've ever had."

"Sorry . . ."—Angela shrugged casually, disbelieving—"but he's never mentioned this purported *friendship* to me."

"I don't know that he would," Abigail persisted. "Our association has been rather . . . well . . ."

"Clandestine?"

"Yes."

"How charming," Mrs. Ford muttered sarcastically.

"I'm very worried about him."

"So am I," his mother allowed. "I have been for a long while."

Abigail was apprehensive about how much to say, but she wanted the entire, sordid story out in the open, so she started with, "I attended the theater, Saturday last, with the Earl of Spencer"—Mrs. Ford perked to attention at Edward's name—"and I caused a row between James and his father. I didn't mean to," she hurried on. "One minute, James was standing before me, and I was so astonished that I behaved atrociously by pretending I didn't know who he was, and the next, he was demanding that the earl introduce us, and then . . . then . . ."

"Yes, yes," Mrs. Ford interrupted, waving away additional clarification, "many, many people told me all about it." Appalled, she deduced, "You're one of the Weston girls, aren't you? One of Jerald Weston's sisters?"

"I am." Abigail couldn't see any reason to sustain her ruse now that she'd been discovered, and she gained immense relief by admitting her identity to James's mother.

Aghast, Mrs. Ford fumed. "You're having a sexual affair with James?"

"We have been . . ." Abigail whispered.

"Oh, Lord," Mrs. Ford groaned. "How long has this been going on?"

"For several weeks now," Abigail acknowledged.

"Well . . . that explains many things."

"Like what?"

"Like why my family is in such a disordered mess," Mrs. Ford responded irascibly. "If you truly know James's propensities as you claim, then you must be aware of his feelings regarding his father. Why would you provoke him while waltzing about on Edward's arm? Do you have any idea of the damage you've wrought?"

"I never planned to hurt him!"

"But you did," she chided, "and several others, yet I'm supposed to gather that you've developed a deep attachment with him."

"I'm so in love with him that I can hardly breathe."

"And what are *his* sentiments about this *amour* that he's never disclosed to me?"

"He loves me, as well. Very much," Abigail contended, but even as she finished the assertion, it seemed terribly embellished.

"Pardon me for being skeptical, my lady"—she shifted forward in her seat—"but I comprehend my son's motives extremely well. Better than you obviously do. James does *not* fall in love, he does *not* have meaningful relationships, and he most certainly does *not* fornicate with pretty women as though there is some higher purpose behind it."

"Don't make it sound so tawdry," Abigail pleaded. "There's so much more between us than mere lust."

"What were you thinking," she scoffed, "embroiling yourself so recklessly in my son's life? Have you any idea of the furor you will cause if you are discovered? You say you care for James. If so, why would you risk putting him in such a predicament?"

"I hardly know where to start. . . ." Abigail attempted to elucidate, but hastily realized that she wasn't very convincing. "From the first moment I met him, I couldn't resist, and with each passing day, my love for him has grown until I can't abide my life without him in it."

The silence was prolonged as Mrs. Ford studied her. Then she rose and went to the sideboard, pouring herself three fingers of a pungent brandy. "Would you like one?" she offered, but Abigail said no. As the older woman pensively sipped, Abigail watched, jealous of her freedom and confidence, of her ability to do something as shocking as enjoy hard spirits in the middle of the day.

Angela Ford was a female who had always lived exactly as she chose, others' opinions be damned. She'd done things and gone places about which Abigail could only fantasize. Where Mrs. Ford reveled in autonomy and adventure, Abigail struggled with routine, boredom, and duty. She was twenty-five years old, and she could scarcely leave the house without obtaining her brother's permission first.

How she wished she could be more like Angela Ford!

As Abigail stared covetously, Mrs. Ford tarried along the wall, sampling her liquor until the quiet became jarring, then she returned to the sofa, and Abigail couldn't resist filling the void. "I apologize for the subterfuge. I just didn't want to be . . . to be . . ."

"Seen on my doorstep; yes, I comprehend your dilemma. You and your bloody kind," Mrs. Ford grumbled, though not uncharitably, as though the same criticism had been leveled at her a thousand times before. "Sorry, Lady Abigail, but I don't understand you. You're here, presumably, because of your concern for James, but considering the fact that you don't want anyone to ascertain your acquaintance, I'm having a bit of trouble in generating any empathy for you. My son is such a dynamic, fine man—"

"I know, I know," Abigail readily agreed. "He is."

"Any woman should be proud to be in his company. For you to be ashamed of him, to try and conceal your connection, well . . ." She swallowed down the remaining contents of the glass and set it on the small table with a resounding crack. "I don't have much sympathy for your problem. *Whatever* it is."

Abigail appreciated how she must appear: a snobbish, wealthy, pampered noblewoman with no integrity, no scruples, and nothing to occupy her time but immoral, destructive liaisons. As she'd recently learned so painfully, she *was* the type of despicable woman who would privately trifle with a man of lower station, but who wouldn't speak to him in public later on, so some of the appalling perceptions Mrs. Ford had of her character were unquestionably deserved.

But I don't want to be this kind of person, she yearned to shout. She wanted to be more like Angela: independent, brave enough to throw caution to the wind, to impetuously plunge forth, conferring free rein to her love for James. But to what end?

Their affair would never be more than a physical diversion for him. He would never marry her, and she wasn't foolish enough to deem such a happy conclusion as being likely. If James could be convinced to recommence with their assignations, they would continue as lovers until the terrifying day arrived when he decided he was bored and inclined to move on, and she would be left heartbroken and alone.

In the meantime, she would have been excommunicated from her family, totally shunned, cut off from everything and everyone. She would never be allowed to see her dear sister again, or the ancestral home, or the smattering of relatives around whom she'd grown up. Labeled as a female of loose morals, she would become invisible, no one would speak to her, no one would associate with her.

Perhaps a stronger woman would forge ahead, heedless

of the consequences and unconcerned over any dreadful future. Perhaps a more capable one could withstand such a fervent upheaval that would never relent or abate. For if she proceeded to her doom, then year after long year, she would suffer unceasingly for her single, rash act of loving too desperately. She'd be cast out forever, and she simply couldn't tolerate the eventuality of passing the remainder of her days as a scorned, solitary pariah.

"I'm not the woman you perceive me to be," she asserted quietly. "Despite how I came here, and how I appear, I'm *not* ashamed of James or what has happened between us. I honestly don't know how I'll persevere without him. I love him with all that I am, but I realize he'll never marry me—"

"I afraid you're right about that," Mrs. Ford concurred gently.

"—and I am too much of a coward to face, on my own, the aftereffects of our romance should it become common knowledge. If I thought he would stay by my side, I would attempt any hurdle."

"That's something, I guess," Mrs. Ford murmured. "So . . . what is it you would have me do?"

"Please . . . just speak to him on my behalf. Encourage him to meet with me on Thursday. He'll know where and when."

"And the reason for this meeting would be . . ."

"That I might apologize, and tell him how much I have loved him."

"I assume you're also hoping to have another chance to be intimate with him." The candid comment caused another furious blush to color Abigail's cheeks, and Mrs. Ford chided, "You've been lucky so far, but perhaps on the next occasion you will accidentally wind up pregnant. Then what?"

Abigail scooted forward and reached out, taking Mrs. Ford's hand in her own. "He has so much anger. At himself. At his father. I can't bear that I've made it worse by my irresponsible conduct. I hate that it's ended like this."

Mrs. Ford pulled away and walked to the sideboard again, pouring another brandy, but then not drinking any. She swirled the amber contents around and around in the glass. "If I could have one wish granted," she finally said, " 'twould be to see James married to a woman who truly cares for him. If I had a second, I would wish he had sons to bring him joy—as mine have imparted such gladness to me, but I am beginning to doubt such happiness will ever occur for him. I don't know . . ."—she shook her head dejectedly—"perhaps if I'd done things differently all those years ago . . ."

"Don't second-guess your actions," Abigail insisted compassionately. "You did what you thought was best at the time."

"Yes, I did," Mrs. Ford concluded halfheartedly, "but I've never been persuaded that I chose the correct path, although, looking back, perhaps there was no *correct* choice. There were only victims; mainly my sons." With a sigh, as though she'd determined to sustain an untenable burden, she straightened her shoulders. "I'm sorry, Lady Abigail, but I'm afraid you've wasted your time by coming here. I won't talk to James for you. He wouldn't listen to me, and I can't say that I'd want him to."

Abigail had erroneously thought they were making headway, and she could only watch in agony as her last chance with James dissolved to ashes. "Please—" she begged.

"No," Mrs. Ford interrupted. "While I long for James to find contentment in his life, you could never be the one to bring it to him."

"I love him!"

"I'm sure you *think* you do."

"I love him more than my life."

"But you've said naught to convince me that James shares your emotional attachment, and, as you've pointed out, he will never marry you. He's well aware of what a disaster such a union would be." With a flick of her wrist, she downed the brandy, eyeing Abigail with a stern expression that silently told her the meeting was over.

Abigail felt as though she were clinging to a sinking ship, that she was fast losing her grip. "I promise that he and I will just talk."

"I understand my son's behaviors. I appreciate what kind of *meeting* the two of you would have, and I won't do anything that might help you create a babe together. I would never want another child to suffer as my boys did." She walked to the door of the parlor. "Forget about James, Lady Abigail. Despite how much you currently wish it, he's not the man for you. Go home and don't come back. I'll have Arthur show you out."

Abigail paced about the bedchamber, her ears straining toward the stairs. Presently, exactly at the hour of two, the front door opened, and her heart skipped a beat. Despite Mrs. Ford's assertions to the contrary, she must have said something to James. Just as Abigail had been hoping she might.

He'd come! He'd really and truly come!

Wanting to appear calm and collected, she hustled to the bed and reclined against the pillows. Leaving nothing to chance, she'd staged the room to entice him. There was a fire in the grate, food and wine on the table, scented candles burning in their holders.

Hoping to tempt him beyond his limits, she'd donned the red outfit he'd sent. Dressed only in the crimson pantalets, stockings, and heels, she'd shed the top that cupped her breasts in such an erotic fashion, leaving them bare, with the raised nipples just visible through the filmy fabric of the robe. The lapels were parted at the center to reveal her cleavage and abdomen.

Her hair was down in the fashion he liked, brushed and curling around her hips; her lips were tinted a rosy hue. Worry had elevated her pulse and flushed her cheeks to a becoming pink. She appeared luxurious, sensual, and ready to provide unceasing pleasure to the man who was about to walk over the threshold.

If only he would let her!

James was furious with her, and would probably refuse to talk candidly, so she had to have a method of breaking through any barriers he erected. Without a doubt, making love was the perfect way to center his attention and ensure that his anger faded. With a little effort on her part, he'd revert to the loving, charming person to whom she'd lost her heart.

As her relationship with James was her one and only dalliance, and this, her first and only attempt at significant seduction, it had never occurred to her that she wouldn't succeed. The possibility that James might be too wounded to accept her apology had not crossed her mind, and she declined to consider that there might be a negative outcome. James would forgive her! He loved her, and she loved him, and in her naïveté she was convinced that their strong emotions could cure all that ailed them.

The door swung open, and she braced herself as he stepped through. He looked as poorly as she felt, which she took to be a very good sign. He'd obviously been suffering! Surely he'd be prepared to set aside their differences.

Gone was the pristine coat, the perfectly tailored trousers, the highly polished boots. He was casually attired in a loose-fitting shirt, leather vest, wool trousers, and a pair of worn boots, making him look as if he'd just been riding or hunting. His hair was overly long and in need of a trim; he hadn't shaved and beard stubble darkened his face.

Without speaking, he moved to the foot of the bed and started a crude assessment. Beginning at the tip of her head and roving down, he rudely perused all that she had intimately displayed. Where before he'd gazed at her with lust that had been a definite mix of fondness and affection, now there was a studied apathy, and she received the distinct impression that it could be she or another lying there so scantily clad. With rising dread, she recognized that she'd already become one of the women from his past.

Prior to arriving, she'd rehearsed a dozen speeches, but now, staring at him across an expanse as vast as an ocean, her contrived words flew out the window. Nothing seemed appropriate.

"Hello, James," she finally said, shattered and afraid.

"You went to see my mother."

This cold, hard individual was not anyone with whom she was acquainted. Sitting before him, nearly naked as the day she was born, she felt foolish and silly. Had she imagined their ardent affinity? Had those handful of heady exchanges actually transpired? Perhaps she had dreamed it all.

Clearly, she'd mistaken his physical ardor for something else. Lady Newton had hinted as much, and Angela Ford had bluntly insisted that any perception of James developing an emotional attachment was erroneous. Apparently, both women had been correct. This stranger, who was so annoyed with her, could never have possessed an ounce of kind sentiment.

What had she been thinking, to offer herself in this manner? She wasn't one of his doxies. Desiring escape—from the room, the house, *him*—she slipped to the edge of the bed, but her clothes were behind the screen, as far away as America. How she yearned for the ability to perform a magical feat whereby she could reappear somewhere else, hidden from his view.

Unfortunately, there was no magic available to resolve her predicament. She'd have to rise and walk past him with his calculating eyes following, and the idea of him watching, while her folly was so plainly evident to them both, was too much, and she couldn't force her legs to take a single step.

So . . . she sat, shoulders slumped, the belt of her tiny robe tied across her waist but not shielding much. Tears threatened, but she'd never allow them to fall because she would never give him the satisfaction of discovering how distressed she was.

He'd rounded the bed, but she failed to notice until she saw the toes of his boots.

"What do you want?" he asked irritably.

"It doesn't matter now." She pretended a fascination

with his footwear, noting the scuff marks, the spots of dirt, the heel that was slightly tattered, and she strove to picture where he'd been in those boots, what he'd been doing; anything to occupy her mind so that she didn't dwell too much on where he was at that very moment.

"You were bold enough to visit Angela. In my home"— he was excessively angry about it—"so it must have been something important. Whatever it is, your *ladyship*—"

"Don't call me that."

"Don't call you what? *Lady* Abigail? Isn't that who and what you are?" She could sense that he shrugged, his furious regard running over her like a hot towel. "Whatever you have to say, say it! Say it all! Unburden yourself. Get it off your chest. I'll not have you badgering my mother ever again."

"I just thought . . ." But as soon as she embarked on the sentence, she realized she couldn't finish it. What exactly had she thought? Her asinine plans were completely idiotic to the situation in which she'd landed herself.

"What?" He prodded like a burr under a saddle.

"I had hoped we could talk," she finally professed. "I wanted to apologize for how I conducted myself at the theater."

"Are you sorry?"

"Don't be cruel, James." She whispered his beloved name, but it felt like crunching down on ice. "You know I am."

"I know nothing of the sort. In my experience, members of your exalted *station*"—his rebuke was stinging—"behave however they please. You'd previously warned me that you would feign disinterest if we met in public; I expected no different conduct from you."

"Well, I expected more from myself. I hurt you, and I'm sorry I've made you so upset."

"Don't flatter yourself, milady," he derided, "into presuming that you have any effect on my day-to-day goings-on. My current mood has absolutely nothing to do with you."

"What is it, then? Why are you acting like this? Why are you speaking to me so horridly?" She found the courage to raise her eyes to his, and she was astonished by what she saw. For the briefest instant, she observed torment, grief, and heartbreak, much more injury than she could have caused by her public slight at the Chelsey Theater. As quickly as she accepted his agony for what it was, he cloaked it behind a frozen mask of ire and ennui.

Quietly, she inquired, "What's happened to put you in such a state? Is it your father?"

He whirled away, lest she discern more of his anguish. Stalking to the table, he poured some wine and drank it down. "My father is fine. So is my mother. So is my whole bloody family." He set the glass on the table so hard that the stem cracked. "Now, was there anything else?"

"Your mother said she was moving out of your home." She pushed at his vulnerable points, driving him to respond. "Did you have a disagreement with her?"

"I don't fight with my mother."

"Who, then?"

"My brother." She was surprised by the admission and, apparently, he was, too. Unsettled, he went to the window, drew back the curtain, and glared down into the street. "My parents have decided to marry. . . ."

She was so startled that she couldn't immediately respond. The Earl of Spencer was finally going to break down and marry Mrs. Ford! What had precipitated their decision? When would the wedding occur? Where would they live? When would the announcements be sent? What explanations would they provide?

Edward had certainly kept it a grand secret, and she wondered if he'd broken the news to his other children yet—and if their reactions had been anything like this!

She was dying to interrogate James as to all the details but didn't dare. He was so distressed that she'd only end up making matters worse, but she wasn't about to falsify her opinion just to placate him. "That's a marvelous conclusion, James. For both of them."

"I suppose you would think so," he mused, glowering at her over his shoulder. "You always were Eddy's greatest champion. I believe I'll introduce you to my brother, so that you can convince him of Eddy's *honorable* intentions. And I'll be certain to call on you to hold my mother's hand when Eddy breaks her heart again."

"He won't."

"I'm glad one of us can be so sure." He left his spot by the window and approached the bed. Without further comment, he pulled his shirt from his trousers, yanked it over his head, and tossed it on the floor.

Gazing up, she saw the swirls of dark hair covering his chest. She could smell his sweat, and there was a musk about him that she associated with desire. Being eye level with his crotch, she couldn't help noticing that he was aroused. Wanting her. Wanting what she longed to share with him.

"Lie down," he commanded, his fingers tugging at the front of his pants. Momentarily, they were loose about his hips.

While she relished the chance to hold him in her arms, she was so uncertain. Of his motives. Of her own. Of what her next move should be.

She was a novice at these love games. Other, more experienced women might be able to jump from cold animosity to physical mating in nearly the same breath, but she wasn't one of them. She couldn't progress to intimacy unless there was affection attached to the joining. Yet if they made love, she felt certain that she could reestablish them in that special place, which was where she desperately yearned for them to be. Still . . .

"I don't know if I can."

"Why?"

"It just seems wrong."

"Then why are you here, dressed like this?"

She flushed bright crimson. "I thought that you might want to . . ."

"I do," he persisted. "Lie down."

"Answer a question for me first." She shifted so she could look him in the eye. "Have you just been to another woman's bed? Because if you have, I couldn't possibly make love with you." Hastily, she added, "Don't lie to me."

"I've been in the country, searching for my brother. There's a whorehouse in Surrey that he particularly likes."

"Oh . . ."

"But he wasn't there"—he kicked off one boot, then the other—"and I didn't partake of any of the females. I came straight back to London."

Nodding, stalling, she tried to quell her careening emotions. She was so confused about what was best! She craved this so much—apparently so did he—yet she couldn't proceed until she ascertained the truth. "With how many . . ." She swallowed, blushed a brighter scarlet, then forced the words on a rush of air. "With how many virgins have you lain?"

"Two. You and my wife." His answer was honest and succinct as he scowled down at her. "Why would you even ask me such an absurd question?"

"Someone said something . . ." She trailed off, unable to describe the strange, hateful conversation she'd had with Barbara Ritter.

"Who?" he pressed.

"Just . . . one of your companions."

"Which one?" he queried, refusing to let the matter rest.

"Lady Newton." She flinched; speaking the name of one of his other lovers was too excruciating. "I chatted with her that night at the theater. She said that you regularly sought out virgins and lured them to bed—just for sport."

"You believed her?"

"Shouldn't I have?" she asked vehemently.

He gave her a mocking bow. "No doubt that is the kind of man you perceive me to be."

No, no, of course not! she longed to cry, but what emerged was, "I'm just so disconcerted, James. I don't know what's true anymore. And what's not."

He reached for her shoulders and shoved the robe down,

baring her breasts. With a finger and thumb, he manipulated her nipple, and her body's reaction was instantaneous. As though they'd never been apart, as though they'd just made love minutes ago instead of weeks ago, she was hungry for him and what he could provide.

He grabbed for the waist of his trousers and started working them off his hips. "I want you now. Lie back."

EIGHTEEN

James stood in front of her, naked, fully aroused, and unashamed of his virility. His male beauty was irresistible, and without pausing to decide the wisest course, she nuzzled her face against the bristly hair surrounding his privates. When James desired her like this, demanding gratification, she simply couldn't deny him.

Whatever animosity remained, whatever issues still separated them, they could resolve their problems later. For now there was only this extraordinary rush of sensation.

Rooting and nestling along his abdomen, she filled her hand with his erect cock, relishing the throb of his elevated pulse through the eddy of enlarged veins. She cupped his balls, caressing the tender sacs. He groaned his approval, and she rewarded him by drawing him into her mouth.

His taste was so intense, a concoction of sweat and man designed especially to inflame her. Automatically, his hips began flexing in the rhythm she enjoyed so much. His hand was at the back of her head, steadying her, and she eagerly complied with his directions, taking as much of him as she could, his satisfaction serving only to increase her own.

The tip of his phallus oozed with his sexual juice, and her level of anticipation grew. During their prior night of loving, he'd refused to spill himself in her mouth, insisting she wasn't ready, but she knew how greatly he welcomed completion in this fashion, and she hoped he would allow her to pleasure him to the end.

But just as she concluded that this would be the occasion she would endure all, he pulled away and settled her against the pillows. His superb, heavy body pushed her into the mattress, the hair on his chest and legs rubbing against her and causing her to writhe with anticipation.

He didn't kiss her, which disappointed her terribly, but

she didn't complain. In his current state, she couldn't predict how he might react, so she forced herself to be content with whatever he chose to share.

With his mouth at her nipples, he labored over her, sucking formidably, inducing her to thrash and struggle against the fierce stimulation. Never stationary, he touched her everywhere: shoulders, arms, breasts, stomach. He clutched at her pantalet and ripped it away, throwing the swatch of red silk on the floor. Then his fingers were inside her, rough and determined, and her hips instinctively thrust in the carnal tempo he set.

He traveled slowly down her stomach, blazing a stormy trail and spurring her to open for him. Licking at her clit, delving into the folds, he buried himself, lapping at her saturated cleft, and he reveled in her flavor as though imprinting it into his very soul.

She wanted to come, she *needed* to come, but he left her hanging on an appalling cliff of exhilaration, begging and pleading for more.

He kneed her legs apart, then grabbed her thighs, the crest of his erect staff at her center, and he hesitated, staring at the spot where their private parts were barely joined, his swollen cock intense and eager, her blond hairs coaxing him in.

Clasping at her hips, he said, "I am going to fuck you so hard."

"Yes, James," she urged, far beyond the point where she would disagree with him about anything. "Whatever you want . . . please. . . ."

"Never forget," he declared, "that I was the first. The only one."

He immersed himself, his reckless member impaling her so ferociously that it felt like a punishment, but it was chastisement she craved. She arched and widened, giving him all the access he could stand. His hips pounded like the pistons of a huge machine, the impact of his momentum propelling her across the bed until she was shoved into the headboard. Grappling to stabilize herself, she gripped the edge, holding on while she received more of his brutal invasion.

She was stretched to breaking, his cock battering her with each incursion, yet he didn't ease up, nor did she want him to. This frantic, savage coupling was so very distinct from what she'd fantasized might occur that she hoped they never reached the conclusion. There was something so joyous about how desperately James appeared to lust after her that she was almost frightened by his intensity.

Perspiration pooled on his brow; his pelvis buffeted hers. His heart was thumping so stridently that she could see it beating against his ribs. He braced himself on either side of her shoulders, his muscles corded with tension, his fists gripping the pillows. From his level of agitation, she recognized that he'd arrived at the pinnacle where he'd spill his seed. At the last second, when he would have stolen his sexual emission from her, she wrapped her feet around his calves, her arms around his back, and she held him as tightly as she could.

With tortured surprise, he glared down at her, but it was much too late to expect that he could hold off. He plunged deep, deeper than it seemed possible to go, then he emptied himself, and she encountered the flaming spray of his semen against her womb.

Closing her eyes, she whispered a small prayer: *Please God, let us have made a babe.*

For that single moment, she didn't care about the future, about Society, its mores, stigmas, or the ultimate disgrace she might bring down upon her family. She was simply a woman who had been thoroughly loved by the man of her dreams, and her body was crying out for the natural consequence to transpire.

With a final, feral submersion, he shuddered and collapsed, his forehead resting on her bosom, his fiery breath spewing across her sweat-soaked skin. As he gradually relaxed, she used the opportunity to calm herself.

Surely, after all that, he'd have purged his animosity and frustration!

She waited for him to speak, but to her dismay he said nothing, and when he shifted away, he had an unreadable expression on his face. It scared her. She'd been so certain that she would finally behold the love burning in his eye once again. Anxiously, she wet her bottom lip, and the corner of his mouth lifted in a semblance of a smile. Her heart ached. He was so beautiful when he smiled.

Gracing her with a chaste kiss, he said, "I shouldn't have finished that way." He shrugged. "I'm always more careful. I'm sorry for my lack of control."

With that, he tipped himself onto his haunches and stepped to the floor. He retrieved her robe and tossed it to her, then he reached for his trousers and began pulling them on.

"What are you doing?" She watched, horrified.

"I'm needed elsewhere," he replied enigmatically, causing a myriad of hideous images to careen through her mind as she contemplated where he might be *needed*. And by whom.

"But . . . I thought we should talk. . . ."

"About what?"

"Well . . . about us . . . about—"

"Lady Abigail," he interrupted, killing her by articulating her title, "there is no *us*. There never has been. You know better than to believe otherwise."

"James, please. I've apologized. Say you'll give me your pardon."

"Certainly, milady. All is forgiven." He grabbed his shirt, tugged it on.

"But . . . you're still so angry with me."

"Truly, I am not. I simply have many, many more pressing matters with which to contend. Now"—he found a boot, jerked it on. Found the other, jerked it on as well—"if you'll excuse me, I must be off. Thank you for inviting me to your bed. The experience was most . . ." He paused, searching for the appropriate word, then concluded with, "Most rewarding."

Their loving had been so dramatic; she'd been so convinced of the outcome! After what had happened between them, how could he consider withdrawing? "You're going to leave? Just like that?"

"Yes, Abby," he responded more gently. "And I must request that you not ask me another time. Don't bother my mother; don't send me any more notes. I won't answer, and I'll not come again. My visits with you have been an extremely pleasant diversion, but they can't continue. There couldn't possibly be an acceptable conclusion for either one of us." When it looked as though she might argue, he added, "You know I'm right."

"But . . . I love you," she whispered in dismay, and to her ultimate chagrin, tears overflowed and coursed down her cheeks.

"I'm sure you do," he retorted, "but that was a grave mistake on your part. For I don't love you in return." He bent over, took one last, quick kiss, then stood. "Goodbye," he murmured, then he turned and strolled out of the room.

Lying there in a stunned silence, she was unable to move, unable to breath, listening to the sound of his foot on the stair, to the front door opening. With the click of its closing, she managed to rouse herself. She pushed her arms into the sleeves of her robe, rushed to the window, and cast open the shutters. Down the street, she could still see him, and she cried out, "James! James!"

The thoroughfare was busy and noisy, with innumerable people and vehicles passing, so nary a head spun in her direction. She called again, but if he heard, he gave no indication. He kept on.

"Well?" Barbara Ritter prompted as the curtain covering the carriage window fell into place. "What do you think about my story now, Lady Marbleton?"

For a long while, Margaret Weston didn't answer. She continued to stare, her gaze drawn to the upper-story window where her sister-in-law had just made a scandalous fool of herself, though no one on the street below appeared to have noticed.

Abigail was a pitiful sight, her hair askew, her breasts barely covered by one of the flimsy undergarments that James had purchased from Madame LaFarge. Weeping and shouting his name, her hand outstretched in supplication, she couldn't have been more heart-wrenching if she'd been on the stage and acting out the latest melodrama. If Barbara had directed the event herself, she couldn't have planned it more perfectly.

Margaret had seen all.

It had taken a great deal of cajoling to induce her to come, and even more sweet-talking to persuade her to stay. Abigail had shown up shortly after they'd arrived, causing Margaret to raise her bushy brows in consternation, but Margaret hadn't actually believed Barbara's strange report until James had also appeared and sauntered inside. Even then, Margaret had remained skeptical, watching and waiting in silence as the hour had ticked away. If Abigail hadn't ended her sexual assignation so spectacularly, Margaret might still be wondering.

But with Abigail's frantic good-bye, there could be no doubts, no suppositions, no uncertainties. While pristine Caroline Weston pranced around London's fancy drawing rooms, her supposedly chaste chaperone was spending her leisure moments fornicating with James Stevens. Through Margaret Weston's eyes, Abigail couldn't have picked a more sordid character with whom to commit her monstrous sin.

Abigail finally put them out of their misery by stepping into the shadows and pulling the shutters closed. At witnessing her despair, Barbara almost felt sorry for her. Almost. But she couldn't help the gleeful smile that begged to burst out, and she had to hide it behind her fan, lest Margaret discover how delighted she was with the afternoon's proceedings.

Margaret surreptitiously observed the house for another thirty-two minutes—Barbara timed every agonizing second—until Abigail departed through the front door. Lost and forlorn, she walked down the street to a parked hansom cab and dejectedly climbed inside.

Once the conveyance rounded the corner and disappeared from view, Margaret's hand dropped away from the curtain, and she settled her massive bulk on the seat. Two bright spots of red marred her cheeks.

"I have to tell you, Lady Newton"—she breathed out a heavy sigh—"that when you first approached me, I didn't credit your wild tale. Abigail has always been such a fine, upstanding young lady; I couldn't accept your account as being true. To find her like this! With *that* man! Of all the scoundrels in the world!" She shuddered in distaste.

"I'm sorry to have been the bearer of such bad tidings," Barbara said meekly, displaying the fawning docility that Margaret expected. "I was so shocked myself when I stumbled upon them that I decided you simply *had* to know."

"You did the right thing by coming to me, dear," Margaret agreed, then grumbled, "Afternoon 'painting lessons' indeed!" She stared out once again, looking but not really seeing anything.

"Your poor husband," Barbara gushed mournfully. "I hate to contemplate how he'll suffer the news."

"This will just kill him," Margaret mused sadly, emotionally. Clucking her tongue, she added, "If I hadn't seen it with my own eyes . . . well . . . I just *never* would have believed it." Momentarily, she shifted her attention to Barbara. "Let's go, shall we? All of a sudden, I'm not feeling very well."

"Of course, Lady Marbleton," Barbara cooed. "We'll have you home straightaway."

James stirred uneasily on the chair in the sitting room of his mother's hotel suite. It was firm and jarring against his back, and he wished that Angela were at home where she belonged, so he could be stretched out on one of the comfortable sofas in his own parlor, instead of here, awaiting her grand entrance, which, knowing her, she wouldn't make until she was bloody good and ready.

The chamber was a bit on the garish side for his tastes, but exactly the type of pretentious, gaudy fashion Angela favored. She enjoyed flaunting her wealth, daring others to see how far she'd traveled from her humble beginnings. While the members of High Society refused to be impressed, the commoners, who were the bulk of her true fans, adored her, and she had the hotel employees tripping over themselves to do her bidding.

In the adjoining bedchamber, he could hear her stirring about, dressing herself—no doubt—in some outrageous garment meant to shock anyone who happened to lay eyes on her later in the day.

She'd thoroughly proven her point: She was furious enough to spit at her two sons and their boorish behavior, so irate that she'd moved out of the house she'd always loved. Whether they wanted her to or not, she was marrying her beloved Eddy. Despite the upset she was causing everyone, she was going to do as she damn well pleased.

She was allowed, he supposed, granting her that much. After the initial shock had worn off, he'd come to terms with their pronouncement. He wasn't crazy about it, but he could accept it. He loved Angela, and he liked Edward, too, when the man wasn't being an absolute bastard. James imagined that he and his father could tolerate one another in a state of companionable aversion that would keep Angela content.

Angela was an adult woman who could form her own decision about marriage to Edward. James had told her as much several times, so he didn't understand why she wouldn't come home, but she continued to insist that her rooms were working out well, and she intended to stay until the wedding.

In order to lessen the furor their union would create, they were delaying the ceremony until after the Season ended and Edward's peers scuttled back to their country estates. Then they planned to sneak off to the Italian coast for an extended honeymoon, hoping that subsequent scandals would occur and that by the time of their return they would have become old gossip.

Their secretive, elaborate scheming was all for Edward's benefit. Angela couldn't have cared less about the members of the *ton*. She'd long ago gotten past being vexed by their convictions, but for Edward and his precious reputation, she would jump any hurdle.

The notion that she was still so in love made James sick to his stomach.

He surveyed the room once again, and he couldn't get over the sneaking suspicion that she was relishing the disruption she'd precipitated. She fancied having him waiting attendance on her, while squirming like a naughty schoolboy about to be disciplined.

Just about the time he decided to leave, she swept through the door in a swirl of bright red. The gown was sinfully low-cut, with a tiny waist and full skirt that emphasized her voluptuous figure. Her glorious blond hair was piled high on her head, her face artfully painted. She was beautiful, confident, successful, full of mischief and trouble, and he was glad he wasn't the man who would have to put up with her for the remainder of her days. He almost pitied Edward. His father hadn't lived with her in twenty-five years, and James hoped that Edward truly realized what he was letting himself in for.

"Have you heard from your brother?" she commenced, never thinking of apologizing after forcing him to cool his heels for the preceding hour while she'd primped and preened.

"Yes. He sent a note." He held it out and observed her while she scanned it.

She was so unconventional compared to the other women he'd known who were also mothers. As she'd never been what one would describe as overly *maternal,* he couldn't help wondering what kind of person he might have grown to be if he hadn't had this flamboyant, charismatic figure as his sole parent.

Her zest for life, and her view of the world, had shaped him into an assertive, powerful, prosperous man, but deep down, he was still the lad who'd always worshiped her. He longed to unburden himself of his woes, yet with a grave certitude, he recognized that if he revealed the smallest tidbit, he couldn't bear to learn what her subsequent reflections might be.

"He doesn't know when he'll be back?" She frowned. "What the hell does that mean?"

"Don't fret, Mother. He's just blowing off steam."

"Where is he?"

James shrugged. "I haven't the foggiest. But he says he's all right, so I'm not concerned. I don't want him about when he's in a snit, anyway. He needs to cool down."

"But what about his job at the club? Are you to limp along indefinitely until he deigns to carry his share of the load again?"

" 'Tis not a problem. Truly." But he was lying. Michael had heavy responsibilities at the club, and he was always missed when he wasn't there, but that wasn't why James detested his absence. Michael was his best friend, and if nothing else, his presence would allow James to pretend that life was continuing on at its normal pace. That he'd never met Abigail Weston. That Angela wasn't totting off with Edward.

"I assume he'll return," she said, "after he's certain he's driven us all mad with worry."

"And not a moment before," James interjected. "You know what he's like. There's no use distressing yourself," and they both smiled at how willful and stubborn Michael could be.

On a sigh, Angela went to the mirror and checked her coiffure. Appearing suddenly unsure of herself, a side she rarely showed to others, she questioned quietly, "Do you think he'll ever forgive me for doing this?"

Considering how adamant Michael could be, James couldn't predict his brother's future behavior, but he'd never hurt her by saying so. "I'm sure of it."

"If I thought he wouldn't, I'm not sure I'd go through with it."

"Mother, if marrying Edward will make you happy"—egad, but he'd fallen into the role of defending his father!—"then that's what you should do. Don't deny yourself because of Michael."

Sighing again, she turned to the mirror and adjusted a comb. "What about you?" she inquired much too casually. "What's become of that girl who called on me?"

"I haven't the foggiest."

She narrowed her eyes. "Tell me you didn't meet with her."

"Yes, Mother, I did."

"I asked you not to!" Worry creased her brow. "You're a smart man. Why would you engage in such craziness? Unless you . . ." She faced him, bathing him in the stare that had ceaselessly caused him to tremble in terror as a child. "She was right! You care for her!"

He shifted uncomfortably. "No. I went simply because I felt someone should talk some sense into her."

When he didn't elucidate, she barked, "And . . . ?"

"I broke it off."

"How did she take it?"

"Fine," he responded cryptically.

"Perfectly amicable? No hard feelings and all that?"

"Yes."

"Did you sleep with her first?"

She liked to shock with bawdy words, so he wasn't surprised by her query, but still, he blushed with embarrassment. "Of course," he responded, trying to seem bored. "I always take what's freely offered."

"You are such a libertine, my dear." She *tsk*ed and shook her head, then stalked across the room and towered over his chair. "Don't lie to me, James Stevens. That girl believed herself in love with you. Very much so. You must have absolutely broken her heart. And don't sit there claiming she was one of your usual doxies, because she wasn't. She was a genuine lady—in every sense. I can't believe that you'd lie down with her, then be so cruel as to give her the heave-ho as soon as you were finished. When did you inform her? When you were lacing your trousers?"

Because that was pretty much how it had transpired, James retreated to the sideboard and poured a brandy, sipping it while gazing out the window so that he'd have somewhere to look besides at his mother. " 'Twasn't as bad as all that," he fibbed.

"You're right," she asserted sarcastically. "I'm sure it was much worse. How could you be so callous? What's come over you, that you would treat such a tender girl that way? I raised you better."

"I did it for her, Mother," he contended, yearning to confess how tragic it had actually been.

He thought about Abby, of how generously she'd offered herself, and how naively she'd expected all to be mended. Until the very end, she'd never comprehended what a bastard he could really be.

He'd gone to the house with the noble aim of finally and irrevocably terminating the affair, but once he'd set eyes upon her, he couldn't remain separate. Even though he'd acted the complete cad by having sex with her, their joining had been magnificent, awe-inspiring, the most intense, dramatic encounter he'd ever had with a woman, and he was so glad he'd taken her that one, final time. Bedding her had been insensitive and wrong, but he had no regrets.

"You did it for *her*?" Angela scoffed, incredulous. "Now I've heard everything. That girl loved you. She'd have done anything for you."

"She didn't *love* me, Mother. I was the only man who'd ever paid any attention to her. That's all. She was infatuated and intrigued; she confused love with desire, but don't be concerned. She'll be over me like that." He snapped his fingers, then walked back to his chair and sat, attempting to appear at ease while desperately hoping she'd drop the entire subject.

He didn't want to discuss Abigail Weston! Not with his mother or anyone else! She was like a pesky insect, buzzing around his heart, occupying his mind. He couldn't eat, sleep, think without her presence intruding.

"I can't believe you're spewing such drivel." Angela moved to his side, falling to her knees and resting her arms on his thighs. Her light perfume wafted over him. "Jamie," she murmured softly, "do you love her?"

"Of course not!" he insisted much too adamantly. He loved Abby more than words could describe, needed her like he needed air or water, but he wouldn't impose himself into her life when she so obviously didn't want him there.

Throughout their last assignation, he'd waited for a gesture, a signal, a sign—anything!—that would have indicated she was prepared to brave a relationship outside their secret hideaway. He'd afforded her every opportunity, but she hadn't grasped her chance to truly make amends. She'd apologized for her behavior at the theater. She'd yearned to mate, but she hadn't intimated her slightest inclination to travel beyond their clandestine *amour*.

Though he cursed having to admit it, she was no different, deep down, from any of the other shallow, immature females of the *ton*. She was too imbued with the social strictures she'd spent twenty-five years cultivating, and she could never cast aside her polite, ordered world for his own.

He wanted to hate her for it, to fault her, but he couldn't. Once, when he was a younger—more foolish—man, he'd assumed that he could overcome the types of burdens a woman like Abby was forced to carry, but transformation was impossible. He'd sworn to never put another lady through such hell, and he'd meant it. If by some dastardly stroke of fate they wound up together, she'd always be miserable, which would ensure that he'd always be miserable, and he refused to inflict that much wretchedness on either of them.

So . . . he'd let her down brutally. He'd abused her terribly and unconscionably. She'd mourn for a time. Then she'd become furious. Then . . . she'd get over him and strive on.

Though it hurt to picture her eventually finding an acceptable partner, marrying, and starting a family with one of her own kind, he wouldn't dwell on the prospect. He'd conducted himself appropriately by crying off, despite his mother's opinion. From the beginning, he'd known that he shouldn't have involved himself with Abby. In his own judgment, he'd behaved honorably for a change, and thus he'd saved her from a predicament she never should have entered in the first place.

Angela laid her palm against his cheek, while searching his eyes for the buried emotion she was so regularly adept at locating. "You're lying again, Jamie. I can see how much you love her. Why can't you let your love flourish? Why must it be so frightening to you?"

" 'Tisn't a matter of *love,* Mother. She simply deserves someone better than me."

"Better than you! Oh, Lord, will you stop it!" She grabbed the front of his shirt and gave him a fierce shake. "Where did you acquire this lack of confidence? Not from me, certainly! When did you grow so bloody timid?"

"I'm not being timid," he contended. "I only want what's best for her."

"But if you truly love her, you'd be what's *best* for her, don't you recognize that?" She ruffled his hair as she used to do when he was just a boy. "Go after her, Jamie. Convince her to have you. You could win her if you set your mind to it."

"Easier said than done, Mother. She can't look beyond our stations to accept me as I am. I attempted such a relationship once before, and you saw what a disaster it was."

"But you didn't love your wife, and she didn't love you! This time, it would be different. I know it would!"

For all her sophisticated ways, she had invariably been a romantic, and he couldn't help smiling. "Love doesn't conquer all."

"That's what you think, laddie," she said. "You'd be surprised what a little love can do."

Just then, a knock sounded on the door. She grimaced that their intimate talk was interrupted. "That's Eddy," she explained, offering her hand so that he could assist her to her feet. "I demand that you be civil to him. I'm not in the mood for any discord among the men in my life."

"I'll try to control myself."

"You'd better!" she warned.

She rushed to the door and opened it, barely closing it again before she was in Edward's arms and kissing him passionately. James observed them for a minute, then forced his gaze out to the street. In his childhood memories, he vividly recalled that his parents had treasured each other's company, that their lives had been filled with gaiety and laughter, but he didn't recollect this blatant, visible current of desire that flowed between them.

It must have always been there, but as a youngster he couldn't have acknowledged it for what it was. Numerous times now over the past few weeks, he'd been with them, and their connection was so obvious that he truthfully didn't comprehend how they'd managed to remain apart for so long. If ever two people had been created to be together, it was they. But that didn't mean he had to appreciate them prattling like a pair of lovebirds. There was something extremely disturbing about his parents' displays of mutual affection.

Edward's voice brought James's focus back into the room. "Any word from Michael?" he inquired.

"He posted a letter to James," Angela answered. "He's well; just not coming home for the moment. Apparently our full-grown son is still having a tantrum."

"Hopefully, it will end someday," Edward said, disheartened.

"Did you speak with your girls?" she asked as he nodded. "How did they take the news?"

"Not well. I left them in somewhat of a state. They swear they won't attend the wedding."

"Brats! Like we'd invite them!" she chided, and, a sign of Edward's devotion, he merely chuckled at her deprecation of his children. "How about Charles? Was he upset as well?"

"Difficult to say. I believe he's withholding judgment until he has the distinct pleasure of making your acquaintance."

"Well, that should be easy. I shall simply bowl him over with my sweet personality." She batted her lashes, and he laughed again, then she went into the other chamber to fetch her bag—and do who only knew what else—leaving James and his father in an awkward silence.

"Hello, James," Edward eventually said.

Their interaction had been awfully clumsy since that dreadful night at the theater. Their contentious comments still hovered in the air, producing a cloud of antagonism and distrust—on James's side, at least. For his part, Edward had proceeded past that appalling evening and seemed prepared to forge ahead for all their sakes. James wasn't quite at Edward's level of cordiality, but he was trying. He longed to please Angela, but too many factors came into play, and nothing seemed simple anymore. The combination of recent events had left him utterly distressed, until he felt like a starved wolf that had been locked in a cage and was being poked with sharp sticks. He was ready to bite anyone who approached.

"Hello, Edward," James responded.

"Considering all that's happening, couldn't you call me *Father* on occasion?"

James pursed his lips, feigning an attempt at enunciating the title. "No," he ultimately said, "I don't believe the word is in my vocabulary."

Edward sighed tiredly. "At least quit scowling at me as though I'd sprouted horns. I've had enough of my glowering children for one day."

"Poor boy," he muttered rudely just as Angela returned. "Did your *daughters* hurt your feelings?"

"Don't be smart," she scolded her son. "I told you I'm not in the mood for it."

"Sorry," he apologized halfheartedly. He was acting more petulant than Michael, but he couldn't arrest his deportment. His brother had been smart enough to leave and stay gone. James had remained, thrust into the middle of all, and heaven help the man who crossed his path—be it his father or no.

"Actually," Edward continued, "I'm glad you're here, James. I was going to seek you out at the club after I visited your mother."

"Why?"

"I received the strangest message. From Jerald Weston." Busy retrieving the note from his pocket, he didn't notice how James and Angela stiffened to attention. "You know him, don't you?" Edward asked. "The Earl of Marbleton?"

"Yes, he's a customer," James replied, keeping his expression carefully blank. "What does he want?"

"He demands that I stop by this afternoon"—he glanced at the writing—"and he insists that I bring you along, but he doesn't say why. I hate to go in blind. Has he run up a great debt on which he hopes to renege?"

Angela glared at James, and he glared back but made no comment.

"You might as well tell him," she finally said. "Or I will."

"Tell me what?" Edward queried, completely in the dark.

A muscle ticked in James's cheek; his eyes glowed red-hot with fury. Clearly, he and Abby had been discovered. But how? And by whom?

The silence became protracted, Edward staring at them in bewilderment, Angela waiting for James to confess his sins. Ultimately, when he appeared unable to, she did it for him. "James has seduced Marbleton's younger sister. The man must have learned of it somehow."

"Caroline?" Edward gasped then collapsed into a chair. "God . . . you've lain with Caroline? Charles loves her! He's all set to marry her. This will absolutely kill him!"

It was so typical that Edward's immediate worry would be for Charles and how the debacle might affect his *real* son, and his misplaced concern was exactly the reason James didn't think Angela should wed him. Edward's loyalty would perpetually belong to others. "Charles can have his little virgin," James remarked crudely. "I'd hardly be interested."

"He debauched the other one," Angela stated sharply, causing both men to wince. "What's her name? Abigail? The girl is madly in love with him, Eddy. 'Tis almost painful to see."

"You've met her?" Edward asked Angela, shocked and amazed.

"She came to the house! Bold as brass! Looking for him"—she nodded toward her intractable son—"but he doesn't have the sense the Good Lord gave an ant. He loves her, too, though he denies it. I've tried to convince him that he'd be particularly fortunate if he was allowed to marry her, but he won't listen to me."

"You seduced Abigail Weston? Oh, James . . ." Edward groaned, discouraged, horrified, rubbing a weary hand over his brow. "Didn't you learn anything from your previous situation?"

"We had a brief affair. That's all." James shrugged, tossing Abby away with utterances that were too cold and calculated to characterize what had actually occurred. " 'Tis over."

"But what are your plans with regard to her?" his father pressed.

"I have none."

"What if there's a babe?"

"There isn't," he declared, though he had to quash a strange flare of expectation that their final coupling might have led to one, which would be the worst disaster of all. A child would obligate Abby to marry, and he'd not bind himself to her unless she truly wanted him for a husband. As she'd already had copious opportunity to decide on his suitability, he had no illusions about where he stood. No matter how they all clamored, they'd never convince him to take any corrective action.

"Oh, son . . ." Edward shook his head in dismay. "What are we to do?"

"Not a bloody thing."

"How do you expect me to explain this to Jerald?"

"I don't *expect* you to explain anything to him. I'm a grown man now. I can speak for myself without any of your halfhearted assistance."

"Then how about Abigail? She's a wonderful woman. I can't bear knowing that you'd abuse her like this." The reproach was lethal to endure. "I'm greatly outraged by the manner in which you've acted toward her. What's come over you . . . to dally like this when you have no compunction to right your wrongs? You—better than anyone—are aware of the consequences."

James fought to seem nonchalant, having learned long ago never to let his father discern how deeply his disappointment cut. "We were extremely discreet. Her reputation is hardly ruined."

"*Someone* evidently knows what you were about!" Edward indicated in a near-shout. "Jerald will be calling for your head!"

"Well, he can't have it," James retorted fliply.

"Have you no honor? No shame?"

"Not much." He casually rose to his feet, though he was dying inside, and he started toward the door.

"Where are you off to?" his mother demanded.

"I thought I'd have a chat with Jerald Weston. I always loathed that pompous bastard, and I'm suddenly itching for a major row." He strolled out of the room and down the hall.

Behind him, his mother exclaimed, "Go with him, Eddy, would you? In his condition, there's no telling what he might do."

"I'll go, darling," his father said, "but I don't know what help I'll be."

"Just don't let him instigate any more trouble than he already has."

James continued on, not slowing in the least as his father raced to catch up.

NINETEEN

Abigail slumped in the window seat of her room, gazing down on the back gardens, but she couldn't find any joy in the view. Birds were singing, flowers were blooming, the sky was bright blue with fluffy clouds. Despite the spring day, all she saw was gray.

James did not love her!

She closed her eyes and rested her head against the wall, wishing she could simply quit breathing, quit thinking, quit being, for she truly couldn't face another day. Her heart was so broken that it might cease its beating. Not that she would care.

During the weeks that he'd refused to meet with her, she'd maintained her equilibrium because she'd been so hopeful that they would have a reconciliation. She'd fully believed that he would forgive her, that they would continue on as they had been, that they would grow more devoted and attached until James came to the same conclusion that she had reached long ago: They belonged together.

Sweet Jesu, but what a fool she was! During that last dramatic, wonderful, hideous assignation, she'd lain there with him and allowed his magnificent presence and fabulous anatomy to overwhelm all reason and sanity. While she'd been fantasizing and suffering her idiotic, girlish dreams, he'd been so bored that, when he'd finished with the sexual act, he could hardly wait to fasten his trousers and be on his way. He'd said that he would never return, and he'd meant it. She would never see him again, and oh, how the knowledge wounded her!

All her plans, all her visions of a perfect life, had been dashed in an instant. Everything was gone but this vast well of love she felt for him, and she couldn't figure out where to bury it now that he'd thrown it back at her This stunning, remarkable mountain of affection was pushing her down, choking her, squeezing against her until she could barely stagger under its heavy weight.

"Oh . . . what should I do now?" she wailed to the un-answering sky.

A knock sounded on her door, and Caroline entered without pausing for a response. On espying her sister across the room, Caroline asked, "Abigail, are you unwell? For the past two days, you've looked absolutely peaked."

"No . . . I'm fine." Uttering the obvious lie, she rubbed at her brow. She didn't want to talk with Caroline! She didn't want to talk with anyone! She simply wanted to be alone while she came to terms with what had happened.

Caroline sidled closer and eased down next to her. "What is it, Abigail? You can tell me."

Abigail focused on her sister, and to her horror, tears welled into her eyes. More than anything in the world, she yearned to confide in someone about what had occurred at James Stevens's hands. Not being able to speak of it seemed the worst torture of all.

"I'm just tired, Caroline," she insisted, while swiping at the lone tear that succeeded in trickling down her cheek.

"Has that man done something to you?"

"What man?" Abigail returned her attention to the yard outside.

"The one you've been seeing. The one who sent you those undergarments."

Abigail closed her eyes again, pressing a finger and thumb against her eyelids in an attempt to hold back a deluge of emotion as she proclaimed the fatal words: "There is no man."

Caroline was silent for a long while, then she vowed, "If you ever need to talk about it, I'm here."

"I'll remember," Abigail murmured vigilantly, lest the entire, sordid tale tumble out. All her regrets, acrimony, and sorrow were perched on the tip of her tongue, begging for the opportunity to spew forth, and making her realize that she had to get control of herself. If she weren't careful, she'd have Margaret up here, as well, though recently Margaret had been markedly absent.

Abigail wished them all to perdition so she could have some peace, but in the large household, privacy was a precious commodity, and she couldn't permit her melancholy to induce others into speculating as to her desperate straits. Caroline had already deduced that something was amiss, so others would start noticing, too, if she weren't more circumspect.

She straightened, fussing with her skirts, while easing the lines of worry that marred her brow. "What brings you upstairs?" she inquired quietly. "You and Charles were going riding."

"You weren't feeling up to it, so we'll try again later."

"I'm sure I'll be ready. Let me know when you'd like to depart." A ride in the park might be just the ticket to lift her lagging spirits. She'd be away from the prying residential staff, and she could travel in the curricle behind the young lovers; she'd be by herself with her lonely musings.

"Abigail, may I disclose a marvelous secret?" Caroline began hesitantly.

"What it is?"

"You must swear you'll keep it until the moment is right."

"I swear."

"Charles intends to ask Jerald for my hand." She beamed with anticipation. "After supper tonight."

It was hardly a mystery! The pair had become inseparable, to the point where other boys had quit calling, certain they'd lost their chance.

"I'm glad for you," she asserted, but she couldn't prevent the flame of bitter jealousy that surged at the awareness that she'd never share the same fabulous news about James.

"So, I've been wondering . . . about our talk." Caroline shifted nervously, the bright sunlight haloing her in a rim of white. She looked so young and pretty, so eager for her future to arrive, and Abigail could only hope Charles would cherish the innocent, gentle girl so that she would never experience anything remotely approaching the type of dreadful despair that now filled Abigail's own veins.

"What will Charles expect of me?" Caroline persisted. "You promised to advise me."

Abigail had stalled Caroline's questions several times now, but quite frankly, she couldn't discuss such a personal topic when she was so distressed. Any descriptions would only serve to remind her of James. There was no method of explaining the sexual act without his image rising to the fore, and she couldn't deliberately conjure him up. It was like jabbing herself over and over with the tip of a sharp knife.

Just the whisper of his name in the back of her mind caused her heart to constrict. He was permanently implanted in her consciousness, and her memories were so vivid that she could smell him, taste him, perceive the sensation of his rough body hair scratching across her smooth, naked skin. The images were still so intense that she squirmed against the cushions.

She could not converse about any of it just now! She absolutely could not!

"I can't this afternoon," she finally said. "I will, though. Soon."

"When?"

"Give me a few days?"

Caroline nodded as one of the serving women stopped by to proclaim the brisk news that Jerald was in his library and demanding Abigail's immediate attendance. Both sisters rose, and Caroline said, "I haven't seen Jerald in ages. I'll accompany you."

"Beggin' your pardon, milady," the maid replied to Caroline's decision, "but the earl requests that Lady Abigail come alone. And straightaway."

Caroline rolled her eyes, out of sight of the maid's assessing gaze, and Abigail flashed her a wan smile as she withdrew. She walked downstairs and encountered Jerald behind his desk, scowling, no papers in front of him, his hands resting, palms down, on the polished wood.

"Close the door," he commanded sternly, and she complied, then moved to one of the chairs directly across from him.

The manner in which he was glaring at her produced a swell of discomfiture. She didn't know him very well. He'd been grown, and his own household established, by the time his widowed father had remarried to her mother. By their age difference alone, they had little in common. With completely diverse interests, acquaintances, and lifestyles, the only factor that truly bound them was that they'd had the same father, but that paternal tie had never blossomed into anything more. They were brother and sister, but not close.

To have him assessing her so meticulously was extremely unnerving. They didn't have the sort of relationship that lent itself to intimacies, and considering her current mood, she wasn't in any condition to delve into serious subjects.

"I've had a situation brought to my attention," he said curtly. " 'Tis shocking and delicate, but I do not apologize for raising it with you."

He stood and rounded the desk. Though he was not an inordinately tall person, their positions caused him to tower over her. His excessive physical bulk, and his angry countenance, made him appear thoroughly menacing.

Apprehensively, she questioned, "What is it?"

"Have you been pursuing an illicit liaison with a man by the name of James Stevens?"

Her eyes widened in perplexed astonishment, her pulse beat furiously, her ears rang. They'd been detected! Her worst fears had been realized! And her first and only consideration was that she needed to protect James from undue censure. Every part of this predicament had been at her doing and none of his own. She'd not pin the blame on him at this late date.

She opened her mouth, but no comment emerged, so Jerald pronounced in her stead, "If you are thinking of lying, don't. Margaret observed the two of you, and she's been positively *sick* with disgust ever since."

Margaret? Where? How? The only place she and James had been together was at the rental house. Why was Margaret even in that neighborhood?

"When?" she appealed stupidly, incapable of formulating a more cogent remark.

"So . . ." he spit hatefully, "you admit it."

Before she knew what he was about, he slapped her with such force that he nearly drove her off the chair. Only her firm grip on the arm kept her upright. She bit back a sob. "Jerald . . . please . . ."

"You little whore!" he hissed. "Do you have any idea what kind of vile creature he is?"

"No . . . no . . ." She shook her head stridently, powerless to stay silent when James was being attacked. "He's a good man. A fine man—"

Jerald slapped her again, harder, and she crumpled to her knees, feeling as though all her bones had melted. Never in her life had she envisioned such treatment, and she was stunned beyond measure.

"Don't defend him to me!" Jerald growled. "Not ever!"

She could hear his harsh breathing as he attempted to rein in his temper, so she hovered on the floor before him, tears streaming down her face, a protective hand pressed to her stinging cheek, while she braced for whatever blow— physical or verbal—might fall next.

Eventually, he stalked to the window, putting distance between them, then he whirled around. "All these years, I've tolerated your remaining single. I've trusted you with Caroline's upbringing, and look what you've accomplished! What form of guidance have you been providing, I wonder? Under your sordid tutelage, will she turn whore, as well?"

"I love Caroline," she protested, but her ardent statement emanated as a whisper. "I would never hurt her."

"You abhorrent hussy, you've already *hurt* her more than you could ever know." He scoffed. "As of this moment, your responsibilities for Caroline have ended."

"No, Jerald, anything but that." She finally mustered the

courage to look at him, and she flinched when she witnessed the repugnant way her regarded her. "I'm begging you."

"*Dear* sister," he asserted scathingly, "your days of requesting boons from me are over." He went behind his desk again and settled himself, nodding impatiently to her chair. "Get up! Straighten yourself!"

She utilized the chair for balance, but her legs had turned to mush, and she couldn't stand. When she took overly long in rising, his intolerance soared anew, and she feared that he might advance around the desk to assault her a second time. With immense effort, she slid her hips onto the seat, then held on as tightly as she was able.

"What have you decided?" she managed.

"You are going to get exactly what you deserve, and nothing less," he replied. "James Stevens—scoundrel, blackmailer, confidence artist, great *lover* of women—will be here shortly to propose marriage."

"James is coming here?" She moaned, shamed and embarrassed that he would observe her like this, with her brother so enraged and her defenses so low. Oh, how could her tremendous affection for him have delivered them to this horrid juncture?

"I expect him at any minute. By tomorrow afternoon, you will be his bride. You will never return to any of my homes, you will never speak to anyone in our family again—"

"Jerald, don't do this. You're angry now—"

"Be silent!" he bellowed. "You are about to behold what you have truly wrought. James Stevens is a man with no honor, no loyalties, who will do anything . . . say anything . . . *fuck*"—she winced at his use of the despicable word—"anything, and he will do it all to you over the years, while you agonize and watch and lament about the bed you have made for yourself. I can conceive of no better, or more appropriate, punishment for this impossible disgrace you have inflicted upon us."

"No one knows—"

"You would be surprised by who *knows*." He laughed meanly, clearly disturbed by the prospect. "I can't believe it's not all over Town by now. I assume that it will be shortly, and when people determine what kind of a *harlot* I have for a sister, I will be scraping the bottom of the barrel to find a husband for Caroline. Are you happy, Abigail, with what you've brought about?"

She started to cry in earnest, for she truly hadn't meant any harm. Particularly not to Caroline, but what Jerald said was true. Once word got out about her liaison with James, Jerald would have difficulty locating a suitable partner for Caroline. He'd probably have to increase her dowry to a staggering height, an act Abigail doubted he would assent to, so Caroline either wouldn't marry or she'd end up in such an appalling union that the result would be beyond consideration.

Entirely because of her impetuous, rash behavior! That she could change the past and erase it all!

"James will not marry me," she murmured, needing to prepare her brother for the eventuality.

"We'll just see about that!" he declared smugly.

"Nor would I ask him to."

"You, Abigail," he retorted caustically, "have absolutely *no* say in the matter."

They lingered in a strained quiet, broken only by the ticking of the clock. Finally, the butler announced that the Earl of Spencer and James Stevens had arrived. Abigail was so mortified to encounter the pair—one her cherished friend, one her precious love—under such appalling circumstances that she couldn't look up as they were ushered in, though she felt James's concentrated attention passing over her.

With a nod from Jerald, the butler shut the door, and the strange quartet was sequestered. Edward and James approached the desk together. Jerald rose to challenge them.

"I will be brief," he started. "I have ascertained from an undeniable source that James Stevens has been having unrestricted carnal relations with my sister Abigail over a period of weeks. His irresponsible actions have ruined her marital chances and very likely left her with child. He has completely compromised her, jeopardized my family's reputation, and destroyed the nuptial expectations of my other sister Caroline. What say you in response?"

"I just learned of the situation myself, Jerald," Edward said, struggling to inject reason. "Let's sit down, shall we, and review the circumstances calmly?"

"We will not *sit*. I do not intend to have that individual"—he rudely gestured toward James, but didn't glance in his direction—"under my roof any longer than it takes him to propose. The two of you will then depart, while I arrange the special license. The archbishop is awaiting instructions from me. A private ceremony will be held here, in my home, tomorrow morning at eleven. I want Abigail gone by noon."

Edward sighed and glared at James. "Well?" he demanded.

"I've already given you my answer," James rejoined, plainly bored.

As Edward was the only one who knew what James's answer was, a long, dangerous interlude ensued. Jerald broke it by slamming his fist against his desk.

"Ask her, damn you!" he ordered, his voice breaking.

All three men turned to her. Jerald's cheeks were so crimson, he appeared ready to suffer an apoplexy. Edward was sad, sympathetic, and apologetic. James seemed totally unfazed, as though the proceedings had no effect on him personally.

She examined him, searching for the tiniest flicker of consideration, the barest hint of fondness. If she'd observed the smallest indication of esteem, she might have thrown herself at his feet and pleaded with him to save her from the fate she would sustain at Jerald's hands. Yet he contemplated her with nothing but apathy and disinterest. They might have been strangers who had just met on the street.

Her heart, already bruised, shattered into a thousand minuscule pieces.

"I don't believe Lady Abigail wishes to marry me," James said. "She never has."

"It is not up to her!" Jerald insisted.

Ignoring Jerald, James inquired, "How do you reply, milady?" His tone was disrespectful and mocking. "Are you prepared to *lower* yourself to wed one such as me?"

The trio held its collective breath. One little word—*yes*—and she would become James's wife. Once upon a time, she'd have done anything for such an opportunity, but as he stared her down with such insult and contempt, she couldn't agree.

Not only did he fail to love her, he apparently didn't even *like* her. How could she compel him to marry when he harbored such profound loathing? If she acquiesced, she'd spend her entire life struggling with the knowledge that he'd never wanted her, pining away while he lusted after one woman and another.

What kind of existence would that be?

"No." She shook her head as she gazed up into his beloved face. " 'Twould be a terrible mistake."

For the shortest instant, she imagined that a wave of regret and hopelessness nearly swept him away. He sagged slightly as though he'd just received a terrible blow, but as quickly as she perceived it, the impression vanished. Her desperate mind had merely been playing cruel tricks.

"There you have it," James said brightly. "Milady, you recall our agreement, don't you?"

"What agreement?" Jerald huffed indignantly.

"When we commenced our affair"—James shifted his focus to Jerald—"I informed her that I would do nothing to salvage her reputation if we were exposed. She understood the terms and conditions of my involvement. From the beginning, I'd resolved to dally, but no more than that." He shrugged as if he'd just explained all the intricate puzzles of the world.

"You advised her up front"—Jerald nearly choked on his outrage—"that you simply meant to dally? What kind of man are you?"

"I am every despicable thing you conceive me to be."

"James!" Abigail scolded. She hated it when he disparaged himself in such a fashion. "Don't act this way." But no one was listening to her.

Jerald leveled his animosity on Edward. "Despite how he was raised," Jerald grimly emphasized, "James Stevens is still your son. Will you let his behavior stand without reparation? Will you tolerate his refusal to make amends?"

"He's an adult, Jerald," Edward returned. "I've tried talking to him, but I can't force him to do what's right. I wish it were possible, but I can't *make* him marry her. You know that."

"He is of your blood! You fathered this . . . this . . ."—his eyes bulging, his nose beet-red, he directed a condemning finger at James—"this contemptible example of manhood. How can you bear to be in the same room with him?"

"I won't dignify that with a response," Edward snapped.

"Get OUT of my house!" Jerald shouted, pushed beyond his limits. "Take your bastard and go! And while you're at it, be sure that Charles never shows his sorry face 'round here again, either."

"No, Jerald," Abigail gasped, "don't punish Caroline. She loves Charles!"

"Shut your mouth, Abigail!" he roared. Crudely, he said to Edward, "The apple never falls far from the tree, does it, Spencer? Well, I'll not have any other of your detestable brood hounding the women of my family."

James bristled and stepped forward. "You know, *Father*"—he emphasized his means of address—"I don't care what this horse's ass thinks about me, but it really bothers me when he denigrates Charles. Would you like me to pummel him for you? I'd be more than happy to."

"No, James," Edward murmured ruefully. "Jerald, I realize you're upset, but please don't make such a hasty decision about the children."

"Go!" Jerald shouted again. "Before I call my servants and have the two of you thrown into the street like the carnage you are."

"Come, James." Edward sighed miserably. "You've caused enough damage here."

They headed for the door, but, startling all—especially Abigail—James moved to her side. She was too humiliated—by her brother's conduct and comments, by her own wanton, lustful comportment that had landed them in the middle of this dreadful scene—to look at him. He cupped her chin, raised her face to the light, and tipped her cheek back and forth. It was swollen and throbbing.

"Did he hit you?" he asked softly, ominously.

Afraid of what he might do if she divulged the truth, she didn't reply, but then, she didn't need to. The evidence was too conspicuous. He spun around, stormed behind the desk, and grabbed Jerald by the lapels of his jacket.

"With the amount of money you owe me, Marbleton," he warned, "I make it a point to know everything that occurs in your petty little life. If I ever hear that you've laid a hand on Lady Abigail again, I will bring a few of your bastard children over and introduce them to Margaret"— their eyes widened at the implication, Jerald's most of all— "then, I will kill you—slowly—with my bare hands." He lifted Jerald off the floor until his toes were dangling and seams were popping, then James tossed him into his chair with a hard thump. "Think about it," he cautioned.

He stomped away, but paused in front of Abigail. "If he touches you again, send me a note immediately. I'll deal with him." Amazing her, he took her hand and placed a tender kiss on the back, but he didn't meet her eyes. "Now I must say *au revoir*, and I apologize for all this upset. I hope that someday you will be able to forgive me." He straightened, but as he did, he was staring at a spot over her shoulder. "Let's go, Father."

They reached the library door just as the butler opened it. Caroline was waiting on the other side.

"What going on?" she queried anxiously.

"I'm sorry, Caroline," Edward expressed.

"For what? What's happened?" She was rapidly growing frantic.

"Your brother will explain."

Edward patted her shoulder in commiseration, then he and James departed as a pall of doom descended on the house.

Jerald righted himself, then stood. "Return to your room, Caroline."

"I won't!" she asserted. "Not until—"

"I will not tell you again!" he screamed. As he'd never raised his voice to her before, the decree had the desired effect. With a final, sympathetic glance at Abigail, she hustled away, her skirts swishing as she stomped up the stairs.

The butler closed the door, and Abigail was perilously secluded with Jerald once more.

"Do you now understand what kind of man you have delivered into our lives?" Jerald seethed. "Do you see?"

"He's not like that," she persisted, remembering the warm chats they'd had, the tranquil moments, the stirring confessions, the ardent arguments. "He's truly not—"

Jerald cut her off. "You will proceed directly to your room, where you will be locked in for the night."

"You wouldn't dare!"

"You will go of your own accord, or I will beat you senseless, then drag you there." He was just outraged enough to carry through on his threat, and evidently he'd worry later about any possible retaliation from James. "You will never speak to Caroline again."

"You can't stop me!"

"Can't I?" he asked gravely. "She will be taken from this house immediately so that she will have no further contact with you. In the morning, you will leave for the country. During the coming month, I will contract a husband for you. To avoid any scandal, you will marry as expediently as the ceremony can be arranged."

In all her ponderings of the viable consequences, she'd never conceived of such a drastic resolution. To be married to another! While her spirit was still aching for James! After what they'd shared, she could never wed anyone else.

The very idea seemed like an atrocious sin. "I won't do it, I tell you! You'll never get my consent!"

"I wouldn't be too sure, if I were you." He nodded toward the door. "Be gone! I'm sickened by the sight of you."

James's carriage rattled to a halt several blocks from the club. Pulling back the curtain, he peered outside. The surrounding establishments were doing a brisk evening business on the busy thoroughfare, so the area was well lit, and it was easy to see that traffic was stalled for quite a stretch. The cool night air beckoned, and he decided to walk the rest of the way. He rapped to signal his driver, and momentarily his coachman released the door and lowered the step.

There were scores of people out, mostly wealthy gentlemen in Town for the Season, so the short stroll was safe enough, but he almost wished the street had been dark and deserted. In his current state, he'd have loved to encounter a ruffian or two. Nothing would give him greater pleasure than the chance to administer a sincere thrashing to some despicable character who thoroughly deserved it.

Two weeks had passed since the hideous confrontation with Jerald Weston, and his heart continued to bleed from the grievous wounds he'd sustained. His level of outrage was so acute that he could barely function. After suffering through Abby's stinging admission that marrying him would be a "terrible mistake," he'd stoically tried to carry on, but her bitter words rang in his ears. Considering the manner in which he'd treated her, what had he anticipated? Love and kisses? Professions of devotion? By her denouncement, he'd gotten just what he deserved.

Still, he couldn't get past the feeling that he should have compelled her to marry him, whether she wanted to or no. At least then she'd have been under his protection and beyond Jerald's wrath. Whenever he recalled the swelling on her face, he saw red. Why he hadn't beaten Jerald to a pulp for laying his filthy hands on her was a mystery, but he'd already convinced himself that he'd caused enough anguish for all concerned, so he hadn't dared go further with Jerald, lest he wind up committing murder. For without a doubt, if he'd thrown one punch, he wouldn't have been able to stop.

Up ahead, there was a break in traffic, and his heart skipped a beat as he thought he spied his father's coach. How he yearned for Edward to relent, to show up at the club, ready to mend fences, to have a late-night drink in James's office as he was wont to do on many previous occasions, but the black conveyance turned the corner, and he realized that it hadn't been his father's, after all.

He missed his father; he'd not seen Edward since he'd exited his carriage in front of his grand Town house after their abominable visit to the Westons'. Edward's disappointment had been so prodigious that he'd asked James not to call upon him for a time—until circumstances were more settled. He'd left without a wave or a backward glance, and James had felt abandoned all over again, as though he were still that six-year-old boy at the flat in Paris, listening for Edward's footstep on the stair.

His relationship with his father had always been tenuous, and he didn't know how they'd ever surmount this latest adversity.

Edward was now thick as thieves with Angela, so he missed his mother, too, since he never saw her anymore, either. In all this, she'd become Abigail's silent ally. Furious that he had refused to ask for Abigail's hand, she wouldn't speak with him or receive him at the hotel. In all his years, he'd never endured any type of ongoing upset with his mother, and he had absolutely no idea how to repair their rift.

He couldn't convince his parents that he'd acted appropriately, that he'd done what was best for Abby. The bottom line was that she could have married him, but she hadn't wanted to, so he didn't care how often or how loudly Edward and Angela screamed their opinions. Abby had chosen the only workable option.

She was tough, a survivor. The humiliation and disgrace would eventually fade, and she'd move on with her life. In the not-too-distant future, he'd be but a bothersome memory, a foolish indiscretion from her past. If that notion was disturbing, so be it. He had no claims on Abigail Weston, or her affection, and never had.

A female voice hailed him from one of the immobile carriages, and he instantly recognized it as belonging to Barbara Ritter. Once he'd gotten over the initial shock created by Jerald Weston's discovery, he'd agonized plenty over how he'd brought such shame down upon Abby. It hadn't taken long to conclude that Barbara had been the one to report their indiscretions. Abby had hinted at a conversation with Lady Newton that made no sense unless Barbara was already aware of their liaison.

While he was acquainted with many women who were sufficiently vicious to effect the damage Barbara had wrought, she was the only one with sufficient gall to carry on afterward as though she'd done nothing. Since that fateful day, she'd been unsuccessfully trying to arrange a tryst, which would have provided him with the perfect opportunity for a showdown, but his fury over her duplicity was so enormous that he'd been uncertain he could control his formidable temper if they'd crossed paths. He'd hoped the passage of time would cool him down adequately so that he could break off their association with some semblance of civility. However, upon hearing her coo and prattle, he realized that courtesy was not a possibility.

Why was she sitting outside his club, waiting for him to arrive? Perhaps this was how she'd learned of his *amour* with Abby. How often had she followed him about? Surely she understood that he was not a man to be trifled with in such a fashion.

"James," she gushed through the window as he neared, and she held the door to the carriage, obviously expecting him to climb in, "how nice that we've run into one another."

"What are you doing here?"

"I was just passing by."

"Really? On your way to what destination?"

The question stymied her, but only for an instant. "You've caught me out, I'm afraid." She blushed appropriately. "I wasn't 'passing by.' I'm attending Lady Carrington's house party. Would you like to join me?"

"Is there some reason I might wish to accompany you?"

"Well, I haven't seen you in ages." Just then, two drunkards stumbled out of the tavern next to them, and lamplight flooded the vicinity, clearly illuminating his face. She was finally able to distinctly read his disposition, and she hesitated. "I wondered . . . ah . . . if you might . . ."

"Might what?" he asked disdainfully, tilting into the doorway, granting her a close-up view of his mood, letting his ire fill the small space in which she was enclosed.

"Darling . . . what is it? What's happened?"

"It appears, madam, that you have involved yourself in my personal affairs."

"What? Who told you such a lie?" She shifted uncomfortably. "Despite what anyone has said to you . . . it's entirely false! I swear it!"

"No one had to *tell* me anything. Your deeds were quite easy to deduce on my own." Intending to frighten, he seized her by the front of the neck, pressing slightly, though not enough to cut off her air.

"James . . . please . . ."

She squirmed, her eyes wide with dread, and he could feel her alarmed swallow against his palm. "I've warned you before, Barbara," he threatened quietly, "but you have a terrible habit of failing to listen. I am not yours to command about." He gave her a shake, then released her, and she shrunk against the squab, massaging her throat. "Never accost me in the street. I don't like being propositioned as though you are some sort of Covent Garden harlot."

"There's no need to be crude." She pretended offense.

"On the contrary, Barbara, *crudity* seems to be the only commodity you understand. So understand this: Do not solicit my company on any subsequent occasion."

"James . . . what are you saying?"

" 'Tis over between us. Don't bother me. I won't stand for it."

"You're not serious!"

"Oh, but I am," he assured her, "but I doubt you believe me, so I've purchased a bit of insurance to guarantee your future conduct." He searched his pocket, retrieved a notebook, and waved it under her nose. "I've been a busy boy the past two weeks. I've gone 'round Town and bought up all your markers."

Startled, she bluffed. "I have no idea what you're talking about."

Unable to stay away from the dicing tables, she was a regular customer at those seedy establishments that allowed women to play. "If you ever accost me again"—lest anyone passing by identify the name he was about to utter, he stuck his head inside the coach and whispered—"if you ever so much as speak Abigail Weston's name to another person, I shall demand recompense on all your notes. You don't have enough to pay, my dear. I'll gladly have you tossed into the streets, and I won't expend a single second worrying about your fate."

"After all we meant to each other! How could you behave so despicably!"

He scoffed then stepped out of range. "It would be such a shame for you to lose your pretty house . . . your pretty clothes . . . your pretty things. . . ."

His threat to her valued material possessions poked a hole in her smooth demeanor, and her true personality was revealed. "What do you care if others know about your little fling with her?" she implored bitterly. "Why is she so special? She was ashamed of her acquaintance with you! The little bitch couldn't lower herself to say hello in a public place! I was with you! I witnessed all!"

The cut was an excellent one, digging brutally at his vulnerabilities, but he was an expert at hiding how thoroughly acrid articulations could wound. "Good-bye, Lady Newton."

"She doesn't deserve your loyalty!" Barbara shouted. "She doesn't deserve you!" He took another step back, and she leaned out for a second, calming herself and attempting to seem more rational. "Don't do this, James. We belong together!"

"Never, milady," he declared evenly. "We've never belonged together."

He started to walk away, and she shrilly called his name. Passersby had noticed their spat and were tarrying to watch. "Pull yourself together, madam!" he ordered, then he glared at her driver. "Do you know who I am?" he asked.

"Aye, sir. You'd be Master James Stevens."

He nodded. "This woman"—he gestured toward Barbara—"has been hanging 'round the front of my club. She's pestering me and my customers. If I observe her in the neighborhood again, I'll confiscate the rig and horse of the chap who brought her." The man gulped in dismay. "Spread the word to the other drivers for me."

"Will do, Cap'n," the driver said. He flicked the reins and forced his way into the line of carriages, relieving James of Barbara's unwelcome presence as quickly as traffic would permit. Many blocks later, she was still screeching epithets.

Disgusted and disturbed, he traveled the remaining distance to his club, used the back entrance, and headed to his private rooms. Already, business was thriving; employees were rushing past in the corridor, and he couldn't help but wish that Michael had returned to London. If ever there was a night when he didn't relish having to supervise the running of the games, this was it.

Without success, he tried shifting through paperwork but couldn't concentrate. Staff members continually interrupted, seeking advice or asking questions. Surrendering to the inevitable, he went to the public rooms, where he arbitrated two disputes between customers, evicted a brawler, and removed a dealer who was having problems with a rude group of gamblers.

Discontented and out of sorts, he circled back to his office, poured himself a brandy, and relaxed in his chair with his feet up on his desk, savoring the amber liquor and wondering if his father might appear. Thinking about Edward caused him to think about Angela, then Michael, then Abby, then the whole sordid mess, which was asinine all the way around, but he got himself so immersed in the miserable loop that he didn't heed the door until it was too late.

Since one never knew what might be occurring in his office, everyone was trained to knock first. It was an unbreakable rule, so one of his crew was in for a serious dressing-down. Irritably, he glanced across, and when he realized the identity of his guest, he nearly fell over in shock.

His half-brother, Charles Stevens, stood there, proud as you please, staring at him with a mixture of trepidation and offense. He was tall, thin, good-looking, with dark hair and eyes, and James recollected that he'd looked much the same when he was twenty.

"My name is Charles Stevens," he said succinctly, introducing himself and offering a slight bow.

"Yes, I know," James replied, struggling for composure, while frantically contemplating what could possibly have drawn the lad into the building against Edward's explicit instructions. Edward had always contended that the prohibition was because he hadn't wanted Charles to grow addicted to the games, but, James had also supposed, Edward had hoped to prevent any cultivation of familiarity with his two older, more world-weary brothers. "Won't you come in?"

He entered and closed the door behind him.

"Have a seat." James gestured to one of the chairs.

"This is not a social call."

"Still, would you like a brandy?" He indicated his glass sitting in the center of the desk.

"No."

"Very well." Slowly and deliberately, he tipped the legs

of his chair to the floor, lowered his feet, and steadied himself for whatever disaster was about to present itself. "What can I do for you?"

"I demand to know"—Charles's fury was barely suppressed—"what injury you committed against Lady Abigail Weston."

Abby was the last topic James had expected Charles to raise. Vacillating, he kept his expression carefully blank while a thousand questions raced through his mind. What had Charles been told? What had he gleaned as gossip? What sorts of comments would Edward want James to provide? There was also Abby's reputation to consider. Through close monitoring, he was certain that no rumors had slipped out, so discretion remained imperative.

He decided to let Charles take the lead until there were more facts on the table. "Why do you ask *me* about Lady Abigail?"

"Don't play dumb. You were having an intimate affair with her."

James didn't acknowledge or deny the charge. The silence lengthened.

"What did you do?" Charles shouted.

James rose and rounded the desk, hoping to ease the lad's distress while he stalled and grappled with untangling a suitable response. Obviously, his younger sibling had garnered some information—none of it good—and he would insist on explanations.

"Won't you sit, Charles?"

"No!"

"All right," he soothed, and he leaned a hip on the edge of the desk, crossed his arms over his chest, and tried to seem unperturbed. "I'm extremely surprised to find you here. What brings you?"

"For the past two weeks, I've been striving to ascertain what transpired between our father and Jerald Weston, the Earl of Marbleton, that has precipitated the untimely termination of my courtship of Lady Caroline Weston."

"I see."

"No, you don't! You don't *see* anything." His fists clenched with hostility; his cheeks burned with rage. "I had learned, in confidence, some time ago, that Lady Abigail might be having an *affaire d'amour*. . . ."

James stiffened. "Who spread such a vile rumor?"

"I would never say," Charles remarked tersely. "Just today, however, I learned that you were involved in whatever had ensued in the Weston home, and in my pursuit of the details, I now have an answer. You compromised Lady Abigail, didn't you? And Lord Marbleton uncovered your misdeed. 'Twas you who destroyed my chances with Caroline."

To James's great dismay, tears welled into Charles's eyes, bald evidence of how much he loved the girl and was shattered by the turn of events.

James vividly recalled every excruciating word his father had recited during the tense carriage ride they'd endured after leaving the Weston mansion on that horrid day.

If you won't think of yourself and your future happiness, Edward had chided, *if you won't think of Abigail and hers, perhaps you could think of Charles and what you've just done to your brother's life.*

Are you proud of yourself? his father had goaded.

Charles, this prized son, who looked so much like James, but to whom he couldn't even be introduced, had hovered over all of James's musings since then. He truly, truly had not intended harm to anyone. Especially not his younger brother, who must now hate him as others did. The idea troubled him exceedingly.

"Yes," he amazed himself by confirming, "I am completely responsible."

"At least you're man enough to admit it," Charles noted scornfully. "Why haven't you married Lady Abigail as duty and honor would require?"

"I had no desire to marry her," James said quietly, for once putting the entire blame squarely on his own shoulders. Evidently, Charles hadn't had the story related in any other fashion, so James opted to paint himself as the villain.

"I had always been told that you were a *bastard,* but that the designation had nothing to do with your birth status, but I hadn't wanted to believe it. Now I am forced to concede that the label is too true. What leaves me curious, however"—he advanced until they were toe to toe and eye to eye—"is why Lord Marbleton hasn't demanded satisfaction from you."

"The subject never came up." Showing absolutely no emotion, he added insolently, "Even if he'd thought to instigate a duel, he wouldn't have obtained much redress. His aim isn't that good."

"Well, *mine,* I assure you, is excellent."

Before James realized what he contemplated, Charles slapped him across the face, hard, with one of his leather riding gloves. James's head snapped to the side; his cheek stung. "What the hell . . ."

"As Lady Abigail apparently has no champion to assist her," Charles harshly pointed out, "I am more than happy to be the one who acts in her defense. Choose your seconds."

"You can't be serious."

"I've never been more *serious* in my life. We meet at dawn."

Brimming with consternation, James balanced on the balls of his feet, distending to his full height, finding that he was two or three inches taller than Charles. Needing occasion to reflect and process, he casually moved to the sideboard and refilled his brandy.

"Don't be absurd," he urged. "I'll not meet you at dawn or at any other time."

"I'm not surprised that you refuse," Charles declared. "A man who would ruin a woman such as Lady Abigail, and then have no compunction to rectify his conduct, clearly has no sense of decency. Perhaps you're simply a coward."

James sighed dolefully. "You don't know anything about me to make such claims."

"Your repudiation of my challenge provides the necessary indication."

"I could no more murder you than I could our father."

"Why are you so certain," Charles taunted caustically, "that your aim would be superior to mine?"

"I'm a marksman, Charles."

"So am I."

"I could never raise a weapon against you. No matter my feelings, no matter the particulars. I can't credit that you'd even ask me to consider it."

"Is that your final decision?"

"Yes, it is."

"Fine"—Charles nodded amicably, a strange, fiery gleam in his eye—"then I shall kill you here and now."

He reached under his cloak and retrieved a pistol. The barrel was long, black, and highly polished, the handle a pearl color with fancy scrollwork carved into it. The weapon looked heavy, expensive, loaded, and leveled with deadly purpose.

"Are you mad?" James was astounded and dismayed. Leaving nothing to chance, he reacted quickly, tossing his drink in Charles's face as he leapt to the side and grabbed Charles's wrist. He squeezed tightly, driving the barrel down toward the floor, and they battled, but Charles was strong as an ox, limber and wiry, and he wouldn't relinquish his grip. James began to worry that he'd have to break Charles's arm in order to compel him to release his hold.

"Let go!" he commanded.

"Never!"

"Let go!" he repeated, yanking strenuously, and he ultimately managed to wrestle it away without its discharging. "Sit down!" he decreed, and when his brother didn't comply, he shoved him toward a chair. "I'm not asking you; I'm telling you! Sit!"

Warily scrutinizing Charles, he stalked around the desk, opened a drawer, and locked the gun inside. "For pity's sake, you could have shot me!"

"I wish I had!" the younger man contended, then his legs folded, and he slid into the chair and perched on the edge. More tears swarmed. "Lord Marbleton is supposed to announce Caroline's engagement tomorrow afternoon. I'll never forgive you for what you've done."

He choked out the last, and a few tears overflowed. As he swiped at them, James observed his suffering, and the ice encasing his heart started to melt.

"I'm sorry, Charles," he murmured. "I didn't mean to hurt you or Lady Caroline. I didn't mean to hurt anyone."

"What about Abby?" Charles inquired quietly but not angrily. Leveling the gun had quashed his bravado; only anguish remained.

"She didn't want to marry me, Charles. I would have made her so miserable. She knew better."

Apparently this was a twist that had never occurred to Charles. "You proposed, then?"

"She said marriage to me"—he gave a self-deprecating grimace—"would be a *terrible* mistake."

"Those were her exact words?"

"Aye."

"Well, now that I've met you"—one corner of his mouth lifted in a hint of the familiar Stevens smile—"I'd say she had the right of it."

"She did," James agreed, totally serious.

Suddenly embarrassed, Charles stared down at his hands as though they belonged to someone else. "I don't think I could have pulled the trigger."

"I'm glad."

Charles shifted uncomfortably, then asked mournfully, "What am I to do, James? Lord Marbleton is preparing to wed my Caroline to another, and I never even got to tell her good-bye."

"Does she know why your visits were curtailed?"

"I don't know what she was informed," Charles said woefully, "but once Lord Marbleton proclaims her betrothal, there will be no method of rectifying the situation."

"Unfortunately, you're correct," James concurred dejectedly, oddly feeling the lad's anguish as his own and yearning to do something—anything!—to help. He was immensely unsettled by these powerful sensations of wanting—to be close, to be liked, to win the boy's regard. They were new and strange, and he didn't care for them at all, because he perceived that they would encourage him to risk impetuous action on Charles's behalf.

"Have you spoken with Father?" He sustained another wave of fervent sentiment that had him desperately longing to share Edward's paternal title.

"Until I'm blue in the face," Charles responded. "I've begged and pleaded for him to intervene somehow with Lord Marbleton, but he said to just 'let it go.' "

"Easy for him to be unconcerned," James muttered, loving the opportunity to take his brother's part against their father, "when he's not the one who's losing Caroline."

"Exactly," Charles concurred. "He's marrying again, and she's presumably his long-lost love, so I can't believe that he thinks I should blithely walk away from Caroline without a fight. He's certainly getting everything he's ever desired." At the offhand mention of Angela, Charles blushed.

"You haven't met my mother yet, have you?"

"No," Charles said, shaking his head.

"Don't listen to any of the gossip. She's quite something, and I expect . . ."—James was abruptly frantic for Charles to like Angela—"I expect you'll be pleasantly surprised."

"I saw her on the stage that one night at the Chelsey," Charles acknowledged. "She has a certain flair, doesn't she?"

"That's putting it mildly."

" 'Tis easy to grasp why Father would . . . well . . ." He blushed again.

"He claims he never got over her. Even after all these years."

"You've discussed his feelings about her?"

Charles was jealous! He was clearly bothered that James and Edward enjoyed the type of relationship where they

were comfortable reviewing such private matters. James
had never considered that his connection with Edward was
different, or deeper, than the one he had with his legitimate
children. The realization swirled through his chest, mixing
ferociously with all the other careening emotions, until he
began to feel dizzy.

"They're very much in love," he inevitably said, prompting dispassion into his voice. "When you see them together,
'tis so evident."

"You've been with them when they're together?"
Charles inquired plaintively. "At home, he just made an
imperial pronouncement of his intentions, but then, my sisters went off on a tirade. They've created such a harangue
that now he won't discuss his plans with any of us."

"That definitely sounds like Edward." James was eminently intrigued to behold his father from Charles's point
of view.

"I wish I could have met your mother that night at the
theater," Charles offered. "And you, too, but the encounter
was so wretchedly strange."

"Caroline was there," James reminded him, unable to
fathom how he'd ended up as the defender of Edward's
behavior. "And Abby. Father couldn't have introduced us
then—even if he'd wanted to."

"I could tell that he'd upset you. At times, I don't understand why he acts as he does. I've been dying to meet
you forever."

"Really?" James preened like a wee child who'd been
handed a favorite treat. "I've asked before, as well, but
Edward always refused. He felt that Michael and I would
be a bad influence on you."

"Did he actually say as much?"

Charles was incensed, and James flushed as a surge of
fondness swelled his heart till it no longer fit properly between his ribs. "Not in so many words, but he's never quite
grasped what to do with the two of us."

"Is Michael here?" Charles glanced around expectantly,

as though hoping Michael would materialize. "I should like to meet him, too."

"No. At the news of our parents' pending marriage, he left Town in a fit of pique."

"Would that I could have joined him!" Charles grumbled so sorrowfully that James chuckled.

He walked to the sideboard and refilled his libation, filled one for Charles, too, and at the offer, Charles accepted, and the two brothers sipped companionably. They smiled at one another, a lifting of the lips that was almost identical, and James grew wistful. He was so delighted that Charles had come, so thrilled that he'd brought his problems here, and he couldn't help but lament over the lost association that had been formerly denied to them.

They smiled again, the pangs of this novel friendship cutting like shards of broken glass. As easy as that, James recognized that his bond with Charles was permanent, solid, and true, a familial loyalty that was indestructible, and he was now duty-bound to protect him, to keep him safe and happy. "So, lad," he nudged, "if you could have anything in the world, what would it be?"

"I'd marry Caroline immediately," Charles declared, without having to ponder his answer.

"You'd dare defy them all? You love her that much?" There hadn't really been a need to inquire. The depth of the boy's admiration was shining through, plainly visible.

"Without a doubt," Charles beamed. "You don't know what she's like."

"No." But he knew Abby intimately, and if Caroline had half of Abby's charm, Charles would never get over her. James couldn't bear to have Charles suffering through the agony that he himself was enduring.

"I wish I could introduce the two of you," Charles said, "so you'd understand."

James *understood* perfectly. Better than Charles could ever guess.

Slowly, a strategy began to emerge. It was scandalous, dangerous, bold, and if it succeeded, numerous parties would be perpetually affronted. Not that James cared. His only concern was for Charles. Aiding him seemed as natural as all the occasions he'd shouldered Michael's burdens over the years. Plus, he was determined to make whatever small amends he could so that at least one person would be content in the end.

"I suspect there's a method for you to win Caroline," he judiciously pronounced, "but you must carefully consider your resolve. This will affect her more than you. Are you confident that she returns your emotions?"

"Positive. She and I have . . ."

Looking abashed, he didn't complete his sentence, causing James to ponder how well his little brother actually knew Caroline Weston. Perhaps he'd be doing everyone a favor by seeing them united.

"Have you . . . ?" he posed delicately.

"Never! She's a lady!" Charles asserted, then he backed off as he remembered James's comportment toward Abby and what had incited him to call in the first place. "Sorry . . . I'm not suggesting that . . ."

" 'Tis all right," James stated, waving away Charles's discomfiture. "I'm not the best role model in these cases."

"I just meant that she and I have sneaked off alone a few times. But I'd always intended to wait for our wedding night."

James nodded, deeming the boy a martyr or a fool, relieved that he'd grown up differently. "Your life will be completely altered, and there'll be no going back. Not for you. Or for Caroline."

"I'll do anything to make her mine!" Charles vowed.

James accepted the gravity of Charles's pledge. He'd have done the same for Abby—had she ever given the slightest indication that she'd wanted him to. "We'll have to proceed with haste. Tonight. With her betrothal so close, we can't tarry till tomorrow. If you're certain . . ."

"I am."

James stepped into the hallway and summoned one of his assistants. They whispered confidentially, the man left, then returned several minutes later, and the whispering continued as Charles watched all with avid curiosity.

"Excellent," James eventually said. "Send Mary up to me, would you?"

The man went to fetch her.

"Mary?" Charles queried.

"She works for me, usually as a housemaid, but as with all my employees, she's extremely versatile." He donned his cloak.

"Where are we off to?"

"Lord Marbleton and his family are attending a soiree at the home of the Earl of Rosewood. 'Tis Caroline's first outing in several weeks." He rested a comforting hand on Charles's arm. "The Westons want her to be seen in public with her new fiancé—a sort of public preview for tomorrow's announcement."

Appalled, Charles asked, "Does Caroline realize what they're up to?"

"That . . . I don't know. But I gather she'd rather be somewhere else. Let's go find out for sure, shall we?"

TWENTY-ONE

Caroline Weston looked from one end of the grand ball-room to the other. She'd been hoping to meet Charles in the crush of people, but so far she hadn't seen him anywhere. If she hadn't been able to get close enough to speak with him personally, she'd thought to send a message through one of their mutual friends, but she'd had no luck. Charles had obviously decided not to attend.

Even if she'd stumbled upon him, she doubted if she'd have been able to chat. All evening, Margaret had lurked by her side as though she were being kept on a leash. Jerald had been hovering, too, but thankfully, he'd finally trotted off, but not before advising her that he was going in search of a young man to whom he wanted her introduced.

Jerald could show up with one of the princes, the royal swain down on bended knee and proposing marriage, and she wouldn't give the highborn suitor a second glance. She just wanted to talk to Charles! Heaven only knew what story he'd been fed by her brother, and she wasn't about to have him assuming that she'd changed her mind. Far from it.

She wasn't exactly sure what had happened that day in Jerald's library when Edward had come to call, along with his illegitimate son, James. But it didn't take a genius to put the pieces together. There had been a shouting match, and Abigail had been sent away in the dead of night, never to be heard from again. Then, as though Caroline had been the one to cause all the trouble, she'd been confined to her rooms, and Charles banished from the house.

For weeks, Caroline had been aware that Abigail was carrying on an affair, but Caroline had suspected that she was trysting with Edward. To learn that it had been the dangerous, impudent rogue of a son, instead! My, but she didn't think Abigail had had it in her to do something so rash.

Caroline had only observed James Stevens on two brief occasions, but that was plenty of opportunity to judge how handsome he was. Not nearly as attractive as Charles, of course, yet dashing in his own fashion. His features were more bold, his shape more broad, and there was a hazardous air about his person that would make any female of good sense shy away.

While her upbringing had been extremely sheltered, she'd still managed to glean some of the gossip about James, plus Charles had fed her various interesting tidbits. By most accounts, his older half-brother was a scoundrel, a villain of dubious integrity and reputation. Charles had heard all the stories, but tended not to believe them, relying on his father's opinion, instead, which was that James was a tough, fair, and honorable individual, who'd been hardened by life experiences.

Despite Caroline's innocent rearing, she hadn't needed anyone to tell her that James had a definite way with the ladies. That night in the theater lobby, every woman in the place had surreptitiously watched him. How Abigail had crossed paths with such a man, how she'd gotten close enough to begin a liaison, or how she'd found the courage to proceed, were questions Caroline was dying to have answered, but she had no idea when Abigail's disgrace would end so that her sister could confess all the juicy details.

Jerald refused to discuss her, as did Margaret, and no one would explain what the future held. All Caroline knew with any certainty was that Abigail was gone, Charles had been turned away, and Caroline ended up spending hundreds of deplorable, solitary hours in Jerald's stifling Town house.

A serving maid who was passing by bumped her slightly, the move precariously tipping the glasses on the woman's tray. Lest the entire mess topple and send wet spray across the floor, Caroline leaned to the side, reached out a steadying hand, and she was surprised to the core when the servant spoke softly to her.

"Charles and James Stevens are outside and request that you join them."

"What?" Caroline gasped on a rush of air.

"Not so loudly," the woman prudently chided. "Will you accompany me?"

"Absolutely!" Caroline verbalized quietly, her eyes wide with excitement.

"Ask me the direction to the ladies' retiring room."

Caroline turned to Margaret and made her delicate entreaty, then mentioned agreeably, "This maid can show me the way."

"Don't dawdle!" Margaret insisted. "And meet me back here in the corner the instant you return."

"Where else would I go?" she asked sweetly, then hurried away while struggling to appear casual.

With the maid leading, they strolled through the crowd and toward the entryway. Once there, they climbed the stairs, passed through a long hall, and the numbers thinned until they no longer encountered any other guests. The maid deposited her tray on a table, and they increased their pace, finally descending another set of stairs, this one narrow and quiet.

"What's happening?" Caroline implored as they started down.

"Mr. Stevens will explain," the maid replied enigmatically.

Moments later, the maid opened a back door, and Caroline stepped out into the fresh night air. "Follow me," the woman said, and Caroline obediently accompanied her. Whirling at the furtive circumstances, her heart pounded with trepidation.

They walked through the garden, fortunately managing to elude anyone Caroline knew. Toward the far wall, the maid paused.

"James?" she asked, her voice barely audible.

"I'm here, Mary."

James Stevens emerged from behind a hedge. He seemed taller than Caroline recalled. Dressed all in black, from his shirt to his boots, and half hidden by the shadows, he looked positively sinister.

"Hello, Lady Caroline," he said politely, bowing in acknowledgment.

"Mr. Stevens," she responded carefully. She wasn't afraid, but on guard, and hoping that Charles's descriptions about his brother's character were accurate. "Is Charles here?" she queried anxiously.

"In the alley. In my coach." Gently but firmly, he counseled, "I apologize for the drama to which we've subjected you, but I must warn you of some disturbing news that we have recently discovered."

"What is it?"

"Your brother, Jerald, intends to accept a marriage contract on your behalf this evening, with the proposal and announcement tomorrow."

"No!" She recoiled, unable to credit what he'd just disclosed.

"Quietly, please, milady," he cautioned. "I realize the information is a great shock."

"Who has he chosen?"

"Lord Welby's son."

"I can't marry him," she declared, holding her fingers against her lips, wondering if she might be ill. She couldn't abide the selfish oaf. "I've already promised myself to Charles."

"I'm glad to hear you say that," he murmured, and though it was very dark, Caroline could see his eyes twinkling. "In order to avoid your fate, Charles requests that you take a drastic step with him."

"Anything . . ." she said, meaning it. She'd do anything for Charles. "Just tell me what it is."

"I have made hasty arrangements for the two of you to elope this evening. To Scotland. After, you'll travel to my country house, where you'll stay until I deem it safe for you to reappear in London." Footsteps sounded on the next path, and they all stiffened, listening to a pair of discreet lovers lingering nearby. The duo moved on, and Mr. Stevens continued. "Unfortunately, there is no time to mull your decision. If you would like to proceed, we must be away."

"Now?" She was shocked by the abrupt turn of events.

"I'm sorry, but yes," he explained. "It must be right now."

Caroline glanced toward the brilliantly lit house, realizing that she had only a few more minutes before Margaret noticed her protracted absence. A few small, precious minutes before others started to search for her. A handful of precarious, valuable minutes during which she could be detected by the wrong person wandering down the garden path.

Yet here she stood, having to make a split-second decision about her future. If she departed with Mr. Stevens, she'd be leaving her entire life behind. Nothing would ever be the same. Margaret and Jerald would disown her, her friends would never be permitted to communicate with her again, most of London's doors would be closed to her.

Did she care?

The answer was a resounding *no,* she didn't care. Not with Charles waiting for her on the other side of the wall. But as she suffered the thought, one face, one person, came to mind, and that was Abigail.

How would Abigail perceive the rash choice Caroline was being offered?

Caroline stared at this man who had brought such unmitigated disaster down upon her sister, this notorious man whom Edward admired and Charles adored, and she vividly recollected Abigail and that day in her dressing room when Abigail had been dancing in front of the mirror with an imaginary beau, categorically exuding intense joy and devotion. Without a doubt, Abigail had loved James Stevens; she wasn't the type of woman who would have given herself freely. Only desperate emotion could have driven her to such lengths.

She pictured Abigail, forsaken and miserable in the country, forever separated from the man she had cherished above all others, and she decided that Abigail would understand her determination. And who knew? Maybe once she was established with Charles, she'd be able to seek Abigail out on her own, Jerald and his stuffy morals be damned!

"Take me to Charles," she declared, feeling reckless and foolhardy.

"With pleasure," Mr. Stevens said.

He presented his arm, and with the maid—Mary—close behind, ushered them to a gate. They slipped through undetected, and his carriage was parked a few feet away. At their approach, the door opened, and Charles leapt down, swinging her into a tight embrace.

"Caroline," he whispered, his warm scent sweeping over her and rendering her giddy with ecstasy. He kissed her long and slow, with Mr. Stevens and Mary watching, but Caroline didn't hesitate to return his affection. Her relief at being in his arms once again was so great that nothing else mattered.

Only the sound of Mr. Stevens clearing his throat compelled them to desist. "You can kiss her as long as you desire," he advised Charles, "as soon as you're safely away."

"You're right, of course," Charles agreed. He turned to her. "Are you sure, love?"

"Oh, yes. Very sure." She smiled, and he smiled, too.

"Up you go, then." He gripped her waist and lifted her in. Mary climbed in after and unobtrusively settled herself in the far corner.

"Are you coming with us?" Caroline asked, surprised.

"Aye, milady," Mary said. "James felt that the trip would be difficult for you, and he didn't want you obliged to travel without a lady's maid."

Caroline raised her brows at the revelation, amazed that the enigmatic man had remembered such a convenience, and glad that he was willing to be so helpful and kind when they'd never even been introduced.

Mary grinned mischievously, obviously enjoying the prospect of an adventure. "Considering the circumstances," she added lightly, " 'tisn't as if we could have your own personal maid accompany us."

"No, definitely not." Caroline chuckled, then she sobered as it suddenly occurred to her that she was fleeing with only the gown in which she was currently attired. "What am I to do for clothing?"

"The first day or two will be rough," Mary said, "but if you can bear with me, James has directed me to get you appropriately outfitted as promptly as we're able."

"I'm certain we'll lump along nicely." She was eager to be off, enthusiastic for the escapade to start. Peeking out the window, she saw Charles huddled with his brother, deep in conversation. At the sight of them, so elegant and dynamic, her heart swelled with love and pride. She let the curtain drop into place and shifted against the squab. On a prayer, she closed her eyes and tried to relax, readying herself for the commencement of the rest of her life.

"Do you have the bag of coins I gave you?" James asked. They needed to hurry, yet he was desperate to prolong the moment. Now that he'd met Charles, he didn't want him to depart.

"Yes," Charles responded, patting the front of his jacket.

"And the directions to the house?"

"Yes."

"Write to me as soon as you arrive."

"I will."

"How about the combination to the safe?"

"Got it." He patted his pocket once again.

"Don't forget to lock your marriage license inside it immediately," he warned.

"James"—Charles laughed quietly—"you're worrying like an old hen."

"With good reason. We're in a rush, which makes it easy to neglect the important details."

"I'll protect our marital proof at all costs."

James paused, imagining what else he might have overlooked. Baldly, he said, "Don't return to London until you're convinced that she's increasing. You can't give Jerald an excuse to reverse what you've done."

"I'll do my best," Charles said, cocky and full of himself, "to ensure she becomes pregnant as rapidly as possible."

"Randy devil," James muttered. "Your surname is definitely Stevens."

Just then, Caroline glanced out the window, gazing expectantly at them both, then retreating behind the curtain, and James couldn't get over how young she seemed, how fresh and innocent. Unexpectedly, he was overwhelmed by a surge of fondness, as well as a wave of protectiveness, for the girl. By all accounts, Charles was a fine lad, but still, with the strict courtship rules of their society, Caroline hardly knew him.

He couldn't help glaring at his brother. "Have you ever lain with a woman?"

"James!"

Even in the darkness, James could tell Charles was blushing. "Well . . . ?"

"Many times," Charles answered.

"I assume they were whores."

"Mostly."

"Then . . . have a care with her. *Try* to restrain yourself. Take your time at initiating her."

"I'll go slowly," Charles pledged.

"For her sister's sake,"—remarkably, he couldn't prevent himself from appending—"and for *mine,* be kind to her."

"I swear to you," Charles proclaimed earnestly, "that I shall love her all my days."

"You'd better," James admonished like a gruff father, "or you'll have to deal with me."

A silence ensued, became awkward, and then, to his utter astonishment and delight, Charles reached out and crushed him in a fast hug.

"Thank you," Charles mumbled into his ear. "For everything."

"You're welcome." James struggled to remain calm and detached, but his heart was booming a thousand miles per hour. Charles pulled away, and they clasped hands. "If you need anything," James expressed, "send a messenger straightaway."

"I will," Charles said.

"When the two of you decide to come back to London, if Father has evicted you and you require a place to stay . . ."—he swallowed and forced the unusual statement from his mouth—"my door is always open."

More footsteps and voices could be heard in the garden beyond the wall, and they froze.

"Good-bye," Charles mouthed.

James nodded his farewell, and Charles vaulted into the coach. The driver, already fully briefed on his duties, pulled away. The carriage jingled to life, and the horses' hooves clopped out of the black alley and toward the street. At the last instant, Caroline poked her head out and waved gaily, blowing merry kisses in his direction. They turned the corner and disappeared, and in no more than a moment he was alone. He stood rooted to his spot, unable to stir long after the vehicle had faded into the night.

Slowly, he walked to the lit avenue, while pondering where he should go next. Briefly, he contemplated heading for home, but in view of his melancholy mood, the silence and stillness of his lonely house was a gloomy option. Not able to stomach the idea of such a solitary confinement, he hailed a cab and provided directions to his club, where the noise and bustle might aid him in keeping his demons at bay.

Abigail strolled distractedly across the sloping backyard toward her family's ancestral residence. The mansion was majestically perched on a hillside, dominating the valley, and it gleamed white in the bright sunshine. Colors and fragrances from the perfectly tended gardens assaulted her eyes and nose, but she paid no attention. The grounds of the Marbleton estate were always beautiful, never more so than in summer, yet she hardly noticed the flowers or shrubbery.

For over a month now, she'd languished in the country. Jerald had sent her down like some sort of recalcitrant child, but she hadn't minded. After the initial shock of her circumstance had begun to wane, she'd relished the isolation and had expended all of her hours in trying to decide what her next move should be.

Unfortunately, she'd had very little inspiration. Money was not a problem, because she could draw funds from her trust. She could go anywhere and attempt anything, the problem being that she had no notion of what she would truly like to do.

In the time she'd been home, Jerald had posted one caustic letter, advising that he was busy finding her a husband, and that she would be obligated to wed once the agreements were finalized. The very idea of Jerald picking her fiancé was as hilarious as it was terrifying. She could just imagine what type of man he'd deem suitable, so she'd written a reply, tersely insisting that she would never marry, that he needn't expend any effort on the fruitless endeavor, but he hadn't drafted a subsequent response.

Due to her advanced age, he couldn't force her, but where did that leave her?

As an unmarried woman, she had no options. Once she refused Jerald's spousal selection, she'd be impelled to vacate the premises without delay, and she'd already discovered that she couldn't remain in the Marbleton area. When she'd arrived at the height of the Season, gossip had rapidly circulated among the neighbors that it must have been due to some type of immorality she'd committed in Town. She couldn't even innocently shop in the village without encountering their malicious disapproval.

So her only other viable course was to go back to London, where she could enjoy a fair amount of anonymity, but it would be an exceedingly pitiful existence. She could purchase a house, employ a companion, then live out her days as an odd, sequestered spinster, but the concept was so depressing that she couldn't bear to dwell upon it.

With the loss of her familial connections and the doors of Polite Society closed to her, she'd have to build new friendships among the demimonde, and such a bohemian lifestyle would place her smack on the fringes of James's world. Wherever she went, his name would be casually bandied about, women would titter over his naughty antics, and—Lord forbid!—she might run into him while he was out and about with his latest lover.

There were definite advantages to being exiled and disgraced, hidden from view and denied all company. She never had to hear a word about him. But in London . . . oh . . . she'd never be safe.

In her sequestration, she could delude herself into believing that their relationship had been an absurd indiscretion, but to encounter him again, alive and in the flesh, would kill her. With a dreaded certainty, she knew it to be so. To be faced with his scorn, to be struck again by his indifference, was too shattering to consider.

"What to do . . . what to do . . ." Incessantly, she ruminated over the question that had no conspicuous answer.

She stepped onto the terrace just as one of the maids came outside looking for her.

"Milady," she announced, "you have a visitor."

"A visitor? For me?" She was surprised and alarmed. With rampant rumors of her ruination circulating the countryside, it wouldn't be any of the local gentry, which only left someone from Town. With the Season's festivities winding down, no one of importance would be caught dead so far from all the action, so most likely it would be a messenger with another angry missive from Jerald.

Had the rat located a husband for her? When she declined to accept his decision, what would be the consequence? Was she to be immediately evicted? Would she be permitted to pack a bag?

"Who is it?" she managed.

"She wouldn't divulge her name, but she's in the receiving parlor. The butler explained to her that you weren't taking callers, but the impossible woman wouldn't listen." The maid nervously worried one hand over the other. "She just barged right in!"

Upon learning that the visitor was female, some of her apprehension lessened. "Don't fret," she irritably told the servant. "I won't tattle to my brother that you've let a guest breach the walls." The maid had the grace to blush at the reminder that the household retainers around whom Abigail had been raised were now acting as her jailers.

Proceeding down the hall, she entered the chamber, then stopped in her tracks as Angela Ford whirled around. Beautiful as always, Mrs. Ford was dressed in a flowing, scarlet gown meant to shock and turn heads. The manner in which it sculpted her voluptuous figure was almost sinful.

"There you are!" she said, smiling and rushing forward. "I was going to give that snooty butler one more minute, then I was prepared to search this mausoleum myself."

Angela Ford was here? In her drawing room? Feeling as though she were having a bizarre hallucination, Abigail shook herself in an attempt to clear her vision. "I must say," she remarked, thoroughly disconcerted, "that you are the very last person I expected at Marbleton, Mrs. Ford."

"Call me Angela," she suggested. "And it's Mrs. Stevens now." She jovially waved her fingers so that Abigail could view her large diamond.

"Since when?" Abigail was smiling, too, and moving across the salon until they met in the middle. Astonishingly, Angela opened her arms and gregariously hugged her as though they were two long-lost friends. Abigail had never had much experience with people who were so flagrantly demonstrative, so she didn't know what else to do but to react with an embrace of her own. Hands joined, they sat together on the small sofa.

"Two days ago," Angela glowed. " 'Twas so romantic. We didn't tell anyone. We just sneaked off and did it."

"I'm utterly thrilled," Abigail said. "Is Edward with you?"

"No. The stick-in-the-mud refused to accompany me. If you want my opinion, he's become entirely too stiff-necked in the years we've been apart. I'll have to break him in all over again." But the gleam in her eye belied her complaint; she would obviously welcome every minute of *retraining* Edward to her liking.

"Where is he?"

"At the tavern in the village."

"But why? I would love to have seen him."

"Didn't I say so?" She rolled her eyes at the stupidity of men. "But he isn't about to do anything that would put your brother into more of a state."

"Jerald is *that* upset?" Abigail was unnerved to learn that he was still so angry. Such a high level of continuing aggravation didn't bode well for her future. "Surely he's calmed a little by now."

"I'm not talking about your predicament. I'm referring to what happened last week. With Caroline and Charles." Angela hesitated, observing Abigail's confusion. "You haven't heard!"

"Heard what? I haven't had any news since I've been here."

"Your brother was all set to marry Caroline to some half-wit, so she eloped with my stepson, Charles Stevens. The scandal is all over Town."

"Caroline's eloped?"

In all the hours she'd passed contemplating her prospects, she'd barely dared consider her sister and what fate Jerald might devise for her. It was clear that he intended to punish Caroline for Abigail's sins, yet Abigail hadn't been able to devise a single method of rescuing her. Not when Jerald was Caroline's legal and financial guardian.

While she was relieved that Caroline had ended up with Charles, she was saddened anew by all the damage she'd wrought on her unsuspecting family. If she hadn't initiated her affair with James, Caroline would be at home where she belonged, planning a grand wedding to close out the Season, instead of hiding in some strange city, secluded and furtively commencing her new life.

Just then, the butler poked his nose in the room, and Angela informed him, "Lady Abigail is shaken by the tidings I've related. Bring us a bottle of whiskey and two glasses. Straightaway."

The man huffed at being ordered about by the strong-willed, flamboyant woman. "Madam," he snarled, "Lady Abigail doesn't drink hard spirits."

"She does now. Go get some!" Angela snapped, and he shuffled away in a snit while she sympathetically massaged Abigail's back. "Are you all right?"

"No," Abigail admitted candidly. "I'm completely stunned. I had always envisioned a magnificent celebration for Caroline's wedding. But to discover that my actions drove her to such a drastic resolution!"

"I wouldn't feel too badly if I were you," Angela advised sagely. "That Charles Stevens has the look of the devil about him, and he's about the age my Eddy was when I first tied myself up with him. She'll not be regretting her choices."

The butler reentered, carrying a tray laden with the items Angela had demanded. She crossed the room and snatched it from him, while pushing him into the hall and closing the door in his face. Pouring them both a glass of the strong liquor, she held one out, and Abigail reached for it with trembling fingers, drinking and letting the potent elixir burn its way to her stomach.

More calm, she queried, "How did they accomplish it?"

"James arranged it all."

"James?" Abigail gasped, loving and hating the chance to speak his name. "Why would he? He and Charles aren't even acquainted."

"I didn't realize they were, either, and Eddy insists not, so I'm not certain how it came about. Supposedly, James snatched Caroline from a party right under Margaret's nose, then she and Charles fled to Scotland in James's carriage."

"Where are they now?"

"No one knows, but word has it that James is concealing their whereabouts." She took a long taste of her libation. "If he is, he's not saying. Eddy wants to wring both boys' necks, and Jerald is fit to have an apoplexy, so that's why Eddy ducked the opportunity to visit you. Considering Jerald's condition, Eddy deems it best if all of us Stevenses stay clear till this latest storm blows over." She smiled naughtily. "Personally, I think we should all tell Jerald to go f . . ."—she paused, then chuckled. "Well . . . never mind."

Angela downed her whiskey while Abigail sipped hers, then the older woman refilled both glasses as she casually mentioned, "Aren't you going to ask me about James?"

"No." Abigail shifted uncomfortably. "Why would I ask about James?"

"I just thought you might be wondering how he's been, what he's been doing with himself."

"Besides orchestrating his brother's elopement, you mean?"

"Yes . . . besides that. . . ."

Both women smiled, but Abigail's faded, and she stood and walked to the end of the room. Unable to face Angela, or the topic she intended to address, she stared out the window, becoming keenly interested in one of the gardeners who was kneeling in the grass and pruning a hedge. "I don't want to talk about him."

"When you appeared on my doorstep in London"—Angela's skirts crinkled as she rose and crossed the room, as well—"you said that you loved him. That you loved him 'more than life.' Those were your very words."

Abigail shrugged. "Foolish sentiments," she murmured, "from a naive, stupid girl."

"I know he cared enough to meet with you even though I urged him not to. What did he tell you?"

"Nothing at all. You had warned me that he felt no attachment to me—or any woman, for that matter—and I should have listened."

Angela rested a gentle hand on Abigail's shoulder. "Did he actually say that he didn't love you?"

"Yes," she choked out on a hitched breath, recalling every hateful, mortifying comment that had sprung from his lips on that dreadful afternoon, "he said exactly that."

"And you believed him?"

"How could I not?"

"Don't you understand anything about my son? He assumed he was being noble!" She grumbled low in her throat, then clutched her fists to her bosom, as though enacting a melodramatic scene on the stage. "He sent you on your way, because he is so *unworthy* of you."

"I *never* thought he was undeserving!"

"Well, James certainly supposes that's how you feel. And why shouldn't he?" she inquired angrily. "What did you ever do that might cause him think differently? You initiated a clandestine affair; you were embarrassed to be seen with him, unwilling to let others know you'd been together—"

"That's not true!" Abigail broke in indignantly.

"The one occasion you could have recognized him—that night at the theater—you gave him a vicious public cut. How else should he regard your behavior?"

"I never meant to treat him badly!"

"Didn't you?"

The damning question hung in the air, and Abigail blushed with shame, unable to lie to his mother. She'd never done anything to show James how important he was to her. At every juncture, she'd denied him.

"Tell me the truth: Do you still love him?"

"Yes. Yes, I do," Abigail confessed.

"Then why are you here, cowering in this house?"

"My brother ordered me home!"

"So?"

"I couldn't refuse!"

"Why not? How old are you? Twenty-five? With your

own fortune and your entire life ahead of you!" She grumbled sarcastically, "Oh, that I had been able to start out with some of your horrid luck!"

Abigail wished she could explain how apprehensive she was over all these alien, drastic alternatives. The future seemed to be a huge, dark hole, yawning loudly, anxious to suck her in and pull her down. " 'Tis not so easy as you imagine!"

"Isn't it?" Angela asked in disgust. "Jerald is treating you like a babe. He decreed that you go to the country, and you scurried away as fast as your feet could carry you!"

"There wasn't any reason to tarry in London! James didn't want me!"

"Oh, you are wrong," Angela said, clucking in dismay. "You are so bloody wrong. I'd like to shake the pair of you!" She took Abigail's hands in her own. "Abigail, dear, what are your plans? Will you stay here until Jerald tosses you out? Until he selects some fishwife of a husband whom you will loathe till your dying day?"

"I don't know what's best," she mumbled dejectedly. "I'm so confused."

"Honey, you don't need to be," Angela consoled confidently. "Let me tell you something: When I was your age, I left Eddy. I was stubborn and vain and completely convinced that I was right, even though when I first became entangled with him, I knew that he would have to marry someday—and it wouldn't be to me. I *knew* how it would go, yet I couldn't stop myself. Then his destiny hit the two of us like a powerful sea wind, and I let arrogance be my guide. We were separated for twenty-five years, and I'm so lucky that fate has given me a second chance. We rushed off and married without even inviting our children to witness the ceremony."

"None of them?"

"No. We were tired of their whining. And guess what? I don't care a fig that they weren't with us. I'm just so relieved that he's returned. Nothing else matters so long as

Eddy remains by my side. The rest of the world can jump off a cliff."

"But I'm not like you," Abigail persisted. Angela had had a lifetime of practice at reaching out and grabbing for what she desired, while the only singular act Abigail had ever committed had been loving James. And look where that had landed her! " 'Tis frightening to consider throwing all caution to the wind. I'm afraid of what might happen."

"What is there to be afraid of? The very worst conclusion is that you couldn't turn James's heart around and you'd wind up with a broken one yourself. But you're already there! Taking a chance can't make things any worse!" She tenderly patted Abigail's cheek. "Will you sit here on your laurels while Jerald organizes a life you couldn't abide? Or will you seize what you genuinely crave?"

"I don't know how," Abigail declared softly.

"Yes, you do," Angela asserted. " 'Tis simple. Just swallow your pride and go to James. Because he's not going to come to you! You'll have to risk that initial step. I realize it's scary, but if you succeed, won't the gamble have been worth it? For what is your other option?" She gestured around the perfectly appointed, sterile salon. "Will you forgo a home of your own? Children? No James to love?" Quietly, fervently, she stated, "I traveled down that road, Abigail, when I abandoned Eddy and fled to Paris with our boys, and it wasn't a pretty trip. Not a single day of it."

The clock down the hall chimed the hour, and Angela straightened and sighed. "I must be off; Eddy will be starting to worry." She went to one of the side chairs, lifted her wrap, and pulled it over her shoulders. "Please promise me that you'll consider what I've said."

"I will."

"If you decide to journey to London, my man Arthur is still at the house, watching after James for me. I've informed him that you might show. He'll let you in and help you get settled." She laughed bawdily. "Move in the damned place; I don't care. You're already a *fallen* woman; go ahead and *fall* a bit further. Just swear to me that you won't leave until James has the opportunity to ask you to stay."

"Where will you be?" Abigail's voice was quaking as badly as her legs, and she eased herself down on a nearby chair.

"We're bound for the Italian coast and our honeymoon. I'd hoped we could visit Paris so Eddy could see where the boys and I had lived, but with all the national upset, we can't stop there. I offered to write to Bonaparte—"

"You're friends with Napoleon Bonaparte?"

"Of course," she answered, looking at Abigail as though she were addled. "I was the *darling*"—she batted her long lashes—"of Paris for nearly two decades. He'd have granted us safe passage, but Eddy wouldn't even discuss it. His *position* and all. That man and his stuffy convictions!" She winked wickedly. "I'll have to work my wiles on him during our lengthy sea voyage. He'll come 'round." She leaned down and kissed Abigail on the forehead. "Goodbye, my dear."

"Good-bye, Angela. Godspeed to you both."

Angela gazed down upon her, then placed her open palm on Abigail's head, as if bestowing a benediction. "Be happy, Abigail. Decide what it is you want and go after it. Don't be timid! You'd be surprised by the small miracles that might occur."

In a swirl of skirts, she departed. Abigail lingered in her chair, too overwhelmed to escort her to the door. Sensing the woman's light perfume, her full-bodied laughter, her charismatic presence, she sat in the stunned silence Angela had left in her wake, and in the blind void enveloping her, she could only focus on one thought.

James! James was alone, and in London, and missing her! Angela claimed it was so.

What was she prepared to do about it?

With all her being, she yearned to storm from the house and march to Town, demanding her rightful place by his side. Angela Ford Stevens made it sound so easy but in all actuality it wasn't so simple to cast off one's past while recklessly plunging forward when there were no guarantees. Yet the older woman had lit a spark that was rapidly igniting into a raging torrent of longing for James. On any terms. Without condition.

Could she, dare she, attempt such a perilous leap for happiness? If she vaulted off this precipice into the great unknown stretching before her, and James didn't deign to catch her, where would she find herself when she hit bottom? Did it matter?

Her pulse pounding in her veins, her mind frantically searching through the possibilities, she quit the parlor and climbed the stairway to her rooms.

TWENTY-TWO

James returned home just as dawn was breaking. His long night of employment was ending, but the rest of London was beginning to stir and face the day. He crossed the threshold and closed the door on the procession of carts and sellers who were slowly going about their business.

By his own request, no one was up to greet him. He was the sole person rattling around in the large house, and he couldn't see any reason to have Arthur, or any of the other servants, hop out of bed to say hello, watch him hang his cloak and eat a few eggs. Competently, he took care of his own outer garments, then stood for a moment in the silent foyer.

By the very nature of their jobs and interests, they had always been a family of night owls. Usually at this time of the morning, he and Michael would have arrived together, animated from all the commotion at the club. Angela would have just arrived, as well, after an evening filled with a performance and parties. On many occasions, she would have brought along friends, and there'd be a loud, chatty, interesting group eating breakfast in the dining room.

More often, it had been the three of them. Fatigued from their endeavors, but unable to rest, they'd unwind by re-hashing the happenings, sharing gossip, exchanging information, and enjoying each other's company.

Now there was only this dreaded stillness. Which he hated.

The hollow ticking of the clock echoed through the empty halls, a constant reminder of how alone he was. Angela had eloped with Edward, then left for Italy without so much as a fare-thee-well. When they returned to London—whenever that would be—they'd reside in Edward's Town house, so she'd never be back. The spirit and vitality she'd breathed into the drafty rooms were gone for good.

Michael was still having his temper tantrum, and rumor had it that he'd gotten himself involved with a woman, but James wouldn't venture to guess what that meant. There was no telling when his brother would reappear, making James wonder if he should simply stay at the club full-time, thereby avoiding these depressing homecomings entirely.

He climbed the stairs slowly, weariness pulling at his mind and body, and he thought about Charles and Caroline. At least one thing had gone right. They were safe at his country house, and the notion made him feel a little better. But then, for the briefest instant, Abby managed to creep into his musings as he pondered where she was and what she might be doing, and he was immediately overcome with misery. Refusing to consider her, he was successful in chasing her away.

No use going down that road!

At the top, he paused, listening to the overwhelming quiet that now occupied the spaces where there had once been so much laughter and gaiety. Strange, but he thought he could hear someone singing, and he shook his head. His mother and brother had only been absent a few weeks, and ghosts were already flitting about.

Still . . . walking down the hall, he couldn't get past the sensation that someone was on the premises, someone whose presence altered the atmosphere, though who it might be, he hadn't a clue. His senses on full alert, he strode into his bedchamber.

The drapes were drawn, candles lit, food and wine on one of the tables, the bedcovers turned down. A lace-trimmed corset, its strings dangling, lay across the foot of his bed. An aroma of roses wafted through the partially closed door to his dressing room. Water trickled through someone's fingers.

For pity's sake! It was six o'clock in the morning, he was dead tired, desirous of a few hours solitude and repose, and there was an unknown woman bathing in his private rooms! Surely this was more than a man should have to abide!

What female of his acquaintance would dare breach the sanctity of his home? Whoever she was, she was brash, bold, and either extremely brave or remarkably stupid. Considering his state of irritation anymore, only a fool would tangle with him. Anger and annoyance warred with one another at the notion that he'd be constrained to endure some sort of ordeal to get her to leave.

While he was willing to tolerate many things from the fairer sex, he was hardly ready to have them sneaking into his bath and bed. Yet, as he traversed the floor, his cock stirred as he contemplated the nude form he was about to view. Since that last, dramatic rendezvous with Abigail, he'd not visited a woman's bed. Not that he hadn't had plenty of chances, but none of those who'd acted interested had titillated his interest the least bit.

It had been almost two months since he'd enjoyed a carnal release, and the lack had added some undesirable side effects to his personality. He was surly, fatigued, irate, and ready to toss this interloper out on her pretty arse, but before he gave her the heave-ho, he was certainly willing to rudely partake of whatever she offered. A quick, heated coupling might be just the ticket to alleviate his stress and bring about some much-needed sleep.

In his dressing room, the smell of roses was stronger. The woman had disrobed in here, and her clothes were scattered about. The tub was shielded by a decorated screen. A lamp burned, illuminating only her profile, and he was treated to an enchanting, erotic exhibition as she steadied herself, came up to her knees, then her feet.

The water lapped against the edge as she exited. She leaned over to grab for a towel, and he hardened at the glimpse of her lush, rounded bottom. Starting at her head, she languidly rubbed her body, working the drying cloth down across her throat, her bosom, her flat stomach, cleft, thighs, calves, toes. Then, she wrapped it under her arms, but not before he noticed that her breasts were flawlessly formed, high and pert, the nipples two taut little buds. Tucking the flap at her cleavage, the long sheeting hung past her knees like a type of native's dress.

He held his breath. Aching. Ready.

She moved from behind the screen.

"Hello, James." Abby smiled. "I didn't realize you were home."

He wasn't quite sure who he'd been expecting, but unquestionably not Abigail Weston. If the Blessed Virgin herself had stopped by, he couldn't have been more stunned.

But for the towel, she was naked, her skin moist, slippery, fragrant. She was the most delectable sight he'd ever laid eyes upon, and as always transpired when she was near, his body reacted with amazing force. His erection expanded severely, and he became so overinflated that he had to grip a chair in order to remain upright, and he struggled to hide his surprise and blatant ardor.

He was furious that she'd come, furious that she'd put him in the position of craving her so badly, of having to chase her away all over again. He wasn't sure he possessed the fortitude to be so overtly cruel a second time.

Angrily, he asked, "What are you doing here?"

"Taking a bath." She stated the obvious as though his stumbling across her while she performed her ablutions was the most common of occurrences. He hadn't moved any closer, so she took the initiative, narrowing the distance until they were toe to toe, and he was assailed by a myriad of feminine bouquets, of perfume and sex and musk.

She flicked that wicked tongue of hers along her bottom lip, drawing his attention to it so thoroughly that he couldn't look away. "The water is still hot. Would you like to bathe? I could wash you."

Her husky voice, the one that sounded more indecent than any expensive whore he'd ever had, flowed over his body as though she were licking him with her words. Vividly, he could picture himself removing his clothes, sliding into the steamy cauldron, and letting her massage him all over. At the thought, his balls clenched and cried out for mercy.

"I don't want you in my home," he contended.

"Really? It seems to me that you've missed me."

So saying, she laid her hand on the front of his trousers, where his cockstand had swelled to a vulgar length, and his traitorous hips, of their own accord, flexed against her. She ground the heel of her palm into the sensitive tip before he managed to yank her away.

"Don't flatter yourself," he said meanly. "I realized there was a naked woman in my bath. I was prepared to *fuck* whoever was idiotic enough to saunter 'round the screen."

"I'm certain that's true." She eliminated the gap between them; her towel tickled his clothing. "Aren't I lucky that I get to be the one?"

Shifting back, creating space, he baldly declared, "I'm expecting my mistress."

"You don't have one," she responded, refusing to heed his protests. "Arthur told me you haven't bedded a woman in weeks. And I was ecstatic to learn"—she flipped that glorious mane of hair over her shoulder—"that you finally had the sense to send that Ritter woman packing. I never liked your being with her, and I'm sure she's the one who caused all our trouble." Appearing entirely too innocent, she inquired, "Would you dry my back?"

She turned and dropped the towel.

For the span of a lifetime, he stared at her, at the ridges and bumps of her spine, the two cute dimples at the base, the cleft of her butt, those velvety cheeks. His fingers tingled, his nostrils flared, but he made no attempt to assist her.

"I don't think so," he ultimately said.

"No matter." She shrugged and twirled past him, headed directly into his bedchamber.

In shock, he didn't follow, tarrying instead next to the tub for many minutes while ruminating over how to proceed. He didn't want her in his personal quarters! He couldn't bear to have her handling his possessions and ingratiating her presence into the surroundings!

What did she intend? Seduction, obviously, but to what end? What did she hope to accomplish?

His mind spun as he sifted through the possibilities, but he couldn't conceive of a single valid reason for her arrival. As he cast about, searching for explanations, he gradually noticed that many of his belongings had been rearranged. On one of his dressers, his shaving equipment had been pushed over, and several decorative combs and brushes were lying next to it. On another, a tray holding his cuff links was shoved back and a jewelry box added. One of his dresser drawers was stuffed full of stockings, garters, and various female unmentionables. Stomping to an armoire, he wrenched at the doors and peered in, only to discover that his shirts were hanging beside several gowns.

"What the bloody hell . . . ?" He gazed around, not caring for these feminine additions in the slightest. Ready for battle, he marched to the outer room.

A cozy fire crackled in the grate, a sofa set in front of it, and she comfortably reclined. She was snuggled against the pillows, his collection of Pierre's lewd paintings propped on her lap, and she was leafing through it as though she had all the time in the world to wait for him to join her.

While he'd stalled and fumed in his dressing room, she'd donned black stockings, mules, and a sheer black robe, but she hadn't tied the belt, so the lapels were open, her breasts and stomach bared for his perusal, and, if he wasn't mistaken, she'd eliminated the womanly hair from her privates! With one knee drooped over the other, her dainty foot lolled back and forth, her heeled shoe dangling, and her clean-shaven pussy winked at him from between her thighs.

Hinting at secret delights, tempting him, he lurched toward her, but caught himself as he grasped that he was being helplessly reeled in like a fish on a hook. He halted immediately.

"Why have you come?" he demanded tersely.

She glanced up from whatever drawing had captured her

attention, impaling him with those startling green eyes. He'd forgotten how astounding they were, how captivating, how far inside they could delve to where his true emotions were hidden. Perhaps he hadn't wanted to remember. Like a coward, he looked away, focusing on her luscious mouth. Another mistake.

"I've been evicted from my brother's home. I have no place else to go."

"What made you consider that it would be all right to show up on my doorstep?"

"Well . . . you *are* the one who ruined me," she said, as though explaining her forsaken condition to a simpleton. "I decided it was only fair that you give me shelter. After all, you wouldn't want Jerald to throw me out onto the streets, would you? I'd be on my own, with no one to watch over me."

"You're not welcome here!" he hissed.

"Actually, I am. Your mother invited me. She insisted I stay as long as I wish." She went back to the stack of naughty pictures.

"My mother?" His blasted mother had butted her nose into this mess yet again? What was it about this situation that she found so intriguing? "Angela doesn't live here. Besides, this is my home. She has no say in who will be a guest."

"Would you like me to leave?" Bored, she was apparently more than willing to depart in her current scanty attire. What had befallen her?

In what he felt convinced was a calculated gesture, her leg fell to the side, exposing her core. He'd been right! She'd shaved! He stalked to her, and she hadn't the common sense to flinch away from his ferocious regard.

"What have you done to yourself?" he queried rabidly.

"Whatever do you mean?"

Mercy, but in one more second, she'd probably be batting her lashes! "You've removed your hair!"

"I hired a new maid. She's French. I had her do my legs and under my arms, too." Holding his gaze, refusing to permit retreat, she seductively stroked her hand over her breast, past her impudent nipple, then pushed her robe off her shoulder. She was silky smooth all the way down to where her stockings were tied. " 'Tis strange to be so sleek all over. But I like it." She raised her brows suggestively, seeking his opinion.

"You look like a whore," he asserted cruelly, lying, finding her sexy and dangerous, and longing to hurt her because of it.

"All for you, darling. I've been informed by a few of your other lovers that you like your women to be a bit nasty." She winked, then lowered her attention to the drawings, and he couldn't help but follow.

The rendering was of Lily, up on her knees and gripping the sides of the daybed. He was perched behind her, fully immersed. Their facial expressions were strained as they struggled toward release.

"You know, James," Abby remarked, "we never finished going through the pictures together. See this one here?" She tipped it toward him. "You never took me in this fashion, and I—"

He ripped the parchments from her hands and pitched them to the other end of the couch, then he grabbed her beneath her arms and shook her—hard. "Why are you behaving so outrageously? What are you about?"

"I told you: I don't have anywhere to go. I—"

"Stop it!" he commanded, shaking her again, his thumbs digging into the soft flesh surrounding her collarbone. "Just stop it! I can't stand to have you acting like this! Or hear you talking like this! Or watch you offering yourself like some . . . some streetwalker!"

"I rather like myself this way," she commented casually. "I think I'm much more interesting. Don't you?"

She grasped his wrists and guided him to her breasts. For the merest instant, he remained there, covering the soft mounds, relishing her nipples as they poked the centers of his palms, then he jumped back as though burned.

He jerked away, brushing his hands across his trousers,

desperate to eliminate the lingering sensation from his skin.
Feeling ridiculous, he recognized that he needed to calm
himself, so he went to the table and poured himself a glass
of wine, clutching his fingers around the stem. Drinking
intensely, he used the opportunity to determine what his
next statement should be, but nothing valuable occurred to
him.

Eventually, he muttered, "You can't stay."

"I don't belong anywhere else."

"People will find out that you're here."

"That's what I'm hoping," she said. "I had Arthur inform the staff that I'd moved in—"

"You did what?" He groaned, bewildered by her folly.
Had she gone mad?

"The word is probably spreading from house to house
even as we speak."

"But everyone will think you're my mistress!"

"Yes, I imagine they will." She smiled and shifted like
a contented cat. "Unless you're ready to make an honest
woman out of me?"

The question caused his heart to pound, the blood to roar
in his ears. Abruptly weak at the knees, he wished there
were a chair close by so he could brace himself. "I'm *never*
going to marry you."

"Mistress it is, then." She shrugged a second time, as
though being married or unmarried mattered not a whit.
"And I must say, from how grouchy Arthur tells me you've
been, you definitely could use one!"

"Is that right?"

"Yes. I'm available." Stretching down toward her feet,
she retrieved the lascivious pictures from where they had
slid under a pillow, and she started leafing through them
once again. "I don't understand why we're fighting," she
mentioned, "when we could be making love instead. We
have our problems, but they're not important when we're
together in a bed."

"There is no *we*."

"If you insist. . . ." She flipped to the last illustration, then she sighed wistfully, as though she'd just finished reading the happy conclusion of a vapid romantic novel. In the painting, he was reclined on the daybed and cuddling with Lily in obvious postcoital serenity. "I'd never gone all the way to the end before," she noted. "You look so satisfied, just the two of you, lying there. The way you're so *attuned* to her is . . . is . . ."

"Lily was a magnificent piece of ass," he concurred, aiming to wound. "I always liked her breasts the best. They were extremely sensitive, and I'd suck at her for hours at a time."

She sighed again, ignoring what he'd said. After staring far too long at the final picture, her gaze slowly rose to meet his. "I miss this closeness," she confessed quietly, running her hand along the image of himself and Lily, as if she could magically force herself into the drawing and actually *become* Lily. "Of all the things while I was away . . . what I missed most was having you hold me like this."

At her wrenching disclosure, his heart skipped several beats. A thousand words flew to the tip of his tongue. Kind words. Cruel words. Loving words. But he didn't articulate any of them. He wanted her gone!

"I'm going to wash," he said, "then I'm going to bed." He started for the dressing room, where the water from her bath would still be warm.

"I'm tired, too." She emitted an unladylike yawn. "I'm not used to these late hours, but I guess I'll have to change my schedule if I intend to welcome you home every morning."

The woman was totally insane; there was no other explanation. "Please don't be here when I'm through. My mother's bedroom is next door, or there's a guest room down the hall. I'll sleep for a few hours; then, when I awaken, I'll find you some suitable accommodations."

Forcing himself to progress dispassionately to the dressing room, he closed the door behind him, relieved at how he'd handled her. He'd showed no emotion save rage, and he'd exercised enough control over his unruly body to ignore her efforts at seduction. Without a doubt, she'd gotten his message and would leave shortly.

Deliberately, he stripped, listening for sounds from the other chamber but not discerning any. Finally naked, he dipped into the tub and had a quick scrubbing. He would have liked a longer soak, but he was too distressed, so relaxation was unattainable.

He stepped out of the water and onto the rug, but as he snatched at the towel, another hand was there first.

"Let me do that for you," she volunteered. His back was to her, and he stiffened when she leaned in and wrapped her arms around his waist, which put her curious hands directly in front of his jutting erection. Without hesitating or requesting permission, she caressed him with one and cradled his sacs with the other. She'd shed her robe, so her breasts were bare, and as she pressed herself against him, he accepted that she'd won.

As long as she hadn't touched him intimately, he'd been successful in keeping her at bay, but he simply couldn't resist the pull of such overwhelming desire when she was standing so close and manipulating him in this manner.

"Abby . . . please don't . . ." he whispered through gritted teeth. It was a feeble attempt at stopping her, but he might as well not have spoken.

He cursed his weaknesses in the damning silence, and she meticulously worked him over, until she had his hips flexing, his muscles straining, and his cock beginning to weep. She circled around his torso and dropped to her knees, nuzzling his balls, then licking a path from the base to the tip until finally, blessedly, she took him inside. His surge of pleasure was so intense that he feared he might spill himself then and there, so he pulled out after only one deliberate penetration.

"Don't order me away," she declared, "because I won't heed your commands. And don't demand that I quit loving you. Because I won't do that, either."

He stared down at her, naked and on her knees before him. Her expressive emerald eyes were open wide, and he

could easily behold her stark emotion. She was so foolish:
trusting him, desiring him, adoring him.

How he hated her at that moment! For coming to his
home and compelling him to remember how much he
cared. For tickling his memory into recalling how much
he'd missed her when they'd been apart. But most of all,
he hated her for making him wonder if it might be possible
to love her, to have her after all.

A wave of fury and frustration swept over him, and he
needed to lash out, to drive her away. With his strong, solid
body. With his harsh, stinging words. What game did she
play, toying with him so heartlessly? She knew *who* he was
and *what* he was, yet she was here anyway, demanding that
he give some part of himself that didn't exist, expecting
him to pretend that he was a different sort of man from the
one he truly was.

Gripping her by her forearm, he dragged her to her feet,
spun her, and bent her over the tub. She braced herself on
the rim, and he kneed her legs apart and positioned himself
between them. He whisked his palm up her flank, her but-
tock, then dipped into her cleft. With her hair shaved away,
her pussy was silky, baby-soft, and he fondled her until she
dampened. Then two fingers slid inside, her inner muscles
clenching around him, and he could sense how tight she'd
be, how hot.

His cock reared, begging to enter, the blunt peak poised
to proceed. With a swift shove, he could be buried to her
womb. A few hasty thrusts, and he could spill himself, his
seed flooding her and, perhaps, producing a babe.

The powerful thoughts raced through his mind, and he
wailed his torment and pushed her away. She tottered, and
almost fell, but he did nothing to help her regain her balance.

In the worst agony of his life, he veered to the bedchamber like a blind man and reeled to his bed, clutching
the bedpost. His pulse roaring, his body on fire, his passion
rampaging to a critical level, he closed his eyes and strove
to stabilize his breathing, but he simply hadn't the mettle

to regain control. His lust for her was so great that he truly believed he might rip her in half if she didn't desist.

He heard her approaching, but he didn't turn to face her. "Go, Abby," he decreed. "I'm warning you. For your own good. Leave me be!"

"I won't," she said, unruffled, courting the danger, obviously not comprehending the peril in which she'd placed herself. "I'm not leaving. No matter what you say or how you act, I'm staying right here."

"What do you want from me?" He moaned in anguish, whipping around to stare her down.

"Just this." She gestured between them. "The two of us. Here, together. On any terms." She moved closer. "I'd like the chance for us to build a family, so I'd be overjoyed to marry you, if you'd ask me. If you can't, I'll stay anyway. I'll be your paramour. For a week, or a month, or a year. I'll remain until this inferno has fizzled out, then I'll go. But only then."

"I don't want to make a family with you," he tried to assert, but the hitch in his voice belied his denial. "I can't be the man you imagine!"

" 'Tis not my *imagination,* James. You're the finest man I know!"

"I'm not!" he shouted vehemently, but the deranged woman just took another step. Then another, until she was near enough to lay her hands on his chest, to tangle her fingers in the thick mat of hair.

"I don't love you," he protested zealously, pronouncing the terrible lie.

"You don't need to," she responded softly. "I have enough love for both of us." She hugged him, crushing her nakedness to his. "Don't drive me away again. I can endure anything but that."

Her breasts were flattened against his chest, his thick, heavy phallus digging into her belly. The warm heat of her, the soft essence of her skin, enveloped him. In one motion, he lifted her and hurled her on the mattress, coming down on top. Roughly, he forced her legs apart, determined to have her, no longer inclined to eschew such a staggering indulgence.

With no more preparation than that, he plunged to the hilt, and she whimpered and arched up off the bed, her body not equipped for his overwhelming size or eagerness, but he wouldn't be denied, and he held her down while he propelled himself into her, over and over again, struggling and straining against her like a crazed man. He did nothing to alleviate the vicious invasion, thinking only that if he could probe deeply enough, descend far enough, he could eventually rid himself of this deadly urgency and find some peace.

Through it all, she cooed reassuringly, murmuring tender endearments. Treasuring him, accepting him. Loving him. In her serene, patient fashion, she took all he so brutally bestowed, letting him fill her to the brim with his loneliness and despair until he'd purged himself of all his heartbreak.

With a fervid rush, he spilled himself, and he intentionally allowed his seed to spew across her womb, some primal part of him yearning to plant a child. He cried her name, crushing her with the strength of his embrace, but he didn't care.

"I don't love you . . ." he persisted. "I don't!" He buried his face against her nape as scalding tears blistered his eyes.

" 'Tis all right, James," she said gently, and she ran her precious hands in a soothing motion up and down his back. "Everything is all right now."

"No, it's not. . . ." He strove to relax his body, his grip, but he felt as if she were the last lifeline tethering him to the world, and he dare not let go, lest he drift away. "Don't make me love you. You'll always regret it."

"No, never. I'll never be sorry." She rested her palm against his cheek. "And neither will you."

He wanted to believe her but couldn't. To have her in his life, to be confident that she would always be his, was a joy too magnificent to count upon. For what if she left? What if he gave his heart to her without reservation, but she tossed it back? How could he continue on? The immense, all-consuming dread, instilled by his father when he was a child, made him too afraid to seize what she was offering.

He only knew of one way to have her, one way that was safe.

Bending down, he found her nipple, latching on and nursing like a babe at its mother's breast. Snuggled there, he suckled for a lengthy time, letting her scent and taste comfort him. But as he shifted to her other breast, he was past the need for consolation, and so was she.

Still implanted, his cock enlarged easily. Ready for her. For this.

He craved to feel her writhing and squirming, wailing out in ecstasy. Physical satisfaction he understood. Carnal pleasure he wasn't apprehensive about sharing. So he blazed a trail down her stomach, to her woman's spot, sinking his tongue into her pliant, wet recesses. The musk and salt of her sex enticed him, lured him, prompting him to long for things that could never be.

Needing her skin next to his, he untied her garters, unrolled her stockings. He savored her shins, her knees, her thighs. Finding her core again, he licked and grazed, causing her to thrash against his mouth. Worshiping her with his lips, his hands, he traveled up her abdomen, dallying at her breasts, then proceeding on.

Finally, he kissed her, and her sweetness and perfection flowed through him. When he eventually centered himself once again, he reached down to steer himself inside, but her hand was there, ready to act as his steady, constant guide.

Diligently, carefully, he entered her, and their hips instantly discovered a matching rhythm. Her verdant eyes locked on his, and he received such an infusion of unbridled devotion that his heart throbbed and ached. She started to come, while whispering his name, and he couldn't help but come with her, sliding into that realm beyond space and time, tarrying there, then drifting back. Together.

As reality tumbled into place, she was crying, and his

heart constricted at witnessing her tears. With his thumbs, he wiped them away. "What is it, love?" His fury spent, his affection for her had seeped in to take its place.

"I'm just so glad I'm with you," she murmured, her voice catching. "Perhaps we made a babe just now. We didn't the last time, and I regretted the loss so very much. . . ."

"Oh, Abby—"

She cut him off. "Don't say that you think it would be wrong."

He couldn't imagine a greater gift. "No," he said, shaking his head and gazing down at her, his love for her shining through, "it wouldn't be wrong."

At his declaration, her certainty soared. "I can't stand to see you so distressed as you've been. Promise me that you won't send me away again."

"I won't." He sighed, giving in, losing the battle. Losing the war. "You're like a bad penny!" he declared, but he was smiling. "You keep coming back. I can't get rid of you."

"That's because I belong here. With you."

"Aye, love, it seems you do." He shifted, so she could stretch out and mold her body to his. They fit like two halves of a whole and, as she put her hand over his heart, the beat slow and firm against her palm, he felt as if the last piece of an unsolvable puzzle had fallen into place.

This sense of completion was what he'd always craved. Love. A family. A wife and children to watch over and nurture. But he'd never dared to envision a better future, believing his reveries impossible to attain.

Linking his fingers with hers, he ventured, "Are you sure?"

"How could you ask?"

"Do you truly grasp what you'll be leaving behind?"

"What would that be?" she inquired. "A few acquaintances who were never close? A brother who refuses to accept how much I care about you?" She cast them all onto the heap that was rapidly becoming her past. "Not much of a loss, in my opinion."

"But your family . . ."

"We'll create our own."

"I'll never let you go," he vowed fervently. "If you say *yes* to me,'tis forever."

"Is that a proposition, Mr. Stevens?" She raised up and covered him with her body, her fists on his chest. "Because if it's not, you'll have to do a little better. I'm afraid you'll have to marry me."

Nothing could make him happier. Nothing would make him prouder, but old wounds were slow to heal. "Tell me it will be forever," he urged.

"Tell me that you love me," she replied in return. When he hesitated, she chuckled. " 'Tis not so difficult. The world won't end if you speak the words."

"I realize that, but after all these years,'tis difficult to change my convictions so readily. I've never believed that true love exists."

"I understand that about you, James. That's why you belong with me."

The final brick in his wall of reserve crashed down. Where she was concerned, he'd never stood a chance of keeping it erect. "I love you, Abby."

"I know you do. You always have, and I love you, too."

"So . . . it's forever?" He sounded expectant as a young child wishing on a star.

"Yes, James. 'Tis forever."

"Will you have me, then, Abigail?"

"Until the end of time . . . and much longer than that." She graced him with a tender kiss.

Sighing contentedly, he nestled against her, and her warm breath coursed across him. He eased against the pillows, and a wave of lassitude swept over him. With his stress alleviated, the weight of the world he'd been carrying had vanished, and he was unexpectedly sleepy. He couldn't stifle a yawn.

Abby sat up and straddled his lap. "You're exhausted, aren't you?"

"Well, proposing marriage does sap a fellow's energy. . . ."

"Devil," she muttered, laughing. "I want you to eat a bit and rest, because when you awaken, you have a busy day ahead of you."

"Doing what?"

"First, we're bound for window-shopping on Bond Street, then we're taking a leisurely carriage ride in the park. With the top down."

"But everyone will see us together!"

"That's my plan," she said, wiggling her brows impishly. "I want to set all the tongues to wagging. By sundown, we'll be the talk of the Town."

"Heaven help me," he grumbled, "but you're starting to remind me an awful lot of my mother."

"What a wonderful compliment," she beamed. "The timid *lady* I used to be when we first met has completely disappeared." She bit her bottom lip, suddenly nervous. "You're not disappointed that's she's gone, are you?"

He gazed upon her, at the beautiful face and the naked, alluring body he knew better than his own. She was smiling wickedly, looking confident and full of mischief, and he decided that she would always be more than a handful.

How had he ever gotten so lucky?

"No," he exclaimed happily, "I'm not disappointed."

He hugged her tightly, cherishing her and loving her. For the first time in his life, eager to hope, content to dream.